For Grace and Ali

PART ONE

FRAN, MARCH 2019

CHAPTER 1

I

After the front door has slammed, I do all the usual things. I take it steady. I make the bed, load the dishwasher, wipe the kitchen surfaces, pat some life into the sofa cushions, tidy the mess from Pete and Harry's football-watching the night before – the cans of beer and pizza boxes – and run the hoover along the passageway to suck up any stray mud-crumbs.

It is only when I pile Suki's bowl with extra food – her tea as well as breakfast – that I realise there is a wobble inside me, ready to reduce me to a jelly if I let it. I am not a risk-taker – life – Pete – has not allowed for that – and yet here I am.

I breathe as much air into my lungs as I can and exhale slowly. Suki appears, threading her black tail between my shins, mewing. I bend down to touch her and she headbutts my hand, hungry for love, as always. Her head is hard as a coconut and her whiskers prickly.

'You'll be fine, you'll see,' I whisper, glad she's just a cat and can't hear the catch in my throat.

Upstairs, I set my phone to Jack's last message and place it beside the suitcase as I pack. I love the shortness of the list, the simplicity, the certainty.

Passport. Phone. Money. Some clothes. Yourself. We can do this. I love you.
Until tomorrow.

Before leaving the house, I check the street like a spy from behind
the sitting-room curtains. If Mrs Dawkins is taking Alfie, her doddery
Frenchie, out, or chatty Dave across the way is on his front step having
a fag, then I'll have to be ready. I have thought of this, of course –
between us, Jack and I have done our best to think of everything, which
is why it's taken so long to get to this moment. If the station wasn't so
close, I'd splash out on a taxi, but money will be tight for a while and
the drama of baggage-loading into a strange car, all that revving and
motion outside the house, would draw attention in itself – crazy, after
all the months of taking so much care.

Better to slip out and brave the gauntlet of the street. Better to have
ready my prepared story about visiting Rob and Jo, my brother and his
wife, and their motley crew of children and animals in the wilds of
Kent. *There's their new baby still to meet, five-month-old little Marcus, and,
of course, it's always lovely to see the twins.* All morning, I have been prac-
tising in my head what I'll say if someone asks, the tone I'll use – jolly
and affectionate. Twenty years of marriage to Pete has taught me that
at least – how to put on a show, how to say what needs to be said, do
what needs to be done. By the time the truth comes out, I'll be gone.

If it weren't for the suitcase, it would be a doddle. But a suitcase
invites questions, even from strangers, and despite having learnt to lie,
it still takes nerve and grit and all the things I do not naturally possess.
That this terrible necessity of double-living, thirteen months of it, is
about to end is one of the things that has been keeping me going. I am
free to make my own choices. My life is my life. Jack has opened me up
to such daring thinking. We are all just tumbleweed otherwise, he said
once, getting blown nowhere, for nothing.

I chose the suitcase from the dusty heap in the loft for its large size;
not used for years and with wonky wheels, I know it won't be missed.
Only after I have finally left the house, passport and phone treble-
checked, the note for Pete propped on the mantelpiece, the one for

Harry half under his pillow so Pete can't get to it first, the front door double-locked, do I discover that the pull-out handle on the suitcase no longer extends properly either. But I am already in the street, sweating inside my overcoat, and it is too late to go back. The coast, mercifully, remains clear.

I set off at a brisk pace in the direction of the high street, the case making a horrible rumpus over the paving stones behind me, shouting for all the attention I am trying my best to avoid.

I'm off to Rob and Jo's, I chant inside my head, matching the words to the pace of my walk, *to meet my new baby nephew; dum-dum-de-dum-de-dumdum.* My brain butts in with an image of Harry twenty years ago, snug in the spotty blue baby carrier, a bag of stale crusts for the pigeons dangling from my fingers; days when I still believed becoming a mum would solve everything.

A man in paint-spattered overalls jumps out of a parked white van, making me start. 'Morning.'

'Morning.'

'Going somewhere nice, I hope.'

Behind him, a kid on a bike, bare knees purple-blue in the mid-March chill, does a wheelie, throwing a glance sideways to check for an audience before whizzing off.

'Yes, thanks.'

I cast a side-look at Annie Smith's front window as I hurry on, grateful to see it empty. I think about her leg ulcer and the carer-rota that keeps changing and have to shove them to the back of my mind. Just as I do Harry, aged just twenty and his father's son these days, but still my boy, and Suki, bless her, found by me in a soggy box under a lamp post a decade before, her black velvet coat sodden and mouldy grey. That selfishness takes courage has been a new discovery.

The bloody suitcase fights me like a sumo, threatening to unbalance us both during its thunderous progress in my wake. But I turn the corner and suddenly there's the postbox on the high street, a red beacon, something to aim for. I slide my resignation letter with its bold, brief outline of the reasons behind my decision into the slot, pausing just long enough to hear the quiet thwack as it lands. I do not let myself think of Camille opening it. There is no going back now. All the big stuff is done.

Jack's voice slides into my head. *Precision planning, my darling Fran, and we shall prevail.* He's got such a voice; low, sonorous, with delicious huskiness on the bottom notes. The moment I heard it, just over a year ago in the auction house, I thought, here is a man who never flaps, who never hurries, who's easy in his own skin. Here is a voice that I could listen to all day. Sometimes, I've teased him about his untapped talent as a voice-over artist, all the money he could earn promoting washing powder and describing four different bits of a cooked rabbit on a plate for a TV cooking competition. He could make a bomb, I've joked, more of a bomb than he's clearly managed from his painting, that's for sure; though I never say that bit. I adore what I have been able to see of Jack's work – he's always reticent about showing me stuff, but it's obvious how brilliant he is. Five dashes of a pencil and he can capture anything; and his paintings, translucent seascapes, burning green countryside scenes, willowy people, are dazzling. But earning money as an artist is hard graft, and he is understandably sensitive about that, given Helena's family millions and how little he and I are going to have to live on.

I've tried to worry about money too, but I can't. For a start, there's my ten grand from Mum, still safe with Santander and in my name, despite Pete's best efforts. And then, between us, Jack and I have vowed to find work, no matter how menial, until some of the new portraits he's been working on – the Rogues Gallery, he calls it – find buyers. A friend of his called Brian is going to look after all of it while we are away, hopefully finding some takers among his rich banker contacts.

Jack already speaks some Spanish, which will give him a head-start, and I'm going to have lessons when we get there. I'd have had a stab with evening classes, but Pete's never easy with things that take me out of the house after working hours. Winning the battle to join Camille's book club for school staff took weeks of pleading and holding my nerve. It's a long time since he really flipped, but the threat is always there, always to be navigated. Even so, each monthly book gathering never fails to cause a rumpus. *Abandoning me, are you? Aren't I interesting enough any more?*

Best of all, Spain means Jack will have the paradise he says he has always dreamed of for his painting: the electric southern sunshine, the big blue skies, the old Moorish towns, the hillside groves of oranges, lemons, olives – in close moments during our few, treasured chances to be properly together, he has talked to me in raptures about such things, his voice a whisper of passion, his strong arms holding me close while his big hands cup my head and his long slim artist fingers comb my hair. Just to recall such times makes my skin tingle. But the far bigger joy is to have found someone whose happiness and self-fulfilment I yearn for even more than my own, with the added luxury of knowing that Jack wants the same for me. Love, in other words, of the sort I had stopped believing in.

With Pete, just using the words 'happiness' and 'fulfilment' is like pulling a trigger. '*Sorry I haven't been as successful in life as Madam would have liked. It hasn't all been the proverbial rose-bed for me either, in case you haven't noticed. Have you noticed, Fran? Do you pay any attention to me – ever?*' It can go either way then, but the old list of life blows will come out during the course of it: the knee injury that wrecked his youthful sporting hopes, the two business partners who somehow both turned out to be backstabbers, the hateful sports-shop management job that was supposed to be a stopgap, Harry dropping out of uni... and some-how, every time, by that last item, I'm the one to blame for it all.

I can feel the old fear and anger rising and I don't want it, not today of all days. My arms and shoulders are starting to throb. Who would have thought a half a mile could feel so long? I divert myself by picturing 'Casa Maria', the gem of a guesthouse that Jack found for us online, with its warm terracotta floor tiles and fresh white cotton curtains fringing the bedroom windows, all centred round a courtyard of cobblestone and hanging baskets, fireworks of colour erupting against soft sandy stone walls. Jack says it's in the same part of Madrid as where his favourite painter, Sorolla, used to live, and that the artist's house is open to the public. Paying the place a visit, seeing all the family beach scenes Jack has shown me on his laptop – gauzy summer heat, shimmering over blue and gold bands of sea, sand and sky, blowy dresses and parasols, bare-legged kids larking about in sparkling shallows – is high on our to-do list. As is moving from the guesthouse into our own home just as soon as we are able; having our own courtyard maybe, our own hanging baskets of flaming palettes.

Suddenly the first rocket of real, hot excitement is shooting up through my innards, one of those electric shocks of rip-your-clothes-off lust and loving certainty which has kept Jack and I going this past year and which we both like to joke will wear off soon, though there's been no sign yet. The idea of just having a room to ourselves makes us both giddy. A basin. A shower. A bed. The chance to breathe the same air, all day, all night. No goodbyes. No secrecy. No heartache.

The need to cross the high street brings me back to earth. The case takes two hands and all my strength, grappling with it over the uneven kerb, round the pothole that has been there forever, and up onto the other side, my overstuffed handbag and carry-on toppling unhelpfully off my shoulders throughout. I grit my teeth as I struggle, reminding myself again of how hard Jack and I have worked to reach this day; the patience it has taken, the good sense, the attention to detail. We are like two parachutists, we agreed last time we talked, every conceivable safety check carried out, every preparation made, poised in the open door of a plane and ready to jump.

When my mobile pings in my pocket, I stop so suddenly that a man and a glossy spaniel bouncing on its lead almost trip over me as they swerve past. I fumble for my phone with shaking hands. Jack and I, needing to concentrate on our separate exit strategies, not wanting any extra risks, have agreed on no communications until the airport, except in the case of an emergency. Dark scenarios are already scudding across my imagination, including Pete, needing something particular – as is his wont – a document from a filing cabinet, or a receipt, or one of his moans about all the crap at work. If I don't reply to the message, he'll call. Then he'll hear the traffic and ask where I am. And if I opt not to answer, he'll try again, and again, and again, Pete not being one to give up, on anything, not even when he should; least of all then, in fact.

Seeing it's from Mel, I let out a groan of relief.

Good Luck! You are the bravest. Remember: LOVE CONQUERS ALL. Can't wait to come and visit! MX

And you're the best friend EVER

I type back hastily, my fingers like spaghetti.

Mel is my rock, a friend since our sixth-form days and with enough issues of her own for Pete not to judge her a threat. She is the only one who knows, about Jack, as well as everything else, which is why she has been such a support in all the madness. It is in her flat that Jack and I have been able to meet, to be close, to plot our escape.

I add a kiss and a fingers-crossed emoji before pressing send, then set off with such a fresh burst of energy that I trip over my own feet and almost go sprawling. I shout a string of expletives, earning a glare from a wan young man at a bus stop jigging a newborn in a papoose. I offer him a sheepish smile, noting that he's in that early crazy protective phase of parenthood. No ugliness allowed. No suffering. No disappointment. Just like me, once upon a time.

I walk on more slowly, trying to shut out thoughts of all the things that can still go wrong: cancelled trains, terrorist attacks, a meteor hitting South London, or the wheels literally falling off my stupid case. I'd have to ask strangers for help then, big time. In fact, I'd probably just hail a cab for the entire journey, blow the cost.

Standing before the train departures board a few minutes later, the illuminated 'on time' notifications glittering at me like miracles, something inside me starts to relax. I catch a glimpse of myself in the glass of an advertising hoarding as I head for the platform. I see a petite forty-two-year-old woman with a pale face, light green eyes and long brown hair. I see a woman in her prime, with a train and a plane to catch.

In the last months of her illness, Mum liked to talk to me and Rob about the importance of having a sense of purpose in life, not wasting any time, her voice wistful from the battles with depression which had kicked in back when our father died and never quite let go. My life-loving, super-smart elder brother hardly needed telling, but I was the one with fewer excuses, the one who has never exactly blazed a trail – marrying at just twenty-one, muddling and fudging through low-key primary-school teaching jobs, bottling in all the secret mess of things with Pete.

I stay by the hoarding so I can keep looking at the reflection. *I think you might root for me today, Mum,* I tell her. *I think you would understand and be proud.*

II

On the day I met Jack, I was still trying to shake off a heavy cold and cough that had arrived through the usual stress of Christmas and was somehow still hanging around in February. It was a Saturday morning and Harry and Pete had gone to a game. I felt so rough, I couldn't even be bothered to slap on any make-up before setting off for the shops.

I took my usual route past the garage and the park, wanting to check out the farmers' market before getting to the budget super-market where I always got most of what we needed, buying in a day-to-day way, as Pete preferred. The last stretch included the old auction house, *Moorlands*, a sprawling red-brick building set behind some railings which I had walked past hundreds of times without a second glance. On this particularly icy day, the sun popped out, a lovely sunlamp of heat on the back of my head, and I dawdled to enjoy it, examining the posters strung along the railings. There was to be an auction that morning. *Victoriana*. Photographs of various items were featured, including a little dressing table the colour of molten honey, set on ornate mini knickerbocker-legs with two drawers and brass keyholes that made me think of a smiley face. Before I knew it, I was wandering in through the gates.

'Got your eye on anything in particular?'

He had taken up a seat one away from me in an otherwise completely empty row, checking his phone and various papers from a weather-beaten briefcase that drew attention to his equally weather-beaten leather shoes – the old-fashioned expensive sort, studded with decorative holes and small laces.

'Me? No...that is, lots of things look nice.' It had taken a while to locate the dressing table, even smaller and more delicate than its photo had suggested. Some miniature silver pillboxes in a cabinet had also caught my eye, on offer as a job lot. Not that there was any question of staying or bidding. I wouldn't have known how, for one thing, and for another, Pete, understandably for once, would have gone into meltdown. Financially, we were in a sound patch, but there was never any question of extras. I had ogled for a bit, then flopped onto a seat just for the chance to blow my sore nose and take in the surroundings. The place was an emporium, high-ceilinged and crammed, like a vast but orderly junk shop.

'I'm here for the books,' my new companion went on easily, absently running his hand over his close-cropped dark sandy beard and pointing across the room. 'Over there, spilling out of the box under the chest of drawers with the blue vase, do you see? The catalogue says a reserve of two hundred, but fat chance, frankly. They'll go for four times that, at least. There's a lot of rubbish among them, not to mention mildew, but also a couple of first editions.'

I hadn't noticed the books. They were in a cardboard box that was indeed falling apart, its sides torn and flapping. Several had fallen out through the gaps, displaying, even at a distance, the grey speckled state of their old leather covers.

'The main thing,' he continued, 'is to have a limit in mind before you start. It's curious how one can get carried away otherwise, beyond the point of reason sometimes. The thrill of the chase, I suppose. A bit like gambling. Not, I hasten to add, that I count that as one of my vices.' He shot me a proper smile then, a glint of mischief flaring in strong blue eyes that caused me, momentarily, both to lament the worse-than-usual plainness of my face, not even the faint teenage acne scars covered up with a dab of foundation, and yet to be aware of the utter absurdity of doing so. He was just killing time, like me.

Get over yourself, Fran. 'So you've already got a limit in mind then?'

'Ah.' The grin became more circumspect. 'Well, in this case, my wife does. And it is on her behalf that I am here.'

'So is your wife really into books?'

'Yes. Or at least, she likes collecting them. Collecting is a hobby of hers. And sending me on errands, that's another hobby.' He laughed with a ruefulness I interpreted as husbandly affection, shaking a mop of hair that was a darker chestnut and much more unruly than his beard. As he pushed a clump of it further back off his forehead, I noticed the wedding band on his fourth finger, thick as a curtain ring and gleaming gold.

There was a faint air of languor about him, or maybe some inner weariness, it was hard to tell. His legs were long, clearly something of a struggle to keep comfy within the tight space allocated between the rows of chairs, and his frame was still notably youthful and slim; though he had to be in his late forties, I decided, thanks to the specks of silver dotting his temples and the creases in the corners of his eyes.

During the course of talking, he had shifted position to face me, one leg crossed over the other, drawing attention to the neat delineation of his kneecaps pushing through the brown material of his trousers. He was wearing a crumpled white collared shirt, the top button open, the sleeves rolled up unevenly to the elbows, displaying lean, pale, faintly freckled forearms. I decided the wife was elegantly pale and slim too; that they were one of those ultra-healthy well-to-do couples who would look the same at seventy as they had at thirty. Unlike me, with my curves all over the place, and Pete's belly, sticking out so far over the top of his belt these days that sometimes I would think to myself, *well, now at least you know what it was like to carry Harry all those months.*

Jack only told me much later that it was the morning after one of their very worst nights. A new low after a history of so many. Helena, using the pretext of a visiting friend to drink all afternoon, had picked a late-night fight, only getting more enraged at his attempts to defuse it. A terrible climax had been reached when she barged into his studio to wreak havoc, using a red felt-tip pen to scrawl the words *your crap* across his best work. The ambiguity of the *your* had almost upset him more than anything, Jack claimed, nobly trying to make light of it; possessive pronoun or misspelling. It was typical of Helena, he said – to be slapdash and doubly cruel.

'And still she does not reveal her hand.' Jack lobbed the sentence across the empty chair between us like a mock accusation, surprising me because I thought we were done. 'I know,' he cried, 'maybe it's the books she's after. Maybe she's a rival. Maybe I am consorting with an enemy. In which case, we should indeed desist from all communications forthwith.' He mimed zipping his lips shut and folded his arms across his chest, the startling blue eyes flashing with faux affront.

I suppose a part of me was already falling. Not that you know such things at the time. It's only looking back that life starts to make any sense. Like Pete, blowing into my small circle of teenage girlfriends like a gust of fresh air, all cheek and cheerfulness, not seeming to mind the still patchy state of my face, like the other boys; not minding anything, in fact, except that I was a willing kisser and a talent scout was talking about him to his league footie coach. Ours was a big West London day school and he was its established star athlete, seventeen, brown-eyed, black-haired and lean as a whippet. I was a year younger and prepared to think that any boy who didn't find me repellent was worth loving in return. My skin was such a constant source of teenage misery that the moment Harry's started to play up, I frogmarched him straight to the doctor and didn't leave till we had a prescription. Making a mountain, Pete said, as per, giving the poor boy a complex; but I could never have explained to Pete, of all people, the burden of feeling ugly, the bad decisions it can cause – like marrying the first person who'd have me – the way it warps one's entire world. I didn't want any of that to kick in for Harry, already in the business of taking himself off to the edges of things, rather than getting stuck in.

When Jack did the mouth-zipping, I couldn't help giggling, which somehow triggered a coughing fit – a truly terrible one, gritty and explosive, that took several ugly old tissues and a sticky cough sweet, dug out from the dusty lining of the pocket of what was my oldest, warmest coat, to get on top of.

'Oh no, your books are quite safe,' I rasped, once speech became remotely possible, keeping my hand in front of my mouth for fear of transferring any of my disgusting germs across the space between us. 'No interest whatsoever. Though I do like books. A lot. For reading. Not collecting.' I had to keep stopping, both for breath and to swallow the continuing impulse to hack my lungs out. 'I'm in a book club. We're doing *Middlemarch*.' I stopped. My chest had settled as quickly as it had got stirred up, but I felt ridiculous suddenly at so much unnecessary disclosure. As Harry might have said, in the unlikely event of him being privy to such an exchange between his mother and a total stranger, 'Doh, Mum', issued with the scornful groan reserved for highest disdain of my embarrassing ways.

Jack was unfazed. Already in love himself, he declared later, when we picked over these unlikely beginnings. Not that I ever quite believed him. Insecurity about looks is one thing; but to accept the possibility of a handsome man, even an unhappy one, falling for a coughing crone with a red nose and deathly face, wearing a coat sporting a layer of cat hair, spewing disease into used tissues, takes quite a mind-stretch. Though, at the time, Jack certainly, to his great credit, merely ploughed on with the subject at hand. '*Middlemarch*. Wow. I gave up on that, I'm afraid. There were just so many... words. And as for the main woman, Dorothy—'

'Dorothea...' I ventured.'

He paused, smiling. 'And as for Dorothea, I actually found her very annoying, getting with that creep of an academic—'

'Casaubon.'

'That's the one. A fossil of a man—'

'Fossil? I like that.' It was impossible not to be pleased that the giving up hadn't prevented a good grasp of the story. Pete only read the sports pages these days, or things on his phone.

'Thanks. Feel free to use it with your club.' He grinned.

Around us, preparations for the start of the auction were gathering pace. An atmosphere of expectation was suddenly in the air. Seats in our row and others were filling up. At the front, a young man was checking the microphone on a lectern and two women at a table next to it were setting up laptops and putting on headphones.

'For the phone bids,' said Jack, watching where I was looking.

'Okay. I see.'

'I'm Jack, by the way, Jack Aspen, nice to meet you.' He reached across the empty seat to shake hands. His was so much bigger than mine, smooth and warm as a glove.

'Frances Grove – Fran. But I must be on my way. 'Nerves about the auction getting underway – being trapped – were overtaking me. 'The truth is, I didn't sit down for anything except a look around. I'm here under false pretences. A fraud.'

'How scandalous. I shall have to report you to the authorities.'

'I better make my escape quickly in that case.' I stood up, spilling and retrieving balled-up tissues.

'Do you like carrot cake?'

'Excuse me?'

'There's a café in the basement that does great carrot cake. If you could wait ten minutes, fifteen tops, the books are early on the list, we could grab a coffee. I'd like to say I won't bother with them, but I must.' The softness in his expression had gone. There was something else there now, a hint of pleading, but also a guardedness, as if inwardly braced to absorb whatever response came back. 'A quick coffee. A piece of cake.' His tone was matter-of-fact. 'What harm could it do?'

What harm indeed, and he was smiling again, so warmly. I sat back down.

The auctioneer stepped up onto the podium and the room fell silent. The man had a waxed handlebar moustache that made me want to reach for my scissors, but he knew what he was about – charging through each bid with quick-fire gabble and banging his wooden hammer like a percussionist. Cake or no cake, it was exciting and I was glad I had stayed, simply for the experience.

It was twenty minutes before the box of books came up. A phone bidder took it to an astonishing eight hundred pounds, but Jack held firm, raising a pencil each time with the metronomic precision of one who knew the game and would not tolerate defeat. It was mesmerizing; a glimpse into another world.

Afterwards, we slid out of the row like truants, slipping down a back staircase I hadn't seen. The café was ill-lit and small, set among stone archways more suited to a wine cellar. We sat across the only spare table, a rickety black plastic one, sporting a single daffodil in a thin glass vase, and shared a slab of mouth-wateringly moist cake – lemon drizzle because there was no carrot left – using two forks, our two cappuccinos mirroring each other across the plate, chatting like old friends. We discussed the bidding and Jack said there hadn't really been a limit, that Helena would have paid anything. Then he apologised again for not liking George Eliot, saying it was probably because he was too dim, but clearly so at ease with the notion, that the likelihood of this being true felt impossible.

'So tell me, what do you do then?' he urged suddenly. 'Do you have children? A job?'

I sensed he had considered asking about a husband and not done so. It made me pleased and uncomfortable all at the same time. But his wife was on the table, so to speak, and my fourth finger, decked with two rings – the tiny single diamond with which Pete had proposed and the thin gold circle that had sealed our union three years after leaving school – was even more obviously encumbered than his, so I decided it was simply because the subject was too evident to raise. We were two random married people having a random coffee.

'One son, Harry, he's nineteen. Gave up on uni after one term and is still not sure what to do next, like many young kids these days, I guess.' I made a what-can-you-do face, like it was just a normal problem, which I kept telling myself it was. 'I teach in a primary school – a new one called Chalfonts, lovely and small; before that, it was a big comprehensive – St Joseph's – and before that, I dipped in and out, covering here and there. All I've ever wanted to do was work with young children. I've got a brother called Rob, who's the high achiever of the family – he advises people on how to invest their money, at least I think that's what he does – it's beyond me, but earns him a packet anyway. What about you?'

'I'm an only child – or as good as. My mother died when I was in my teens and my father remarried a woman who didn't rate me much. They had more kids and moved to Canada. And no offspring of my own,' he went on quickly, like he didn't want any sympathy. I didn't know what to say then either, having no clue whether that meant years of failed effort or not wanting to be a parent anyway. It was an impossible enough question between proper friends, let alone total strangers. Even with Mel, single and childless, I always trod carefully. 'I think teachers are the most important people in society,' he continued thoughtfully, before adding, like it was something that needed owning up to, 'I paint. Or at least I try to. I am not what you would call successful – private sales to friends, that sort of thing. Though it's hard to know what "success" really is when it comes to art, don't you agree?' There was a sudden defensiveness in his tone, such a wariness of being judged, that my heart went out to him. 'What I mean is,' he went on, 'it's one thing to know a work is supposedly "valuable" and quite another to be truly absorbed by it. Like with a painting worth millions, you can stare at it till your eyes boggle, but if it isn't pushing your buttons, it isn't pushing your buttons.'

'No, that's so true.' My mind was skittering back to the husband thing, whether to just say Pete and I had been together since school and have done with it, but he hadn't finished.

'Does George Eliot push yours for instance?'

'My buttons?' For some reason, the question made the blood rush to my face. 'I suppose it helps that my reading group are doing it,' I replied quickly. 'There's this strict club rule about having to read the actual book.'

'Ah. Now there's a good rule for a book club.' And suddenly we were both snorting with laughter, so that people at the other plastic tables turned to look. We laughed till our eyes streamed, till we had to not look at each other. It was a laughter that had nothing to do with book clubs or books or anything except the unlooked-for and thoroughly inexplicable pleasure of the moment in which we found ourselves. I didn't mind the turning heads. In fact, I rather relished them. They reminded me of all the times I had watched other couples seeming, effortlessly, to enjoy each other's company – the sense of wonder it had evoked in me, of envy; and now, here on this blowy, bright, unlikely February morning, sitting in a dungeon of a cafeteria, it was happening the other way round. It was happening to me.

III

A wonderful calm infuses me once I am inside the airport. The wobbly wheels of the case run more smoothly along the hard, polished floor and it makes the dodgy handle easier to manage.

All flights are on time. I am earlier than we have agreed by almost an hour. I go to the toilets and check myself over in the mirror, resisting the urge to swipe on more lippy or start fussing with my hair. Jack likes me as I am. 'What scars,' he said, the first time I dared to mention them, which was the first time we made love, the first time we laid ourselves bare. We were in the empty flat belonging to a friend of his called Hugh, a mad snatched couple of hours on a Saturday in May after weeks of calling, texting and brief agonised hand-holding across tables in shadowy corners of wine bars and coffee houses. Helena was having lunch with a girlfriend and Pete and Harry were at an end-of-season game. Jack had jumped on a tube from Islington and I had headed up the Northern line. Six stops each from opposite directions, meeting in the middle. We had drawn the curtains to block out the daylight – the world – and were sitting on a white leather sofa in the sitting room, holding hands, trembling and happy, in no rush, despite the magnitude of the occasion and time, as always, being so pitifully short.

'As a schoolgirl, I had bad skin, you see,' I said. He let go of my hand and brushed the side of his index finger down my cheek. 'But you certainly don't now,' he said. 'You are beautiful, Fran, glowing. You have an inner light.' He took my face between his palms and began kissing every inch of it, slowly, gently, methodically, working his way down over my forehead, my eyes, my cheeks, my nose, my ears, my chin. When he reached my throat, I found myself moaning softly. 'Your scars are only visible in your own mind,' he murmured. 'As are mine. We all have them.' He pulled back, waiting till I opened my eyes and then smiled. 'All I see is you. You. Frances. Fran, the warmest, most loving, sincere woman I have ever had the fortune to come across.' He shifted closer and placed his mouth on mine as I had ached for him to do, sliding his tongue between my ready, open lips. He tasted sweet and his beard was silky and warm against my skin. We undid the buttons on each other's shirts as we kissed, pulling them from the moorings of our trousers. His shoulders were broad and contoured by muscle, but the rest of his body was boyishly lean and pale, with a shield of light brown hairs on his chest. 'Let me look,' he said, when we were both down to our underwear. 'Let me take you in.'

I had only ever been with Pete, and it was always in the dark; *I could be anyone*, I often thought; *I am just a body*. And though what Jack asked of me made me shy, there was such unquestioning, tender, loving acceptance in the way he stared that overcoming my shyness became integral to the desire of wanting him in return.

I stood up and unclipped my bra and slid off my pants. My blood pounded in my ears. It was like setting myself free, from the version of me to which I had clung for two and a half decades like a ball and chain. 'Oh my goodness,' he said, his voice full of loving wonder, and it was like a part of me had jumped inside his head, able to see and share the pleasure of what he surveyed: my strong hips and a firm round belly, my short shapely legs, the breasts that had always troubled me for their size, ungainly but still pleasingly full, their shimmering silver threads offering testimony both to my forty-two years of living and all the rigours of bearing and mothering Harry.

'I like how you look too,' I whispered, shy still of my own daring.

'I will do anything you want,' Fran, he said. 'Anything.' He was stroking my forearms, his eyes still drinking me in. 'We can even call a halt now, if this is all too much. We can put our clothes back on, just talk. It's okay. Everything is okay, so long as I am with you.'

A whoop of laughter flew out of me. I threw my head back, my arms shivering under his touch, my body burning. Right from the get-go, Pete's approach to sex was to assert his superior strength, to take what he wanted when he wanted; my role was to acquiesce, feigning the pleasure that his needy ego required. Survival, like love, can make you do many things. Any form of mutual, loving desire had never been in our lexicon; let alone the revelation that it could take the form of these tremulous, precious moments that Jack and I were now savouring, barely having touched each other.

Emboldened, I took a step back and said I wanted him to take off his boxers. I said if he dared do anything along the lines of calling a halt, I would self-combust into a pile of dust and he'd have a lot of explaining to do to his property-tycoon friend, Hugh whoever-he-was, who had so generously offered us the flat and who, I could tell, from the minimalist pristine gleam of its decor, didn't like mess. I added, rather more ruefully, that, by my reckoning, we had precisely thirty-nine minutes before we had to be putting our clothes back on again.

'It's McKay, Hugh McKay, and he doesn't live here,' Jack said huskily, standing up and removing his boxers in one swift movement, and then lifting me onto his hips. I locked my legs around his back and we began to kiss again, in earnest this time, any notion of stopping utterly forgotten.

Afterwards, I lay on top of him – the narrowness of the sofa necessitated it, but it was where I wanted to be, my smaller body on his longer, broader one, contained within the frame of him, skin-on-skin, leg-on-leg, arm-on-arm, my head turned sideways on his chest so that I could feel his heartbeat matching mine. I told him I loved him, which was the first time I'd said it, but not his. Then I told him properly about

Pete, just so he knew, I said, and not because I was expecting any answers.

IV

I park myself at a table in one of the walk-through cafés near the check-in desks with a coffee and a muffin, even though I don't really want anything. But I was too rushed and tense to manage breakfast and not eating gives me a headache, which is the last thing I want. I need my wits about me. I also want to see, think, to *feel* every instant of this once unimaginable day. After all the years of putting up, holding in, bowing to, cajoling, *navigating* Pete, I've found this man, this courage, this chance, and nothing is going to get in my way. I have become the heroine of my own romantic story. I am taking control, just like Dorothea and all heroines across the centuries must learn to do, of my life. *My* life.

I drink the coffee and eat the muffin which is studded with blueberries. They stick to my teeth and taste too sweet. Time, displayed on the big airport clock, seems to have gone into slo-mo. As the sluggish seconds pass, I am aware of all the calmness seeping out of me, drop by drop. Soon, I am checking and rechecking the inside zipped compartment of my handbag for my passport with such feverish compulsion that I loop the bag strap across my chest like a satchel, clasping my arms over it to stop them twitching.

My brain flips to Harry, getting his rucksack nicked at Heathrow on a post-GCSE school trip to Barcelona. So quick, he said, that the thief was out of the airport doors before he or any of his group could properly register what was going on. The rucksack had contained everything that mattered, including a new laptop Pete and I had given him for his sixteenth. Reporting, sorting, replacing it all had been expensive, not to mention inconvenient, what with having to turn round and head back down the M4 when I had only just dropped him off. 'These kinds of things seem to happen to Harry,' said the master in charge helpfully, before rushing off to passport control to join the rest of the group. Instead of Barcelona, Harry spent the half-term in his room, gaming and driving both Pete and I up the wall.

Someone has left a newspaper on a seat and I try to read it. Three immigrants have drowned trying to swim the Channel. A new species of butterfly has been identified in Papua New Guinea. Scientists have photographed another black hole thirty million light years away, a glowing doughnut with a dark nothingness at its heart that gives me the shivers. In Penge, police have arrested a terrorist suspect. Only five miles from my own front door... except it's not mine any more, I remind myself with a jolt. It's just Pete's. And Harry's, of course, bless him, until he gets properly on his feet and can make his own way in the world.

An ache for my boy flares, so bad that I have to squeeze my eyes shut until it passes. Leaving him is temporary, I remind myself, a necessity, until everything gets worked out.

In the meantime, I am asking for nothing – not even a divorce – and neither is Jack. That guilt and desperation can make you big-hearted has been yet another recent discovery, but the truth is, neither of us can face the messy horror of it. Jack says Helena would deploy hotshot lawyers and tie him knots for being a 'kept man' – which I can fully believe after all that he has told me about her quantities of money and the constant attempts to belittle him. While Pete... But I can't even bring myself to imagine Pete's reactions. Another reason to be as far away as possible. It's been a while – many years – since he really flipped out, but the possibility hovers, a dark cloud, over everything. It's a bit like living with an unexploded bomb, I explained to Mel once, when she was on one of her beefs about how I should leave; the one sure thing to set it off would be me trying to walk away.

Jack's distress on the subject of Pete is so acute that I tend to avoid it. He says things like we should be going to the police rather than Spain, and that if the man ever lays so much as a finger on me, he will personally ensure he rues the day he was born, which is nonsense – I can't imagine Jack being violent with anyone – but sweet all the same. Sometimes, in lighter moments, we joke about how well our hard-hearted, manipulative spouses would get along; how handy such a coupling would be, leaving us to be free of both and with each other. Although, in truth, I wouldn't wish Pete on anyone, not even Helena.

I check my emails. No emergencies. No unforeseen problems. I have seen off a lot in the last few weeks, unsubscribing from pointless things, winding down in every possible area without doing enough to provoke awkward questions. Mel, superstar that she is, has promised to help with any part of the inevitable shitstorm that crosses her path, stonewalling and fighting my corner, particularly with Pete, who is bound to come knocking.

On the work front, Camille won't get my letter until she returns from her Florida family holiday, a few days before the start of the summer term. She'll be astounded – rock-solid Fran Grove doing a runner – and furious. She'll say, why not have given her some private warning, and 'what sort of friend and colleague am I'. She'll say, what is she supposed to tell my Year Ones, all those trusting little five-year-olds I claim to care about, not to mention their parents, taking the plunge with Chalfonts. She'll say, because she isn't sufficiently briefed to deduce anything else, 'what the fuck, Fran, throwing away a perfectly decent life for what – some unhappily married loser *artist*?'

And then there's Pete and Harry. Finding their letters. My heart pumps. I can picture Pete's thick fingers ripping the top of the envelope off, the snarling disbelief and outrage; how he'll yell at Harry, at the entire street, at anyone prepared to listen. *I always knew she was rotten; she never really loved me or treated me right.* But it is the image of

Harry's eyes travelling down the page that really tears at my heart. Despite my painstaking efforts at explanation, my son's already hurtful sea-change teenage decision to start hating me will find reinforcement with every word. I wonder if he'll see the smears on the paper and realise how hard I wept. I wonder if he will guess how the pen slid in my trembling fingers, how my chest nearly burst, how the room spun.

I had been losing him already, I remind myself; my beloved boy, whose every murmur I once knew like my own name, whose every small sock I folded with the loving awe of one who recognises herself, at last, to be truly blessed; the child who arrived at the head of a little ghostly procession of siblings lost to miscarriages; a baby who liked to curl in my arms – and my arms only – every night, long into toddlerhood, breathily sucking his thumb, clinging with such mad motherlove that it was this early period of the marriage that saw Pete at his worst.

People who say babies draw couples together know nothing. I was once one of them. At twenty-three, I truly believed Harry would solve all our difficulties. Instead, his arrival just shifted and intensified their focus. From the start, the three of us were like a triangle of points that never quite connected, not altogether anyhow. The distance between Pete and me was already there, and it was like Harry fell into it, stoking his father's envy as he went.

I check my watch and suddenly, ridiculously, I'm in danger of being late. My phone rings as I leap to my feet and I throw it against my ear. 'I know – I'm here – I'm on my way...'

'Frannie?'

'Rob?' I can't keep the disbelief from my voice. I had been so sure it would be Jack.

'Are you okay, sis? You sound odd.'

'No... yes... I'm fine. All well with you and Jo?' I stammer, desperate to deflect any interrogation.

'Yeah, grand. Look, I just wanted to—'

'And the twins? And little Marcus?' I am scanning the concourse as

I speak, juggling my mobile in order to sling the carry-on securely over one shoulder before grabbing the case.

'Oh yes, all good. Except, of course, the little bugger doesn't sleep,' he adds, his voice soft with love. 'Jo and I take it in turns to wear earplugs at night, pillow-talk generally being about why the hell we had another, as if we didn't learn our lesson with Tilda and Billy—'

'Rob, this isn't the best time...'

An announcement on the airport speaker system almost drowns me out.

'Where the hell are you? Sounds like... Are you at an airport? Where are you going? Don't tell me that great ray of sunshine to whom you are married is whisking you away for once?'

'No, I... I'm meeting Mel...' I falter. 'She's been to... to Barcelona. She's hurt her... foot – her ankle – so I'm helping out.'

I am cursing myself for not ending the call at the get-go, for dithering. And now the absurd nonsense about Mel, all while I am scanning the crowds which are starting to gather round the EasyJet desks. My brother's voice, so familiar and trusting, so blissfully ignorant, is making me feel bad in the last way I want or need. He will be the first to get a full and proper explanation, once the deed is done.

'Mel really is something else,' he goes on in his booming energetic manner. 'I mean, I know you two go way back, what with all that business at school, when you helped her through after that boy—'

'Ed Caulder,' I say automatically, my eyes travelling from face to face, 'he was lucky just to get expelled, and that was because Mel didn't press charges.'

'Though nothing actually *happened*...'

I can't believe I am having a Mel conversation. I am fully aware of Rob's reservations about my best friend, stuck in their usual groove, despite not having seen her for years and being partly founded, I cannot help suspecting, on the fact of Mel's size – the elephant in the room, he once joked, for which he knows I have never forgiven him.

'All I'm saying,' Rob goes on quickly, 'is that you always put yourself out for everyone else. Not just Mel, but that husband of yours and all those old ladies you visit—'

'One lady. Annie Smith.'

The queues are so thick that it is getting impossible to tell where one starts and another begins.

'Mother Theresa of South London... Hasn't Mel got anyone else she could have asked?'

'It's the holidays and I am happy to help,' I snap, immediately feeling bad and adding in a softer tone, 'Look, Rob, I've got to go.'

'Well, what about later then,' he ploughs on, in his obstinate, winning way, 'after you've done your chauffeur act? I'm in London with some time on my hands for once – not one but two meetings cancelled – I suppose I could just jump on the train home, but, being the loving brother that I am, I thought, why not see that little sister of mine—'

'Rob...' I cut in, exasperated.

'Okay, okay, I'll let you go. But just so you know, Jo and I want you all to come for Easter.' He's talking at treble speed now. 'It's been an age and I'm very fond of that waster of a godson you produced – who also runs you ragged, by the way – and you can at last meet the monstrous Marcus – one dribbling grin and you'll be a goner like the rest of us – Frannie? Did you hear? Are you still there?'

I am still scanning the throng of travellers so keenly my eyes are beginning to water. Rob's words have receded into the mass of white noise inside my head, part of a jumble that now includes images of my nephews and niece in the most recent Christmas card family collage; the twins in pom-pom hats and stripy wellingtons, the new baby swathed in a yellow blanket, his pink, round face topped by a tiny knitted white skullcap that gives him the look of an exotic fruit dunked in sugar.

Suddenly, at last, I glimpse the back of Jack's head through the throng and start to run. 'Sorry, Rob, but I've really got to go. I will be in touch very soon, I promise. I love you.'

'I love you too, sis,' he says as I cut him off, a trace of bewilderment in his voice.

* * *

An hour later, the EasyJet queues are thinning and I am still hovering nearby, pinned into my coat by my satchel handbag, phone in one hand, the suitcase handle in the other, the carry-on parked between my feet. It wasn't the back of Jack's head. It was quite a different person, a man with brown hair, as tall as Jack, but beardless, several years younger and from Germany, as it turned out, once he started speaking to a blonde woman who strode towards him from the direction of the toilets.

I have checked my phone perhaps thirty, perhaps eighty times, but there is nothing there apart from a message Rob left after our call, which I can't bring myself to listen to just yet. Not until Jack is safely at my side.

I have texted him now. Twice. First with the word, *Emergency?* And then saying, *Worried. pls call*. I have also tried ringing, but it cuts out straightaway.

It dawns on me that Jack must have lost his phone. These things happen, and I am not going to panic. It is probably in the back of the taxi that he had to take from the place where he was staying last night, seeing the person he had to see before making his way to the airport. The person with whom he was leaving all his precious paintings. A person whom Helena reputedly does not like and whose name I cannot, for some reason, now summon to mind. Helena herself is in Cornwall, with her father and sister. The mother is dead, the father is called Ralph and has Parkinson's, which must be hard on Helena. On all of them. The sister is called Christabel. She is older and expecting a baby. My brain is like a flapping sail, untethered.

Brian, that's it. Jack spent the evening with Brian, who knows there is a plane to catch, but not the reasons behind it. Helena is returning to London this afternoon, by which time we will be long gone.

I can feel the muffin sitting like glue in my stomach. I need, badly, to pee, but dare not leave my post. If Jack has no phone, then even a few minutes away could be fatal. He might turn up and think I have already checked in, or gone through passport control. Worse, he might imagine I have changed my mind and have his own panic attack. He will be in a lather somewhere, and it is my job, my own act of love, to stay contrastingly calm. Whatever we face, we face it together. That has been our mantra. Nothing about that can, or ever will, change.

There is only one girl now at the EasyJet jet desk advertising our Madrid flight. She is busy on her phone. On the main noticeboard the 'final call' sign has started flashing. My heart hammers. My phone slides in my gripped fingers. I could still go for it – leg it to the girl, to the gate, to the plane, plead with the crew, on my knees if necessary, to make the plane wait. Jack is coming. I know he is coming.

I stare at my phone. We are two hours beyond the agreed meeting time. He would contact me now if he could. He would never, ever, leave me like this, hanging. That is why I know his phone has been lost or taken. But maybe other things have been taken too. Maybe he has been mugged. Maybe he is lying in an alleyway somewhere, unconscious. Maybe he has been stabbed. Maybe he is bleeding out, with no one at his side to tell him he is loved.

I am so hot inside my coat. My head is exploding. I cannot move. The big digital airport clock is playing tricks again, speeding up now, hurtling me towards a point of no return. I need the seconds to stop. I need a delay. I squeeze my eyes shut and pray for a fault to be found with the plane. Brakes. Indicators. Wing flaps. Toilet blockage. I don't care what. I pray harder than I ever have in my life for anything. Except Harry, of course, most precious cargo after all the years of early bleedings and dashed hopes.

When I flutter my eyes open, the flashing sign has been replaced by the words *Gate closed*. A different girl is sitting at the check-in desk with a new flight number behind her head. A fresh group of travellers is starting to queue.

I could barge through them. I could plead.

Or I could remain waiting. I watch the new crowd thicken. I decide that when the chance arises, I will ask about the next flight to Madrid, when it leaves and the possibility of securing two seats. Jack will come soon, I know he will. I picture his face, the haggard look he gets when the stress with Helena is bad and he is trying to hide it from me; the mournfulness, like a weight, in his beautiful blue eyes. He will be so relieved to see me here. So happy. His expression will light up as he kisses me, leaving the tingle of his beard on my lips. The apologies and love will pour out of him. *You are my brave darling girl, Fran,* he will say in his sweet, slightly grand way. *Thank you for waiting, for keeping faith. I would be nowhere without you. Nowhere. I have found you now and I will never let you go.*

V

I am on the train, not sitting, but standing by the door, hunched inside my coat, hoicking my case out of the way of the steady traffic to and from the buffet car. An icy draught is blowing in from somewhere, cold steel on the back of my neck. It is only four in the afternoon, but the skies are pink-tinged and murky with the promise of nightfall. I cannot look out. I cannot bear to see the same landscape sliding past, the same world of this morning but utterly changed. I drop my gaze to my feet, to the scuffed suede tips of my boots, the slight bulge of my big toes, the grey smudge left by a dribble of olive oil the day after I had bought them.

'Don't move,' instructed Jack, seeing what had happened. We had entered the phase of occasionally using Mel's place for a couple of hours and I was frying onions for a Bolognese. Jack was sitting on a kitchen chair, reading out funny snippets from a newspaper he had picked up on the tube. We were like a proper couple. An ordinary couple. Spaghetti and a bottle of rioja. As comfy chatting as silent. The luxury of normality infusing us both like balm.

Jack grabbed a roll of kitchen paper and knelt at my feet, pressing piece after piece against the blob of oil, 'to soak up the worst', he said, while I stared down at the neat circles of rich brown hair spiralling out of his crown, laughing and saying, 'A beautiful man on bended knee, what more could a girl want.' Then suddenly he was tossing aside the bits of kitchen paper and kissing the boots instead, followed by my calves and shins, working his way up until the hem of my skirt was brushing his face. 'You might want to turn those onions off for a moment,' he said.

Near me on the train, leaning against the toilet door, two young men in crumpled city suits swig from beer cans and whisky miniatures, discussing, volubly, the unlikely existence of God. One had been brought up a Catholic. 'I mean, the flames of hell, for Christ's sake.' They move onto black holes. The glowing doughnut picture in the airport newspaper burns in the back of my mind, returning me to the slight stickiness of the café table under my forearms, the excitement churning in the pit of my stomach. It is like remembering another person and I yearn to return to her, all her wild excitement and hopes still intact.

I press my eyes closed and speak to Jack. We have had moments of telepathy in the past, calls at exact times they were needed, nights when our imagining of each other was almost as intense as our actual love making. I can feel him thinking of me now. I can *feel* it. *It is all right*, I tell him. *I know that something terrible has happened. I do not even need to know what it is to forgive you. We will regroup. We will find a second chance.*

The train, suddenly and for no discernible reason, grinds to a standstill, reminding me, with a sickening lurch, that I am in a race against time. Even now, Pete and Harry, whose two-week work experience in the sports shop has somehow run on for eleven months, will be closing the tills, checking their pockets for their phones, preparing to lock up. Their commute east is roughly forty minutes, an hour if I am lucky. My remaining journey time, with no glitches, should be half an hour. At best, I will have a ten-minute window before they get home. Only an idiot would have gone for it.

With each passing minute at the airport, it had got harder to think straight. There were too many options. Whether to carry on waiting.

Whether to make my way to Madrid on my own. Whether to flee to Mel's, or simply scramble home while I still could; regroup until Jack could explain what has gone so badly wrong. Bridges were burning, but it seemed to me, standing dazed and alone in the swirling maelstrom of the departures concourse, that I could still put the fires out, still do enough to buy Jack and I more time.

I wasted precious minutes hauling the suitcase to a Left Luggage locker and then changing my mind. I badly wanted to leave it – it was so big, such an encumbrance, somehow it had started to feel integral to the failure of the day. And I also longed to leave something solid in the airport, some marker of intent to return. It was the image of all the telltale little gaps on the shelves at home that stopped me – the silver knick-knacks of my mother's that I had been unable to resist packing, along with a couple of treasured family photos, including the one of Harry blowing out two candles on his second birthday, his little cheeks puffed as golf balls, his face creased with an expression of earnest intensity, reserved these days for sessions on his laptop. I might be able to bluster responses to queries about the odd half-empty drawer and extra wardrobe space, but Pete, eagle-eyed, despite the obsession with his own needs and miseries, would spot such a quantity of obvious blanks in an instant.

One of the suited young men widens his eyes at me and I realise I have been staring. *Jack, sweetheart, where are you? Have you died?* I tighten my throat muscles to stop the threat of tears. I cannot cry. Not now. Not yet. My phone is quiet as a tomb, my fingers round it cold. But Jack may yet contact me. All can still be well. Even the possibility of returning to Gatwick remains. We could sleep at the airport if necessary, propped against each other, like the two weary travellers we are. The delay might even be fun. Part of the adventure. My frayed heart canters.

With creaky sighs, the train at last starts to move. I stare bleakly at my phone screen. The notification of Rob's message is still there. I recall all Jack's and my painstaking efforts to be sensible about how we corresponded: deletions of messages, no voicemails, no photos. We ruled out getting second phones, reckoning that the risks of being tripped up, especially for me, outweighed the advantages. It wasn't for long, we reasoned and we had our brief encounters at Mel's place to keep us sane. Our priority was to stay in control of the situation until we could escape it. There would be no avoiding the explosions, the carnage, that would eventually follow, but at least we would be in charge of – and at a safe distance from – the detonation.

I press on Rob's voicemail message and put the phone against my ear.

I just hope Mel appreciates you, is all I can say.

I can hear the edge of hurt in his voice.

Let me know about Easter, okay? You are all welcome for the whole weekend if you fancy it – you could apply your talents to clues for the Easter Egg Hunt – remember how Billy and Tilda loved that last time? And, look, would you be Marcus' godmother? That's why I was hoping to see you today actually – to ask properly. It will be a naming ceremony like with the twins, but this time Jo and I've decided to throw godparents in for good measure. The other two might even get some retrospective ones while we're at it. The more people looking out for your kids, the better, right? And Jo's got all those God-fearing sisters to keep happy. Anyway, call me when you can, okay?

There was a second of silence before the message cut out, as if a part of him had half hoped for an answer.

VI

'So what exactly does your pal Hugh use this place for? I mean, it's still so clean and empty, like no one is ever here.'

'It's just one of his investments, for renting out, but he hasn't got around to it yet,' Jack explained ruefully. 'He's already got a house in Hampstead, a flat in New York and a place in Toulon, which he jokingly calls the shack, even though it's got eight bedrooms and a swimming pool.'

'Wow. How does anyone even have time for three homes?'

'I guess he doesn't,' Jack laughed.

'And, in the meantime, he gives you a free pass to come here because...'

'Because Helena helped with the furnishings. He doesn't know about us,' Jack admitted with a sigh. 'All I did was sneak off and get an extra set of keys cut, from Helena's...' He shook his head, an expression of dazed disbelief clouding his face.

'I know, it's all crazy,' I murmured, squeezing his hand, loving him all the more for how at one we were in hating the thickening duplicities.

'Hugh's more Helena's friend than mine actually,' he confessed.

'They grew up in Suffolk together, went to the same birthday parties as kids, that sort of thing.'

An image of Helena floated across my mind, pieced together from other such fragments and the occasional glimpse of an elegant blonde woman in pictures on Jack's phone. I envisaged her now, skipping through her rose-tinted life, apparently taking all that she wanted as she went, including men. Including Jack. A woman clearly brought up to believe the world was there to do her bidding. Jack must have liked that about her once. A part of me wanted to ask him if that was the case, but also not to know. Knowing would have brought Helena into our precious space, defiling it. It did make me wonder though, just for a moment, what he didn't say, the degree to which he filtered things, just like I did about Pete.

It was a gleaming breezy June Saturday morning and our second time at the flat. On this occasion, we had carved out the luxury of a full hour and a half. I was supposedly at Mel's having a crisis coffee about her overdemanding mother and Jack had a big chunk of freedom thanks to Helena going to visit a great-aunt in Cambridge. We had sat in a square of sun on the sofa for ten minutes and then ventured, hand in hand, down the corridor and into the third, smallest bedroom, where I had spread a small bathroom towel on top of the covers for us to make love on, a detail of precaution and planning which had prompted Jack, seeing me pull the towel from my shoulder bag, to gasp with admiration. 'You think of everything, Fran,' he cried, pulling me into his arms. 'Christ, how could anyone *not* love you?'

The spare room was the plainest in the apartment, little more than a chic box, with ceiling lights and several large landscape paintings ranged round the walls like windows. It felt blissfully sealed in and safe, a wonderful contrast to the gnawing and increasingly demeaning sense of stealth still dogging our other encounters – so snatched and furtive, brushing hands and kissing in grimy corners, behind trees in parks and one terrible, quickly abandoned attempt to have a cup of tea at mine, when I couldn't relax for fear of Pete barging in through the front door. It was no way to be with someone you cared about, let alone someone you were starting to love with every ounce of your being. At home afterwards, scrubbing the traces of Jack's aftershave off my face, so much bolder and sweeter than anything Pete ever put on his body, I would gawp at my ruddy cheeks and guilty eyes, marvelling at what my heart was making me do. Only when Jack and I were actually together did everything make sense.

The bedroom was warm and the towel downy under our nakedness. Jack talked softly as we touched, as fearless with his words as the positions he nudged and rolled and shifted me into for our lovemaking. The effortless pleasure we took in each other was stupefying.

'I don't understand it,' I said, as we lay side by side afterwards, our bodies damp, only the knuckles of our nearest hands lightly touching.

'Me neither.'

'It's like you've unlocked me.'

'That's good.' He laughed softly. 'I don't think I've got the words for what you have done to me. Made me hope, perhaps.' He picked up my hand and kissed the fingertips, one by one. 'Love is a lot like hope, don't you think?'

'Yes, I do. I totally do.' I rolled over and nuzzled his arm before flopping back so we were side by side again. 'But I still don't really understand how – why – it is happening. We couldn't be more different. You with your arty genius and me stuck in a classroom...' I said the words fondly. Jack knew I loved my job, the respite it had provided over the years. 'You don't even like children,' I added softly.

'I've never said that,' he murmured.'

'I guess you haven't.'

'Helena couldn't, but was clear she never wanted to anyway. And I was okay with it. I mean, as an artist you have to lead quite a selfish life in many ways – putting the work first.'

'Oh, I see.' I hesitated, curious, but wary, again, of pushing too hard about his home life, not wanting to intrude beyond what he wished to share. 'And now?'

'Now I'm not okay with anything. Except you. Thank God I met you. Talk about luck, that day at the auction house...' He rolled onto his side and pulled me closer, clasping me so tightly it hurt.

'Or serendipity,' I whispered.

'Oh yes, that's a better word. Fun to say, too.' He loosened his grip and shouted 'Serendipity!' at the ceiling several times.

'I just want to occupy the same space as you,' I giggled, 'like animals in a burrow. And I love your smell. That's pretty animal too, I guess. In fact, I could eat you, right now.' I pressed my mouth into his shoulder, biting gently.

Jack kissed the top of my head. 'That's a quite-recent one of mine, by the way.' He pointed across the bed.

'That picture?' I wriggled upright. He was indicating a canvas I had barely noticed, smaller than the rest and hanging in the corner. 'Really? Oh my goodness.' I clambered over his legs to look more closely. 'You should have said.'

'I'm saying now. Best to look from further away. Try by the door.'

I slithered off the bed and, within moments, the streaks of yellow, pink and green, floating on pillows of soft blue, coalesced into picnickers at a flower-fringed lake dotted with little sailing boats. The figures were in his usual willowy style, and translucent, apart from the occasional highlighted detail – a crimson ribbon flashing on a sunhat, a sparkle of a bracelet round a wrist.

'It's beautiful.'

'Ah, but you would say that, wouldn't you?' He scowled at me affectionately. 'It's an old one I've reworked, based on a photo of a lake in a park in Madrid. I'm quite pleased with it.'

'I wish you'd let me see more of what you are working on.'

'I know, but it's not my way. And taking snaps on the phone...' He shuddered.

'It's okay.' I bent over and kissed the tip of his big toe, which happened to be the nearest bit of him. 'So, this escaped the dreaded red felt pen anyway.'

'Yes.' He answered absently, still scrutinising his own picture, critically by the look of it.

I rubbed the arch of his foot. I hated to think of the insulting gashes of red wounding his treasured painting. How could Jack be with someone who treated him so monstrously? The fragments had included references to similar outbursts over the years – histrionics, drunkenness, brinkmanship – despite having everything, Helena clearly loved to fight, and I found it mystifying. She had everything a woman could want and yet evidently didn't appreciate it. She was a constant liability too. A recent night of binge-drinking, Jack had reported bitterly, had ended with a dawn dash to A & E because of her tripping over on their patio and cutting her head. Little wonder he talked of having found peace with me. 'Well, thank god for Hugh, is all I can say,' I offered brightly. 'If he likes your paintings then I like the man right back.'

'Oh yes, Hugh is a big fan.' The hint of self-mockery was there as always. Jack made no secret of his deep discomfort at selling only to friends. Apparently, there had been an agent and some exhibiting once upon a time, but somehow it had fizzled out.

'Never give up, will you?' I blurted. 'I mean, I know I'm no expert, but this...' I flapped my hands at the dazzling lakeside scene, 'well... I think it's as good as any impressionist, Renoir, or any of them.' I was aware of sounding lame. I had made no pretence of any knowledge of art beyond a GCSE coursework project on the Renaissance and a couple of visits to big London galleries with Harry's Primary class when they needed parents to help out. 'All it takes is one break,' I said fiercely, hating my powerlessness, but aware of some hunger in Jack, hanging onto my words, 'the right picture, the right buyer, the right time.'

He sighed. 'Thank you, Fran, for your faith. All artists need a bit of that from those around them, those they hold dear.' The heaviness was back in his tone. He meant Helena, of course, and it made me hate her. It was odd and horrible to feel such antipathy towards a person I had never met. A person to whom, on the face of it, I was doing a great wrong. But it didn't feel like a wrong. It felt like a right. If she did not love Jack, or treat him with love, then why should I not be allowed to love him in the way he deserved, and be loved in return? The same went for Pete and me – I was worth so much more, as Jack always said.

I gazed at the painting. It seemed to glow with all the vibrancy that Jack himself possessed, all the energies that his wife seemed so adept at crushing.

'But I've no intention of giving up,' said Jack firmly. 'Not even Van Gogh was properly recognised in his time. Though I have to say that being able to pay my own bills from time to time would be nice.' He laughed sharply and my heart went out to him again.

Apart from dividends from a few modest investments, it was clear he had no regular income at all. Helena paid for everything, and it was painful to see how much he loathed it. Her father had made a killing in the city and apparently loved to spoil both his daughters. Helena had spent her youth working in picture galleries, he had explained – it was how they had met – and now dabbled in interior design, but never once in her life had she actually needed to earn a living.

'Maybe posthumous global fame awaits me,' Jack went on, much more cheerily, 'you never know. Maybe even the felt-pen episode will become famous, like Van Gogh's ear. Hey, are you coming back to bed or what?' He patted the towel.

'Definitely. Right this minute, in fact.' I was eager to hold him again, to be held by him. But as I turned towards the bed, a door slammed. I froze, one knee poised on the edge of the mattress. Jack, too, had gone rigid and was sitting up, head cocked, eyes frozen. It had to have come from another flat. My heart was sprinting so hard it hurt.

I widened my eyes questioningly at Jack, hoping for an answer that I knew wasn't there. Had we got too lost in ourselves? I glanced at my watch. Twenty precious minutes of our mutually allocated time remained. Except, of course, that was irrelevant, since if this was Hugh paying a visit, he had no idea we were in the flat. He was a landlord coming to check on his property. We were interlopers whose luck had run out. Unless we were very quiet and the visit was quick. Maybe he had dropped by to pick up some post. Had there been post? I couldn't recall any.

The splash of a running tap exploded into the silence, eradicating our last hopes. It was clearly coming from the kitchen, the first room off the small vestibule by the front door. Jack leapt off the bed as if he had been shot and began tunnelling his legs into his trousers and scooping on his socks.

I seized my bra, flung with such sweet casualness onto the floor less than an hour before, fighting with its twisting straps. Neither of us spoke. Jack was dressed in instants, but I was way behind, my pants snagging on my toes in my eagerness to get them over my feet. Hopping, I lost my balance and fell with a thump against the built-in wardrobe.

Jack groaned softly. He was holding my things for me – clothes, shoes, handbag, the towel – frantically trying to straighten the creases out of the bedcovers at the same time.

Footsteps had started down the far end of the passageway, slow taps on the parquet, with pauses for the opening of each door. I had my shirt on and was doing up the buttons. Jack was watching me, ashen. As my fumbling continued, he jerked his head in the direction of the dark narrow space under the bed, his blue eyes stricken with a fear that was far worse to witness than the experience of my own palpitating chest.

'Please.' He mouthed the word, gesturing again, more vigorously, at the narrow gap. Something in me had stuck. I didn't want to hide under the bed like a thief. We weren't criminals. We were just two people who had found each other in an ugly world; a world that survived on appearances and clinging to things that did not matter. Despite the embarrassment of my half-dressed state, a part of me yearned for the strength to stand my ground and tell this Hugh person exactly that. He was partly Jack's friend too, after all, a man of the world, surely capable of understanding the situation.

The footsteps had paused again, so near the door now that they could have been in the room.

Jack was looking as if he might throw up. 'Please, Fran.' His lips stretched unnaturally wide to mime the words, a silent scream. Then, in one quick motion, he rammed all my stuff under the bed and tugged on my arm. 'It's our only hope', he whispered.

Tears flooded my eyes as I obediently sank to my knees and rolled into the slice of dusty darkness. I lay on my back unblinking as Jack threw himself onto the bed in the same instant, bringing the sag of the mattress to within a couple of inches of my nose.

The door opened and two slim, shapely bare legs, rising out of tall, thick-heeled shoes the colour of tangerines, slid into my line of vision.

'Jack, what the fuck.' The voice was breathy with shock.

The mattress moved, bringing a dangling cotton thread nearer my left cheek. Then a version of Jack's voice I had never heard before, more expansive and slurring with feigned sleepiness, said, 'Darling, good god, what the hell are you doing here?'

There was a laugh, high-pitched with incredulity. 'I might ask the same of you.'

'Stupid, I know, but I wanted to see the Hugh picture in situ. Then I'm afraid I couldn't resist a snooze. Slept like crap last night, didn't you? Those fucking foxes...'

'You gave me such a fright, Jack. I thought there was a bloody squatter or lunatic or something.'

'I thought you were on a Daphne mission.'

Oh god, Helena. *Helena.*

'She cancelled, the silly, when I was halfway there. A text. Said she was ill, when she probably just didn't feel up to it. Extremely annoying – not that I could tell her that. So then I decided to check up on a window blind Hugh's been going on about...though it was fine...'

'Maybe Daphne really is ill.'

'I bet she isn't... Look, how did you get in here anyway? I mean, I've got the keys.'

'Hugh gave me a set too, just in case, remember?'

There followed a fraction of a pause. I wasn't sure when I had last breathed. Stars were pricking at the edges of my vision. Helena didn't sound as I had imagined. Her voice had a harshness, but was mostly bewildered.

'So you came to look at your own picture? My God, Jack, that's sort of tragic.'

'Yup. That's me. Tragic.'

'Well...' The shape of the mattress shifted as she sat down. Every beat of my heart hurt. 'You could take me to lunch, I suppose, now that I am here.' She had dropped her voice so much that I had to strain my ears to hear. 'Unless...' The bed creaked faintly as the orange shoes disappeared from view. 'I mean, darling, we do also have other options, seeing as you've already messed the place up.' There was a sweet, teasing laugh. 'Why not, my Jackadoodle? A bit of *spontaneity*? Like in the old days, when...'

I watched the thread of cotton. I was aware of the blood pumping round my body, of my toes and fingers tingling. Out of the corner of my eye Jack's feet dangled into view, then disappeared again. Tears tracked steadily over my lower eyelids, across my cheeks and temples, and then slid, cold and tickly, into the hollows of my ears. I placed my palms over them and pressed hard so I wouldn't have to hear any more. I thought about my phone and what I would do if it rang. I thought about the hopelessness of loving Jack and the need to bring it to an end.

VII

The unlit windows tell me that Pete and Harry aren't home yet, and that my ten-minute window is secure. I barrel into the hall like superwoman. I know what needs to be done. Adrenalin is pumping through my veins. I run up the stairs, lugging the albatross of a case behind me, but still managing to take two steps at a time. I plunge into the bedroom and throw it onto the bed, unzipping it in three quick movements before starting to unpack, unearthing the ornaments and pictures first, treasures buried among the soft wads of T-shirts and socks. They need putting back in their rightful places, but next I move onto pulling out shoes, clothes, toiletries. I am a whirlwind. I dart between drawers and cupboards, opening, slamming, ramming.

Five minutes in, and I remember the letters. *Oh god, the letters.* I race downstairs to snatch Pete's off the mantelpiece.

I have felt for some time now that we have grown apart. I think we met far too young, before I had begun to know who I was.

Platitudes had come to my rescue. It makes my flesh crawl to think how much Pete would hate them; what they might make him do.

The sight of the spaces on the sitting-room shelves sends me charging back upstairs for the ornaments, still sitting on the bed – a small silver owl, a porcelain deer, a silver cigarette box that had belonged to my father – but as I reach the landing, Harry's letter pings back into my mind. My brain is starting to bounce. I am not doing things in the right order. I am misfiring.

I fly on up to Harry's room, on the top floor, and snatch the envelope out from under his pillow. Suki is there, as she always is, curled into a dip in his duvet like some sleek Cossack hat nestling in tissue paper, her tail curved round the O of her body, head buried under her dainty paws.

My darling Harry, this has been the hardest decision of my life. Do not think it is because I do not love you...

Only the truth for my darling child.

I can feel my superhuman powers ebbing, the chaos rushing in like a tide. I charge back down to the first floor and across the landing into Pete's and my room. There is so much still to do. The case isn't quite empty. The ornaments are still there next to it, along with the birthday picture of Harry that lives on the landing windowsill. It is all a question of priorities. I stuff both letters into the very back of my underwear drawer, gather all the ornaments off the bed and turn to head back downstairs. I am starting to feel as if I have been running forever, that I am trapped in one of those nightmares about competing in a race that never ends.

Jack, help me – I shout the words in my head. A dumb longing to check my phone swells, but there isn't time.

I race out of the bedroom, not seeing Suki, who has descended from the top floor in order to stretch and roll across the middle of the landing in silent ecstatic celebration at my return. The toe of my heavy suede boot makes hard contact with her body and she lets out a blood-curdling yowl. I pitch sideways, falling painfully against the banisters. The cat scampers back up to the top floor, her velvet ears flat with suffering and indignation. I track her through the receding bannister posts, grateful she is at least still capable of movement, that the failures of the day have not encompassed murdering the family pet. Meanwhile, somewhere deep inside, I am aware of a chasm opening up, of the danger of falling in.

I realise I still have my coat on. I slam the birthday photo into its rightful place, tear downstairs to the sitting room, where I restore the knick-knacks to their correct positions, then run back into the hall, tugging my arms free of my coat as I go. At the sight of the row of pegs behind the front door, I stop. I breathe. The nearest peg is allocated as mine. This is the place where my coat belongs. Slowly, carefully, I loop the toggle over the hook. There is such consoling precision in the action. I can weather this storm. All I have to do is keep things where they belong, do what I always do.

I check my watch. Twelve minutes and still Pete and Harry aren't back. Maybe they have stopped at the pub, though that only ever happens on a Friday, and then rarely. I go back upstairs, slowly this time, hauling myself by the bannisters. I just need to get through the next few hours. Then I will be able to think straight, decide how to feel, what to do.

It is only seconds later, when I am kneeling in front of the almost-empty suitcase, that I hear the key turn in the front door. There is no time for the loft and its cumbersome unfolding ladder. No time for anything.

'Anyone home?' Pete calls at once, as he always does, even when he can see me straight ahead of him fiddling with something in the kitchen. He likes a reception does Pete. A homecoming.

'Hi! Be right down!' I throw the words over my shoulder, shoving the case under the bed, pushing it as far to the middle as it will go. As I do so, the unspeakable incarceration in Hugh's flat ten months before rushes back at me. The worst of times. Jack had got rid of Helena eventually, being so resistant to her idea of the two of them going off to do something – lunch or an art exhibition – that a bit of a row had broken out. I kept my hands clamped over my ears throughout, hearing only snatches, frozen with wretchedness and humiliation.

When she had gone, the door banging and the tangerine shoes stalking back down the passageway like the distant ack-ack of a machine gun, Jack went after her before returning to the spare room, where he lay down on the carpet and reached under the bed for my hand. I stayed where I was in the dusty dark. I asked if they had kissed at all and he said no. I asked if they ever made love and he said no, not for years. I said I couldn't do it any more, that we were finished. Jack said he couldn't do it either, that we had to find another way. He said if he didn't spend the rest of his life with me, he would never know happiness again. He said I was his oasis in a desert, his calm in a storm. He rolled onto his side so that we were looking at each other across the carpet, his hand still outstretched. I let his eyes hold mine, hold me, it felt like. We interlaced our fingers.

He told me he wanted, literally, to make a new life with me, to run away together – fix a date and make a plan. He said Pete was a controlling bastard who didn't deserve me, and that for years, Helena had done nothing but delight in causing him pain. We each had one life, he said, one chance to be happy. It was when he mentioned tumbleweed, and wrong choices and getting blown off course. All he wanted, he said, if I would accept, was to devote his whole life to making me happy.

I started crying again, but only out of joy this time. Jack helped me wriggle out from under the bed and we held each other tightly, me making sure my tears didn't smear mascara streaks on his shirt.

Helena was extremely clever, as well as volatile, he warned, but we would be cleverer. We would outwit her. It would take caution and patience, but our reward would be each other. And so, the worst of times became the best.

'What are you doing?'

'Hey Pete.' I turn so fast, I crick my neck. The pain shoots like scalding liquid up under the base of my scalp. 'An earring fell off, but now I've found it.' I scramble to my feet. I hadn't expected him to come upstairs. He never comes upstairs straight after work. He goes into the kitchen and gets a beer from the bottom of the fridge. When the supply of cans is down to one, I have to replenish the stock, but not before.

'An earring?' Pete starts to scan the carpet. The sheer familiarity of his face is somehow a shock. The slightly protuberant ears, the smooth full cheeks, the deep-set brown eyes, the lean legs, which are starting to look weirdly skinny under the bulge of his stomach, no matter the style of trouser he wears. He's in tracksuit bottoms today, black ones with a thick silver stripe that make me think suddenly of the days when he still wore regular trousers. Days when there was still some residue of a deep, buried hope that I might yet prove to be the wife that he wanted, the one that would make him happy. My thoughts flicker to Jack and his collared cotton shirts and well-fitted trousers. He wouldn't be seen dead in tracksuit bottoms, unless he was taking exercise. Pete, for that alone, would call him a posh twat.

Pete flicks on the bedside lamp for extra light and the silver stripes gleam like blades. I know they will have come from some new stock for which he hadn't been able to resist deploying his manager's discount. I hang onto this train of thought because it makes me angry instead of panic-stricken about the half-unpacked suitcase just a few feet from his legs. If ever I buy new clothes, I get a grilling, but Pete's rules for himself are always different.

'I found it,' I repeat, because Pete's eyes are still on the floor and I have a sudden terror that he might choose this moment of all moments to put on a show of husbandly concern and drop to his hands and knees and continue the search. 'Look.' I lift my hair off my ears so he can see. I smile and shake my head a little as if to make the earrings swing, except they can't because they are studs.

I am aware of a sort of envy for Pete's normality, the ignorance that allows him to be innocent. I am the opposite of innocent. An ache for Jack is sitting in my belly like a stomach cramp. I know I must not acknowledge it. There is too much danger to navigate first.

'Good day?' I ask.

'Same old, same old.' He slumps onto the bed and kicks off his shoes, using the toes of one foot to lever the heel off the other. 'I'm knackered. All right for some.' He shoots me a look as he throws himself back against the pillows, crossing his hands under his head. 'God, what I'd give for school holidays.'

I swallow the usual reflex of hurt irritation. That Pete thinks being a primary-school teacher is the cushiest of jobs is old hat, a battle long since lost after arguments that have never led anywhere good. 'Why not have a bath,' I coax. 'Relax.'

I can't help noticing that Pete does, in fact, look pretty terrible, pasty-faced, the bags under his eyes wrinkled pouches, the bracket lines round his mouth deeper indents than I can ever remember, seeming to drag his entire face downwards into one permanent grimace. I recall, in the manner of one summoning to mind a distant stranger, that once, such observations would have had the power to affect me deeply, both out of fear and the belief that if I could only soothe my husband's manifold sorrows correctly enough, tenderly enough, I could ease them out of being. I would have offered a shoulder-rub. I would have worked on his neck too, gently kneading my thumbs up and down the nape while he grumbled. I would have eased off his socks and run him a deep, hot bubble bath, chivvying the water with my hands to make just the right amount of foam. Now, it is all I can do to stay in the room.

'Yeah, right, like a bath is going to make any difference.'

It is a challenge just to have to talk. I can feel the weight of my phone in my back pocket, on silent and non-vibrate. Jack could have sent a message and I wouldn't know. I think of the coat peg. I must do normal things. Say normal things. 'So did Harry get to any of those applications today?'

'Here we go.'

'I don't know what you mean.'

I know exactly what he means. And he knows I know. Harry is one of the regular minefields. Eleven months on from dropping out of his social studies degree, our son appears to be sleepwalking down a cul-de-sac, all his aspirations, the ones I worked so hard to instil in him against the put-downs of his father, forgotten. Instead of challenging him, Pete is lapping it up – another victory against me – treating Harry more and more like a co-worker and a pal.

Those tech courses he used to talk about,' I go on quickly. 'He's so good at tech, isn't he – I still think it would be the perfect thing for him. I'm wondering whether he's said anything to you, since he never speaks to me these days.' Longing for Jack rises in my throat like nausea. I sway on my feet and reach for the back of my dressing table chair. 'Of course, the job in the shop is a great stopgap,' I say carefully, 'but I just think he should keep looking around for other things, not imagine that doors have closed.'

'Like his father,' he sneers.

'I didn't say that.'

'You didn't have to.'

'You've done loads of other things in your life, Pete, and you run the whole show at the store now. We both want what's best for Harry, right? So all I'm saying—'

'I know exactly what you are saying, Fran. It's what you always say.'

'I'll have a word with him myself then.'

'Well, there's an idea.'

I turn for the door.

'He's gone out.'

'Really?' Harry's social life, never lively, has been practically non-existent since he gave up on his degree. 'With Dylan? Is he back then?' Best of friends at school, the pair had set off for uni at the same time, Dylan to Nottingham, Harry to Warwick, the only difference being that Dylan was well into his second year and, by all accounts, having a great time.

'Not Dylan.' Pete, mercifully, is on his phone now, half-concentrating. 'Looking after that horrible creature over the road. *Again.*'

'Alfie's not got long and Mrs D needs a break,' I say, the reflex of defending Harry firing, despite the potential for further provocation it might cause. 'And he says it's good, easy money,' I add quickly, grabbing at the one tack with a chance of eliciting Pete's sympathies.

'What's for tea anyway,' is all he says, tossing his phone aside. 'I'm bloody starving.'

My stomach flips. I had not thought of food. I am supposed to be in Spain, sitting opposite Jack at a rickety table with a bottle of chilled wine and tapas, prawns in chilli perhaps, and patatas bravas, and crispy rings of calamari, and a basket of bread for dunking in the sauces. 'Fish pie,' I say, forcing my concentration to the contents of the freezer, steadily stocked over recent weeks. Leaving my husband and son hadn't meant wanting them to starve.

I continue for the door, surreptitiously patting my back pocket where my mobile sits.

'Leaving me, are you?'

It takes a long, heart-stopping moment to realise this is just Pete being Pete. 'Yup,' I quip, quite loudly, to disguise the tremor in my voice, 'and I might not be coming back.' My bravado astonishes me. I feel a rush of strength. I even think, madly, of Helena – not a doormat, like me – always the one to pick the fight. All is not lost. Not yet. I know Pete well enough to ride this out, to find a way through.

'I suppose I'll have that bath,' he concedes with a sigh.

'Good idea. I'll get supper going.'

Once in the kitchen, I quickly put the fish pie in the microwave to defrost ready for browning in the oven, and check my phone. There is still nothing. I send Jack another message, a question mark, a single kiss, and the words Going mad, with no conviction it is even getting through. Then, when I hear the bath taps running upstairs, I quickly text Mel:

It's all gone wrong. He never showed. Am back home. Total nightmare. Need to talk. Not now.

The microwave pings and I transfer the pie to the oven and start to lay the table. Exhaustion is seeping through me, weighing me down. I pour a glass of wine and drink it in three long swigs and, before I know it, I'm on my knees, sobbing Jack's name, gripping the edge of the kitchen table. But I cannot do this. Not yet, not now. It is playing with fire, despite the upstairs gurgles of the hot-water tank as Pete runs his bath. I grope my way along the hall and into our box of a downstairs toilet. Sitting on the seat brings my knees to within a few inches of the door. The tiny basin is right next to me. I turn the taps on full and tug on the ceiling light rope to make the fan whirr. Then I allow my crying to start, keeping an eye on my watch to be sure there's time to patch up my face before we eat.

* * *

'Mum.' Harry says the word uncertainly, clearly disconcerted at finding his least favourite parent sitting at the kitchen table in the middle of the night. He hovers in the frame of the kitchen door, a tall reedy silhouette against the blaze of the hall light.

'Couldn't you sleep either?' My voice is a croak and I hope he thinks it's from fatigue. 'Don't put the light on, there's a love,' I add quickly, fearful of him seeing my blotched and swollen face. I had managed supper, forcing lumps of fish and mash down my throat while watching telly next to Pete, and then, in bed, feigned sleep until I heard Harry's late return, around ten, and Pete started his snoring, by which time the tight misery in my chest was again ready to explode. 'There's some tea if you want.' I pat the pot next to my mug.

Harry shakes his head. It is perfectly clear to me that all he wants is to go back upstairs, but that some vestige of filial duty forbids it.

The size of him still throws me. As a boy, he was always so delicately built, a waif compared to his peers. Until, sometime around his seventeenth birthday, after all the on-off battles with playground bullies and his own teenage neuroses, this adult version of him burst into being – the soft downy hair on his cheeks morphing to stubble, the muscles on his arms and chest thickening, the length of his legs jutting out several inches below the hems of his trousers. He started refusing haircuts during the same period, allowing his mousy curls to grow into the straggly mane which he keeps now in a thick bushy ponytail off his shoulders. It isn't tied back tonight and is on fire from the hall light, a wild halo round the narrow face that is so clearly mine, rather than his father's. Though it is Pete's brown eyes that gleam under his dark brows, still with the animal intensity that I found such a joy when he was little.

'You okay?' The question is lobbed out quickly, in a grudging tone that seems to communicate both resentment at having to ask and dread at what the answer might demand.

'Oh fine. Just wanted a cuppa.'

He moves to the fridge, standing in the triangle of light it throws out, eating whatever is within reach; in the first instance, a rugged square of cheddar.

'There's some fish pie if you want.'

He makes a noise that means no, while continuing to feed on the cheese.

'So Dad says you looked after poor Alfie again for Mrs Dawkins?'

His ponytail dances between his shoulder blades as he nods. I want to stroke it. I want to stroke him, press him against my chest and tell him that the one good thing – the *only* good thing – about the nightmare of this endless day is the chance to have him once again in the same room. I find myself wondering in the same instant when exactly the delicious privilege of mother-intimacy ended. Had Harry edged me out, or had it been a sudden decision? It seems absurd that I cannot ask even this simple question without the certainty of pushing him still further away, widening the distance that I can never, for one moment, stop wanting to close.

'I heard you come back. Dad and I went up early. So, couldn't you sleep either?' I press, when still he says nothing, unable to resist pushing for something that might bind us, no matter how small.

Harry shrugs. 'Wasn't tired.' He picks a Granny Smith from the bottom drawer and leans back against the fridge door to eat it, studying the fruit as he noisily chisels big holes in its sides. His Adam's apple bobs as he swallows. I can dimly make out a mark next to it, what looks like a faint red smudge of a bruise. 'So, what's wrong with Suki, anyway?' he mutters.

'Suki?' I sit up, forgetting I am trying to hide my face. 'Why?'

'She's got like, this limp, I mean, really bad. And when I tried to pick her up, she went all weird. She's under my bed now. She never goes under my bed.'

'Oh dear. I'd better take her to the vet.' I clasp my empty mug more tightly. Suki may yet be mortally injured and it will be all my fault.

I try to imagine the following day. I had expected to be waking up in a Madrid guesthouse, sliding into the strong, warm circle of Jack's arms, the purple bougainvillea we had so admired in the image gallery online, bobbing round the windows. I had expected to be gone, to be free. Instead, I have to go to the vet, and lug the suitcase back up to the loft, and wait and wait and wait, and hope and hope and hope that Jack will make contact to tell me what has gone so badly wrong. The thought of that, the effort it will take, is almost unbearable.

I dig my nails into my palms, remembering there is the letter to Camille to worry about too. By tomorrow, it will be sitting in the Chalfonts postbox. I have to decide whether to try to intercept it. Or to wait, in case Jack gets in touch. A pulse in my left eyelid starts to flutter.

'She's probably been in a fight,' I offer feebly, rubbing my eye. Harry has reached the core of the apple and is nibbling down through it with his big strong front teeth. When he gets to the stalk, he will be gone. 'You know I only ever want what is best for you, Harry.'

'Yup.' He tosses the stalk into the bin.

'So, whatever happens, just remember that, because—'

'Mum, I *know*, okay?'

He has his face in the sink and is drinking from the tap, not, I am certain, because he is thirsty, but because it is a way of drowning me out, keeping me at bay. For a moment, my throat is too tight to speak. There is no question of crying in front of Harry. He would be appalled and I would have no acceptable justifications to offer. I reach for Jack in my mind. One day he and Harry will be friends, I tell myself. One day everything will work its way through and come good. It's just going to take a little more time than we planned.

Harry is swiping his mouth dry on the back of his hand, readying himself to go back upstairs. I am surprised he has stayed so long and get the sudden impression that he wants something from me but cannot put into words what it is.

'Just don't give up on your dreams, okay?' I know it is corny and clumsy.

He nods, shooting me a look from under his eyebrows before taking himself up to bed.

I am rinsing the teapot, in a daze, when my phone vibrates. A moan escapes me as I grab it and crouch behind the fridge. But it's a message from Mel.

Oh you poor love. I am here whenever you need me. Just call. Xxx

CHAPTER 2

I

The sun drills through our thin pale bedroom curtains, highlighting the wobbly lines of my stitching round their edges. Having to make do doesn't mean you are always good at it. My eyes ache and there is a strange metallic taste in my mouth. The other half of the bed is empty, and the silence in the house suggests Pete and Harry have left for work. For an instant or two, I hang in a state of blissful emptiness before everything rushes back in. The airport. Being back home. Camille. The vet. The need not to fall apart.

I roll onto my side to reach for my phone, switched off as I crept back up from the kitchen, grateful as ever for Pete's capacity to snore through thunderstorms. My entire body hurts, as if I have spent the night being punched instead of trying to sleep – a real possibility back in the day, before I got the hang of things; though I am not sure any blows from Pete ever left me feeling so bruised. Holding the mobile in my palm, I am aware of a tendril of hope, so welcome, so needed, that I delay the moment of switching it on. But then the screen lights up and the tears spill, because there is not the message I need, only the growing clutter of ones that I simply cannot face.

I crawl to the window and part the curtains, squinting at the glare of the morning. Down in the street, the spindly cherry trees, planted by the council a decade before, are popping their buds, pink candyfloss tufts clustering every branch like some crazy cartoon. I stare at them till my eyes blur, seeing not the flowers but Jack, me nestling in the crook of his arm on Mel's sofa as he summons a favourite Van Gogh onto his laptop, one of pink blossom on a silver tree. 'Geniuses see beauty and paint it,' Jack says in the reverent tone he reserves for any discussion of art, absently brushing his lips across my hair; 'Van Gogh only ever knew joy with a brush in his hand,' he adds, and 'Christ this is so joyous you just can't stop looking; I mean, you could eat it, couldn't you?' He nibbles the tip of my ear.

A car shoots down the street, bouncing over the bumps designed to slow it down, shattering my trance. In the flash of its number plate, I spot the letters J and X and my heart leaps, deciding, wildly, that it is a message – a kiss – from Jack to me. And then the tears really start, because seeing communications in car registrations is proof I am truly losing my wits.

I drop the phone on the floor and flop onto my back, making a cave with the duvet over my head. I lie very still, my breath heavy and hot, wondering how long it would take to suffocate, whether I would have the willpower. It occurs to me in the same instant, something like relief as well as despair surging in equal measure, that Jack must have died. Our pact was so strong, so painstakingly planned – it is the only possible explanation for his silence.

I throw back the covers and retrieve my phone. My hands shake as I yet again break every rule we have ever had and dial Jack's number; but there still isn't even a ring, just a single, continuous flat tone. Feverishly, I google recent car accidents near Gatwick and then, when that produces no results, hospitals south of the M25. There are three big ones. Fresh energy is pumping through me. Jack may have experienced some terrible medical emergency but still be breathing. Most likely, he will be in no position to make or take phone calls; and everyone knows hospitals are funny about mobile usage anyway, because of how it interferes with their systems.

I prop myself against the pillows, swiping the sleep-grit from my eyes and clearing my throat as I dial the number of the first hospital. I am good at getting to grips with things, I remind myself; it is just a question of recognising what needs to be done. When Pete's first business venture went under, it was me who sat down with our outgoings, working out where we could save, what we could sell, seeing what mattered while he sat hunched, cursing, imploding and ashamed. I was the one to phone the bank, to cancel standing orders, to call the credit card people, and then collect Harry from nursery, swinging him onto my hip and chatting with the other parents like I didn't have a care in the world. When I got back, Pete was still in the chair, grey-faced, on his fifth beer. I told him I was returning to work and that we would survive. Which we did, financially anyway.

When the hospital switchboard answers, I explain that I am trying to ascertain the whereabouts of an injured relative. I am put through to someone else to whom I give more details of my predicament, only to be told that names of patients cannot be divulged without certainty as to the identity of the enquirer. I grow angry and tell them that I am Jack Aspen's very dear friend, and that I am certain he has suffered an accident or been taken ill somewhere in the area of Gatwick, since he had been due to meet me for a flight out of the South Terminal the day before, but never arrived.

'You need to phone missing persons, by the sound of it, love.'

I cut off the call, reality and hopelessness sweeping back in. I have lost something I cannot even own up to. I am Jack's secret, as he is mine. Whether he is dead or alive, it is as if I am bereaved without a body. I have no rights, no power. I cannot even mourn. I picture Helena, seated at Jack's hospital bedside like the gaoler she is, sinewy limbs crossed tightly, grilling and bossing the medical staff in the voice I heard in Hugh's flat ten months before, as I lay staring up at the shifting mattress, my ears pooling with tears. It takes every scrap of my shredded strength to dig past the image and remind the small sane corner of my brain that something unforeseeable and less calamitous might have occurred, that Jack may yet be in touch. In the meantime, there is this moment, this hour, this day, that must be lived.

* * *

'Oh dear, nothing serious, I hope?' calls Mrs Dawkins, appearing just as I reach the car.

'Hopefully not, Mrs D,' I trill, carefully sliding the cat box into the passenger seat, aware of Suki's yellow eyes fixed wretchedly on mine through the little barred door. The three deep neat scratches she engraved across the top of my hand are still glistening. She hadn't wanted to be prised out from under Harry's bed, and I didn't blame her. Harry with his long arms and placid demeanour would have managed it easily. Whereas I had pondered and cajoled for too long, giving the cat time to register my anxiety, so that when I made my move, she was already braced to defend her ground. It didn't help that, in the moment of lunging for her, I had the sudden image of yet again floundering hopelessly on a dusty carpet under a bed. The realisation made me feel idiotic, as well as hopeless, as if my life had got stuck on some peculiar loop that was making someone, somewhere – a malign deity sitting at a screen perhaps – laugh their heads off. It also reminded me that the suitcase was still in its lame hiding place under Pete's and my bed; but the vet had said come at once and so there simply wasn't time.

Mrs Dawkins is peering at Suki's box through the car window, clucking compassionately. There had been a husband once, Donald, taken from her by pancreatic cancer when their son, Len, was little – diagnosed on a Friday and gone by the Monday, as she told it. It was one of her favourite stories and referred to often, along with pride at how Len had turned out, twenty-five years later working as a trader in the city. 'Ah, bless,' she says, clearly in the mood to chat, pulling her vaping stick from her pocket and pushing her thin bleached hair out of her eyes. She inhales deeply, tightening the little drawstring lines that sit along her upper lip, before blowing out a blue-grey cloud that floats up, dispersing among the blossom. 'I don't know what I'll do when Alfie finally goes. He's hanging on, the love, but I need a break some-times. Harry is such a dear to help out. He's got a gift, I'd say, that boy of yours.'

'Really? Yes, I suppose he has.' I have the driver's door open, but she hasn't finished.

'I saw this film last night – ever so clever – the monsters only eat you if you make a sound. Never known a cinema so quiet.' She laughs her husky laugh. 'Home by eight, which was nice – plenty of time to fix myself a bite and give Alf a cuddle. Can't do late nights any more.'

In spite of my rush, I pause. Harry hadn't come in until much later. I find myself remembering the little red mark on his neck. He's never mentioned a girlfriend or brought one home, but that's hardly surprising. 'No, me neither,' I offer absently, getting into the car.

'So you weren't off on a trip then – yesterday?' Mrs Dawkins flings the question out before I can shut the door, as if she has been wondering about it, saving it, which of course she has.

'Oh my – *that*.' I am glad I am now behind the wheel, sitting down. I can feel the blood draining from my face and my brain racing to compute the best response. Worst is a sudden twist of dread that she might already have made some passing comment to Harry. *Where was your Mum going yesterday morning then, with that big old suitcase?* A need of Jack flares like heartburn. There is so much to manage. Tripwires everywhere. 'Long story,' I say wildly. '*Very* long... helping out a friend who'd hurt her ankle.' The lie I told Rob arrives like inspiration. 'Total fiasco – what are friends for, eh?' I pull a goofy face and shake my head. 'But, really gotta go now – the vet's squeezing us in.' I slam the door at last but wind the window down to add, 'Thanks again a million for giving Harry the work – you know what they're like, always needing more pocket money!' And then I'm swinging the car out into the street, almost running over a squirrel in my haste.

Ten minutes later, kerb-crawling for somewhere to park up and down the busy section of the high street that houses the vets, Suki yowling because she hates the box and the car and is in pain, I find myself shrieking at Jack and thumping the steering wheel. I tell him it is not fucking fair and I don't know how I am going to cope and if he is dead and there is an afterlife, could he, at the very least, kindly organise a parking space.

A large van vacates a spot right next to me and I experience a rush of absurd exhilaration. I reverse smoothly into the space, enjoying the sudden silence from the cat box caused by the shock of my shrieking. 'Everything's going to be just fine, Sukes,' I whisper, 'just you wait and see.'

The vet is one I haven't encountered before, a gentle giant of a young man with a lilting Caribbean voice. His mouth contains an array of sparkling teeth and a smile so vast and kind that just being with him is soothing. Despite her injury, Suki clings to the inside of her box with the dexterity of a gym champion, but he extracts her in seconds and is soon cradling her in his arms like a new-born, telling her to calm down so he can take a proper look. I watch in awe as he gently sets her on the examination table and runs his hands over her sleek black fur. She trembles but stays still. His hands are the size of spades and their palms so pink I find myself thinking of the blossom. 'This poor little lady has a broken leg,' he says softly. 'We are going to have to take some X-rays, but I am pretty sure it's the back-left femur. Broken at the hip, I'd guess. Any idea how it happened?'

'No.' The lie sticks between my teeth. I cannot own up to my crime. It is too tied with owning up to other things. 'Could she,' I venture slowly, 'perhaps have fallen out of a tree?'

He shakes his head doubtfully, rubbing Suki between the ears in the way that makes her do her thing of half closing her eyes, like she does for Harry when he slings her round his neck in the manner of a feather boa and kneads the downy fur just above her paw pads. 'More likely to be a car,' the vet says thoughtfully. 'Though cats' reactions are so quick, it's normally their heads rather than their legs that get damaged. They hear the engine, you see, and then turn at the last minute and... *wham*.' He releases the word which such force that I jump, and before I know it, mortifying tears are streaming down my cheeks and he is reaching for a box of tissues from a shelf beside the consulting table. 'Hey, but we can totally fix this,' he reassures me kindly, tactfully keeping his attention on his patient, while I dab at my face and blow my nose, my shame heightened because of knowing I am crying for myself rather than my cat. 'A couple of X-rays, an operation...' He carefully transfers Suki back into her box while he talks. 'So long as there are no unexpected complications, and with sensible post-operative care at home, she should be right as rain in eight weeks or so. Do you have insurance?'

I shake my head, my tears stopping in their tracks, not because of the lack of financial cover – a luxury never even discussed – but because eight weeks is two months. Jack could make contact any time. I need to be ready to leave at a moment's notice. I love Suki. I was her rescuer after all, fishing her out of the soggy box and taking her home, riding out the subsequent battles with fleas, litter training and Pete, growling criticisms and protests from the sidelines. My inspiration through it all was Harry, aged ten and visibly in need of some comfort and fun to break the fluctuating tensions between his parents.

'But she'll be getting back to normal long before then, right?' I ask weakly, imagining the longed-for sound of Jack's voice in my ear, the impossibility of telling him that our already delayed escape has to be deferred further by the necessity of nursing the family pet.

Alone in the car ten minutes later, Suki's plaintive mews at being left echoing in my ears, I sit numbly. The operation, the overnights, the meds are going to cost the earth. The Santander money – Jack's and my money – will almost certainly have to be raided.

My phone stares up at me from my lap, full of notifications, but still not the one I need. Around me, the world streams: shoppers, walkers, runners, drivers, cyclists. Only I am stuck; in purgatory.

* * *

'If only I knew what had happened,' I wail at Mel, stumbling across the threshold of her flat half an hour later, having messaged an SOS from the bleakness of the car outside the vets. I fall against her, talking incomprehensibly through my sobs, while she strokes my head, murmuring the sort of words I used to comfort Harry when he was little and his world had come crashing down. She steers me to the sofa.

'I know it's only mid-morning, but we're having gin,' she says firmly, once I am seated and a little calmer. 'Sometimes only gin does the necessary. Then you are going to tell me everything properly, from the very beginning to the very end. And you can strike Suki off your list of Things To Worry About right now. If it comes to weeks of cat-care, I can help out, okay?'

I cry some more because she is so kind-hearted, and burrow into the sofa, hugging one of her big soft scatter cushions. The sounds of plinking ice cubes and fizzing tonic float out of the kitchen.

'It is the uncertainty,' I say when Mel re-emerges, in a voice so lost and hoarse I hardly recognise it as my own, 'the inability to make contact, the not-knowing, the terrible waiting.' I clutch the glass tumbler she has pressed into my hands. A day ago, I was stepping into the future of my dreams; a turning point worked for with every fibre of my courage. Now I am spinning in reverse, with nothing to hang on to.

Mel parks herself at the other end of the sofa. She is wearing a loose purple dress that accentuates the glints of blue in her beautiful grey eyes. Her eyelashes are long and coated with the heavy mascara they do not need, but which Mel applies assiduously anyway, deploying the mesmerising tactic of separating each lash with the point of a pin to maximise the widening effect. Her glossy hazel hair hangs half across each side of her face, a pair of shining half-drawn curtains through which she prefers to regard the world. She nudges these aside now, to give a clearer view of my face as she addresses me.

'Okay, honey, let's have it, the blow-by-blow.' She sips her drink and holds my hand, displaying the graceful patience and generosity which she has demonstrated for all the woes I have laid at her feet over the years, and which, I know, is a reflection of her own rich acquaintance with life's difficulties. Difficulties which she rarely complains about and which currently include a job which pays well but which she hates, in the finance department of a PR company, a demanding cantankerous mother in Amersham, as well as the ongoing lack of what Mel likes to call a 'significant other' – an ancient and entrenched source of disappointment, based not on a lack of willing partners, so much as Mel's inability to find someone she can truly connect with. Indeed, I am the least of Mel's worries, though she never for a moment allows me to think so.

'Get it off your chest,' she prompts, when I – bewildered suddenly at having to decide where to start – find myself hesitating. 'Then we are going to make a plan.'

'Oh yes, a plan,' I whisper. 'A plan would be good. A plan is what I need.'

A slither of lemon bobs among the ice cubes in my glass. I prod it with a fingertip and then swig deeply, relishing the hit of the alcohol at the back of my throat. I am struggling with the realisation that I sat with Jack in this very spot just a couple of weeks before. It was the last time we actually saw each other. We had made love and then lounged on the little sofa afterwards, arms round each other and drinking tea. We had counted the remaining days. We had talked of my opening a kindergarten and him renting a gallery. We had been exuberant. I can hear our laughter. I can smell Jack's skin. I press the cold glass against my hot forehead.

Occasionally as I speak, Mel squeezes the hand she is holding. Otherwise she doesn't interrupt, except to whisper, whenever I falter, that she is here for me and everything is going to turn out fine. It is a blessed relief, like lancing an infection, just to disgorge the horror of the last twenty-four hours, to the one person in the world fully apprised of the situation and therefore equipped to understand; the one person who, thanks to her great kindness in facilitating Jack's and my need to be together, has actually met him, telling me afterwards that he was dear and handsome and she couldn't think of two people who deserved each other more.

We were to consider her spare room 'ours', she had said the moment I took her into my confidence, assuring me that, if given a few days' notice, she would always do her best to organise her schedule accordingly, joking that more motherly visits to Amersham might secure her an otherwise questionable place in heaven. She even took to leaving a spare set of keys under a loose stone by the front door so we could let ourselves in. On every visit, there would be fresh flowers on the bedroom mantelpiece and plump towels on the chair next to the shower. In return, Jack and I left gifts – wine, chocolates, gin – and little notes of gratitude. She and Jack met on a couple of occasions, when her exit and our arrival overlapped, but Mel was too tactful and aware of our relentlessly tight time-slots to hang around for long. It was only to me afterwards that she would confess how happy it made her to be able to help, how it restored her faith in love, renewing her own long-cherished hopes of one day finding someone special for herself.

When I have finished, I drop my head onto the back of the sofa, staring at the ceiling, which is swirled and peaked, like meringue. 'Do you know, I nearly got on that fucking plane.'

'I don't think that would have been wise,' Mel says drily. 'And there has literally been no message since,' she asks in a gentler voice, 'not one word?'

'Nada.' I slowly sit up, regarding her solemnly. 'Something terrible has happened to him, Mel, I just know it.'

'Maybe it has, darling.' There is a different sort of gentleness in her tone, one that contains a hint of doubt, and though it has every right being there, I do not like hearing it. I need Mel's faith in this. Only she knows the full picture of the last two decades – all the bad stuff with Pete, the difficulties with Harry; only she understands why Jack and I finding each other has meant so much

'What do you mean, maybe?'

'Oh, *something* terrible has most definitely happened. All I'm saying is, we don't know exactly what. So we're going to have to find out. Together. I promise. Or maybe,' she continues quickly, 'we won't have to because Jack will get in touch, and oh my word, darling, there is nothing I want more. But, in the meantime, you have to stay strong and carry on exactly as you are – being brave, being *normal* – because if Pete suspects something, then you could really be in trouble.' Her eyes are pinned to mine, glittering with warning and compassion. 'I can't imagine how hard this is for you, Fran.' She grabs both my hands in hers, making the bangles round her wrists jangle like wind chimes.

'Very hard,' I echo.

I know that everything she says makes perfect sense. I manage a feeble smile, marvelling, as her big gentle moon of a face holds my gaze, at the still enviable flawlessness of her complexion. I remember too, as if it was yesterday, the lithe, impish sixteen-year-old who sashayed into the sixth-form some twenty-five years before, daughter of an ex-army father and exuding all the attitude and confidence of one who had seen something of the world. Heads turned and Mel flashed the cheeky grin of one unsurprised at causing a stir. Even then, lost as I was in the maze of my own teenage insecurities, my ogling had contained a sort of sympathetic wonderment at what it must be like – the unimaginable pressure – being the centre of such admiring attention. And later too, after the thing with Ed had happened and he had been expelled, it made perfect sense to me that Mel should start to eat with the dogged determination of someone building her defences, thickening her walls, doing all she could to stop the world from ever looking at her in quite the same way again.

For a while, she was the talk of the class, but then it died down and everyone left her alone instead, like she was hazardous goods. It was then that our friendship had found its roots. Two girls who didn't quite fit, who took refuge in each other. And even when Pete started coming on to me, with a charm and a swagger that makes me have to pinch myself now, inviting me to cheer him on at his matches and for rides in his father's car, he seemed to clock from the outset that Mel and I were non-negotiable; that his controlling possessiveness could run whatever course it liked, but this was one friendship I would never surrender, and there was no point in trying to persuade me otherwise. It helped, too, that, from the first, Mel was equally prepared to accept and fit round him, the most unimposing of best friends, the most unthreatening.

I leave Mel's flat clutching a list she has sweetly written on a page torn from a notepad, under a big smiley face and the heading: THINGS TO DO. Her writing is just as it was at school, like lines of tidy knitting. In the car, I hold on to the paper like a lifeline, crumpling it. A strong coffee followed the gin and my pulse is racing. I read it several times before driving off.

> *Get back your resignation letter.*
> *Or just tell Camille you've changed your mind…*
> *Put suitcase back in loft.*
> *NB: Be extra nice to Pete, for now.*
> *Stay strong. Stay calm. This WILL work out*
> *Phone me WHENEVER you want.*

And, right at the bottom, there is a line she added at the last minute, folding the page so I would only see it later.

> *Check the balance in that Santander account. I couldn't say it to your face, sweetheart, but your Jack's no-show at the airport might – MIGHT – just be because he was not what he seemed.*

II

The gold lettering on the big blue board still gleams: *Chalfont Junior School, Co-education for five- to eight-year-olds.* Camille chose the name, she said, because Chalfont was her maiden name from her Brummie father, and much as she loved her Norwegian husband, Erik, and delighted as she had been to take the surname Larsson for herself and their three impossibly beautiful, blue-eyed, caramel-skinned boys, she wanted to keep a chunk of her original family roots alive and firmly kicking.

Behind the sign, the school itself, a big Victorian building that was once an old people's home, looks slightly ramshackle but very welcoming, thanks to an assortment of Easter bunnies, bonnets and eggs dancing across its windows and various bright orange finger-pointing signs positioned around the drive, advertising information about parking and goods entrances. The main gates, however, part of a wrought-iron fence skirting the entire front of the property, are visibly and formidably padlocked.

In a way, I am relieved. It is one difficult decision delayed and it is not as if there is a rush. Camille is still on holiday and there is still two weeks until the start of term, with Easter to get through first. *Though I could be long gone by then*, I assure myself. Somehow.

I idle for a few minutes in the car, pondering the miracle of Camille, running the Maths department at St Joseph's one minute and Head of her own little school the next. Twenty months in and there are still just three year groups of two classes in each, but plans are already well underway to expand into a fully-fledged primary, from reception to year eight, by extending into some of the spacious garden at the back. With an architect brother and her proven ability to secure funding, tapping into the surge of city interest in investing in free schools, I am in no doubt she will make it happen. The way she set everything up while still working at St Joseph's, unblinking in the face of pressures that would have flattened me in seconds, holding her nerve with the money side of things, the preparation of the building, the recruitment, before finally leaving, persuading a couple of the juniors' staff, including me, to go with her, was a revelation. Indeed, I should take heart from such impressive single-mindedness, I tell myself now – the proof that if you want something – or someone – badly enough, you can make it happen. It is all a question of holding firm, of keeping faith.

And yet being outside the school, with its doughty little sign, a beacon against the grey March sky, is also a sobering reminder of what I have been prepared to give up. St Joseph's, so big, so noisy, was enervating. My five terms at Chalfonts have been sheer heaven in comparison. I love my eager little class and they love me. I had teaching plans that would take us and a hundred future Year Ones into the next century.

A plastic bottle rattles noisily into view on the pavement, making me start, before bouncing out of sight into the gutter in front of the car. Love, the real thing, requires sacrifice, I remind myself. It is never simple. It must be seized.

The bottle makes a crunching sound under my wheel as I drive off. Mel's piece of paper sits on the seat next to me, like a wagging finger with its dire final warning. Of course, she is right. Mel is always right. But Jack is also the sweetest, most honourable man I have ever met. I wouldn't love him otherwise. Indeed, it struck me early on that it was precisely these qualities that had kept him loyal to the monstrous Helena for so long. A lesser man would have walked out years before.

Physical, visceral longing rises in me like a tide, not for sex but just to hold and be held – penned, safe from the world, in the firm circle of his embrace, the curve of his rangy body fitting in its miraculous, easy way around mine. The interminable tears spill again and I swipe them away to keep the road in focus. I am like my resignation letter, I decide grimly, picturing it sitting in the school mailbox – in a state of suspension. Nothing finalised. Nothing sorted.

Mel calls just as I pull into a slot outside the supermarket.

'Just checking you are okay.'

'I went to the school and it's all locked up. But Camille's not back till next week anyway. Now I'm about to brave Costcutters.'

'Good girl. Hang on in there. This is a nightmare, but it will work out.'

'Are you sure?'

'Yes, I am. And I've been thinking. You know where Jack lives, right? It's in North London somewhere, isn't it?'

'Yes… Lavender Grove… though I've never been there.' I whisper the words, guessing the direction of her questions.

'I'll come with you is what I am saying,' urges Mel, realising I get her drift. 'Surely anything is better than sitting around wondering what might be going on. I'm not saying we do any doorstopping. I'm just saying we take a look. Maybe over the weekend. I can do Saturday or Sunday. Tell Pete I'm in dire straits about Mum or something, as per usual. Look, just have a think about it, okay?'

'Okay.'

'You are my dearest friend,' adds Mel fiercely, suddenly sounding close to tears herself, 'and if this guy has fucked you around, then I want to know about it. And I am sorry if that is hard for you to hear, but there it is.'

III

'A broken leg? How the hell did that happen?'

'I knew it was something bad, I told Mum.' Harry is triumphant, his dark brown eyes fixed intently on his father for approval; as they always are, I realise with a tug. 'She was, like, so weird last night, Dad. I could tell she was in massive pain.'

'Yes, well, the vet says that they need to confirm with X-rays,' I interject evenly, 'and then they can do an operation to set it with a pin.' In truth, I am glad at having poor Suki as fodder for conversation, something I can speak honestly about. Every other subject feels like a minefield.

'Blimey.' Pete is staring at me, his round pale face flexed with concern, his voice edged with warning, so I know, even before he goes on, what he is going to say, what the concern is really about. 'And how much are they going to charge for that privilege?'

I have a full mouth and chew slowly, buying time. We are seated at the kitchen table, eating my home-made chicken and pork pie, an erstwhile family favourite which I realised, drifting along the supermarket aisles after talking to Mel, I hadn't cooked for so long that I could no longer summon to mind the exact ingredients. I remembered enough to buy sausage meat, chicken, apples, chutney and herbs, but, checking the recipe at home afterwards, found I had the wrong kinds of each and in unnecessarily large amounts. The pie is nonetheless close to perfect, its pastry crisp, the innards moist and layered with the precision of rock strata. The aroma floating out and filling our small kitchen is as sweet as a summer meadow. On seeing the hefty slices I carved and slid onto their plates, Pete and Harry released involuntary groans of pleasure, immediately helping themselves to the two vegetable dishes I have also prepared, one of roasted squash, dotted with butter and peas, the other of mash, whisked into soft waves with the aid of an egg, butter, a dash of cream and several bulbs of crushed garlic which glisten now, specks of half buried treasure, under the ceiling lights of the kitchen.

I am aware that I am wooing my son and husband with food, diverting them like a magician using sleight of hand. It seems to me the only weapon I possess in this new terrible holding pattern of a battle to keep them as relaxed – as happy and diverted – as possible. No glimpse must escape of my true mindset, which has progressed during the course of the last two days into a state of tautness so extreme I feel like an elastic band stretched to the point of snapping. Within this, however, there is, this evening, a thread of crazy exultation going on too – the scent of progress – because, aided by the boost of Mel's checklist, the suitcase is back in the loft at last and the Santander account has been examined and not found wanting. My ten thousand pounds and eight pence are there in full, just as they were two days and a million years ago, when Jack and I were going to meet at Gatwick. And yes, I am awash with relief about that, because, as Mel had clearly suspected, I had given all the passcodes and account number to Jack months ago. He had said no, but I insisted. Because, as I told him at the time, 'you never know and I trust you with my life, and as far as I'm concerned it's already "our" money anyway.'

I had phoned Mel at once with the good news and, while I was at it, took the plunge about her North London proposition, saying Sunday might work. She told me well done, but also expressed incredulity when I clarified that, while knowing the address, I'd never once been to Jack's street, the early fraught cup of tea at mine having convinced us never to risk meeting on our respective home turfs again.

'We'll be like cops, doing a stake-out,' she had said, a bit gleefully for my liking, before ringing off. I had laughed, because I knew she meant well, but also from terror at what we might find.

'I don't know exactly yet what the total vet bill will be,' I tell Harry and Pete. 'The vet was so nice though – a new one.'

'Ah good, well that's all right then – a nice vet, we can all relax.' Pete chops and shovels at his food, talking with a full mouth in the way I hate, his chipmunk cheeks bulging. 'Let's write a cheque now for thousands and tell the man to have an exotic holiday on us while he's at it.'

'Well, there's not really any choice, is there, Dad,' ventures Harry, in such an unusual show of solidarity that I want to throw my arms round him. He eats with less drama than his father, occasionally pressing his lips with one of the paper napkins I've put out, while Pete, who thinks napkins are a waste of time and energy, leaves his untouched on his side plate. 'I mean, all that matters, surely, is—'

'And that's my whole point,' Pete barks, cutting across his son, in the way he cuts across everyone. 'They have you where they want you, these people – like car mechanics and private doctors – they can charge the earth just because they know a bit more and hold all the cards. We're at their bloody mercy.' It is a pet rant and Harry and I endure it stoically.

I consider mentioning the obvious option of dipping into Mum's money to shut Pete up but decide to see if he dares to raise the matter first. I watch my husband impassively instead, trying to recall if there was ever a time when he was interested in anything but his own opinions. A deep dark part of me is even glad he's being so Pete-like and prickly. It feels normal. It also helps validate everything that has happened between me and Jack, the need to escape. One of his Mr Bountiful charades would have presented a far greater challenge.

'So how does the vet think it happened?' Harry persists, once Pete has run out of steam and gone to get the wine bottle from the fridge.

He tops up my barely touched glass without asking and fills his own to the brim before sitting down.

'A car was his best guess,' I reply carefully, noting in the same instant the now fading red bruise of a mark on Harry's neck, just visible among the hairs sticking out round the neckline of his T-shirt. I wonder if it could just have been a flare-up of teenage skin trouble and feel a twist of the old guilt.

Harry snorts. 'But Suki doesn't often go out the front. She mostly likes the back.'

'Who knows what she gets up to?' I counter weakly. 'Remember that *Secret Life of Cats* thing on the telly? They do all sorts after dark. Now, pudding anyone?' I push back my chair, even though Harry hasn't quite finished, and fetch the honey and lemon cheesecake I have made from the fridge. It is another recipe I haven't done in years, using hobnobs for the base, and with icing sugar and raspberries scattered across the top.

Both Pete and Harry are staring at it in gratified wonderment when my phone rings. I move too quickly – I know I do – but I thought I had switched it to silent and the shock is too great. I set the dessert down with a clatter, making the raspberries tremble, and am across the kitchen in two strides to the ledge where I've parked the phone, deliberately far from prying eyes.

Harry and Pete stay at the table, exchanging glances across the cheesecake. Seeing an unrecognisable number, my heart leapfrogs. I answer it with a strong 'hello', waving a hand designed to communicate rueful apology to my husband and son and a command to continue the meal without me, which they ignore. Phones at mealtimes are not allowed. It is one of my own – rare – rules, not theirs.

Inwardly I am ablaze. Jack is calling me from a new number. This is where it starts again – the hope, the new planning. The risk is insane, but I am braced to reply with something innocuous and bland, along the lines of it not being a convenient time and could he call me back tomorrow – any old gobbledy-gook. All I want is to let him know that I am still open to contact, still ready, still desperate, still his.

'Bloody hell, Fran, what on earth is going on?' It is Camille booming in my ear, with her unmistakeable orchestra of northern vowels.

'Camille... I thought you were away... I thought...'

'No, we had to rejig the dates because Erik had a work thing. And I'm on his phone because mine is at the bottom of a bloody lagoon in the Florida Keys, in an alligator's belly by now, I shouldn't wonder...and then I get back to this letter of yours...leaving your job and your husband...to move to *Spain*? Are you there now, with this new man? Fran, what the hell? Have you lost your mind?' Her sentences are galloping and incredulous, and so loud, I fear they will travel across the kitchen.

I manage a whoop of laughter. 'Look, Camille, we're in the middle of a family supper – so sorry about your phone and glad you're back safely, but can we talk tomorrow? And I haven't forgotten the book I'm supposed to be reading for after Easter either,' I blather, thinking of the book-club communications among my unanswered emails and needing to toss something into her stunned silence. In truth, such is the pressure of the moment that I am close to forgetting my own name, let alone what is supposedly the next subject of a reading group I had thought never to attend again.

When Camille next speaks, her voice is a shrunken version of its exuberant self. She tells me any time is great, and she doesn't know what is going on but hopes I'm okay.

I surreptitiously switch the mobile to silent before returning it to the ledge and skip back to the table. 'Dramas, dramas,' I sigh, picking up the knife and starting to carve soft fat wedges out of the cheesecake, 'they're back early because Erik has a work crisis. Oh, and Camille says a Florida alligator ate her phone.'

This prompts a bit of laughter, but there is nonetheless an odd atmosphere in the kitchen, the sense of something being off-kilter. Harry feeds it by breaking the habit of his entire young life, not only clearing the table without being asked, but loading the dishwasher and washing up. He then announces he is meeting a friend for a drink and shoots out of the house. My heart plummets as the door slams. Harry is such a useful buffer. With him gone, there is nothing to hide behind.

'I wonder if he might be seeing someone,' I venture.

'You mean, seeing to someone?' Pete quips, chuckling at his own joke. 'And about bloody time too. So long as he doesn't start taking the piss with work. If he does, he'll have me to answer to.'

'I'm sure he won't,' I answer levelly, knowing it is an idle threat. Pete likes digging at Harry, but saves all his real outbursts for me, behind the protection of at least one closed door. 'Tea?' I make a big show of yawning as I get up to fill the kettle.

'I'll have another glass of this, I think. I expect it was pricey.' Pete studies the bottle – chosen at random from a special offer shelf at the supermarket – before emptying it into his glass. 'Nice meal.'

'Really? Oh good. It was only four pounds.'

'Are we celebrating?' He performs a half-shuffle half-dance across the kitchen and slides his arm round my waist, nuzzling the back of my neck between taking swigs of his wine.

'It's just nice to do things properly sometimes.' The inward flinch has to be disguised, as always, but never has it felt so hard. 'There's that thing on the telly tonight – the murder whatsit with those people stuck in the Arctic somewhere. Do you remember, we liked it last week?'

I ease out of his hold and fetch the milk from the fridge for my tea. I can feel him watching me, weighing up what to say next, how best to get what he wants, which is sex.

Instead of going into the sitting room and putting the TV on, he sits back down at the table and twiddles the stem of his wine glass, swirling the wine like the experts. 'Rob's worried about you.'

'Rob?' I cannot disguise my surprise and dismay. My husband and brother rarely communicate. Two years ahead at school, Rob was at university by the time Pete and I got together and the pair have never got along well anyway, thanks in part to Rob's total lack of interest in sport, but also because of Pete's wariness of the undercurrents of our sibling closeness. An only child himself, out of touch with his own long-since divorced and remarried parents, one of Pete's favourite sayings has always been that it is the family one creates that matters, not the one into which you are born. Rob's obvious business acumen has never helped either, Pete bristling, as always, at the whiff of success in others. 'Well, I can't think why.' I lean against the kitchen counter, hugging my mug of tea.

'He phoned me. He said he's been trying to sort us going there for Easter and you haven't answered his emails or returned his calls.'

'I wanted to talk to you about it first, that's all. I was going to mention it tonight.'

'I see.' My answer is the sort Pete likes, but he is looking at me intently. Above his head, I notice a small spider's web across the corner of the ceiling, a teeny fly dangling from its centre, still alive and struggling.

'So, I'll say yes then, shall I?' I blow at the steam floating out of my mug. 'Rob suggested the whole Bank Holiday weekend, but if you wanted, we could just do Saturday to Monday morning to avoid the worst of the traffic?' My voice is brittle-bright. Committing to Easter in Kent in ten days' time makes me feel faint. I had been banking on Rob's normally laid-back approach to social arrangements. He and Jo are complete last-minute merchants, managing somehow to be spontaneous in the process rather than pissing each other off.

'I suppose. I'll let you sort it with that brother of yours.' There is still something in Pete's manner, an alertness that shoots me back to the dire dark days before Harry, when he hadn't given up on trying to get his knee fixed and the first business venture was in its early days and already floundering. I'd ask some perfectly straightforward question and his jaw would tighten as he'd fix me with an unblinking look, his pupils going huge and black, like Suki's when she's crouched with a prey in her sights. I was usually between pregnancies, the string of early ones that never took hold. It meant the punch would land on my arms or chest or shoulders – places that were easy to hide – so fast that there was never time to anticipate how to respond, let alone dodge out of the way. It was his pain meds, he would claim afterwards, often sobbing more volubly than me as he held me close, stroking my head like I was a pet; and also my fault for driving him mad, he'd say, hijacking him with questions to which he had no answers – grilling him. And I did sort of understand what he meant, because I did go on about things then, being always worried and not having learnt the trick of keeping my mouth shut.

'Okay, great. I'll tell Rob. First thing tomorrow.' I gulp a mouthful of tea, even though it is still way too hot, a part of me relishing how it scalds, the displacement of pain. I badly want us to go and sit in front of the telly as usual, but Pete is still in his kitchen chair and I sense that if I walk out of the room, he's in the mood to take it badly. 'I can't wait to meet little Marcus,' I say cosily. 'Did Rob mention they want me to be godmother?'

'But no call-up for me.' Pete laughs drily. 'Paragon of fatherhood that I am.'

'You're a wonderful father,' I say quietly, trying to mask the dogged-ness in my tone, the hint of insincerity it would betray. 'And you'd hate it anyway – all that vow stuff – it just makes you cross.'

'Yeah, well, I thought the great Robert and Joanna weren't big fans of God either.'

'They're not. It's still just a baby-naming thing, Rob said, but with godparents as a sort of back-up, should anything happen to him and Jo.'

'Oh, they'll live to be a hundred those two.' His tone is one of lament rather than celebration. 'With their bloody green living – organic this and that. And there is nothing up with you?' The question flies out like the missile it is, the glower back in his eyes.

'With me?' Inside, I am flailing, caught on the back foot. 'Of course not. A bit tired maybe.'

'Tired? You're on bloody *holiday*. In fact, I don't know what you do all day. What *do* you do all day, Fran?'

'Well, some cooking for starters,' I counter lightly, aiming to remind him of the meal that he has so recently applauded, and evidently succeeding, because he stands up at last, draining the final mouthful of his wine before heading off to the television. He leaves the glass on the table and I wash, rinse and dry it, making the job last as long as I can, before slipping my phone into my back pocket and going after him, as I know I must if there is to be any hope of keeping the peace.

The football season is over, but Pete has found a game to watch, as he always does, some Spanish clubs by the look of the names. I pluck a magazine from the weekend newspaper off the table and flop into the armchair, instead of our little sofa, where Pete has parked himself, arm along the back, ready to pull me nearer when I join him.

I wasn't supposed to sit in the armchair. I know this, but – as with so many things – I have learnt to pretend not to know it. I keep my head down instead, feigning interest in the magazine, until my page-flipping lands me at the monthly horoscopes. All nonsense, but in my stricken state, I find myself scanning every word. My world has imploded. Who's to say a stargazing nut might not help me understand why?

Despite recent setbacks, being a Libran, you are courageous and positive and will get what you want in the end.

I race to Jack's.

Like all Leos, you are affectionate, warm and generous, and can be counted on to keep your promises, bringing sunshine into the lives of those you love.

I read the lines over and over, feasting on their pitiful crumbs of hope.

'So, what's the book anyway?'

'Pardon?'

'For your *ladies'* book club.' He says the word in a posh hammy way. 'Or am I too dumb to be told?'

For a moment I cannot think of a single book I have ever read in my entire life. Indeed, so empty is my brain that I say '*Middlemarch.*'

He frowns. 'I thought you'd done that one.'

'Yes,' I say weakly, 'but we are re-reading it. It's one of those that you get something new out of every time – lots of layers going on.'

His gaze is already drifting back to the television. My pulse settles. I cannot broach the subject of Sunday now. I feel too shaky. The evening has at last found a familiar path. I have done enough to reassure Pete and he wants sex on the back of it. Once we are upstairs, he will follow through on that wanting and I will deliver. To keep him sweet. To keep Jack's and my dream safe. And at least the lights will be off, I remind myself. Anything is manageable in the dark.

CHAPTER 3

I

'So how come Easter's always on a different date?' Harry is lounging on the back seat of the car, trainers off, headphones askew, his anorak bunched up against the window by way of a pillow. He has not shaved and the darkness on his chin and cheeks is already strong enough to suggest the delineation of the beard he would have if he chose to grow one. It might even suit him, I decide, glancing over my shoulder and thinking – as I do, still, most minutes of most hours, despite trying not to – of Jack. I had never been a fan of beards, and had enjoyed confessing as much. He should judge the extent of my feelings, I used to tease, by the fact that I was prepared even to kiss him.

I happen to know the answer to the Easter question, but Pete pitches in first, quickly demonstrating, to me at least, that he doesn't really have a clue. 'It's to do with the tides and the moon,' he says, throwing looks at the rear-view mirror, even though Harry is too horizontal to be visible, 'one of those stupid things fixed centuries ago that nobody bothers to question.'

I gaze out at the undulating fields of rapeseed that have replaced the grey south-eastern suburbs of London, a whizzing slide show, so dazzling that I am tempted to reach for my sunglasses. My eyes ache anyway, from the still regular, covert activity of crying and the continuing strain of having to hide the fact.

'It is always the Sunday after the first full moon after the March equinox,' I say absently, once Pete has dried up, to which Pete himself says nothing and Harry emits a bemused 'Oh', before retreating behind the protection of his headphones.

The Easter question – the willingness to communicate – is further proof that Harry is in remarkably good spirits for a twenty-year-old being subjected to a long weekend in Kent with relatives, not one of whom falls anywhere near his age bracket. That morning, I had been astonished to see his rucksack packed and parked by the front door before breakfast. For the meal itself, a brunch, as it was Saturday, he laid the table and sat down before being asked, going on to eat as if it was the last meal of his life, mopping up the last drizzles of egg yolk with wads of extra bread and then checking for permission before demolishing the two leftover sausages, bringing his total sausage tally for the meal – I counted out loud, amused – to five. Pete, from behind the shield of his newspaper, grunted, 'Those would have made a good sandwich,' but all I could think, with a burst of excitement, is that if there is someone giving my son love bites they are clearly making him very happy.

I close my eyes, shutting out the violence of the yellow crops. The idea of Harry having a girlfriend is wonderful, for all the obvious reasons, but it also dawns on me that it will be good if he has something, someone – other than his father – to hang on to if I do ever get to be with Jack. And if he is truly smitten, then he might even understand a tiny bit more about his mother's need to follow her own heart, the difficulties between me and Pete, though settling into something like normality over the years, hardly having been a secret. In fact, I would probably have to rewrite my goodbye letter to him in the light of it, I muse, a certain wonder pushing through my distress at how life, once on such a flat line, seems to be bouncing in new directions every day.

I open my eyes to find the rapeseed has been replaced by open fields, displaying the occasional grazing horse, nose-deep in the soft mossy spring grass. There is freshness to the unfolding countryside but also a hazy stillness suggestive of the start of the unseasonal spring heatwave about which the weather pundits have been warning – new records predicted in all parts of the country, especially the south-east. Pete has already flicked our air con on and keeps fiddling with the dial, as well as various other switches and buttons in the dashboard – the satnav menu in particular, even though we know the route to my brother's and have no need of it. Pete likes cars. He also drives fast and well, as deft as a pilot in a cockpit. I remember suddenly that I like this about my husband, and have done so ever since the first spin in his father's Vauxhall twenty-five years before. 'Relax and enjoy the ride,' he said cockily once I was strapped in, and to my surprise, I did.

'I've got lots of eggs,' I say, by way of an offering in the now established game of pretending to be the me that Pete expects and knows. 'For the hunt. Rob said he wants me to help with the clues and hiding, like last time.'

I get a half nod by way of response and then whatever Harry is listening to hums quietly into our silence. I think I hear my phone buzz, but I am not certain and dare not check, for fear of drawing a comment or question. I remember in the same instant, my spirits tumbling, that Rob and Jo's place has lousy connectivity. In the past, Harry has been castigated for spending so much time sitting on a fallen tree at the top of the field behind the house, claiming testily when challenged that it was the only spot that provided a decently steady signal. What did being offline for a couple of days matter anyway, I had hissed, cornering him alone, never imagining that one day I would share the same desperation.

It has been nearly two weeks now, and still no word, despite me continuing to break all our old rules and trying repeatedly to call and send messages, without any clue if they are getting through. I have become an automaton, functioning on the outside, hollow on the inside. Each night, I sleep fitfully, drifting between increasingly gruesome imagined scenarios and self-recrimination for holding onto my hope; but the grey light of dawn always brings an obstinate flurry of certainty. Still barely any time has passed, I tell myself. Jack loves me. He will contact me when he can. The prospect of this taking place when I am buried in one of the few remaining black spots in southern England makes the inside of the car spin. Jack might think I have lost heart, lost faith. I grip the shoulder strap of my seat belt and press my face against the window, steaming the glass.

Pete shoots me a look and, for one mad moment, I am tempted to shout that he needs to turn the car round and take me back to London – because I am ill, or have left the bath running or the oven on. Any old thing. Instead, I stare bleakly ahead, fighting the sensation that every yard is taking me further away from the place I need to be.

Twenty minutes later, we all catch sight of Rob signalling and waving from a track above the road that leads to the winding wooded drive to the house and fruit farm beyond. Beside him, the Jack Russell, Skipper, bounces in and out of view, while a larger, more recent arrival, a mixed mutt called Pooh rescued from a local pound, lopes on ahead.

Harry immediately winds down his window and waves back, shouting, 'Hi, godfather.' Pete honks the horn and I yodel a hello, cupping the word between my hands to help it travel, some of my distraction easing at the sight of my brother's familiar tall, lean frame, his easy gait and gingery hair, looking in need of a cut, as always, and blowing up in stalks that show the growing bald patch on his crown. We could be any old family, I think suddenly, hooking up with relatives for a jolly Easter Bank Holiday weekend. No one can see the bad stuff. No one can see what's true.

II

The visit to north London with Mel had taken place on the Monday in the end, because of me not wanting to stir anything with Pete. We set off in high spirits, chattering about safe topics like Harry's new invisible love life and poor Suki, now confirmed with a broken femur as well as a hip, almost like we were going on some sort of fun road trip. We had even managed to share a joke about it being a spying mission, Mel at one point breaking into a diva rendition of Adele's 'Skyfall' that had me laughing properly for the first time in what felt like months. Finding that I could still let go like that, even for a few moments, felt fantastic, despite the bubble of hysteria which I knew was only half a beat behind. It was also a relief to be bombing along in Mel's little blue Yaris, *doing* something at last, as opposed to moping about like a zombie, clutching my phone.

Jack's street proved easy to find, as did the house itself, of handsome white stucco with an arched portico of sandy bricks round its entrance, all of it fizzing with white and pink roses and looking so exactly like a small painting of Jack's that he had shown me on his phone early on, that I promptly burst into tears, the reality of our mission slamming into me like a wall. To think of Jack possibly being inside this very building – so close, but so untouchable – was just too much. The sobs came with such violence, it was like throwing up.

'All righty,' Mel murmured, craning her neck to get a good look as she drove past, but then doing a smart U-turn and pulling into a space a good fifteen yards away on the opposite side of the street. 'Let's have a cuppa.' She switched off the engine and reached for a small cooler bag on the back seat. 'And maybe a bite.' She unscrewed a smart little stainless-steel thermos as she talked, pouring some steaming tea into its lid and handing it to me along with a neat tin-foil parcel. 'Tuna.' She peeled back the foil, as if I was a hopeless child, exposing four neat plump brown-bread triangles, trimmed of their crusts. 'No sugar for the tea, I'm afraid, only these.' She rattled a little tube of sweeteners, adding, when I shook my head, 'I'm on a diet actually.'

'Okay. Though you are totally gorgeous. You know that, right?' Distracted as I was, I felt a stab of affectionate concern. Whatever my theories about her formative years, Mel was indeed beautiful, and had long since, correctly, stopped caring what a set of scales might say.

'Nothing drastic,' she went on, ignoring my remarks and starting to nibble on the first of her own sandwich segments in the manner of one consciously prolonging a treat. 'Just no meat, fewer carbs and less sweet stuff. And I only put a tiny bit of mayonnaise in the tuna.'

'It's delicious. Thank you, Mel.' I drank and ate methodically, my eyes pinned on Jack's house. Helena's house. I focused on the windows, squinting for any hint of movement inside, dreading it and wanting it in equal measure. A glimpse of Jack... it made my heart pump. I wasn't sure what I would do. I stared down the street, picturing myself running like the crazy person I had become, screeching his name, all the neighbours' curtains trembling as they enjoyed the show.

In front of the house, there was a large square of grass and a strip of empty tarmac clearly designed for a car; but there was a garage too, with closed doors, so who knew what was inside. It could even contain Jack himself, I decided wildly, chained up, gagged, near death from dehydration.

'Seems pretty quiet,' said Mel. 'Maybe they've gone away...'

'Or maybe Jack is locked up somewhere,' I blurted. 'That is the sort of thing Helena would do. Starve him to death. For a laugh. No wife in the world could treat a husband more cruelly.'

When Mel remained silent, I started listing the injustices Jack had relayed to me during the course of our time together, even though she had heard it all before – the relentless jibes about his lack of prowess, as a man, as an artist, the chain-yanking over money, the vicious drunken assault on his work.

Mel seemed to grow more impassive and inscrutable as I talked, chewing her way through her tuna triangles till I was close to screaming.

'Well?' I demanded at last, determined not to show my own awareness of how crazy I sounded.

She sighed heavily, turning to me and blinking her Bambi eyes. 'She's almost certainly still with him though, isn't she, Fran? Just like you're still with Pete. People put up with crap all the time – I'm sorry, but they do. You are living proof. You could have just left – I've told you that enough times. You could leave now.'

'But it's never been that simple,' I gasped, 'as you well know, not with Pete... and the fact is, good people endure bad things, often precisely because they *are* good people. You learn to handle what you have to. And there's never been enough money anyway...' I was close to tears again, '...which I also thought you understood. I tell you what, Mel, it's fucking hard to separate when you're broke. People don't realise that. And then there's Harry. Despite everything, he has needed – *needs* – his Dad.' I folded my arms tightly across my chest, reflecting, with the usual wrench, on my son, so many years in the making, so treasured, but so integral to the complications. 'Jesus, Mel, putting Jack first has been the hardest thing I have ever done, I've *told* you that.' The fact of Mel, currently partner-less, as well as childless, was somehow hovering in the air between us. Not wanting kids was one of her declared life certainties and I had always admired her for it; but as her clock ticked and the years passed, I sometimes sensed she might be finding it a harder conviction to hang on to.

'Yes, I get that,' Mel replied evenly, having waited for me to finish, like some kind of maddening, unflappable therapist. 'And you've been a total saint, hanging on in there all these years. When Jack came along, no one could have been happier for you. Remember?' She licked her fingers and crushed up her empty tin-foil wrapper into a tight ball. 'But here's the thing...' She shifted in her seat slightly so as to be able to face me more squarely. 'Don't you think it might be time to consider the possibility that Jack has simply chickened out? I'm sorry, Fran. Don't shoot the messenger and all that. It's what married men do – they get to the brink and change their minds.' She was still kneading the foil, compressing it into a silver bullet. 'I hate to say it Fran, but maybe he has just ghosted you. It's hardly uncommon. Nothing speaks greater volumes than total silence. If he popped out of that door now and you confronted him, maybe he would even deny knowing you. Maybe he'd call the police and accuse you of stalking. People do all sorts to save their marriage.'

I didn't speak. I couldn't. I wanted to push my palm into the middle of her wide, flat, placid face, offload some of the chaos that was pulling me apart. A heavy quiet fell between us. Mel took my empty wrapper and her bauble of foil and put them in the cooler bag, zipping it shut.

'Jack loves me,' I whispered. 'I know he does. And he knows that I love him. If there was any way he could make contact with me, he would – even to tell me it was over. He would *never* shut me out with this hideous... *nothingness*.'

Mel shook her head despairingly. 'Like I said, it's called ghosting.' She unzipped the cooler bag again and pulled out two bananas, putting one back when I shook my head. She broke off the end of hers with her teeth before starting to peel it, her long lacquered nails like little pink tweezers. 'And besides, love doesn't get anybody anywhere.'

'And how would you know, never having found it?' The words were out before I could stop them. Mel flinched, seeking refuge in the view through her near window. 'Mel... sorry... I shouldn't have said that. I'm a total mess, a total bitch and—'

'No, you're right. Thanks, Fran. Friends must speak the truth.' She finished peeling the banana in two swift swipes and ate the last quarter steadily. 'But you know what?' Her voice was shrill. 'I would choose my life over yours. Any day. I can, and do, walk away from things that don't work. Also, I might not love my job, but it pays well and I have my independence. Whereas you might like how you earn a living, but on all other fronts... you're just trapped, Fran, and always have been from what I can see.'

'Yes.' I hung my head, castigated and mortified. 'You are right, and very special. Please forgive what I said.'

'It doesn't matter.'

I wanted her to look at me, to soften, but she kept her head averted, the sense of injury still blazing out of her.

'I'm not myself,' I admitted quietly.

'No, you are not.'

Both our gazes drifted back to Jack and Helena's house. It seemed to stare back at us, silent and still. The patch of grass was long and whiskery, I noticed now, and I could just make out what looked like the yellow heads of several dandelions sprouting through the hard surface of the drive. Round the doorway, the rose briars were laden and low-hanging. Jack would have to duck to avoid their thorns tangling in his thick hair. 'I don't think anyone is home.'

'Shall we go then?'

'A bit longer, if you don't mind.'

'I don't mind.' There was still a harshness in her tone.

'Sorry again for what I said. It was unforgivable. I just don't know where I am at the moment. I'm so confused. I can't think what can have happened. It's like a death with no body.'

Mel reached across the gearstick and patted my knee, turning her kind, candid gaze on me with a relenting sigh. 'I know, babe. You are so sad. Just remember, I am on your side, okay? I love you so much.'

'Okay. Thanks, Mel. I love you too.'

We waited ten more minutes and then left. The house had stayed still - lifeless, I couldn't help thinking. We were much more subdued on the return journey. Inside me, I was aware of something shifting, starting to give up. It felt like there was nothing more to say, no more theories to come up with, no consolation to be had. I took the opportunity to phone Camille, apologizing for the delay in getting back to her and explaining – because it seemed the right thing to do – the humiliating bare bones of what had happened, how I was now back with Pete. I said I would love to continue in my job, but would understand if she wanted to fire me anyway. She told me not to be an idiot, that Chalfonts was where I worked until I said otherwise.

'Though, all of it to my face next time, okay? Bad news should always be delivered in person, is my view, and I would say the same to this vanishing man of yours if I could...' She paused, as if there was a lot more she would like to say on the subject, and I could hardly blame her. The need, even for this conversation, was mortifying. 'But look,' she went on more gently, 'call me again after the Easter weekend, okay, so I know how you are doing? In fact, let's meet before the book group that week, so we can have a proper talk. I can't tell you how much I need you, Fran. Everything is taking off and I want you on board. And, besides, relief teachers cost the earth.' She was trying to be funny and nice, and I couldn't have been more grateful, but it was hard to laugh.

'Let him go,' said Mel after parking near my house and getting out of the car. She held me in the longest hug she had ever given. 'Just let the fucker go.'

III

'Could you take him?' Jo is already turning back to the fridge as she hands me my godson, fishing out things for the picnic in the woods that has suddenly been announced as the day's lunch plan. 'We'll fill a couple of baskets with bread and leftovers from last night, take some sunscreen, as well as lots of water and plonk ourselves under the oak by the river. Easter Sunday al fresco – it'll be lovely, and anyone brave enough can swim. I'll tell Rob to sort some wine and dig out the plastic glasses. Do Harry and Pete like quiche? Do you? Oh, and look, and there are the strawberries too.'

She is loading stuff from the fridge onto their pine-topped kitchen island as she talks, her long hair sprouting attractively out of its various clips and her white cotton shirt still untucked from the latest breast-feed, a process which she manages without any fuss, simply dropping into the nearest chair whenever Marcus's fretting becomes serious, and tucking him up under whatever top she happens to be wearing. At supper the previous night, she had fetched him from his cot for feeding at the dining-room table, and then continued to eat and talk through his noisy chomps and guzzles, able to do so with just a fork, since Rob, without saying a word, had got up to cut her chicken and vegetables into bite-size pieces the moment she left the room. They are so in tune, my brother and his wife, so aware of each other, that it is like watching two dancers, lost to their own private choreography. I have always known that they love each other, but never seen it so vividly. It makes me happy, but also, now, shamefully jealous. More than ever, Pete and I seem such clumsy failures in comparison. Whereas with Jack, I can't help thinking fiercely, it would have been us who stood out for our closeness; us whom people envied.

'I don't know how you manage everything, Jo. You are a marvel.'

My sister-in-law pauses in her sorting to laugh, the dusting of freckles round her strong green eyes disappearing into the deep crinkles at their corners. She is so much younger than Rob, so much more physically beautiful. 'Thank you, Fran.' She sounds genuinely touched. 'I blunder along. And after the twins, this one is a breeze, even if he hasn't actually learnt the meaning of the word *sleep* yet.' She crosses her eyes in the direction of the baby before returning her attention to the fridge. 'And you're back at work next week, presumably? I must say, I can't wait to get rid of my two. School is a total lifesaver.'

'Yes.' I try to sound positive. Inside my head, the days stretch ahead, a dark tunnel. Jack has been my pinpoint of light, and now he is gone.

'And we've settled on the second weekend of the summer half-term for the baby-naming,' Jo chatters on, 'June the fifth – did Rob tell you?' She is arm-deep in a bench freezer on the other side of the kitchen, pulling out frozen baguettes.

'No, but that sounds... Thank you both, again, so much for asking me to be—'

'We might do it somewhere in London, as it seems fairer on all the guests. We really aren't sure. Could we use your place as a base if necessary?'

'Yes... of course.' Oh god. I sway, powerless, again, against life's currents. I want to give up on Jack, but it is so very hard.

The baby blinks uncertainly, casting a look at his mother.

'Does he need changing?' Jo hops closer to sniff in the direction of his nappy. Satisfied that it is clean, she turns her attention to a heap of carrots, nimbly peeling and slicing them into long segments. For dunking into dips, she explains, abandoning the pile to pull out various plastic tubs from the fridge.

Marcus, snug now on the ledge of my hip, eyes me steadily. He is square and chubby-limbed, dressed only in a stained T-shirt and a nappy that neatly contains the bulge of his tummy. His upper lip pouts comfortably over the lower one and his cheeks glow like polished peaches. He has spent most of the morning either asleep in his pram or sitting, a bobbing Buddha, on a padded blanket in a little pen in a patch of shade on the front lawn, watching his elder siblings twirl and shriek their way round the garden filling their flimsy home-made Easter baskets with the aid of the easy clues I helped to compose and write on large pieces of paper, hiding them under big stones and empty flowerpots.

> I am near a big pipe, but it does not smoke.
> I am in a house that is green, but you can see right through me.

The primary-school teacher bit of me had enjoyed herself. Watching the twins, quickly figuring out the answers, I had found myself wishing that life's signposts could be so simple.

When a fracas broke out, triggered by Tilda's basket collapsing and Billy pouncing on her eggs as they spilled onto the grass, claiming them as his, Marcus clapped his little dimpled hands like a delighted theatre-goer. And after the hunt, when Harry, at Rob's request, stopped throwing sticks to distract the two exhausted dogs and hoicked Marcus awkwardly out of the pen for carrying at a somewhat lopsided angle back to the house, the baby had eyed his big cousin with a look of bemused curiosity, swiping gleefully at all the passing objects this new and unexpected manner of transport brought within his reach.

'Animals are loads easier,' Harry had said with a rueful grimace, handing his charge over with evident relief to Jo, waiting with arms outstretched at the kitchen door.

'I'll take him on a walkabout,' I tell Jo now, leaving the kitchen and going into the sitting room, where Pete is standing in front of the television, hands in the pockets of his baggy beige shorts, his big feet splayed in the open sandals that make no secret of his aversion to the use of toenail clippers. We had both slept badly, rolled into the central dip of the old springy mattress in the spare room. I had felt envious of Harry, alone on the fold-out sofa next door, crammed between the filing cabinets and desk from which Jo somehow finds time to run a flowers-for-events business on top of everything else.

Pete throws me a quick, dismissive glance before returning his attention to the cricket game on the screen.

I stay where I am. For all that has passed between us, all the hovering fear, there is still a deep, obstinate reflex to make him at least acknowledge my existence. 'By the way,' I say, addressing the back of his head as the players in yellow tracksuits suddenly swarm around a team member like angry bees, 'Jo was wondering if we could help host the baby-naming ceremony if they decide to do it in London.' I see the muscles in his wide neck tighten. 'It would be nice to help them if we can,' I plough on, trying to sound enthusiastic, fighting the dawning realisation that nothing in my life is about truth, that for years I have been lost in a maze of deception. 'I said I'd talk to you...'

'Fine.'

I chew my lip, alert, as ever, to the danger of pushing him too far. 'Apparently we are having a picnic lunch now. In the woods. By the river.'

He swings round at this. 'Really? Isn't that a bit unnecessary?'

I shrug helplessly. Marcus is growing heavy. I shift him to my other hip. 'Jo says it will be under the big oak by the bend. I think Rob might need a hand carrying stuff down there.'

'You mean you want me to go and help Rob?'

'Well, I—'

'So why didn't you just say so?' He speaks quietly and viciously, wary no doubt of being overheard. 'Why do you pretend that you came into this room for any other reason?'

'I didn't—'

'Forget it, Fran.' He turns the TV off with an angry flick of the console and marches out into the passageway.

I nuzzle Marcus's neck with my nose, sniffing his milky sweet skin. 'You see why I fell in love with Jack?' I whisper. 'You see?'

'Hey, sis.'

I spin round. 'Hey, Rob.' Marcus releases a wet coo of happy recognition at the sight of his father and then grabs my necklace, a sturdy string of tigers' eyes which Jack had always admired. 'Pete just went looking for you – to help carry things for the picnic.'

'Did he? That was kind, but it's all done.' Rob does a jokey strongman flex with his slim pale arms and then bends over his son, brushing the tip of his big nose against Marcus's very small one. 'I see you got landed with The Monster.'

'My god, he's so gorgeous.' I plant a light kiss on top of the baby's head, which is bald apart from a downy layer of near transparent hair, more like fur and silky on my lips. 'He keeps reminding me of Harry as a baby. They're kind of similar, don't you think? Harry turned dark, but his hair was white-blond at the beginning.'

'I guess they are, a bit,' Rob concedes, laughing, 'though we're expecting a hint of red to grow through with this one. Harry seems to be coming along, by the way. We had a bit of a chat after supper last night. He says he's thinking of starting his own business.'

'Is he? Goodness. What sort of business?'

'Animals – pet-care, he said. Sitting, walking, grooming. He's saving to go on some sort of course.'

I am truly astonished. 'Well, he hasn't told me, or Pete – as far as I know.' I should be long used to Harry shutting me out, but it is impossible to keep the trace of hurt from my voice.

'Ah, that's families for you,' Rob replies quickly and kindly, 'poor communication with those closest. Jo says I am hopeless – the proverbial clam – always in need of being prised open. Talking of which, you are all right, are you, Fran? It's like you've been... I dunno... slightly off-radar recently. Is something up?' And suddenly he's looking at me properly, my big brother, and inside me a hair-trigger – to spill twenty years of unspoken difficulties – is trembling. There is our ancient closeness, but there has never been any question of being confidantes. Our lives have been too divergent, and Pete, a master of putting on appearances when required, has never given Rob undue cause for concern.

'No, I'm great.' I'm aware of the words coming out a little too fast, and before I know it, some rogue tears are spilling down my cheeks. I swipe at them furiously, hating the new, appalling leaky state of my tear ducts.

'Frannie? Hey, now... I didn't mean to upset you.' Rob touches my shoulder.

'Just a bit tired, not sleeping too well...' I force a smile because he is still scrutinising my face, making me uncomfortably aware of the now permanent telltale purple smudges under my eyes, getting harder to conceal, like everything else.

'There, now.' And, next thing, he's got his arms round me and Marcus, holding us both tight. The baby tries to grab his ears, while I bury my nose in his T-shirt, inhaling him and the entire history of our childhood, it feels like, the sense of security that underlined all the minor ups and downs, understanding, as if for the first time, the sheer luxury of its normality. Our parents were older than most, and old-fashioned with it, but they did a good job.

Rob holds me at arm's length, fixing me with the piercing light blue eyes that look so fine against his bright red hair. 'Do you miss Mum?'

'No...' I falter, caught out both by my brother's touching determination to discover the source of my low spirits and the sudden recollection of my naïve imaginings that Mum would have been happy for me and Jack. It is difficult now, to conceive of her being anything but bitterly disappointed. 'I mean yes, I do miss her,' I assure him hurriedly, 'sometimes, but I'm fine. It's been nearly three years, after all, and she was so ill, wasn't she, when it came back. I sort of wanted her to hang on, but also sort of didn't.'

'Yes, that's what I think too.'

'And she was never quite the same without Dad, anyway, was she?' I murmur. 'In fact, I think she fell apart without him more and more as the years passed...'

'Hey, you're not ill or something, are you Frannie?' Rob interjects sternly.

'Not remotely.' I sniff, pulling myself together properly and giving Marcus, who is getting restless, a little jig. 'But, actually, a proper brother-sister chat might be nice.' I grin at him, high on his brotherly kindness. 'If we get the chance. In the meantime, you should watch me closely with this one, just in case I kidnap him for myself.'

Rob relaxes at once, laughing his bass laugh. 'Ah, the Marcus Effect, don't say I didn't warn you.' He waggles the baby's toes, so dainty in his huge fingers.

'Warn her of what?' Pete is in the room suddenly enough to give me the unsettling hunch that he has been loitering and listening.

'Marcus's magic powers,' says my brother easily, tenderly cupping the back of his son's head before giving my husband his full attention. 'When I called Fran to pop the godmother question, I warned her about it. I would have preferred to do so in person of course, but she was at the airport.'

'The airport?' Pete looks from Rob to me. 'When was that then?'

I am glad I have Marcus in my arms. It allows me to feign preoccupation with something other than the topic of conversation. 'Oh, it was a crazy day – I meant to tell you...' I pull a face at the baby and go on breezily to recount the story of Mel returning from her mythical trip with her mythical bad ankle, a lie deployed so often it is starting to feel like fact. For a second, I wonder if that is all it takes, believing in something to make it real. 'I knew you would think I was mad,' I chatter, 'Rob certainly did, didn't you, Rob, both of you being united in the view that my oldest school friend is, and always has been, a waste of space...' I swing my hips as I talk, rocking Marcus harder. He starts to cry. I chuck him under the chin, which distresses him even more. I know my tension is to blame, powering into his little body like electricity, upsetting all his innocent equilibrium.

'You drove Mel to the airport?' Pete persists.

'No, she collected her,' explains Rob, plucking the baby from my arms. 'There are a couple of deckchairs I'd love a hand with, if you didn't mind, Pete?' There is wonderful authority in my brother's voice and I am not sure I have ever loved him more.

'Sure, lead the way,' growls Pete throwing me a glare as he follows Rob out of the room.

An hour later, the deckchairs are propped unused against the oak tree and we are all sprawled on an assortment of picnic rugs, exactly as Jo must have envisaged, replete and sleepy, the remnants of the meal scattered around us in Tupperware containers, the sun dappling the ground through the leaves of the branches, which vault over our heads like a mighty parasol. The dogs have been left at the house – not being good with picnics, Rob had admitted with a regretful expression after a warning look from his wife – and Harry has taken himself off to the top of the back field with his phone. The twins are a little deeper among the trees building a den, their gingery blonde heads bobbing as they charge about with sticks and feathery fans of fresh bracken, Tilda taking charge as usual, issuing the occasional high-pitched command that has her brother, younger by two hours – though it sometimes seems more like two years – rushing to do her bidding.

The spot is by a big lazy bend in the river, thick with bankside brambles and trees, apart from a handy gap offering a yard or so of reedy bank that makes easy access for swimming. Rob and Harry braved the cold before eating, taking charge of the intrepid twins, who squealed first in protest at being made to wear their armbands when they can both swim, and then in delight at the clinging squelch of the river-mud round their feet as they paddled through the reeds. Being neither proficient nor enthusiastic in water, let alone an icy river, I had refrained from joining them, as had Jo, while Pete had made a big to-do of borrowing some comical pink and black Bermuda shorts of Rob's, only to change his mind at the last minute. He then ate and drank more liberally than any of us – his reservations both about the picnic and my airport rescue of Mel thankfully forgotten – before being the first to fall asleep, rolling off the blanket onto a patch of grass and putting his shirt over his face by way of an indication of his intentions.

Soon, Jo and Rob were following suit, stretching out separately on the largest of the rugs, with their arms reaching towards each other, fingers touching, making a natural protective archway for the baby, lolling on his back between them, arms and legs splayed. I have a smaller tartan rug to myself and lie on my side, watching the sunlit water, such a perfect mirror of the trees and sky overhead that it is impossible to tell them apart. The children's voices recede to a murmur, and all I am aware of is the occasional buzz of an insect and the faint chink of the bottles – water, wine, beer – which Rob has tethered among the reeds for cooling. Through half-closed eyes, I track a wisp of cloud, a lone sail on an indigo sea. I drift with Jack in my head, unable to resist thinking how he would have loved the relaxed day – egg hunts, picnics, the glassy beauty of the river. I picture him getting out his pencils and thick pad, starting to sketch, the expression of furrowed intensity on his face that I so love, especially when it is aimed at me. Let me look, he always used to say, let me just drink you in.

Mel's command to give up on him – the good sense of listening to her – tries to block my path, but I kick it away.

Oh, my darling, are you thinking of me? Are you coming for me? Are you still alive...?

I have no idea I have fallen asleep until I am woken by a shout. I roll heavily, reluctantly, still drugged with fatigue, onto my side and sit up. I blink as Rob leaps past me, doing a running flat belly-flop of a dive into the water. Jo is kneeling up, rubbing her eyes, her hair lost entirely from its clip and hanging round her face. I stagger to my feet, noting that the grass where Pete was lying is flattened but empty of Pete himself, save for the crumpled heap of his shirt.

There is some sort of commotion going on in the river, intermittent shouting, of Rob, by the sound of it, but it is just beyond the turn in the bend, behind the wall of brambles and out of view.

I clamber to my feet and slide my feet into my sandals, still feeling sluggish. I haven't slept so deeply in weeks, months. Behind me, I hear

Jo say, 'Where is Marcus?' I turn to see her hobbling round the big tree, one flip-flop on, the other in her hand. 'And the twins... Billy, Tilda...' She calls their names, sprinting towards the den-building area and then back again, hopping to put the second shoe on. 'Children!' This time, the word is a roar.

'Mummy!' It is Billy, emerging from the riverside tangle, lumbering because he is carrying his baby brother, who bounces between his arms like a beach ball. It is a relief beyond words to see the baby turning his head to look over his little shoulder, his bright blue eyes, blinking in bemusement. 'I think he got stung by the nettles,' Billy sobs. His fair hair is a flat black, wet cap and his face mud-streaked. Marcus looks unscathed, apart from a scattering of pink dots on his chubby forearms, but bleeding scratches crisscross Billy's stick-thin arms, legs and chest like ghoulish tattoos. 'We found a new path to the river from the den and decided to take Marcus for an adventure, but Tilly fell in, Mummy. She fell in.'

Jo scoops the baby from his arms and pulls Billy against her in one swift motion. 'What do you mean Tilly fell in?' Her voice is glacier calm. 'Where is she now?'

'Uncle Pete came. Uncle Pete was there. And then he called for Dad.'

I have found a hefty branch and am thrashing at the nettles and brambles to carve the quickest route through the dense foliage separating us from the next section of the river. I hack manically, but Jo pushes past me, heedless of any stings and thorns.

'You stay,' she yells back at her eldest son, standing miserably among the wreckage of the picnic, his legs smeared with blood, his little brother sitting at his feet. 'You stay and look after your brother.'

For all the noise of my scything and Jo's shouting, I am aware that a silence has fallen on the other side, where we are headed. I slash all the harder and suddenly the river lies before us, still bathed in sunlight, but offering a much wider, choppier version of itself than at our picnic spot. The current is immediately visible, a series of swirling eddies carrying sticks and leaves downstream. Pete is in the middle of it, doing his slightly lopsided breaststroke and aiming towards the bank in front of us. On his back, draped like a sodden doll, is Tilly, her arms trailing in the water, her head on one side, her hair matted, her eyes closed. Rob is swimming alongside them, performing an awkward one-armed doggy-paddle while using his free hand to keep his daughter's mouth clear of the lapping water. They are making slow, concentrated progress.

Jo issues a single scream, which rings in the silence.

CHAPTER 4

I

'I simply cannot imagine... if one of mine...' Camille presses her hand to her chest, where a small gold cross gleams in the v of her white silk shirt, and shakes her head fiercely, as if to eradicate the image, making her explosive black curls swing across her face.

As if on cue, the sitting-room door swings open to reveal her middle son, Lars, hanging off its handle. A gummy impish smile displays two missing front teeth and his sun-bleached hair is like liquid gold against his toffee skin, burnished darker by the recent Florida holiday.

I think again of Tilly, of the miracle that is the life of every single child, and their own oblivion to the fact. I also cannot help worrying a bit for the door handle, rattling and loose in the little boy's grip.

'Lars, I said no interrupting, remember?' Camille scolds.

'Yes, but Papi is still running and can I have ice cream. Pleeeeeese.' He is clinging to the entire door now, like a mini rock-climber.

'No, you may not. Go to bed and clean your teeth. He knew he didn't have a hope,' Camille says drily as soon as the door is shut, topping up my wine, which I have barely touched, and refilling her own glass, despite having said she would hold off until the rest of the group arrived. Around us lie the usual platefuls of mouth-watering food she always warns she won't have time to do, along with neat piles of crockery, cutlery, napkins and condiments. In the middle of it all sits a copy of that month's book, a fat thriller with an embossed silver jacket called *City Blues*, which I have neither bought nor read – a fact which keeps pinging me back, unhelpfully, to Jack's and my very first laughing conversation in the basement of the auction house; all the simple joy before the storm.

I am perched on Camille's black needlecord sofa, the bay window behind her dark, handsome face displaying a London garden big enough to suggest that whatever Erik actually does in the oil business, he is paid well for it. As agreed, I have come early so that we can talk properly, a daunting enough prospect without the recent trauma of the Easter weekend.

'Water terrifies me,' Camille says softly now, sipping her drink.

'Apparently she lost her balance in the mud and got swept away. Both the twins swim, but the current was so strong. Pete happened to be nearby having a pee. He was incredible.' There is genuine awe in my voice. Four days on, and I am still mesmerised by the image of my husband staggering out of the sludgy riverside, the ridiculous borrowed trunks clinging to his thighs like sodden wrapping paper, the hair on his big belly sleek and dripping as he swings Tilly, floppy as a doll, off his shoulders and lays her gently on the scrubby ground. As Jo and Rob threw themselves at her, slapping her hands, rubbing her arms, calling her name, I shouted that I'd ring for an ambulance and started thrashing my way back through the way we had come. My heart surged with relief when I saw Billy sitting quietly on the picnic rug, wan and shocked, the baby tucked against him, sleepily sucking on his thumb. In the same moment, Harry emerged on the far side of the clearing, asking what on earth was going on.

'Dad just rescued Tilly from the river,' I said in a voice that I tried to keep matter-of-fact. 'Run to the house and call an ambulance, sweetheart. Quick as you can. Take Billy and Marcus with you. I need to get back. Everything will be okay,' I assured Billy gently, as the little boy clambered obediently to his feet, looking dazed, while Harry, with a swiftness that told me he was in no doubt of the gravity of the situation, gathered up the baby.

I hurried back, stopping in my tracks at the sight of Pete on his knees and pumping at Tilly's skinny chest with a professionalism I had no idea he possessed, using visible, rhythmic force, both palms layered one on top of the other. He counted out loud as he worked, breaking off after each ten to open Tilly's mouth and blow into it with the same determined rhythm. Tilly's little body bounced unresponsively, the thin straps of her turquoise bathing costume falling off her knobbly shoulders. Rob had fallen silent, rocking on his heels, his face in his hands. Beside him, Jo was moaning, a keening sound that made the hairs on my neck stand on end. I watched numb and transfixed, sick with the certainty that Pete, for all his heroic efforts, would fail. Life is a plan that goes wrong, a plan full of pain. Trying to be a good person is no protection against anything, not even for an innocent child.

But then Tilly made a groaning sound and gullies of cloudy liquid started spilling over the edges of her mouth and down her chin. Jo and Rob went mad, shrieking her name and grabbing her, but Pete barked at them to hang on, and turned her onto her side, carefully using his fingers to clear her mouth and throat as she carried on being sick. Only when Tilly sat up, looking about her and crying normally, did he move away so that Rob and Jo could have her, and their joy, to themselves.

'I once did a course,' he said to no one in particular, batting at a fly diving round his head, paying no heed to the hand which I had found myself placing on his shoulder. 'Back in my sporting days. Never put it to the test before. She'll still need checking over, I should think.'

I took my hand away and we both watched Tilda weeping softly in the tangle of her parents' embrace, while they crooned – 'nice to have you back,' 'you gave us quite a scare' – words of comfort designed to give no inkling of the end-of-the-world sorrow into which they had, briefly, been plunged.

'Dad did mouth-to-mouth,' I explained to Harry, when he reappeared, the ambulance summoned, Marcus pinned under one arm and Billy clinging to the other. 'He saved her life.'

'I was just taking a leak,' said Pete, as if this explained everything.

* * *

'What a time of it you have been having, girl,' Camille murmurs. She has come to sit next to me on the sofa and has put her arm across my shoulders.

'It's not been great recently,' I admit grimly. In truth, I am starting to feel as if I have opened some sort of Pandora's box; that by daring to try to jump the tracks of my own life, I have unleashed a chaos that now seems to be encircling – infecting – everyone else's. 'I can't apologise enough for all the trouble I've caused you. I'm embarrassed, actually.'

'You've caused me no trouble. Yet.' Camille's expression is kind, but there is a steely undertone to her voice. She has three young children and a school to run. The summer term starts in four days. She needs me to be on top of things and part of the reason for my mustering the courage to be in her sitting room – when it was the last thing I felt up to – is the hope of reassuring her that I am. 'I need to check on something in the kitchen,' Camille says suddenly, handing me my wine. 'Don't move. I'll be two minutes.'

The quietness with her gone is soothing. I let myself drift back to the dramas of Sunday; the weird steamy April warmth of the evening, the kids worn out and tucked up, us five adults sitting out on the patio at the back of the house with the pizza and champagne that Jo and Rob had bought after getting the all-clear from the hospital. We had all drunk a little too much, Rob man-hugging Pete so many times, with increasing resistance from Pete himself, that it had become a joke. 'No words, mate,' Rob growled, his voice a little looser each time, his embraces a little wilder. 'No words. And if there's ever anything Jo and I can do... anything... you only have to ask.'

Jo was more silent, holding my gaze from time to time and shaking her head in wonderment. She had unpinned her hair and brushed it out, showing off its natural streaks of blonde and copper, making her look impossibly young and radiant for a mother of three, let alone one to have endured a near-catastrophe. Giddy with my own exhaustion and relief, I was also aware of my chance of talking to Rob sliding out of frame. Everything felt different. I had had my glimmer of opportunity. Now, the very last thing my brother would want, or need, was a bombardment about my own, relatively trivial woes, sucking him into a war against a man who has just saved the life of his child.

Upstairs later, tipped together in the deep springy dip of the mattress, things felt different too. When Pete, in his inimitable way, tugged me into position, kneeing my legs apart to make his intentions plain, something deep inside me acquiesced. He had saved Tilly. It was an act that needed acknowledging, that deserved reward. Tenderness. Even though Pete himself was, if anything, rougher than usual, asserting his greater physical power, his right to take rather than give – a stamp of entitlement which had been there from the beginning and which I had never felt able to question, until Jack.

But there was no room for Jack that night. The spongy bedsprings sagged under us as Pete moved on top of me, like some widening mouth threatening to swallow us whole. At some point, a component in the bed's old joints began to squeak. I prayed for Pete to be done with it quickly, hating to think of Harry, ears wagging on his sofa bed next door; and Rob and Jo, a few yards further along the passageway, imagining we were making passionate love when we weren't; when it was so much more complicated.

Afterwards, Pete fell asleep at once, but I lay wide awake, the sheets sticking to my clammy limbs, my heart fighting the new, confusing notion of having somehow betrayed my lover rather than my husband

'I guess such near misses put all kinds of other things a bit more into perspective?' says Camille, giving me a start as she re-enters the room, crossing to pull the curtains shut against the darkening evening sky.

'Oh, my goodness, yes.' I sit up to attention, grateful and a little in awe of her power to be both candid and gentle at the same time. Mel, in contrast, when I phoned after the weekend, had somehow managed to hit the wrong note, sounding more thrilled than anything, not seeming, fully, to understand the trauma of it all, both over what happened by the river and between me and Pete afterwards.

'So. This other man of yours?' Camille has folded her arms and is fixing me with her big dark eyes. 'Far be it from me to judge, but—'

'He was never mine. It was madness. It's all done with.' It is good to hear the certainty in my voice. 'His name was Jack. I still haven't heard from him and I don't think I ever shall. I'm putting it behind me. I am focusing on Pete, who has no idea...our relationship has always been a bit up and down, you see...though now I am determined to make it work.' I bite my cheeks. It is no moment to start pouring out the full story of Pete. Humiliation is washing through me, again. Camille is a friendly wonderful woman, but most of all she is my employer. 'I cannot thank you enough for your understanding in this, Camille.'

'Oh lordy. Okay.' She sighs. 'Well, I am sorry – about all of it – and sincerely hope you and Pete can find an even keel. But also – selfishly – professionally – I am pretty glad not to be losing you... though Jesus, Fran, aren't you furious?' she exclaims. 'For this Jack to give you no explanation? Just to leave you dangling?'

'I suppose... I mean, sometimes...' I flounder. I have been drowning in feelings, but not always, it seems, the right ones. 'The thing is, I truly believed it wasn't just some sort of dumb fling...' I stop abruptly, assailed by the full weight of the past tense. It really is over. And suddenly anger is indeed pushing through everything else. Have I been nothing but an idiot? Have I been played? Jack knew my existence with Pete was a balancing act. He knew how much our relationship meant to me. He said it meant the same for him. He helped me build a road out of both our lives and then left me standing on it alone. Abandoned.

I am trembling. Camille has come to stand behind the sofa and has a hand on my shoulder. I know she means well – the woman deserves a bloody medal – but it is simply too much.

I struggle free and stand up. 'I think I'd better be going, actually.' My chest hurts from the effort of trying to speak normally. 'I'll be fine by next Tuesday, I promise. The start of term. I can't wait actually. Just to get on with life. You've been amazing, Camille. *Amazing.*' I stride round the room as I talk, looking for my bag.

'Fran, there's no need to go—'

'And by the way...' The bag was back by the sofa, right where I had been sitting. 'Please be assured, that if Jack ever does get in touch again...' I am sounding decisive now, almost merry, 'then there will be no more attempts to run off into the sunset. I mean, that never happens anyway, right? It was just some idiotic fantasy.' I love how jolly I sound, how buoyant. *I can do this*, I think, *I can totally do this*. Life is just one big charade; it's all a question of how well you play the game. I know that really but had somehow been in danger of forgetting it. 'I promise I won't let you down.'

Camille is eyeing me warily. 'I know you won't,' she says softly. 'No marriages are perfect, Fran,' she adds, dropping her voice and casting a glance at the door. 'A while ago now, I nearly blew it with Erik – an old friend of his from Gothenburg, about as mind-blowingly irresistible as you can imagine – a national skiing champion, for god's sake.' She laughs, but her eyes are black and grave. 'I had to dig so deep to stay on board, but I couldn't be gladder that I did. I look back, incredulous, at what I almost threw away. So, hey, maybe it can now work out for you and Pete? I truly hope so.' She opens her arms, as if to say the possibility really could be that simple. 'In fact, why don't the pair of you come over here for a bite one evening? It's ridiculous I haven't met him yet and Erik would love it too. And it might help, you know?'

I smile and nod, knowing already that whatever she suggests will be refused and that it will fall on me to make excuses. The battle for a normal social life is one I gave up on long ago. Pete has his football mates and Harry. I am allowed Mel, book meetings and family, but not too often. That is the deal, worked out over the years with barely a word uttered.

I am almost across the room when the front door slams and female voices fill the hallway.

A moment later, Erik bounds in, his short blonde hair in spikes, his muscular frame conspicuously evident in running gear, loose shorts and T-shirt, a sheen of sweat covering his big-boned Nordic face. Following behind, chattering and laughing, are several of the group, women whom I had thought I would never see again. Beatrice, Zoe, Cara. Only two are missing, Aditi, and a woman called Graciella who's always late and whose recommendation was the thriller. On seeing me, they leap to hellos and air kisses and I find myself putting my handbag down. The warmth of these fellow teachers, fellow women, is genuine, and soothing. They know nothing, I remind myself, and never need to.

'What a lovely crew to find on my doorstep,' says Erik, raising his booming voice with its perfect English inflections above the mêlée. He grins, waving at me. 'Hi, Fran, how are you doing?'

'Great, thanks Erik.'

'I can't kiss anyone because I need a shower,' he jokes, tweaking at his sweat-dampened shirt and making a pretend lunge for Camille, who pushes him away with a look of affectionate disgust. 'You go be a father,' she commands. 'And watch Lars because he's full of it tonight. And ladies,' she addresses the room, 'Fran here has had a fraught Easter and is to be totally let off the hook for not having got around to this, which by the by...' She picks up the thriller from the table with her thumb and index finger like some kind of suspect package. 'With apologies in absentia to Graciella, but I just could not get along with it. Oh lord, all the blood and guts. Who needs blood and guts?' She hugs the book, as if forgiving it. 'Now, tuck in, won't you, and remember to be extra nice to Fran.'

They gather round me, asking what has happened, reeling with disbelief and sympathy when I start to tell them about Tilly. There is no question of protestation or escape; no question of doing anything but giving in. I could have been like these women, I think, unable to resist basking in the warmth. In a parallel life, with a different partner, I could have been one of them.

It is nearly eleven by the time I get home. To my great relief, Pete has gone to bed and I assume Harry has too until I almost trip over him lying on the kitchen floor, phone in one hand, the other draped over the edge of the makeshift cardboard pen he has built for Suki who, in her new convalescent state, is not allowed to do anything except eat and rest. We collected her from the vet after the Easter weekend, Harry sweetly taking the morning off to give me – and the cat – as he put it, 'morale' support. She is crouched now with her nose in the palm of his hand, licking and purring, despite the lampshade of a collar framing her little black face and the thick blue strapping round her back-left leg and hip.

The litter tray in the pen has been cleaned and freshened, I note with some surprise, while the pink fluffy mouse and miniature toy football Harry insisted we purchase at the vets both show heartening signs of use, the mouse missing one eye and most of its tail, and the ball bitten into on one side like a discarded apple. Only the bowl of deluxe top-priced, low-cal cat food, recommended by the vet to prevent weight gain, looks completely untouched.

'I've been giving her some bits of roast chicken,' says Harry. 'She loves it.'

'Well, there's a surprise.' I am too pleased at having him there to tell him off. The chicken had been supper for him and Pete, left to keep warm in the top oven in a moat of mash, peas and roasted parsnip, part of the unwritten code around my book-club nights – and indeed any other demands on my time – being that the provision of a decent evening meal must never be compromised. 'Will that be your approach to running this business of yours,' I tease, 'spoiling animals rotten?' I bustle round the kitchen as I talk, kicking off my shoes and putting the kettle on, still buzzing from the simple conviviality of my evening.

And now here was Harry, all cheery and receptive, just like the old days, before the aftermath of the whole uni fiasco knocked him – and what was left of our closeness – for six. The endearing plan of starting his own pet-care company had bubbled out of him with only the slightest prompting during our trip to the vet: walking, house-sitting, vet visits, grooming. He hadn't minded Rob mentioning it to me, he said, because he had been on the verge of doing so anyway. He was saving madly from his salary, he had declared proudly, to fund various animal welfare courses that would give him the qualifications to set him apart from the crowd. Only Pete, briefed over supper later that day, had been predictably lukewarm, saying Harry was never going to get rich that way and if he thought he was going to start filling the house with creatures, he had another thing coming. I had stepped in where I could, walking the usual tightrope of loyalties, feeling desperate for Harry, so obviously in need – as always – of encouragement rather than a slapping down. But it was also sort of nice, having my son properly back on my side.

'How was your book thing?'

'Good, thanks. I'm making a tea, do you want some?'

'Yes please.'

I quickly add more water to the kettle, knowing better than to express my surprise. Part of the prolonged Cold War offensive has involved Harry refusing all such offers, and then, pointedly, making his own. It is the detail of life that matters, I muse, the tiniest signs that are so telling.

I bring the teas to the table, pulling out another chair to use as a footstool and putting my face over my mug to enjoy the gentle waft of its steam. 'Do you want yours down there, Mr Animal Man?'

'No, just coming.' He stays where he is, running his long slim fingers up and down Suki's spine, making her shiver with pleasure despite her wounded state. Above them, the wall clock ticks companionably and the window next to it is a big dark square against the glow of the kitchen lights. I am happy, I realise. Right now, without warning, out of all the crap, I am happy. Harry was why I have steered a way through life with Pete for two decades, and here he is, still my loving darling boy.

'Did Dad go up a while ago?'

'Ages.' Harry turns onto his back, making a pillow of his hands under his head. 'I guess what he did was pretty awesome, wasn't it? With Tilly.'

'It certainly was.'

'It's also cool how he doesn't make a big deal of it. Don't you think?'

'Absolutely. I mean, Dad was totally amazing. A superhero.'

He laughs, liking this. 'Hah, yeah.' He carries on staring at the ceiling, and I muse what I would have given to know that even these simple, fleeting moments of companionship lay ahead; how they would have made the terribleness of the last few weeks so much easier to bear; how they would even have made the decision to run away with Jack more harrowing. At the time, it felt like I had lost Harry anyway. Now, I can't imagine a better reward for staying.

'Sorry if I've ever made you feel hounded, sweetheart, about all the university business. You tried it and didn't like it. I can see now that I could perhaps have been better at showing how much I respect that. It's also clear to me that working with animals will suit you far better than some sort of stuffy internship. You're brilliant with them – everybody says so – I mean, Mrs Dawkins was going on about it just the other day. And dogs are so in fashion now – as you say, needing walking grooming, sitting – you could do really well.'

'And cats.'

'And cats.' I watch him fondly as he carefully strokes the fur near the big shaven area around the scene of Suki's operation. The cat goes very still, her yellow eyes widening.

'Dad thinks it's a waste of time though,' he mutters bitterly.

'Don't worry about your father.' I ponder how simple these words are to say, and how hard to act upon. 'Just do what you want to do. I will support you, okay?'

'Okay. Thanks, Mum.' He gives me a brave grin that tears at my heart.

When his phone vibrates with a new notification and he doesn't move, not even to glance at the screen, I venture, 'So, you've been going out a bit more recently.'

'I suppose.'

'Is Dylan still around? Or has he gone back?'

'Yeah, we've met a few times.'

'Ah, you're still friends then?'

'Yeah, why wouldn't we be?'

He isn't looking at me any more and I can feel the atmosphere tensing, but I press on. A mother ought to be able to talk to her son and it is so long since I have even felt able to try. 'And tell me to mind my own business, love, but have you by any chance met someone?'

'I meet people all the time, Mum.' He has extracted his arm from the cardboard pen and is still lying on his back, staring at the ceiling.

'You know what I mean. Someone special—'

'Why does it even matter?' he snaps, sitting up. '*Meeting* someone. Like that is what everyone is supposed to do.'

'Mind my own business, you mean,' I counter quickly. 'I did give you that option too, remember?'

Harry peels himself off the floor with a grunt, picking up his phone and folding and unfolding his rangy limbs like a piece of garden furniture. He shuffles to the biscuit cupboard, pulling out one of the several packs of Party Rings it contains – his snack of choice since the age of three and a half – tearing the packet open with his teeth as he joins me at the table. 'By the way, those came.' He nods over his shoulder,

Only then do I see the sturdy square brown paper bag, parked in the gap between the bin and the wine rack. Ruffles of white tissue paper stick out of the top of it, affording the glimpse of a few heads of flowers. I glance at Harry, busy now with eating and with his mobile, while also forcing swathes of his hair into one of the horrible old rubber bands he likes to use, creating a messy off-centre bun. 'When did they arrive then?' My heart is doing a slow, agonised cartwheel.

'Just after you'd gone out.' He holds a biscuit in his mouth, his thumbs dancing across his phone screen, dainty as a pianist.

I approach the bag like a bomb-disposal expert. Wanting, not-wanting, I am back in the thick of all the adrenalin rush of hope and despair I have vowed to leave behind. A full cluster of yellow roses comes into view, swathed in blue clouds of forget-me-nots and blue and yellow freesias, all the stems neatly sealed in a pouch of water to keep them fresh. I crouch down, drinking in the aromas, looking for a note, which I fully expect not to find. Jack had a soft spot for yellow, especially roses, and knows freesias are my favourites; what better flower to go with them, given the circumstances, than forget-me-nots? It is the sign I had given up longing for. The gift of apology, of reassurance. With no note, I can say it was a wrong delivery – laugh it off. How clever of him. How glorious. But then Jack is clever, and thoughtful and...

'The card is over there. I opened it. I hope you don't mind.'

I stand up so quickly, I see stars, flecked with the colours of the flowers. Harry is pointing out an envelope on the windowsill, propped between a little photo of him in his purple primary-school uniform and a thick bristly thumb of a cactus, bought for a science project and still alive eight years on, despite resolutely refusing to sprout new limbs.

'They're from Uncle Rob and Aunty Jo.'

Of course they are. Hope is such a dumb beast, popping up after every slapping down. The note is written in Jo's big looping hand – *A million thank-yous from us all.* Underneath are the twins' signatures, childish squiggles among hers and Rob's. The entire page is fringed with hugs and kisses that look like Tilly's handiwork.

'By the way, Mum...' Harry's voice is bright enough to suggest that my earlier interrogation has been forgiven. 'I could help towards Suki? If you wanted? From my savings? I know the vet bill was massive and you had to use some of Granny's money.'

'Don't be silly. You mustn't do that.' I set the card down, and drop the envelope into the bin. It takes a moment to bring Harry into full focus, my heart swelling at how achingly naïve he is, for all his manly hairiness and grand efforts to demonstrate otherwise. 'I've always said that money is there for special things. And Suki is worth every penny. As are you.' I kiss the top of his head as I cross behind his chair. 'I'll put the flowers in a vase in the morning. I'm too tired now. Goodnight, darling. Turn the lights out, won't you.'

In bed, I ease myself carefully under the duvet. Pete is sleeping on his front as usual, one arm thrust up under the pillow, the other hanging loose over the side of the mattress, his face tipped upwards, his mouth open like a drunk, though he won't have had more than his usual beer because he seldom does during the week. I know the pose so well, I could draw it. I think about the oddness of being so close to someone and yet so distant, the contradiction of it, and wish suddenly that I could share the thought with Jack. He wanted to understand the world, that was one of the things I had loved; to enjoy it, to capture it with his pencils and paints. If he asked me something, he remembered the answers. Pete never asks me anything or listens to what I have to say. He is not interested in the world. He lives like one under siege, bent on keeping threats at bay, including, and especially, me.

I long to sleep, but the usual inner voices are hectoring me, warring jurors about how to feel, what to do. *Hold fast*, says the loudest voice of all, *hold fast to what you have, count your blessings, better the devil you know. Stay put. Take no more risks.*

I roll carefully onto my side, needing to have my back to Pete, and close my eyes. I will let Jack go, but decide it doesn't have to be right at this moment. At this moment, I shall treat myself to remembering, how we were together, how good it was. I try to picture one of our walks, only to find Helena striding into view instead. Jack's nightmarishly volatile wife, difficult always to think of and only ever glimpsed in fragments, but here she is. And in my half-dreaming state, it is as if I know her, standing resolute on the other side of the invisible wall that separates us. A woman prepared to roll her sleeves up, to call the shots. Fearless. Adversarial. The opposite of me, as I realised the moment Jack ventured a proper description of her nature, that guarded, weary look clouding his blue eyes. I will the image away, but something flutters, something removed from the old reflexes of hate, and closer to an acknowledgement of a strength vastly different to my own.

It requires willpower to reach beyond it, to a memory of Jack and I walking on Hampstead Heath. I take my time, viewing every frame affectionately, like an old favourite film: a chilly, blowy afternoon, our heads bowed against the brunt of the wind; a section of path so deserted that we dare for once to hold hands, eventually tucking them, fingers entwined, deep into one of Jack's big coat pockets because the air is so cold. We sit on a bench and he brings out the sketchpad that goes everywhere with him and starts to draw me. As the pencil moves, he asks me about my work, the 'tricks' I use, as he puts it, why I love my small charges so passionately, before suddenly dropping the pad and pulling me into his arms. Even sitting down, he is so much taller that I have to tip my head right back for our mouths to meet. He cradles the back of my skull as we kiss, bearing the weight of it so I don't have to, his fingers threading my hair. Our noses bump and we giggle. His beard is rough and full of heat against my icy skin. He tastes of the mint he has just sucked. *'Never leave me, Fran,'* he murmurs, breaking off to whisper in my ear. *'Whatever happens, never leave.'*

III

'You were late last night.'

'Was I? Yes, I suppose it did go on a bit...' My voice is croaky with sleep, which came in the small hours, deep and dark. Pete is moving round the bedroom, a bath towel slung round the swell of his waist, whistling under his breath.

'I'll be taking the car today. You don't mind, do you?'

'No, that's fine,' I say at once, knowing from his tone that I am being challenged rather than asked a question.

'I made you tea.'

I peer at the bedside table, noticing the mug of tea, made as Pete likes it himself, which is near-white with milk, when he knows full well I prefer mine dark brown. 'Fantastic. Thanks.' I struggle upright, squinting at my wristwatch, which tells me it has just gone half past six.

'I mean, you don't need the car, do you?' he presses again. 'Unless, of course, you have plans I don't know about?' An undertone of menace has entered his voice.

'No, I—'

'It isn't school yet, is it?'

'No, that's tomorrow.' I sip the tea, which I would have traded in a heartbeat for just a few more minutes of sleep. 'So, are you and Harry driving in today?' I make sure I sound chatty, to deflect whatever storm might be brewing.

'No, Harry will have to look after himself for once.'

'I see.' I offer the comment brightly, but I do not see. Inside, a great weariness heaves. Pete likes to make everything difficult. He does not divulge things. He likes them to be extracted. And, in the process, lays tripwires across my path. I am supposed to play the game, with more questions, but I am too tired. I let my eyes fall closed, trying, still, to cling to the notion that any man who saved a child's life is worthy of some patience, some love.

Pete's voice breaks through, demanding my full attention. 'This dog idea of Harry's is a total joke. I don't know why you are humouring him. You, of all people: Mrs I-Want-My-Son-To-Be-the-Next-Prime-Minister. Hah.' He is standing in front of the mirror, energetically knotting a tie as he talks. The tie is a real silk one I gave him several Christmases ago, yellow, dashed with white, and looks crisp and smart against his white shirt. Otherwise, he is wearing boxers, red and white checked, and thin black socks, pulled to their full stretch halfway up his calves and looking faintly comical, as socks always do.

'I couldn't think of anything worse – or unlikely – than Harry becoming a politician,' I counter lightly, hoping to dodge the confrontation he seems bent on having. 'Hey, Jo sent some lovely flowers – did you see?' As I speak, he reaches for his smartest dark blue suit and starts pulling on the trousers. Despite the thick atmosphere, it is impossible not to be curious at this, as Pete well knows, which is why I in turn know he will offer no explanation. If I dare to ask why he is dressing up, he'll say something opaque. If I don't ask, I will be accused of lack of interest. The weariness churns again. My marriage is a game of chess – with forfeits – and I am a poor player. Mel is so right. A braver, cleverer, richer woman would have left long ago. I needed Jack for my courage, and now he is gone.

'Flowers?' he growls. 'Nobody tells me anything.' He turns back to the mirror and begins unknotting and redoing the tie.

'What you did – saving Tilly - it was a miracle, Pete, truly,' I plough on. 'Harry can't talk about anything else.'

'Hah.'

The tie is done, the knot a bit broader, the ends more even.

'You look very nice.'

'For a change, you mean?' He spins round. The old familiar trace of tension is unmistakable now, the clamp of his jaw, the darkening of his eyes – signs I learnt long ago to recognise and dread.

'No,' I cry. 'That isn't what I meant, Pete...' I catch my breath. It has been a while, but I decide suddenly that I am ready, that I don't even care. I grip the mug handle tightly, pretending to take a swig when I have in fact already finished it. 'I am just saying you look nice,' I repeat dully.

'Actually...'

I brace myself, but when I look up, the hints of menace have dissolved into an expression of boyish eagerness that for one moment makes him the unnerving spit of Harry.

'There is some stuff going down at work – big stuff – wheels within wheels – a sort of internal coup that could open new doors. I don't want to say too much yet, jinx it, but, well... it might be good news for me.'

'Pete, that is wonderful.' I laugh a little wildly, as the tension inside me unspools. 'I mean, wow.'

'Fran, I think my luck might have turned.' He's at the bedside grinning, and I find myself reaching for his hand and giving his fingers an awkward peck. He pulls them free, shooting me a strange look, like he knows I'm being fake. 'And what are the Lady of Leisure's plans for the last day of her long holiday?'

'Oh, so much...' I babble, '...pre-term stuff, looking in on poor old Annie Smith, who I haven't seen in ages... oh, and a bite of lunch with Mel...' I reach for my dressing gown off the end of the bed as I talk, absurdly afraid that nerves might make me blurt out the one thing that must not, at any cost, be blurted out; namely, that on this, my last day of relative freedom, I am going to pay a second and final visit to Jack's house. The idea arrived as the grey tinge of dawn was fringing the curtains. I am going to go on my own. No fanfare. In search of 'closure', as everyone calls it these days – a tiny and annoying word, it strikes me now, for something so momentous.

'But with time to cook breakfast for a working man, I hope? Your wage-slave.' He moves towards me as he speaks, tugging the bow of my fastened dressing gown cord like a bell-pull and thrusting himself against me when it falls open. 'If I wasn't already spruced up, I might be after an appetiser...'

I let him nuzzle my neck, only stepping away when I am sure he is ready for it too, that he was just fooling around. 'One full English coming right up.'

'Good girl. And car keys?'

He is looking for my handbag, but I get there first. It is sitting on top of my half-open underwear drawer, at the back of which, I remember suddenly, with a shiver of disbelief at my own reckless ineptitude, are still buried, among my old pairs of tights and ancient shapeless bras, the two goodbye letters for Harry and Pete, never rewritten, still not destroyed.

I toss the car keys across the bed, a bad throw, too low, but Pete snatches them from the air with the casual ease of the sportsman he once was, dropping them into his trouser pocket as he strides from the room. I open the curtains, letting in the blue-grey light of morning, before pulling on some clothes and heading after him.

There are sausages, thank god, and bacon, as well as eggs. I resolve to cook the best of breakfasts, making enough for Harry when he surfaces. *Hold fast to what you have*, chants the voice inside my head, *and don't let go.*

IV

The moment I see the straggly meadow of the front lawn, the big dandelions flourishing in the tarmac, the archway of pendulous, now shrivelling roses, over the door, I feel an idiot for having returned. I stand on the pavement gawping and helpless, the front windows staring back at me, cold as an empty gaze. Gingerly, I approach the front door. On the wall beside it, wads of junk mail stick out of the postbox.

I step back and make my way round the side of the house, peering in windows. The first room is protected by frosted glass, the second, much larger, has long curtains hanging sufficiently far apart for me to make out an elegant sitting room, furnished with a large blue sofa and chairs and mustard-coloured cushions. Along the back wall behind it, there are rows of books in two tall handsome bookcases, old-looking ones with leather spines – Helena's collection, no doubt, I deduce grimly. Between them hangs a large gold-framed picture, one of Jack's, I realise with a start, recognising the style, fresh hurt flooding the chaos already whirling inside me, along with self-loathing, for it to have come to this, peering into Jack's marital home – Jack's life – like some voyeur.

Even at a distance, I can see the painting is a stunner: a lustrous wheat field under a blue sky, with a little girl racing through the middle of it, long hair in sunny arrows, her white dress full as a sail. This is not a work Jack has ever mentioned or shared with me, not even during one of the rare, lovely sessions when he let me peek at pictures of his work on his phone. My mind flicks to the famous drunken scrawling of Helena with her red felt pen. This one was clearly safe from the fray. Or had the incident ever even taken place? I drop my forehead against the windowpane with a thud, breathing hard. I don't know what I can believe about Jack any more. Nothing is certain.

Turning slowly, I slide down into a sitting position, leaning against the brick wall, soothingly cool and hard against my back. My feet are throbbing, thanks to my heels, black ones to match my jacket and already a cause for regret by the time I tottered out of dear Annie Smith's ground-floor flat and headed for the tube. Under the jacket is my fuchsia summer dress, its first airing of the year and a garment I had picked in the daring knowledge that Jack would recognise it, his own clumsy fingers having tussled with its fiddly zip.

Given the potential perils of my mission, it had seemed important to look good, ready for the hideous eventuality of Helena or Jack, or both, blowing out of their front door just as I was walking past. I had found a lipstick to match my dress and even got the tongs out – once the post-breakfast coast was clear.

Annie had noticed my efforts at once, clapping her crooked hands with delight as soon as she had wrestled open all the locks on her front door. 'You are a looker, as well as the sweetest soul,' she had chirruped, pressing her powdery cheek against my mouth before turning to lead me down her narrow passageway, doing her drunken sideways roll with her Zimmer because of her hips. 'I have cake,' she announced, pointing at a chair for me once we were in the kitchen and not letting me move from it while she proceeded with her laborious shuffle to assemble plates and cups and saucers. 'Such a pale-faced little thing when you first came to the street,' she went on when we were seated in the front room, letting me pour because the pot was heavy, 'seems like yesterday to me. But my, how you've blossomed, especially in the last year or so. Kids leaving school, that's when it happens. A woman gets her life back. Her inner glow. I notice these things, you see.' She tapped her bird-beak of a nose, and did one of the big grins that made her dentures click. 'Good things come to those who wait, Frances, my love. Never forget that, will you, dearie. Life is a long road. If you're lucky.' Her kind grey eyes had shone.

'Hello?'

I am on my feet in two seconds, clasping my bag to my chest, my face aflame.

'Are you the cleaner?'

'Cleaner? I... No, I'm a teacher,' I flounder, in no control of what comes out of my mouth while my mind implodes with the new and terrible information that the unoccupied house was occupied after all, not by Jack, or Helena, but this tall, lean man with staring hazel eyes and glossy jet-black hair, cut close enough to his head to show the contours of his skull.

'Might I ask what you are doing here, in that case?' He remains by the archway of browning roses, hands on his hips in the manner of one with all day to sort the mystery out. He sounds irritated, but also faintly amused to have cornered a trespasser.

My brain gallops. There is nothing I can say, no possible explanation, except the truth, which is impossible. 'I am so sorry. I just needed to sit down.'

His hauteur disappears in an instant, his face creasing with concern. 'Oh dear, do you feel unwell?'

'No. At least, not any more. I am sorry to have... trespassed.'

'Oh, I'm only house-sitting. I was told a cleaner would come. And a gardener.' He casts a rueful look at the front lawn, running wild in the April sunshine. 'Look here, would you like a glass of water or something?'

'No, I'm fine, thank you. Many apologies again.' I am already walking fast, past him, down the strip of path between the tarmac and the grass, my sore feet forgotten in the urgency of the need to get away, an urgency heightened by the sudden realisation – various photos of

Jack's shuffling like a pack of half-remembered cards – that the man addressing me is none other than Hugh; Hugh, whose property investment Jack and I exploited ruthlessly until Helena's intervention; Hugh who is more Helena's friend than Jack's; Hugh who has houses in France and somewhere else that I cannot quite recall because I am walking with such speed that all my concentration is focused on the importance of not tripping over a paving stone and compounding my ignominy by falling on my face.

Behind me, Hugh has travelled to the middle of the long grass to watch my departure and I can feel him tracking my progress down the street, scrutinising and puzzling over the strange behaviour of a forty-something woman with crimped hair and crumpled smart clothes, whose claim that she needed to take the weight off her feet did not preclude the urge to peer into his friends' house like a would-be thief. If he saw me looking. Did he see?

I had intended to go home and change before meeting Mel, but a delay on the Northern line meant there wasn't time. I have had to hurry straight to the vegan café where she suggested we eat – a new place near her flat called 'The Grasshopper' – my feet now pulsing with discomfort and my brain conjuring wild worries about what Hugh could be reporting, at this very moment, to Jack.

Catching sight of her, lounging on the low wall skirting the café entrance, my first thought is that the new four-day week she recently mentioned negotiating is clearly making her very happy. She is engrossed with her phone, her legs stretched out in front of her under the big panels of a long sleeveless lilac dress I have never seen before, her dainty feet flatteringly encased in salmon-pink, wedge-heeled espadrilles that look equally fresh off the shelf. A wide pink silk shawl is slung loosely across her back, leaving her upper arms and shoulders bare, while her hair has been wrested into a bundle of shining coils on top of her head, all held in place by chopstick-style accessories that I know at a glance would have been way beyond my own expertise. During recent phone calls, there has been some chat about sticking to the diet started before Easter, but nothing has prepared me for the transformation now before my eyes.

'Mel—'

'Hey, you.' Her face lights up with a sunny smile. She drops her phone into her bag, a pale blueish leather one that goes well with the dress, slinging it over her shoulder as she stands up.

'You look amazing.'

'Thank you kindly, I'm sure.' She performs a twirl, making the panels of the dress fly out like a carousel. 'But, so do you. A million dollars, in fact.' She cocks her head in admiration at my outfit before kissing me on both cheeks. 'Was there a school meeting or something?'

'No, I've just...' It never crossed my mind that I wouldn't tell Mel where I have been. The desire to share the shock about the encounter with Hugh has been building throughout my journey. But in the unexpected oddness of the moment, I say only that that I have called on Annie, who appreciates a brush-up.

'Oh yes, the poor love with the leg ulcers.'

'They're a lot better actually...' My discombobulation won't go away. 'That dress is such a beautiful colour. Is it new?'

'Needs must. I've dropped two sizes. Nothing fits.' Mel laughs, her exultation ringing. 'No one tells you losing weight can get expensive. But, blimey, I'm starving all the time. I mean – *all* the time.' She turns to reach for the café door, but a man coming out makes a big to-do of holding it open, smiling at us both with unabashed appreciation.

Mel loops her arm through my elbow as we find a table. The energy coming off her is palpable. The new diet has inspired her to start an Instagram account, she explains excitedly as soon as we are sitting down, which she has been saving to tell me about until she was sure it was going to take off. She is posting her weight and daily selfies – 'in my bra and knickers', she squeals – along with photographs of every single thing she eats. She reinforces the point by grabbing her phone the moment our food arrives – a nutty salad and a glistening bowl of beetroot risotto, both for sharing – and taking snaps from several angles before carefully – meticulously – dividing the portions between our plates.

'I'm sharing my "journey",' she declares gleefully, as we both start eating, painting quotation marks in the air with her knife and fork, which, like all the cutlery, are made of wood and have little images of grasshoppers studded into their handles. 'Guess how many followers I've got.'

'Four hundred?' I hazard.

'Three *thousand* and rising,' she shrieks, grinning at the expression on my face. 'Insane, right?'

'Insane,' I cry, as astonished as she expected.

She raises a palm and I dutifully high-five her, thinking how this, too, feels weirdly hyped up and strange. I ask her more questions, saying I can't wait to follow her too, all the while fighting down the unforgivably envious notion that, just as my dreams have hit a wall, Mel's are starting to take off. What is also disconcerting, I realise, is that I am getting glimpses of a version of her I haven't seen in twenty-five years – the cocky pre-Ed Caulder version with a heart-shaped face, jutting cheekbones, and a figure exuding an athletic elegance that has nothing to do with exercise. They are just snapshots, based on memory – Mel, as she keeps now saying herself, 'has a long way to go' – but I cannot quell a spark of envy that the old Mel is emerging, being set free; while I remain trapped.

Mel is loving my interrogation. She is going to stop being at the beck and call of her mother, she declares, and make the absolute most of her weekly one day off, maybe start posting recipes and touting for advertising and product placements, become an *influencer*. 'And if it takes off, then you can be bloody sure I'll stop sorting other people's pay packages for a living.' Her big grey eyes flare with outrage and I get another, vivid flash of the eye-popping teenager with the hitched-up skirts, laddered tights and swagger, the one who had the entire sixth form in her thrall.

'I'm even thinking I could turn it all into a book – you know, one of those ones with daily recipes – offering a path to physical and mental health.' She paints an imaginary headline in the air: '*One woman's journey back from trauma...*' but then breaks off with a quick laugh. 'Not that I want to rake up any old stuff. So, you can stop looking like that.'

'Like what?' I counter, appalled to think my selfish flutters of unease might actually be visible.

'All bug-eyed, like you think I am finally dealing with my *issues...*' She's hooting with laughter suddenly and so am I. 'Oh god, Fran, it would just make a good selling-point for a book, is all I mean. You know – these days, everybody needs to have their own tear-jerking story to share. *That's* the way to make money.'

It feels great to laugh. This is Mel, I remind myself, most beloved of friends and deserving of nothing but all the luck in the world. 'Well, I think it all sounds brilliant. And I couldn't be happier for you. Except... Mel... please never forget that you are beautiful as you are. Okay?'

'Okay, darling. And ditto.' She puts her cutlery together across her empty plate, and sits back, the restlessness gone suddenly. 'We are two wonderful, strong women who can take on the world. Right? Fran?'

'I went back to Jack's house this morning,' I blurt, 'just to see.'

'You should have told me,' she cries, throwing her arms in the air, all the placidity gone.

'I am telling you.' I sound snappier than I mean to.

'You've got to let it – *him* – go. You bloody have to, Fran.' There is desperation in her voice. 'It will drive you mad otherwise.' She looks close to tears suddenly.

I reach for her hand across the table. 'I know and I am, I promise. Going there this morning was part of that. Actually, it really helped. The place was totally overgrown and neglected – much worse than when you and I went. I just wanted to find some sense of a proper ending. In my own head. And now I have.' I don't even bother mentioning Hugh and that feels good too. Who cares what he might or might not say to Jack? All of it really is done with.

'Good. Jack doesn't, *didn't* deserve you. And neither does Pete, for that matter,' she mutters, squeezing my fingers and sounding more herself. She signals to the waitress for the bill. 'I'd love it if you came to mine now? For a coffee?'

I protest that I have too much to do with term starting the next day, but she won't back down, or let me contribute to the bill.

Once we're in the street, she loops her arm through mine, pulling me close. She'll lend me some flip-flops, she says, when I confess to the mounting agony of my pinching shoes, 'just to get you home. Blisters are so gross and take weeks to go.' She plants a kiss on the side of my face, adding excitedly, 'I've got this neat tripod for taking pictures – it's awesome – and lots of new stuff for the kitchen. I know you've always been a serious cook, Frannie, that's like one of your *things,* but I get it now, I really do. I am looking after myself properly at last. I hope you're proud of me.'

'So proud, Mel.'

'I think you've inspired me, Fran, if I'm honest.'

'Don't be crazy.'

'Having the guts to change tack, try for a fresh start. That option is there for all of us.'

'Except my option failed,' I point out grimly, touched, but also a little put out by the clumsiness of the compliment.

'But you have other choices, Fran,' she says earnestly, 'never forget that.' She pats my arm, still threaded through hers. 'And besides, what you were prepared to do – for love – how you've held it all together since it all went wrong, *is* a bloody inspiration.'

We have reached her front door, part of a lower row of attractively converted erstwhile council flats. 'And, whatever happens, I'm always here for you, okay?' She rummages in her bag for her house keys and my eyes drop to the loose stone under which she used to leave a set for me and Jack. For a moment, his shape fills the air next to me, the curve of his head, the square set of his broad shoulders, his long legs, before vanishing; a ghost. A pot beside the stone contains a new plant, an azalea of the deepest pink, erupting into flower along every stem. 'You've got me, Fran, is what I am saying. Never forget that.'

'Thanks, Mel.'

'I mean it, okay?'

I can sense her wanting something more of me and I am not sure how to give it. 'I know, Mel, and I am so grateful. But I am sort of coping, for now. Harry has mysteriously decided to be his old sweet self and even Pete is being strangely all right – well, manageable anyway.'

'Because of his lifesaving act, do you think?'

'Maybe. It was truly amazing...' I pause, still a little in awe myself at the memory of the Easter weekend. 'But there's something going on at work too that he's really excited about. He won't tell me, of course. But when Pete's happy, he's nicer. So, it's like we're all in... a slightly different place.'

'Really? Fantastic.'

'I've made a sort of resolution. To sit tight and hold on to what I have... for the time being anyway.'

As soon as the door opens, I can see at once that Mel's flat is as transformed as its owner, with the furniture in the main room pushed against the walls to allow space for a tripod, parked in the middle like some giant leggy spider, and surrounded by various accoutrements, including two large circular silver reflectors, half-unfurled rolls of brightly coloured drapery and several bowls of gleaming fruit and vegetables. It looks more like a film set than a home. Through its half-open door, I note that the spare room has been sucked into the changes, resembling a storeroom now, with its own stack of boxes and the bed piled high with clothes.

My thoughts fly back to the dandelions running riot through the cracks in the drive at Jack's house, thicker, bigger, self-seeding. Soon, every last trace of him and me will have been overlaid by new realities. Life is rushing on, taking over, submerging the past, as it must. Before long, there won't even be ghosts; it will be as if none of it ever happened.

CHAPTER 5

I

The sweet, heady smell of freshly cut grass wafts in as I open the door, making it easy to forgive the stop-start buzz of the lawnmower that has formed an annoying backtrack to the morning classes. I make an arch of my arms to keep the door open while the children pass underneath, holding hands in pairs as instructed, jostling, hopping and chattering, their clipboards and attached pencils dangling carelessly in their arms. Ellen the gardener, her blue mountain of hair shining in the strong May sunshine, trundles past with an empty barrow, giving us a cheery wave.

Six weeks into term, and I have been finding something like a new rhythm, a new normality, the After to the Before. Back with my little class, so eager, so in-the-moment, life has started to make some sense again. Jack, the background drip-drip pressure of waiting, is utterly gone. Recently, I even, at long last, got around to burning my farewell letters to Harry and Pete, the final link with my old hopes, standing in the kitchen watching the edges of the papers curl on the plate I used for the task, the flames licking my words to ashes.

Pete, arriving home half an hour later, had nonetheless managed to wrong-foot me by sniffing the air like a dog, tracking the scent to the bin even after I said there had been something on the bottom of a saucepan. Luckily, I had changed the bag, and he wasn't about to start foraging in the wheelie. I had carried on stirring my white sauce throughout, gripping the wooden spoon, unable to suppress a certain weary awe at the precision of my husband's instincts, his nose for gaps in my defences.

As the last two children, Joey and Stella, are filing through, I catch sight of Camille rounding the bend in the corridor. She hurries towards us beaming.

'Hang on, everyone,' I call out to those already outside. A lot of hilarity and exaggerated bumping into each other ensues, though they settle quickly, clustering back round the door, at the sight of their headmistress, commanding, always behind her cheerfulness.

'Hey, this looks fun,' says Camille, bending down to address the pair nearest her. 'What are you all doing?'

Joey blinks importantly, preparing to answer, but Stella chips in first. 'It is science and writing and art,' she says, 'and also a treasure hunt. We have to find leaves and stones and feathers, and draw and write what they are and then we are going to make a collage.'

'Well, that sounds wonderful.' Camille tweaks the brim of Joey's cap. 'I like your hat, Joey. Is that a bear on the front?'

'Yes, a grizzly one. My Grandad went to America and he got it then.'

'Super. And a good idea to wear it when the sun is strong. It's like we've been in midsummer forever, isn't it,' she says to me, standing up. 'Apparently June and July are going to be just as bad.'

'Don't worry, they've all got sunblock on and we're heading for the shade. I just thought it would be a nice treat, with half-term starting tomorrow.'

'Absolutely. We should use the garden as much as possible – before it gets turned into a building site.' Camille beams. The architect's model for the next stage of the school now sits on a table in the middle of the entrance hall for all to enjoy, as appealing and ingenious as a Lego project, with its miniature jigsaw of buildings and open spaces, laced through with tiny interconnecting stairwells and pathways. 'Oh, and I'd love a word, Fran, at the end of the day, if you have time?'

'Right, okay – sure.' Camille's expression, so bright and inscrutable, causes me a momentary unease. The dinner she suggested that I thought would never happen had finally taken place the night before and I wonder suddenly whether she detected something untoward between Pete and me during the course of it. Or maybe it is about a work problem. I am not sure which would be worse. 'Thank you again, for having me and Pete round last night – it was lovely.'

'My pleasure,' she calls over her shoulder, already striding back towards her office, her loose black linen trousers swinging as she moves.

I return my attention to marshalling my jigging five-year-olds, steering them towards the coolness of the arching trees in the far corner of the garden for a final talk-through on the tasks on their charts. As we proceed, Pied Piper fashion, across the grass, the events of the previous evening continue to play on my mind. It remained a wonder that it had taken place at all, but already there have been signs of a price to pay – the stoking of old problems, threatening my fragile equilibrium.

'Yeah, why not,' Pete had said, much to my surprise, when I first, cautiously, mentioned the invitation and the dates Camille had suggested. Throughout the evening itself, he then behaved so impeccably, alternating between intelligent interrogations about the City investors in Chalfonts and Erik's navigation of the recent volatility in the oil industry – with passing references to his own struggles with high street retail thrown in – that it was all I could do not to stare, boggle-eyed, across the table. Pete's sociability and cleverness – his 'niceness' – so clearly existed; it was just me he was determined to keep it from. Erik and Camille, understandably, had appeared nothing but charmed.

'All people like that want is to show off,' he said as soon as we were in the car.

'But I thought you had a good time...'

'Oh really,' he sneered, 'and what gave you that idea?'

'Well, you certainly made a real effort then,' I replied quickly, 'and thank you for that. Keeping my boss happy means a lot to me.' I was glad I had offered to drive, that I had a clear head, that it gave me something to do.

'So now you're calling me a liar.'

'No, I... Come on, Pete.' I threw him a look of friendly incredulity, inwardly reflecting that it made no difference to have the 'good' and still exasperatingly mysterious things going on with the shop, or that seven weeks ago he had hauled Tilly out of a freezing river and blown oxygen into her lungs. Pete was Pete, especially after a glass or five: antagonistic, as unyielding as cement and needing to prove it.

'And don't think I didn't notice how you looked at Erik.'

'I did not look at Erik,' I protested, my heart plummeting. 'I have no interest in Erik.' This was how it used to be, why the going out had to stop. 'Or any other man, for that matter.' I heard a terrible false clang in my voice. I had come to a halt at a red light. There were no other cars around and the air between us felt leaden.

'Because you love only *me*, right?' There was icy sarcasm in his tone.

'Right.' My teeth were starting to do that thing of sticking to my inner lips. My pulse was sprinting. *Here we go*, I thought, *here we go. It's been so long, but it's always there.* 'Look, thank you for agreeing to tonight, Pete. I know it's not your thing and I am really grateful—'

'Well, you and she are clearly thick as thieves, that's for sure. Whispering on the sofa. Talking about me, I shouldn't wonder.'

'Talking about work more like, and how glad she was to have met you at last, how nice you were—'

'And *books* presumably, because of your *girls'* club.'

'A bit, yes.'

I tried to inhale through my nose, quietly, since anything resembling a deep breath – a sigh – a hint of patience being tried – would, I knew, have been inflammatory. He was already on the edge, picking for a fight, a reason to get angry. I instructed myself instead to be grateful that Jack was no longer in the mix; that Pete could poke and snarl and lash out, but that there was no longer the added terror of what he might discover. I told myself, too, how lucky I had been that the dinner-party chat hadn't included Pete or Camille inadvertently exposing my dumb, needless lie about the club having read *Middle-march* twice. The risk of this inane falsehood spilling out had dawned on me during an awkward break in the conversation, as Camille was fetching dessert, a shining mound of fresh strawberries, and I had pressed my palms together under the table in silent prayer, to a god I did not believe in, for protection. What an easy trip-up that would have been. What a field day Pete would have had.

'But hey, it was great to hear you talk a bit about work tonight,' I forged on, knowing I sounded too eager. Enough flattery, however, enough enthusiasm, had been known to get me out of holes in the past. 'In fact, I was rather hoping you might spill the beans on what on earth *has* been happening – you know, since that meeting when you had to get all spruced up? I've tried not to bother you with questions about it, just like you asked...' I hesitated. That day, fraught enough with the Hugh encounter, had ended badly, with me misreading the spring in my husband's step as permission to ask how the meeting had gone. I was to stop haranguing him, he had snarled, everything was still to play for and he'd tell me about it when he was good and ready. 'It's hard not to be excited, that's all,' I murmured now, 'given what you said then about your luck changing.'.

'Yeah, well, telling you everything might just jinx it. You, Fran, are my *un*lucky mascot. Hah.'

'Oh, I see.' Despite everything, I felt crushed. 'Well. Fair enough.' It wasn't fair. It was hateful and upsetting. I clung onto the steering wheel. I reminded myself that after drinking everything was always worse. Even Pete, during one of his early bouts of repentance had been forced to acknowledge that, hence the rigidity of the usual nightly beer allowance. 'I'll just carry on keeping my fingers crossed in that case.' The lights changed and on we ploughed through the near-empty streets.

He had his hand across the top of my thigh, tightening his grip every time I worked the clutch. After a few minutes of silence and feeling his fingers loosen at last, I dared to glance sideways and saw he had fallen asleep, his chin bouncing on his chest like a baby. A loathing, as well as relief, filled me then, not so much for Pete, as for my own complicitous cowardice in never standing up to him, for still being there after all these years, always looking to other people for answers and happiness.

I drove as steadily and smoothly as I could, not wanting to wake him up. It was a beautiful summer night, the final one of May, the quiet streets gleaming black, the moon, low and golden. A glossy fox darted across the road, pausing on the kerb to stare directly at me, its orange eyes like lasers, before ducking under a hedge. Turning into our road a couple of minutes later, I could find nowhere to park near the house, and before I knew it, I was accelerating on, past Mrs Dawkins, past smoky Dave, past Annie Smith's, remembering, with every passing yard, my attempted escape three months before, the raucous, trundling suitcase, all the worry about the things that didn't happen and didn't matter.

Instead of doing a simple circuit, I kept on heading south, encountering less and less traffic and eventually skirting the perimeter of a huge park I hadn't even known was there. The moon's golden face came and went, popping up over the tops of houses and from between thin streaks of silvery cloud. Beside me, Pete's head lolled more heavily, his nose emitting the buzzy nasal sounds indicating his deepest state of sleep.

It was almost an hour before I turned back into our street. A space had become available right outside our front door. I gave Pete a tentative nudge. He growled with irritation and directed a bleary-eyed grimace at his watch before stumbling into the house and up to bed without even bothering to clean his teeth. I locked up, following slowly, relishing the sense of having got one over on him, albeit in the smallest of ways. One step at a time.

II

Camille's office combines the cosiness of a front room with the seriousness of a library. It is the end-of-day meeting she had requested and we are sitting with cups of tea on our laps on the honey-coloured sofa parked in the bay window overlooking the front drive and street.

'How was the garden lesson?' she asks.

'Fantastic. They loved it. All a bit distracted by the excitement about half-term, of course.'

'Of course.' There is a moment of stilted silence as we each take a sip of tea, Camille clearly building up to whatever she has to say and me with fresh dread as to what it might be. 'Any plans for half-term?'

'Not really. A christening – or rather, a baby-naming ceremony – at my brother's next weekend.'

'Ah, that would be the brother you saw at Easter when...?'

'Yes, the one with Tilly. I don't think they're quite back to normal actually. When my sister-in-law phoned the other day about the arrangements, she sounded a bit subdued. They were going to do it in London, but are now keeping it in Kent – very small and simple...' I stop abruptly, aware that the disclosure of so much information was not called for, that uncertainty is making me chatter.

Camille pauses, before saying kindly, 'The bad things that nearly happen can traumatise us just as much as the terrible things that do.'

'Oh God, that's so true...' A gasp of recognition escapes me and I drop my gaze to my tea. My home life is a prison. Did I fall in love with Jack? Or with the opportunity for escape? No. I had loved Jack. I grip the little handle of my cup.

When I look up, Camille is staring at me with her customary candour, her dark brown eyes flashing. 'You're a bit of a mystery to me, if I'm honest, Fran.' She picks up a tiny white feather off the back of the sofa and flicks it to the ground. 'So brilliant at your job – the kids, the parents, adore you – so much ability, and yet, forgive me, but, even before your recent... difficulties... during our St Joseph days, I have always had the impression that there is something holding you back. Like you don't have as much faith in yourself as you should.' There is a question mark in her voice, but when I don't say anything, she continues quickly, 'For what it's worth, both Erik and I really enjoyed meeting Pete last night.'

I glance out of the window and catch a glimpse of a man walking past the front gates. Tall, rusty brown hair, a beard. Like Jack, but not Jack. The reminders are sparse these days, but exhausting. I wonder who the man is, where he is going, whether he is happy. I wonder what Camille would have made of Pete's and my conversation in the car after her lovely dinner. In my shoes, she would probably have given him the finger and told him to get out and walk. In my shoes... Except a woman like Camille would never be in my shoes. She would have long since left, or filed complaints; stood her ground. The shadow of Helena brushes across my mind. She wouldn't have stood for Pete's antics either. Not for a second.

Camille is talking about dear Steven Mason, the deputy head, who is suddenly quitting because of ill health. 'There is an opportunity for you here,' she continues briskly, 'to apply for the deputy headship,' she adds, when I stare at her blankly. 'There are no guarantees, of course, I shall be formally advertising the job, and I think Beatrice and Aditi might want to throw their hats in, but the reason for this talk is that I want one of the applicants to be you.' She drains her tea and stands up to put the empty cup and saucer on her desk. 'Think about it.' The words are a command, cutting through my stutters of astonishment and thanks. 'Oh, and there is one more thing.' A softer, much dreamier look is suffusing her face. 'Come the autumn...' She is wearing a loose cream shirt that hangs below the waistline of the linen trousers and has placed both palms across her lower stomach. 'Well, let's just say I shall be needing rather more support from my deputy than I do now – till the weaning is done with anyway.'

'You mean...? Oh, Camille, that is wonderful news.' I clap my hands in a reflex of delight, aware in the same instant of my phone – on silent – vibrating in my bag next to my left leg.

Camille is grinning, still lost to her own pleasure. 'Terrible timing, but there you go. Erik and I specialise in that. With Lars, Erik's dad had just got his diagnosis, and before that, with Per, we were moving house, and with Max...' She frowns. 'Oh yes, I'd just landed my first job – I knew there was something,' she laughs.

'Wow, four... I cannot imagine...' I stand up. My phone is bouncing again, which means it's probably Pete – never one to accept silence as an answer.

She sighs, shaking her head as she opens the door for me to leave. 'It *will* be fine – I've always wanted a large family – but fourth time around, it's not like there are any illusions about what lies in store. Lars didn't sleep through until he was three. And his brothers were almost as bad. Max had a horrible biting phase, which only stopped when I bit him back.' She bursts into more laughter and then composes herself suddenly, fixing me with one of her piercing looks. 'I love being a woman, but there is a hell of a lot to cram in, don't you think?'

'A hell of a lot.' I laugh. The phone has fallen quiet. 'Thank you so much for the encouragement about the job. I will have a go. I mean, I can't think of anything I'd like more, frankly.' As I swing my bag over my shoulder, my mobile starts another round of vibrations. I want to savour everything Camille has been saying, her wonderful declaration of faith in my abilities, but all I can think of is the power of one human trusting another, the utter shattering of self when it is denied or lost. 'Have a great half-term, Camille, and thank you so much. I can't actually tell you how much this means.'

'Well, it would mean a nice pay rise for a start,' she quips, breaking out of her headmistress mode to kiss me warmly on both cheeks. 'And, do you know, I am guessing Pete might be really proud.'

She holds my eyes with hers for a moment and I keep my smile fixed. 'Yup. I am sure he will be.'

I hurry down the corridor. My screen reveals four missed calls from Pete. In the entrance hall, I encounter Aditi and Beatrice studying the model of the new buildings; Aditi in her cycling shorts, rucksack across her slim shoulders, Beatrice in one of her big-print floral dresses, car keys jangling in her hand.

'We're going to Wendy's,' says Beatrice, referring to the wine bar on the corner of the street, favoured by all members of the staffroom. 'Why not come. Just this once?' she urges, long used to the refusal already on my lips.

'Just an orange juice,' Aditi chips in. 'Come on, Fran, it's half-term.'

'Sorry, but I can't.' I am too distracted to muster even a proper show of regret. If I don't call Pete soon he will go mad.

'One quick drink? Winding each other up about the big job strictly forbidden...' She throws a conspiratorial look at Beatrice and then breaks off as my phone starts buzzing in my hand.

I waggle it, rolling my eyes, and head on towards the door, answering it as soon as I am out of earshot.

'I make the point of getting home on time and you're not here.' He speaks slowly and coldly, like a disappointed parent.

'Sorry, Camille threw a meeting at me... it turns out she—'

'You never said.'

'Well, that's because I didn't know...'

'Don't you worry, I'm used to being bottom of your priority list.'

I bite my lower lip. This is no moment for a conversation about the Deputy Headship – I can sense he's already too wound up to give anything like the response I would so love to hear. 'With half-term starting, there was a bit to wrap-up, but I should be home soon.'

'How soon?'

'I'm just leaving. So, half an hour, max.'

'Good because we're celebrating.' He still sounds annoyed.

'We are?' I pause, fingers round the brass handle of the school's heavy main door. On the wall beside me is the small gallery of staff photos – cheerful, informal, colourful, professional – the photographer had carried out Camille's characteristically excellent brief to perfection. My own image beams at me, my skin strikingly pale between the neighbouring portraits of Camille and Aditi, my even teeth shown off in a grin, my long hair brushed back to reveal my straight stare and wide eyes, looking their sharpest green against the olive-coloured top I had chosen for the day. *When will I ever become that person*, I think, *the one sitting there, the one everyone else has no trouble bringing into focus.*

Pete's voice, full of thrill and pride now, bursts through my thoughts. 'A new branch and I'm going to be running the whole show. Share options thrown in, the lot.'

'A new branch? Oh, my goodness. How fantastic. Where?'

'Edinburgh.'

'Scotland?'

'I believe that is where Edinburgh is located. Jesus, don't go overboard, will you?'

'No... Pete, I'm just surprised... I mean, obviously, that is really exciting...'

'I've splashed out on tickets to fly up there, so we can take a proper look – tomorrow, because next weekend we've got that bloody non-christening of your bloody godchild.' He laughs. 'Well, you've been nagging to know what's going on and now you do. There's a lot to sort out still – a hell of a lot – but come the autumn, barring catastrophe, it should all be in place. We'll have to sell the house. It will be a whole new life for us, Fran.'

'A new life?' I echo, aware of my own new hopes starting to spin out of reach.

'Blimey, you really aren't getting carried away, are you.'

'No... I... that's so... Oh my goodness... I'm just pretty stunned, Pete, I mean – it's such big news. But, congratulations. And flying to Scotland tomorrow – that really is splashing out. What an adventure.' Each word is an effort. All I want to do is scream. Pete dictates what happens. Protesting never leads anywhere good.

'I dipped into the Santander. You said it was for important things and, luckily, Harry knew the password.'

'He did?' I turn the door handle, aware of my fellow teachers approaching down the corridor. In my head I watch my own good news dropping out of sight, like a pebble thrown from a clifftop.

'I booked a hotel while I was at it – nothing fancy, Christ, they're pricey – but I'll get it all back on expenses, of course. For tonight, I was thinking steak and a nice red. Assuming your frantic schedule will allow you to pick up such things on your way home? Maybe with that nice mushroom sauce thing you do.'

I have managed to push my way outside, spurred on by the very real danger of Aditi and Beatrice catching me up. The door clanks shut behind me. Pete claiming the money back just means he will keep it for himself, so it is gone for good. What I have to concentrate hardest on, however, is not thinking about Harry at my elbow in the vets, memorising my username and password as I settled the bill. Pete will have pressured him, that's for sure. Pete will have made it impossible for him to say no.

I hear myself say, 'Steak and mushrooms, no problem,' then I get into the bread-oven heat of the car and resolve, with the phone still against my ear and the leather seat scalding my thighs, that something has to change. Not with the help of anyone else, but inside me. Me.

'Well, be quick about it,' Pete barks, terse as always when it comes to his appetites. 'We don't want a late night as we'll need to be off by five. Harry was going out, but I've told him to cancel all his plans. I've told him he has to learn that family always come first.'

CHAPTER 6

I

The journey from London, with its dawn train ride to the airport, went like clockwork and with little communication, Pete glued to documents and his laptop, and Harry virtually somnambulant, wrapped against the world in the hoody he pulled on over his smart shirt and the ear-wires connecting him to his phone; like some creature on life support, I kept thinking, tenderness and dismay punching me with equal force every time I tried to catch his eye and he pretended not to notice. Suki was the only one he paid any attention to, filling her food and water bowls to the brim before we left and assuring her we would be back soon.

We had eaten our steak and mushrooms in front of the television in the end, saved from the burden of real conversation by a thin drama of murder and mayhem set on a Caribbean island. Both Harry and I knew enough to declare enthusiasm for the Scottish adventure Pete had laid before us, but the air thrummed with all the things thought and not said. Pete grumbled about the sharpness of the cheap Rioja I had bought, but then drank it eagerly enough, either not noticing or not caring that my own, calculated, abstemiousness meant he consumed almost the entire bottle. The strategy got me what I wanted, which was one of his deep snoring sleeps the moment his head fell onto the pillow. It gave me time to think – about my precious, raided stash of money and the chance of a job that I found myself believing I could do. By the small hours my head had been going round in circles, thrashing for answers that wouldn't come.

After leaving our bags with Reception at the hotel Pete had booked – it being too early in the day to check in – we found our way to the proposed shop-site, a huge space on the ground floor of a still half-finished multistorey shopping mall fifteen minutes' walk from the city centre. A project so close to conclusion, Pete explained eagerly once we got there, bouncing between firing questions at the smart young woman waiting to show us round and rapping on bits of wall like some expert builder, that the rental costs had come right down to encourage the final takers required to fill all the slots.

Subdued all morning, and a little hungover, no doubt, the arrival in Edinburgh had brought him to life. Indeed, during the tour, it occurred to me that I had never seen him so hyper. It was nerves, I realised. This was his big third chance, inducing a sweat of desperation that went way beyond the light grey damp patches spreading steadily under the armpits and across the back of his smart blue shirt as he quizzed our guide.

Neck-deep in my own dilemmas, a reflex of something like pity stirred nonetheless. Pete's biggest fear was being a loser, and yet the very fact of that always seemed to make the possibility of failure more likely. Within the pity, however, faith in my own contrasting strength was also starting to take root. Mel said I had inspired her. Camille believed in me. I had certainly weathered the Jack storm – held everything together even as I fell apart. So I would find a way out of this new impasse, somehow. It wasn't Scotland I was against, though turning my back on the wonderful chance of the Deputy Headship job was hard to contemplate. It was the terrifying notion of committing to a whole new phase of life with Pete, hundreds of miles away from all the support – Mel, Rob, Camille, my work – that helped keep me afloat. There had to be a solution, but it was going to need courage as well as inspiration; maybe I'd even have to dig for some Helena belligerence to lend a hand, I reflected wryly. In the meantime, the immediate priority was not to aggravate Pete, to buy some time and space in which to think.

'You go and enjoy yourself,' Pete instructed once the site inspection was done, his voice ringing with condescension and magnanimity even though it had already become clear that, while Harry and the woman in the trouser suit would be joining the lunch meeting, there was no question of it including me. 'See the sights,' he added, in the same insultingly authoritative voice which I realised was purely for the benefit of the young woman. 'We'll meet back at the hotel at three o clock, check in properly. Keep your phone to hand, there's a good girl.' I was sure I sensed Harry flinching, but he had been hovering at Pete's elbow all morning and was looking at his shoes.

Walking out of the shopping centre, turning right as they turned left, I pretended to appear a little downcast, to paint the picture that Pete most wanted to see: Fran having to do as she was told, submissive, but wishing she was more at the centre of things. I hung my head. I clung onto the strap of my bag. Inside, I wanted to run and jump. I had time to myself at last. I could breathe, I could think. Life was just an act, I reminded myself firmly, doubling my stride as soon as I was out of sight, it was just a question of staying on top of the script.

As always, it was the walking away from Harry that was tough. After the last couple of months, to be confronted again by this pale, woe-begone mask of his was like having a door slammed back shut in my face. I couldn't wait to get him alone, tell him there wasn't a jot of blame, that no one knew better than me that he wouldn't have given up the stupid Santander password without a fight. Most of all, I wanted to ask how he was really feeling about all this new railroading by his father. Not once had Pete referred to the tentative animal-care business ambitions; the crushing implication being that they weren't worth mentioning. And when I had dared to raise the subject the night before, saying, as conversationally as I could, while sliding the steaks, soft and succulent from the butter in the frying pan, onto their outstretched plates, that there would be just as many animals in need of looking after in Scotland, Harry had angrily cut me off, saying it had been a lame idea and didn't matter anyway. I noticed him sling the usual hungry glance at his father as he spoke, the plea for praise, but Pete was busy helping himself to the sweet-potato fries I had already pulled out of the oven, taking way more than a third, as usual. I quickly scooped just a few onto my own plate, so that Harry knew he could have the rest.

Alone now, the beauty of Edinburgh explodes into my consciousness, its gritty grey buildings tall and majestic against the brilliant blue new June sky, its streets such a hubbub of energy and colour, that I have to keep dodging tourists and flier-distributors to maintain my pace as I head back towards the centre. The day is hot and the sun high, but there is an enjoyable trace of northern freshness in the air and, every so often, a feisty breeze whips into the back of me, teasing my hair and puffing at the hem of my cotton skirt.

I stop at a café down a little alleyway, taking a seat at one of the rickety pavement tables and ordering a cappuccino, which is brought quickly by a slip of a girl with cherry lipstick and a red spotty scarf, knotted on top of her head like a bow on an Easter egg. Sticking out of my bag is the tourist booklet kindly provided by our hotel, offering a parade of options for someone with over two hours of free time – the Golden Mile, the castle, Waverley Gardens, as well as the National Gallery, home to the famous Landseer stag blazing out from the booklet's slim front cover. I study it carefully, finding a moment to lament the fact that Pete and I had never, not even during the very early better days, gone out together to enjoy such sights. We had been so young, and like two planets spinning separately, right from the start.

The coffee is so lukewarm that I have to stop myself downing it in one gulp. I want, badly, to call Mel, but I make myself log into Santander instead. My heart sinks, even though I have prepared myself. After Suki, and now Pete, it is down to six thousand eight hundred and forty-two pounds instead of ten. But still not nothing, I console myself. Still something. Vital assistance, just as soon as I have settled on the path to take. I can feel myself faltering, and make a conscious effort to think back to all the intricate, patient waiting and planning I did with Jack. I was good at it. I can do it again.

Slowly, squinting at my little phone screen as I bring the right menus in and out of focus, I go through the security checks necessary for changing my account password. *Place of birth. Favourite food. Mother's maiden name...*

And suddenly my mother is filling my vision, clearer than the Scottish summer daylight, before she was ill and on a good day, looking up to greet me in the doorway of her tiny greenhouse, brushing the tendrils of hair that have escaped her ponytail with the back of her muddied hand. It has been three years and, though inevitably missing her from time to time – sometimes wistful that, as with Rob, we had never had the sort of relationship that invited confidences – the rush of loss that engulfs me now is as extraordinary as the even stronger rush of love that follows. I even glance over my shoulder, half expecting to see her standing there. I catch the eye of the crimson-lipped waitress instead and signal for another coffee, forcing my attention back to my task. I settle on *hcr@melddɪM* as the new password, pleased to have thought of something so easily memorable for me and so unlikely to cross the imaginative reach of my husband.

I then try Mel, who doesn't answer, so I check her Instagram as I do most days, liking the latest post with a smiley face and shaking my head in wonderment. In the last couple of weeks, swimwear selfies have been replacing the underwear ones. Gone is the early, like-me-as-I-am stance of Mel facing the camera with the defiance of a prisoner confronting a firing squad. In its place are poses suggesting the confidence of the catwalk, a toe pointed, a hip cocked, her head thrown back, showing off the cascade of her long light brown hair, streaked with its beautiful gold highlights.

Today she is in a blue and white striped bikini of hugging shorts and a half T-shirt top that shows off the newly evident ribcage. She has adopted a side-on position, leaning up against the door frame of what I think is the spare bedroom, and is staring directly at the camera through the window created by the casual circling of her near arm round the curve of her head. Her eyes are as mesmerisingly enhanced as I have ever seen them; playful, bold, sparkling. If life is indeed an act, then Mel has really got the hang of it – or is rediscovering the hang of it – I reflect tenderly, but with a little pulse of worry too, because I would hate her ever to feel she had to put on an act with me. I remember suddenly what Annie Smith said about good things coming and life being a long old road, and decide no one could be more deserving of good things than Mel.

I quickly take a selfie for my own fledgling Instagram account, posting it with the caption, *Edinburgh on a sunny day,* and then check my emails, where I find an unexpected message from Rob under the subject heading: *CEREMONY-POSTPONEMENT*

Dear friends,

Due to various unforeseen circumstances, Jo and I are going to defer naming Marcus until later in the year. Sorry for the late notice and thank you for bearing with us!

J & R.

'What unforeseen circumstances?' I have phoned their home number and had been expecting Jo, but it is Rob who answers.

'Hey, Fran.' He sounds weary and flat.

'Has something happened?'

'Not exactly.' I hear him sigh heavily. 'Jo's got the can't-copes. I can't really talk now, actually. I'm taking a bit of time off. There's a lot going on, what with half-term and so on.'

'The can't-copes? Why, what's happened?'

'I don't really get, it to be honest. I mean, it's since Tilly... The whole thing really seems to have thrown her. The doctor also thinks there's some postnatal stuff in play. She's been put on tablets and has started some therapy.'

'Rob, I'm so sorry.' I try and fail to imagine my charismatic, capable sister-in-law not coping with anything, let alone her three beautiful children.

'She cries all the time. Doesn't want to do anything. Nothing I do or say helps. It's completely... it's intolerable, actually.'

'That's terrible, I—'

'Could you still come next weekend, Fran? It might be a bit chaotic – you know what a bloody lost cause I am in the kitchen. Though I am learning quite fast,' he mutters, 'necessity being the mother of invention. The fact is, it would cheer me up to see you and I'm sure Jo would like it too. You're so sweet and calm, Frannie, so... unthreatening.'

'Am I?'

'I mean Jo's got dozens of local friends, of course, but she says she can't face them – they're all so busy, she says, with hectic, functional families, that it makes her feel like a failure. And all the bloody sisters have been banned. Not to mention the parents – reducing everything to God, which, as you know, drives her mad. I'm at my wits' end, to be honest. And the kids... well... Bloody hell, sorry...' It takes me a moment to realise he is in tears.

'Rob, of course I'll come.'

'On your own might be best. Seeing Pete could set Jo off – though I feel a bastard just saying that, given what he did. Mind you, I suppose he won't be keen, will he, lending you out, so to speak. Pete likes you to do things together – I've gathered that much over the years, for all Jo's claims as to my emotional obtuseness. I may be an idiot, but I do notice the occasional thing.' He laughs bitterly.

'You are not an idiot, Rob, you are wonderful. And, yes, I will come, no matter how much it pisses Pete off, okay? Give Jo my love. Tell her... tell her, that never mind how bad things seem, there is always a way out. You just have to keep faith in yourself.' The words tumble out of me, as much counsel for my own position as for my poor sister-in-law, grappling with this new, utterly unexpected plight. As we are about to sign off, I find myself adding, 'By the way, Rob, I had the strangest thing just now, when I felt so close to Mum suddenly – I mean, closer than I ever did when she was alive – almost like she was standing next to me.

It was amazing. I know it's not the moment, but I just wanted to tell you. I mean, you're always so careful to ask if I miss her, and I don't think I really have been, not properly, not till now.'

'I'm glad, Fran. That sounds good. Better go. Hope to see you next weekend.'

II

An hour later, I am standing in the National Gallery, transfixed not by Landseer's *The Monarch of the Glen*, regal though the creature is, but before a much smaller oil painting of a Victorian reverend, dressed in his black church clothes, skating alone on a Scottish loch. There is such solitariness, but also such poised self-containment in his slim dark figure – the body leaning forwards, the back leg lifted, balletically – that what hits me most about the painting is the sheer joy of the skater, enhanced by the stormy lowering backdrop of the big Scottish sky.

It had seemed important suddenly to look at some art without Jack at my elbow; to show that I did not need him in order to know what to think and what to like. The thrill of finding the clergyman in ice-skates is as much about that as anything else – luxuriating in the certainty that nothing Jack – or anyone else – could say would make me enjoy the picture more. It makes me hungry to carry on exploring the gallery's other gems, and the Portrait Gallery too, which is just next door, but I notice, with a start, that it is already quarter to three and set about following the exit signs instead. Given my hopes of keeping Pete mollified, it would be stupid to rile him by being late.

The crowds are thick and I have to keep apologising as I elbow my way out, inwardly cursing myself for having allowed the time to slip through my fingers. I had stayed at the café for a sandwich, that was the trouble, and then my route to the gallery down through the Waverley Gardens had come up against a sudden and unadvertised 'closed' sign on the only path for getting back up to street level, necessitating a U-turn which had wasted valuable time. I am itching to buy a postcard of the skater, but the queue for the till in the gift shop is a winding sluggish snake and I know I mustn't risk it.

Outside, the sunlit streets are swarming. A young woman on stilts is threading her way through the tourists juggling big gold balls, while the flier-distributors are out in force, so numerous and insistent that it is easier to accept their offerings than refuse. By the time I am heading up the hill, free of the worst of the crush, I have a sheaf of papers, which I shove into the bottom of my handbag. It is now three o'clock and the hotel is still a good twenty-minute walk away. I break into a jog, clumsy in my summer sandals, telling myself that I am panicking needlessly. The lunch will have run on. Pete, in his new high spirits, probably won't be too bothered anyway.

The hotel, a functional, sparsely furnished town house, has its reception on the first floor. I use the stairs rather than the lift, and then have to press the bell several times before anyone appears.

'Oh, they've already checked in,' says the girl who eventually ambles out from the back room, making a big do of wiping her mouth and swallowing so I know I have interrupted her snack time. 'It's the family room, 28b, third floor, left out of the lift and at the end of the corridor. I'd give you a key card, but we only issue two and they took both. Don't forget your bag.'

'My bag?' She's pointing at my carry-on, left along with Pete and Harry's rucksacks when we came by in the morning and still sitting behind the reception desk, sporting its big paper tag with our surname on. 'Oh, thanks.' But somehow, even as I set off, swinging the bag over my shoulder and taking the stairs because they are nearer and more obvious and reliable, I know that this is not a good sign. To leave my bag, but take his. Pete is always good at making sure I feel neglected over the smallest things.

I have to knock several times and it is Harry who opens the door. I say hello, but he doesn't answer, or look at me, shuffling sideways instead to stand by the window, which offers a view of the fire escapes and backs of taller neighbouring buildings. A grey sodden sock hangs out of a gutter. Pete is in the only chair in the room, an ugly low-backed beige seat with high arm-rests which he has positioned to face the door, sitting square on, like some sort of courtroom judge, his face as glacial as the atmosphere in the room. The rest of the space is taken up with a plain single bed and small double, arranged on either side of a door to what must be the bathroom. There is a thin dark brown carpet on the floor and the faint smell of ancient tobacco.

'Hey, Pete, sorry to run late. I went to the National Gallery. It's got so many great things; I forgot the time.' I drop my bag tidily against the small wardrobe fitted into the wall behind the door. Hurrying along the streets, I had felt a strong need to pee, but for some reason the urge has completely disappeared. 'How was the meeting and the lunch? Did it go well?'

Harry seems to be looking at the sodden sock. I can see the rigidity in him, the misery, and it is worse than anything.

When seconds tick by and Pete keeps his eyes nailed on me, still not uttering a word, I burst out, 'Look, being a bit late isn't a crime. And if you are angry, can we at least save it for later, so Harry doesn't get dragged in?'

'Oh, but Harry is already dragged in,' Pete says quietly. 'You *dragged* him in.'

'What on earth do you mean?' My thoughts fly to the Santander account – whether the change of password has already been discovered and the hapless Harry blamed for not knowing it.

Pete has shifted forwards so that he is sitting on the edge of the chair and I see for the first time that he is clutching a creased piece of notepaper. 'So…' He pauses to take a long breath; 'I have always known that I married a whoring slut who'd jump into bed with half the world if I let her; but, thanks to you, our son, god bless him, now knows it too.'

'Pete, stop this. We've all come here for fantastic reasons. Let's try and enjoy it. Not let—'

'You deceitful, lying *bitch.*' The words hiss out of him.

Harry has dropped his head into his hands.

Pete holds the paper higher, and at some distance from his face because of the long-sightedness that he still hasn't got around to reporting to an optician. 'At least we think so, don't we, Harry? Putting the pieces together from this list, we've had to be quite the detectives, haven't we? There's no date, which is annoying. But there is the suitcase that needed *hiding*. And being *extra nice* to me. Well, that was actually quite promising, until we got to *your Jack*. Now, that had us racking our brains, didn't it, Harry? We had to put our thinking caps on there, because neither of us could summon to mind anyone we know called *Jack*. Unless… is it the postman? I mean, there's a thought. A strapping young lad, the last one I glimpsed – I tend to be out at work too early to catch them, you see, not that you appreciate such things – a ginger, though not much older than Harry here. So that would be a bit… But then, as I am realising, anything is possible with you, Fran. Absolutely. Fucking. Anything.' He lands on the last two words with a stamping force.

Harry is whiter than the window frame behind his head. He has folded his arms and is gripping himself, as if to stay upright. I have edged back so that I can lean against the small wardrobe for support. I recognised the piece of paper just as Pete started reading from it and, in the flooding terror of the moment, had experienced a visceral stab of pure rage at Mel, for the thoughtlessness of setting down so incriminating a checklist, a small, unwittingly poisoned dagger, among all the layers of minutes, hours, days, weeks, months, years of my fastidious caution. I am also trying to remember what the hell it actually said and whether there is a scrap of a hope of conjuring some plausible, appeasing explanation.

'Personally,' Pete says, laying the note down flat on the arm of his chair, ironing out its little creases with his fingertips, a document for reference as he continues to speak, 'I think it is good that Harry, beyond all reasonable doubt, now knows his mother to be an unfaithful fucking deserting slag. Wouldn't you agree, Harry?' His tone has become light and conversational.

Harry stares back at him, saying nothing. He is sucking in his cheeks, reminding me of when he was little and playing the game of seeing how long he could hold his breath.

'Leave Harry out of this,' I whisper. 'I love you, darling,' I add, turning to address him, 'please do not ever forget that.'

He drops his gaze, clutching himself harder and mauling his lips with his big teeth.

'*Love.*' Pete snorts. 'Now there's a thing you, clearly, know absolutely fuck all about...' The crescendo of anger in his words is audible, but he reins it in, closing his eyes and issuing a deep shuddering breath instead. 'We think the author of this delightful list is Melanie, your *bosom* pal. Like I say, we have had to be detectives. Are we correct?'

I see no option but to nod. My brain has frozen. And a part of Pete is enjoying himself, I realise, sickened, playing the cross-examiner, complete with dramatic pauses.

'So. What happened. And when. Tell us, please. We are on tenter-hooks to know. Aren't we, Harry?'

'It's all over,' I burst out, 'and I'm so sorry, but... yes, there was... briefly... someone—'

'This... Jack?'

'Yes...' The confession was hard enough, but I find that actually saying Jack's name – once so private, so precious – out loud is beyond my capabilities.

Harry has swivelled to look out of the window, as if literally unable to bear either the gruesome confessional being played out between his parents or the sight of me, his loathsome traitor of a mother.

'And you packed a suitcase...' Pete goes on. He consults the paper, 'Resigned even, from your beloved job. My goodness.' He raises his eyebrows. 'And then...' He frowns, scanning Mel's words, which I am still fighting my freezing brain to try and recall, vowing to withhold any detail I can. 'What, so this Jack never made it to the airport? Changed his mind on you, and wise old Mel thought it worth checking the Santander account. Which was safe, right? I mean, thanks to Harry here, I was able to see that for myself only yesterday. Unless there was more from your mother than you told me? Was there more, Frances?'

'No, of course there wasn't. Look, I am so sorry, Pete, but it was all madness anyway... I mean, it was never going to happen, and thank goodness.' I rush with the words, as if skimming over them might lessen their blows. 'I am truly sorry and I promise it couldn't be more over and done with. I think I was just very confused, very unhappy – a stupid midlife crisis – and if you give me the chance, I shall explain everything properly, right from the beginning. If we could just—'

'Oh, you will, will you?' Pete is suddenly on his feet. 'Well, that's rich, because I'm not sure I want to hear your pitiful excuses for behaving like a total cunt. And I don't think Harry wants to either.'

I detect a shrinking in Harry's broad shoulders. I am used to this particular word flying from Pete's mouth, but our son is not, at least not without the protection of a closed door. 'Pete, please, I think it would be best if you and I talked this through alone. The main thing, like I say, is that it's all done with – a brief and terrible mistake, which I deeply regret, because of not being honest, and now, obviously, for causing you – and Harry – so much distress.'

Pete appears to listen intently. He puts both hands in his pockets and rocks back on his heels, back in the guise of a courtroom professional, weighing up evidence. 'I see. So, the gist of it is, you were unhappy, almost ran away with someone called Jack – who you met fuck knows when and where, but we'll get to that – and now you are sorry. And we should all put it behind us.' His tone is calm and reasonable. He is nodding his head, as if the matter has almost been cleared up to his satisfaction. 'And maybe,' he goes on with faux brightness, 'you even wanted to be found out, because they say that can happen, don't they? And why, otherwise, would this piece of *litter* have been sticking out of your bag? And when did Mel write it anyway? When, Frances? So many questions, so few answers.' He flaps the paper.

'Months ago.' I whisper the words. To my surprise and relief, this appears, for the time being, to satisfy him. He folds the paper once, twice, three times, making a neat flat square before putting it in his pocket.

My eyes have fluttered to the carry-on; leather, roomy, with zipped outer compartments. I use it frequently for work, shopping, as well as travel. It had been to the airport and back on the fateful day back in March, but only dimly do I recall hurriedly sliding Mel's page of prompts deep into its outer sleeve, it not being a convenient moment to carry out its destruction, but vividly aware of the importance of it not being found. I had remembered to deal with every potential hazardous loose thread among so many, but not that. Even so, I reflect bitterly, most husbands would not have given a piece of paper poking out of a wife's travel bag a second thought. But then, Pete is not like most husbands. The note almost certainly wasn't even sticking out anyway; he probably just decided to have a dig-around and found it.

'Do you know,' Pete says, patting the pocket where Mel's words now reside and resuming his tone of chilling jollity, 'I think Mum might be right after all, Harry. She and I would perhaps be better off talking through the rest of this alone.' He reaches for his wallet, which is on the bedside table and plucks out a twenty-pound note, handing it to Harry, still such a pallid statue at the window that it's all I can do not to throw my arms round him. 'Find a cinema or a pizza or something, there's a good lad. And leave that key card of yours while you're at it. We'll both be here when you get back, I can assure you of that.'

Harry does not immediately move and for a few terrible moments I think he might refuse to go. I know what is coming, but it is unthinkable that Harry should have to know it too. It's been a long while, but Harry's ignorance has been my way of keeping him safe.

'Go on love, Dad and I need to talk.' Inside, I feel very calm. This is what I have dreaded and now it has arrived. There is some strange comfort in the certainty of that. Here is the storm.

Harry moves at last and has barely closed the door when I see Pete's hand slide to his belt. It's his favourite, the one with the big brass buckle.

III

'Either of you want anything? A coffee? A tea? I can't believe how quickly we got here. Sunday morning, I suppose, no traffic on the roads – that bus took half the time compared to yesterday. Hey, anybody home in there?' Pete playfully raps Harry on the head. 'Your father is asking you a question.'

Harry offers a quick reflex of a smile, adjusting his headphones to release an ear. He is still behaving as if I am not there, as if he can't bear even to set eyes on me, and given what he now knows, about Jack, I do not blame him. 'No thanks, Dad. I'll just sit here.'

'Fran? A cappuccino?'

'Thanks, Pete, that would be lovely.' He leads the way to a small airport café and I follow, meek as a well-trained dog, keeping a white-knuckled grip on my two bags, the carry-on over one shoulder, my handbag over the other, because of the pain. I try to move steadily, marvelling at how integral ribs are to the business of normal motion – breathing, walking, lifting, turning – even a fixed smile, it turns out, demands an effort that somehow feels connected to the middle of the body.

Watching Pete's belt slide out of the loops of his trousers, I had thought I was ready, that I knew what was coming, but it turns out that the brain is better at recalling the fact of physical assault, than its specific sensations. The first whipping sting of the flat leather across my back, even with the protection of my clothes at that stage and the door barely closed behind Harry, drew a low growl of a shriek that was as much about the shock of the pain as the pain itself. I had forgotten how much something could hurt, had buried it, as mothers do the agonies of labour, nature's way of granting strength for the ordeal to be endured again.

It took a good while, not until my clothes were off and the buckle end was landing before the thwack of the leather, for me to be back in the old familiar rhythm of it, so deep inside myself that I was on the outside too, watching as much as receiving. Even when Pete had finished, wiping the belt clean on some loo roll, stepping over me to draw the curtains against the darkening sky and then going to wash his hands, a numbness held me for a while, keeping the worst of it at bay. I was glad it was over. I was glad too, to be able to concentrate on the voice inside my head, a voice I had never heard before. *No,* the voice shouted back, *this is not what happens to useless people. No, this is not what I deserve. No, I have not 'made' you do this. You are doing it, Pete. You. Are. Doing. It. TO. ME.*

By the time Harry knocked on the door, Pete had tucked me under the covers and was lying fully clothed beside me, watching telly and eating the sandwiches that he had sweet-talked the girl at the reception desk to procure for him, on the grounds that I had been taken ill. The room was lit only by the light of the TV and the low-wattage lamp on the small table on the far side of our bed.

'It's open,' Pete had called out, having thought to put the latch on before settling with his food. 'We've talked it all through and Mum's tired,' he reported, the moment Harry opened the door, putting his index finger to his lips to reinforce the point.

Harry threw a furtive glance in my direction, a lump under the bedclothes, before gingerly picking his way to his corner of the room and then disappearing into the bathroom.

I was indeed tired. Sleep – oblivion – would have been blissful, but my throbbing body kept grabbing me and pulling me back. Through half-closed, eyes I let my gaze travel between the blur of the TV screen and the grey curtains. A vertical strip of light shone where they didn't close properly and I found myself thinking of the grey sock dangling from the gutter, wondering to whom it belonged and hoping they were all right. To throw a sock out of a window was not a friendly act, I reasoned, however you looked at it. To have to walk with one bare foot, it made me want to weep with pity.

When night fell properly and the telly was off, I found myself focusing on Harry's soft, even breathing over Pete's noisier rasps. My son's abhorrence towards me now was without question, and wholly understandable. Somehow, when Jack had been integral to the equation, I had thought this was something I could sort out, firstly through my 'farewell' letter, with its clumsy effort at explanations, and then with an imagined idyll of a future scenario in which Harry, observing I was happy and that Jack was a good man, forgave me everything. The naivety of this now, the sheer *delusion* to which I had treated myself, would have been enough to make me laugh out loud, had I not been a captive, pinioned under the bedcovers. Instead, peering down the line of my nose over the top of the thin, lumpy duvet, I acknowledged bitterly the tightrope between innocence and stupidity from which I had now truly fallen. To think that, at the height of my excitement, I had even entertained the wild notion that elopement with Jack would make me the heroine of my own 'story', conveniently – idiotically – overlooking the crucial difference that books are fabricated to have happy endings, while real life is not.

I took my turn in the bathroom long before Harry or Pete were awake, shoving two paracetamol tablets from a dusty packet in the bottom of my washbag to the back of my throat without water, and trying to keep my involuntary whimpers muted as I peeled off my nightshirt. My first thought at the sight of my torso in the small basin mirror, the welts and bruising spreading and merging like spilt paint, purple, black, red, orange, dotted with clots of sticky scarlet where the skin had broken and the blood congealed, was that the pale pink T-shirt I had brought in with me, by way of a change of clothes, might not be up to the job.

Under the shower, I used the hand-held attachment, keeping the water flow gentle and lukewarm, and clamping my teeth against the vicious stinging as each patch of torn skin received a drenching. I then dabbed myself dry with one of the hand towels, rinsing it out afterwards to erase the dots of blood. At every glimpse of myself in the mirror, it was hard not to marvel at the precision of Pete's efforts – it was like ghoulish body-art stopping just below my mid-sternum and just above the middle of my thighs. My arms were fairly clear too, apart from a scattering of angry risen lines that made me think of the jellyfish stings which had ruined Harry's first foray into the sea, aged six, when I had persuaded Pete out on a rare bucket-and-spade trip to the coast.

'Sprinkle of chocolate?' Pete asks now, bringing me back to the airport and the charade of normality in which we are all engaged.

'Yes please.'

'I'll carry it for you, shall I?'

'Thanks. I need to pee, actually.'

'Okey dokey.' Pete looks around for the toilets sign, which I have already located. 'I'll come with, hold your bags while you go in.'

'No need,' I say dully, as he follows me, grateful for the crowds, which I know will shame him into acquiescence on the bags at least. I walk slowly, pain stapling every step, and feeling unpleasantly hot in the cagoule I have put on to hide the possibility of blood smears soaking through the thin pink top. 'I won't be long,' I say and keep my word, even though I don't pee but use the time, sitting on the closed lavatory seat, to check all my notifications – grimly considering the irony of receiving a message from Jack now – and hastily messaging Mel to the effect that the really bad stuff is hitting the proverbial fan and she is not to make any sort of contact until I have given her the all-clear. I then delete the message I have sent her, getting a stab of a flashback to all the precautions against discovery that Jack and I took, and thinking how nothing is truly safe, least of all love.

When I emerge, I can sense Pete wanting and resisting the urge to ask for my phone. He has checked it enough times already, and will do so again.

'All right?' he says.

I nod and he leads the way, carrying the coffees, back to the row of seats where Harry is sitting, and then settles behind his laptop. I close my eyes, not because I am tired – I am the opposite of tired, in a state of such hyper alertness that I am afraid it might show. The airport is steadily coming to life on this Sunday morning, and every part of it, the kaleidoscope of the departures and arrivals boards, the rumble of trollies and suitcases, the announcements, the myriad snatches of conversations, is flooding my senses, a cacophony, and yet each component note as clear-cut as glass. The past is assailing me too, the same orchestra of sounds in a different airport three months ago, the exultation ready to burst as I scanned and rescanned the seas of faces for Jack, while, overhead, the information board clicked through its updates like a ticking bomb.

'Unhappy, were you?' Pete had growled, during the course of the commentary that had accompanied his work with the belt. In the foetal position at the time, on the floor, I had observed through the tangle of my hair that he was pausing to wipe the sweat from his forehead on the sleeve of his shirt and been grateful for the respite. 'Un-*fucking*-happy? And what do you think I was, eh? What do you think I *am*, now? Working my arse off and living with a fucking ungrateful fucking cheat of a fucking cunt.' He swung again and I knew it wasn't yet about wanting proper answers. That would have required real conversation and even in happier circumstances he was reluctant for that.

It was only later, after he had cleaned himself up and was holding back the bedcovers, watching me put my nightshirt on, that he asked, 'So how did you meet anyway, you and this Jack?'

Without a beat of hesitation, I pattered out a story about Jack stopping me in the street to ask for directions. It was six months ago, I said, and it had gone from there. In the grilling that followed, I continued to offer complete fabrications. I said Jack was an antique dealer from

Wales. I said we had met only a handful of times and reiterated that it had been a stupid whirlwind midlife crisis of a thing for him as well as me, and I was glad it hadn't worked out. I said I had been hurt, but mostly consumed by remorse at my own idiocy – risking everything on nothing. I said he and Harry were my world and I wanted only to be forgiven and for life to carry on. I said I loved Scotland and couldn't wait to make a fresh start there. I said I loved him and always had. I said any damn thing. Because the pain was not yet a memory and I would have hurled myself onto the rooftops to join the dangling grey sock rather than endure another second of it.

IV

I find myself praying for a delay – a glitch – just as I had at Gatwick, but again the processes – security, the departure gate, the queue to board – go smoothly. As we walk down the embarkation tunnel towards the small, waiting mouth of the plane door, Harry in front, Pete second and me last, my leaping brain flicks to a novel the group had read about a man getting trapped while potholing; wriggling forwards in the hope of a way out and becoming fatally sandwiched between the layers of rock, while, outside, heavy rain falls and his woman waits. The June sun is hot through the airport Perspex and no one is hanging on for me. No one, that is, except my inner – my other – self, the one who dared to defy Helena and love Jack, the one who shouted back at Pete in her head as the belt kept landing.

'Welcome on board. You're in the middle on the left.' The air hostess has a strong Scottish accent, sticky red lips and hair moulded into a tight blonde bun, perched like a gleaming doughnut on the crown of her head. She is already looking over my shoulder at the couple behind me.

Pete and Harry are a little ahead, picking their way along the plane aisle, which is busy with settling passengers trying to negotiate the overhead storage space. I proceed more gingerly than my husband and son, to protect my tender body from any unnecessary contact. By the time I reach our row of seats, Harry and Pete are already in their places, Pete by the window because that is his preference and he would not consider offering even so trivial a treat to anyone else, and Harry in the middle. As I start to ease my bags off my shoulders, it is impossible not to grimace.

'Mum, do you need a hand?'

The offer is made in a pinched, reluctant voice, but I beam at Harry nonetheless. 'No, don't worry...' I look back at the knot of passengers filling the aisle behind me. 'Actually, I need to go to the toilet.'

Pete looks up from his phone. 'Don't be ridiculous. You can't go again now, while we're still on the ground.'

'But I've got my period,' I hiss. When Harry cringes and Pete starts shaking his head, I go on, much more loudly. 'In fact, I'm wondering if it's early menopause, it's so heavy. There will be the most terrible mess if I can't get to a toilet.'

People are staring and pretending not to. Only a young woman with dreadlocks, sitting right in front of Pete, throws me a direct eye-roll of sympathy. Harry has hunched lower in his seat and Pete is looking appalled.

'I am sure they can make a small exception when I explain,' I continue, louder and so strident now – so not me – that I have one of my wild thoughts about Helena. She would make a scene. She wouldn't be afraid. 'They certainly won't want to deal with the consequences, I can assure you of that. Blood everywhere. I can feel it coming now. Gushing.' Pete is ogling me in incomprehension and disgust. 'I'll be as quick as I can,' I add, managing to switch to a tone of cheery ruefulness as I start to make my way back up the plane.

It is not a popular choice with anyone. The aisle is packed and I have to withstand several elbows brushing against me as I fight my way through. I can feel Pete's eyes on my back and am grateful for the crowd, especially the two family groups near the front, waving boarding passes and having an argument about who is in whose seats. The second air steward, a slim young man with peroxide hair, has to

join in to arbitrate, helping to block the view of me, I hope – I dare not
look back to check – as I dodge past the hostess and step back out into
the embarkation tunnel. I think I have got away, but she hurries
after me.

'Madam, you cannot leave the plane now. We are departing in five
minutes.'

'I know. I am leaving my husband.' I speak very quickly, hoicking
up the cagoule and my pink T-shirt to flash her a glimpse of my
bruised stomach, and adding, as she gasps, her big green eyes flaring
with shock and concern, 'I've told him I've come on and urgently need
the toilet.' Then I set off at a run, weaving through the stragglers still
boarding, and finding that adrenalin has many miraculous benefits,
including the numbing of extreme pain.

Questioned at various other points as I swim back – the wrong way
– through the tide of the airport, I offer the simpler explanation of a
family emergency and needing to catch a later flight.

My phone, predictably, leaps into action within minutes.

Where the fuck are you?

From Pete, and

Where r u dad's going mental

From Harry.

They are hard messages to read, so I turn the phone to silent.

Soon, I am back in the main concourse of the airport, where the din
of travel already feels more normal, as if I am lost within it rather than
sitting outside it. I go to stand in front of the departures board,
watching as it performs its regular updating flips, needing to see with
my own eyes that the London flight has progressed from *gate closed* to
departed.

Pete might have barged his way off anyway, I know. But, somehow, I
have faith in the air hostess, with her blazing sympathetic eyes and no-

nonsense hair. And when I venture, at last, to check for messages, there is only one more from Pete, his favourite over-used four-letter word, sent ten minutes before and sounding a little weary, I decide, grimly, like the last flutter of one who, for the time being at least, has no more moves up his sleeve.

I don't have much left in me either, apart from six thousand eight hundred and forty-two pounds, a dirty set of clothes and a toothbrush. I glance back up at the board and the word 'Madrid' blinks at me from the middle of the listings, scheduled to leave in three hours. Keeping my gaze fixed on it, I reach into my handbag, down through the crushed jumble of fliers, until I feel the rectangular shape of my passport in its inner zipped compartment, still safely stowed after all the frantic checking and rechecking three months before. Ninety days ago. Another universe; one in which I still believed I needed someone to hold my hand instead of being able to jump alone.

PART TWO

HELENA, FEBRUARY 2018

CHAPTER 7

I

'Damn, it's Hugh.'

'Did you ask him?'

'No, I'd have told you if I had. He's so needy since Paula, it's heartbreaking. I could send him on the Victoriana Auction mission tomorrow, if you like, give him something to do?'

'No, I'll do it. South of the river will make a change.'

The doorbell rang again, louder and longer. I dropped the curtain from behind which I had spied Hugh's metallic blue Aston Martin and reached for my shirt, pulling it quickly over my camisole and stepping into my skirt before slipping my feet into my blue velvet pumps. I was still bare-legged and the skirt short, but there wasn't time for my tights, still in an inside-out balled-up tangle by the foot of the bed. I strode to the bedroom door, pushing what shape I could back into my tousled hair. 'I'd better go down and let him in.'

Jack, still naked, rolled onto his side. 'Daaaarling, don't leave me this way.' He made a jokey show of clutching a pillow.

'Bloody hell, needy men – I'm surrounded.' I pulled a face. 'Not that there was that much to be saved from, was there, sweetie? *Again...* though you know I'll love you always, don't you,' I added quickly, blowing him a kiss before I bolted down the stairs, tucking my shirt in as I went.

By the time I got to the hall, Hugh was shouting through the letterbox.

'I know you're both in there. I'm freezing my bollocks off. I've got fizz.'

'He's got fizz,' I yelled, both so Hugh would know I was almost at the door and by way of a further sweetener to Jack, whose claim to like my straight talking was seldom borne out by how he dealt with it. I offered the flat of my cheek up for Hugh's hello kiss, playfully wresting the bottle from him, which was still wet and cold from his palatial wine-fridge a couple of miles away in Hampstead. 'Ten minutes' notice would have been nice. I'll have you know you've interrupted a spousal siesta.'

'Well, you two should be ashamed, having time for such things on a Friday afternoon, let alone the inclination – after all your decades.'

'Age jokes are *verboten,* and *inclining* is the key to a happy marriage,' I quipped, casting an eye at the landing, hoping Jack wasn't going to sulk and not come down

Hugh followed me into the kitchen, a huge glass-walled add-on running along the entire back of the house which had taken twice the time to get permission for as it had to build. I handed the bottle back for opening and perched on one of the chrome bar stools positioned along the granite-topped island facing the garden.

'Ciggie?' I waved the packet and Hugh shook his head. I pulled one out for myself, lighting it with the hob igniter, left out from Jack's and my poached egg breakfast, together with our used plates and the big hand-painted French coffee cups bought on one of our early trips to Hugh's place in Toulon. It was already gone two o'clock, but a late start and no commitments meant we hadn't got around to lunch.

I inhaled deeply and blew a plume of smoke towards the glass panels, privately lamenting the February drabness of the garden. Even the quince blossoms were starting to fade. The same quince that Jack had grandly pronounced his 'waterlilies' when we first moved in, proceeding to capture their every nuance at his easel until his interest faltered, as it always seemed to.

I squinted at Hugh, struggling with the cork. 'You better not be on a self-denial kick. I need my partner in crime, especially on a dank winter day.' I tapped my ash onto a bit of egg yolk, where it sizzled faintly before blackening. 'I'm not sure I could bear it if you went all clean, green and virtuous on me, darling.' For some reason, there was a lump in my throat, which took effort to swallow away.

'I already am all those things,' Hugh grunted, through the scowling demanded by his labours with the bottle. 'I own a water carbonator. I recycle my empties – of which, it is fair to say, there have been a good many lately... that bloody woman, it's my bank she wants to break more than my heart...' He paused to breathe. 'Rest assured, I remain your partner for all crimes, Helly, and when I am finished here, I intend to smoke you out of house and home.'

'Oh, you do, do you?' I was glad he hadn't noticed my wave of sadness.

He flashed a grin at me, one of the big ones that made his temples move and his light brown eyes sparkle.

'Hugh, what an expected pleasure,' announced Jack drily, appearing behind us, shuffling in the old-man mules which he was well aware I loathed and which therefore told me he was still not entirely happy. I knew I'd been my usual blunt self about our recent sexual half-mast efforts, but maybe it was simply that he wasn't in the mood for Hugh. I wasn't in the mood for Hugh either, but that was the way it was with old friends. Sometimes they had to be endured, supported, especially if a greasy-pole-climbing actress half their age had chewed them up for five years and then spat them out. And, besides, champagne would definitely throw light at what was in danger of feeling like a very gloomy afternoon. Jack must have reached the same conclusion, I mused, relieved and pleased to see the speed with which he swiped three flutes off a top shelf and arrived at Hugh's side.

'To Hewie.' I raised the full glass Jack had put beside me, choosing the same moment – shooting him a penitent look – to swap the breakfast plate for an ashtray. 'With good riddance to Paula.'

'Good riddance,' Hugh echoed, but without conviction and looking suddenly so boyishly forlorn himself that I was momentarily cast back to the shared Norfolk years of growing up, Hugh trailing behind his elder brother Felix in all our silly games, just as Christabel, despite being the elder, had traipsed behind me. Some were followers, some were leaders, I mused, at least to outward appearances.

'It will get better, Hugh.' I slid off the stool to give his shoulder a squeeze, aware as always when I stood next to him of my own superior height. It took nerve and veuve to be a small man and I was never sure Hugh had it. Of all my suitors, only Jack had ever really towered above me; indeed, it had been a small but integral part of the decision to say yes when he finally popped the question, thirteen years before, after months of shilly-shallying. He could *contain* me, I had thought, only discovering later that it was mostly the other way round. 'Paula was a child and a bitch and you can afford it,' I went on to Hugh, firing Jack a look of affection, which he still chose not to acknowledge, 'and no, I know that does not make any of it easier right now, darling, but it is all true. In the meantime, let's withdraw to the *withdrawing* room and drink some of your lovely gift, shall we?'

'Smoke-free zone,' Jack cried, as I knew he had been dying to, opening a crack in the passageway window as he strode on ahead, but then doubling back to the kitchen, saying he was starving and would make us all sandwiches – an offer which I knew was as much about giving us a little space to talk as his desire for food.

Hugh and I both called out our appreciation, before settling ourselves in the respective corners of the blue velvet sofa that formed the centrepiece of the room. I unfurled a leg so Hugh could rub my foot and flicked on the latest jazz playlist Jack and I were into. 'Clever darling to gate-crash a dreary and empty afternoon.' Hugh kneaded the foot in his usual businesslike way, beginning at the heel and working up towards the ball. 'And I'm truly sorry you're so miserable, but Paula really *isn't* worth it, you know. A total gold-digger... better than the dreaded Claudia, though,' I added slyly, wanting badly now to make him smile.

'Ah, but anything's better than the dreaded Claudia.'

We both burst out laughing, Claudia dating back to our East Anglian teens and the Claudia stories being plentiful and colourful, having encompassed a good decade of disastrous roller-coaster liaisons, including an early one with Hugh shortly after he and I had split.

'I wonder what became of her. I hope she's all right.'

'Oh, Claudia will be *fine*,' I replied hastily, sensing Hugh's mood in danger of dipping again and knowing only too well how badly one could sometimes need the positivity of friends to stay afloat. 'Word would have got out otherwise. And anyway, she's that sort – a survivor.' I paused, hoping suddenly that the same might be said of me. I certainly never shied away from things. I was always prepared to do what it took.

'And so, life is obviously hectic for you,' Hugh remarked wryly, draining his glass with quick steady gulps, and then refilling it from the bottle.

'Don't start trying to shame me.' I pretended to glare, waggling my other foot for attention. 'Today, I'll have you know, was an oasis of much-needed quietness. I've been run ragged for weeks helping Madeleine with this Mayfair gallery she's so determined about – the place is a complete wreck. Next week, Jack and I head off on a Cornwall stint, and tomorrow – as I've got my monthly Daphne meet – Jack's chasing down a couple of first editions for me from Moorlands, that little South London auction house that throws up the occasional gem. I find keeping my husband busy tends to make me less infuriated with him.'

'Ah.' Hugh set my foot to one side.

'Life certainly isn't hectic for Jack,' I murmured, tucking both my feet in and sitting upright, 'he just doesn't *do* anything any more, Hewie. I have to bully, or nothing happens. It drives me mad. Do you remember how he used to be? I mean, look at my gorgeous wedding present, for heaven's sake.' I flung an arm at the painting above our heads, hanging in perfect equidistance between the two bookcases behind the sofa, a labour of love – literally – based on an old family photograph of me running through a field as a little girl. 'Just *look*. I honestly do not think there is a single thing we possess that I love more. Sometimes, now, it makes me want to weep. Metaphorically, that is.' I grinned. Talking to Hugh always made everything seem better, because of the shared history and not having to explain anything. He knew I adored Jack – that my moaning was never about more than getting things off my chest.

'Don't weep, old girl, metaphorically or otherwise. Say you'll do me a favour instead.'

'Oh yes?' I eyed him with faux wariness, thinking for by no means the first time how relaxing it was to have a friend with whom all the possibilities of romantic entanglement had long since been explored and jettisoned. 'I should have guessed there had to be a reason for the visit, let alone a foot-rub that has lasted well beyond your usual thirty seconds.'

'I protest. I came by because you are my oldest friend and because I love both you and your wildly talented husband.'

'Get to the point.' I reached for my glass, stretching both legs back out and tucking the toes under the side of Hugh's thigh because they were in danger of getting cold. 'And by the way, you need a haircut, you've got that Superman curl going on, which I can't stand.'

'It's the new flat,' Hugh said, pushing the offending clump off his forehead, only for it to drop back down again. 'The sale has gone through and I was wondering if you could work some of your magic on the interiors. For a handsome fee, of course. I'll be able to get top-whack rent if you do.'

'You greedy landlord, you.'

'Okay, lovebirds,' announced Jack, bounding into the room bearing a large plate on which he had assembled a perfect, closely interleaved pyramid of open smoked salmon sandwiches, lemon wedges draped round its edges like bunting.

'You are a marvel, husband,' I cried, scrambling to clear a space on the coffee table in front of the sofa. 'An artist, as well as a gourmet. Food, glorious food.'

'Thank you, wife, whom I adore,' pronounced Jack, whisking out three napkins with the flourish of a conjuror as he set the plate down and then tossing them onto our laps. Tinged with age, they were from the trousseau that had belonged to my maternal grandmother, part of a linen set stored in an overcrowded cupboard of inherited treasures which I had only recently complained we never used. 'Because beauty in life matters,' he added softly, giving me one of the piercing, tender looks that had made me fall in love with him and which could still topple me, fourteen years on.

* * *

'I'm just saying...'

'Well don't,' Jack batted the air separating his armchair from the sofa as he cut across me. I was now stretched out fully, a cushion instead of Hugh's legs keeping my bare feet warm. On the table were several bottles, empty of champagne and the wine that had followed it, but still containing various amounts of water for a game of guess-the-tune using musical bottles, which I had devised but then quickly banned when inane squabbles broke out between the men about names of songs and note-pitching, somehow causing copious amounts of water to get spilled in the process. The sandwich plate sat among this detritus, long since picked clean.

'...just saying,' I continued, with an implacability I was drunk enough to hope would aggravate, 'that I married a man of immense talent not knowing he was a lazy arse. *Just saying.*'

'A man, yes,' snarled Jack, 'not a pet seal – performing to order. The muse doesn't arrive like so many thrown fish.'

'Hewie agrees with me, don't you, Hewie?' I swivelled my gaze to our guest, who, a while ago now, had slid onto the floor to demonstrate some yoga moves – a legacy of his recent ex for which he had admitted grudging gratitude – but then pronounced the carpet so comfortable that he had remained where he was. I had to blink to bring Hugh's prone body properly into focus. It must have been only four or five hours since his appearance on our doorstep, but it was starting to feel like it could have been four or five weeks.

'Leave off, you two,' Hugh groaned in the tone of a weary parent. He had summoned an Uber and was tracking it intently, holding his phone screen right up against his face because a bout of itchy eyes had seen the removal of his contact lenses.

None of us had been bothered to draw the curtains and only a single wall light lit the room, flickering slightly because the bulb fitting was loose. It had been because of that, and with the windows having become big, black, depressing Rothko squares of darkness, that I had found myself suddenly turning again to Jack's sunny arresting painting of my childhood self and hailing it as the only true source of light – and joy – in the room. The declaration had burst out of me like desperate inspiration – a truth, as well as a spur – to make Jack see again what he was neglecting in himself. But, within seconds, predictably, offence had been taken and the usual row was kicking off.

'The little car has arrived,' shouted Hugh, triumphant, and relieved too, perhaps, given our bickering, though he, of all people, was used to it. He levered himself to his feet, with remarkable grace, given his extreme state of inebriation. 'It is outside *now*,' he exclaimed happily, still gaping at his phone, 'a picture of a car and a *real* one, all at the same time. Isn't the technological world a marvel? As are you two,' he added glibly, swaying only slightly as he pulled on his jacket and patted his pockets to check for his belongings. 'Be kind to each other, won't you. It really is all that matters. I will collect the mean machine tomorrow. At some stage. Possibly in the afternoon. To be realistic.'

'I'll see you out,' Jack grunted, hauling himself out of his armchair.

I blew a kiss off from the sofa. 'Safely home. And thank you for the exercise class,' I giggled. The yoga display had been as earnest as it was inept, making Jack and I laugh till our eyes streamed.

Hugh gave me a wave from the doorway and I watched Jack follow him out of the room, walking in the slow stiff manner of one drunk enough to be aware of the need to micromanage his movements.

Alone, I reached for the only bottle still containing a little wine and poured it equally between Jack's and my glasses, before flopping back to marshal my thoughts. I wanted Jack to understand the point I was making. He was neglecting his genius and I needed him to see it. I did not want the sun to go down on anger, mine or his. I wanted to thrash through what was at stake, ideally with a spot of rampant make-up sex to follow. It really was rather a long time since anything truly satisfactory had taken place in that regard. How long? Weeks? Months? My tipsy brain wouldn't cooperate, but it was an age anyway and hard to pretend it didn't matter. Not to feel properly wanted. It mattered like hell.

I heard the front door slam and the dim, tinkling sound of Jack peeing in the downstairs loo, followed by the flush of the cistern.

'I don't need any more,' he said, spotting the two refilled glasses the moment he reappeared, 'and I don't think you do either.'

'Don't tell me what I need, there's a good boy. And, besides, please acknowledge that there is a world of difference between needing and *wanting*. Now, come and sit next to me and stop being grumpy.' When he remained leaning against the door frame, scowling, arms folded, I decided to try a new tack and clambered to my feet on the sofa, holding out my arms. '*Pleeeease* come here, Jackadoodle. We could dance. I *love* dancing and we *never* do it.' I fired the console at the speakers to set the jazz going again, rolling my hips and beckoning with my hands. When he still glowered, I began to undo the buttons on my shirt, hamming it up like a stripper. 'Maybe you will want me properly this time, eh sweetie pie? If I do it right... make it sexy enough...' I began tugging at the zip on my skirt, but couldn't seem to get a proper grip.

'Stop it. Please, Helena.'

'*Helena* is it? Oooh, the man is seriously vexed. What happened to the wife you adore?" I gave up on the zip and continued to shimmy, despite the struggle to keep my balance.

Jack stayed where he was, an iron rod, his face a mask, not under-standing how this stoked my desire to break through his defences and force a response. The men before him had been putty in comparison – easy to manipulate, to trample on sometimes, especially dear Hugh, yielding, collapsing, leaving little to get hold of or – on occasions – to respect.

'Once you couldn't get enough of me, remember...?'

'Stop, Helena, okay? Just stop. The way you go on so, it doesn't help. I mean it *really* doesn't help.'

I switched off the music and let my legs buckle, dropping into a cross-legged position in the middle of the sofa. 'Most men would be happy at such interest,' I mumbled. 'I could have had any man I wanted...'

'Oh, don't worry, I am well aware of that.'

'But I chose you.' I felt empty suddenly, with a little bubble of anger sitting in the middle of it. 'You never think about how I feel.'

'I *always* think how you feel, Helena. Indeed, I think of little else. Because you never let it be otherwise.'

'Oh, fuck off, Jack.' It was a throwaway mutter, but I would still have retracted it if I could.

'Yup. I think I shall. To bed.'

When he didn't move, I was glad. 'There isn't someone else, is there, Jack? Someone who *does* turn you on like I used to?' It was a ploy, but good nonetheless to see the surprise on his face and hear the hint of genuine softness in his tone when he told me that of course there wasn't and not to be silly.

'Not that I wouldn't have grounds,' he added sharply, as if he remembered we were arguing, 'with you and Hugh canoodling like bloody teenagers.'

'You're not jealous of Hugh.' The row was coming back into focus for me too. A second wind.

'Is that so?'

'Yes. You've never been jealous of Hugh. Because you know there is nothing to be jealous of. You *know*. So, don't play that card when what's really pissing you off is what I said about you being a lazy arse.'

'Funnily enough, that did piss me off, Helena, yes. Because how dare you judge me like that, when you have no idea – *no idea* – what it takes to create something?' The patches of cheek above his beard had gone very red and the veins in his neck were standing out. 'When all you've ever done is spend Daddy's money and collect things other people have made or written. When all that's really pissing *you* off is how I haven't turned into quite the cash cow you envisaged when you married me.'

'Cash cow?' I hooted viciously. New energy was ripping through me. My sister Christabel was the one who couldn't stand on her own two feet, not me. Massive financial backup was always on hand – our father's generosity could be overwhelming – but I at least always tried to keep working, to be my own woman. Not succeeding as much as I would have liked had never been from lack of effort. 'No-hoper, more like. Loser.' I formed the shape of an L on my forehead, sticking my tongue out.

I could feel the bubble of anger growing, filling the emptiness, the wonderful liberation of it, allowing things to be said – and done – that should never be said and done between two people who have sworn to love each other until death did them part. I was standing again on the sofa, my knees shaking, but this time as much from being fired up as the effort of maintaining my balance. The hairs up my arms and on the back of my neck felt shivery and upright. We were sliding into the territory of home truths and I could beat Jack at those any day, because he was afraid of them and I wasn't. And though he kicked all the way, I also knew that it was our big rows that occasionally galvanised him, almost as if the rage in me could become a channel for him, finally, to shut himself in his studio and at least try to prove me wrong.

Steadying myself, I reached down to the table for my wine glass and drank it in one gulp. I then tossed it to the other end of the sofa, and wiped my mouth on the sleeve of my shirt.

'I'm not playing, Helena,' he said stonily, 'not tonight.'

'Playing what, sweetheart?'

'Punchbag.'

'Diddums. You'd be nowhere without me. Nowhere. Daddy's money – my money – in case you hadn't noticed, keeps you in the manner you so need.'

'The terrible thing is that you have got me believing that. But, actually, it's about being kept in the manner *you* need. Not me. I need very little—'

'Is that so? Excuse me while I laugh.' I made an ugly braying sound, aware suddenly of being as sad as I was angry and the impossibility, somehow, of communicating that.

'And though you bang on about me not working,' Jack ploughed on, 'you have no interest or faith in anything I produce anyway.'

'Bollocks.' I could tell he was getting drawn in in spite of himself. He wanted to walk away, but he couldn't – because we were at the nub of things now and he cared as much as I did. The no-sex was nothing compared to this. 'The problem, Jack, is that there is nothing now for me to have faith or interest *in*—'

'There is,' he cried, wagging his finger at me like a headmaster. 'There's loads of stuff... or at least, there has been over the years. You just don't really pay attention any more—'

'I do. You've got two things on the go, a vase with some roses in it, and a view of our front door. More fucking roses. Talk about twee. Talk about vapid. Worthy of a greetings card. Where's the man who did this, that's what I want to know.' I jerked my thumb at the picture behind me. 'Where's the man I married?'

'You bitch.' The words were a hiss of exhaled air. His hands were balled into fists. 'You drunken bitch.'

'It's because I know you.'

'Like fuck. I'm going. To the spare room.'

'Don't you dare turn your back on me, Jack Aspen.'

He laughed bitterly. 'Oh, I dare.'

He turned and I leapt off the sofa, elbowing my way past so I was out of the room first. 'I'll show you what I think of your work. I'll show you.'

The bubble had exploded now and I was flying up the stairs to the top floor, nimble on the balls of my bare feet. I could hear Jack's heavier footsteps behind me, chasing, panicking. His studio was his sanctum, his bolthole, an airy, asymmetrical room built into the roof of the house, with views towards the Heath and the northern suburbs. We had spent a lot of the money he was so quick to despise making it as perfect a space as it could be, installing extra windows for light and building cupboards into the eaves for canvas storage, thereby maximising the room available for the several easels from which he liked to work at simultaneous projects (never concentrating on one properly, in my view) and the various paint tables scattered in between. Against the central wall was a small beautiful Jacobean desk that had belonged to my mother, hidden under a shameful mess of unsorted papers and pots of pens and brushes, with his laptop, freckled with paint, in the middle of it.

Having charged into the room first, it was from out of this mayhem that I plucked a large red felt-pen, tugging the lid off and turning to face Jack with it as he appeared in the doorway.

'Get the fuck out.'

'No.' I took up the pose of a fencer, lunging forwards, pointing the pen's fat red tip like a sword, the other arm raised up behind my head for balance.

'You are so plastered.'

'Maybe. But at least, as somebody once said to somebody, I shall still be beautiful in the morning, unlike... *that*.' I swung round, using the pen now to indicate the half-sketched, half-painted blue vase of white roses on the nearest easel, untouched for so long that specks of dust had settled along the top edge of it.

'You disgust me,' he said, which I thought was pretty good in the circumstances; so good indeed, that I found the hand in charge of the felt-pen stabbing at the half-painted vase. I had intended the motion only as a threat, but somehow the tip made contact with the canvas and before I knew it, I was writing – scrawling – the first words that came into my head. Cruel words, like a bleeding gash in the paint. *Your crap.*

Jack let out a roar and I dropped the pen, the spell of anger shattered, remorse flooding in. In the same moment, the door thundered shut and Jack's footsteps thumped down the stairs, heavy with his fury and unhappiness.

I stood still for a while, my head pounding and the insipid vase glaring at me with its open wound. Picking up a cleanish rag from a paint table, I spat on it and began, feebly, to wipe at the red letters, only succeeding in smudging them into something even worse. The alcohol was felling me now, weighing me down.

Downstairs, the spare-room door banged shut with a force that sent a tremor up through the floorboards. I picked my way to the corner of the studio, where a small yellow sofa, half covered in an old blanket, was tucked under the slant of the eaves. I clambered onto it, curling onto my side in a tight ball and tucking the blanket under my chin and round my bare legs. I shut my eyes, but my brain held on for a while, flinging out worries as it spun, about the next day and coping with Daphne's London visit and whether Jack's inevitable seething would extend to a boycott of his promise to attend the Moorlands *Victoriana* auction for me.

I vowed not to mind if it did. A few old books didn't matter. Not many things did in the end. Regret was lapping at the edges of my consciousness, but I shoved it back. *At least I've shown him,* I thought, *at least he knows that beneath all the crap I, too, am raw and full of caring.*

CHAPTER 8

'Hello, stranger.'

'Christabel.' I kissed my elder sister, too used to her digs about the infrequency of Jack's and my Cornwall visits to rise to the bait. She had clearly just arrived herself – on foot, to judge from the absence of her car and the fresh mud on her wellingtons. Living near our father, she got the brunt, coming by most days; but she loved the area and owned a dream house for her pains – a sizeable picturesque cottage in the next village, bought by Daddy for her when the ridiculous candle-making company imploded with debts. 'How is he?'

'Not great this week. They've readjusted the meds. But looking forward to seeing you,' she added, such a light of fondness, as well as a trace of envy, scudding across her big blue eyes that I felt a spurt of guilt and grabbed her again for a proper hello-hug.

Across her shoulder, my gaze feasted on the slope of ragged coast-line fringing the shimmering grey seascape and our father's house, parked among terraced lawns on the clifftop – an extraordinary rectangular, multi-levelled glass box that seemed to merge with the majestic beauty of its surroundings. Commissioned by him during the passion for avant-garde architecture which had seen the decampment from our old sprawling family house in Norfolk twenty years before, the designers had won several awards for innovation.

My mother had at first resisted strongly, dubbing it the Ice Cube, but then had quickly grown to love the place once they moved in, not just for the daily panoramas of earth and sea and sky, but because after decades of patching up mercurial damp patches, crumbling floorboards and ancient pipes, the plethora of smooth-running modern conveniences made her swoon. And she felt so safe there, she said, which was terrible and ironic given that it was a local teenage joyrider who had managed to put her in her grave within a year of the move, knocking all of us to pieces in the process.

It always meant a lot to me that my mother had loved the house. I loved every inch of it too. Which was why, whenever Jack gave vent to the bee in his bonnet about getting a bolthole somewhere in Spain, I reminded him we had Cornwall in the wings – if it came my way, which I had every reason to believe it would, what with Daddy's hints on the subject over the years and Christabel never being afraid to say she loved her cottage and found the Cube far too big and impersonal for her own tastes.

'Hey Jack,' Christabel said, releasing me and ambling across the gravelled drive to where Jack was still busy pulling our bags out of the boot and making enough of a to-do of it for me to know that the silent treatment during our long car journey had still not seen the end of my punishment. After the Friday-night row and red-pen incident, the weekend had been predictably sticky, with him holed up either in his studio or the spare room, between taking himself off for long walks on the Heath. But the *Victoriana* auction had at least been attended and the book lot secured (I had exaggerated my gratitude), and there had even been a couple of cursory enquiries about my time with Daphne. I had responded as engagingly as I could – my godmother, with her scattiness and predilection for extravagant, peculiar headgear (an ostrich feather in what could have passed for a blancmange had been the choice for Saturday) was an easy target for humour – but nothing I said had so far succeeded in evoking the remotest inkling of relenting in my husband's granite mood.

Then, that morning, despite a plan to leave London first thing, he had gone on another, sudden, maddeningly long solo walk, so long indeed that I had progressed rapidly through see-if-I-care irritation to a state of near panic. Finding he had locked the door of his precious studio hadn't helped. Never, in our thirteen years of marriage, had Jack turned a key to keep me out of anywhere. A slap in the face could not have stung more.

'Still painting?' Christabel asked him in her hapless way, as if Jack might have taken up juggling or plumbing instead.

A caustic reply would have been justified, but Jack merely grinned and pecked her on the cheek, saying, 'Yes, still painting, Chrissie, and how goes it with you?' before slinging his artwork bag over one shoulder and picking up both our suitcases. The amount of luggage was because we were staying for a full two weeks, the idea being to give Christabel a proper break, though quite what she was going to do with it, other than hang around us, remained unclear.

'Welcome all,' hollered my father, which was what he always said, waving his stick from the front doorstep.

I let Christabel get to him first, scolding that he would catch cold as she hurried along the long narrow shingle path to the house, her muddy wellingtons crunching on the stones and her long straggly hair flying over the shoulders of her big old green coat.

I followed with a show of eager cheerfulness that belied the twisting of my heart. It was only three months since our Christmas visit, but there was no denying the increased gauntness in my father's once broad, handsome face and the new looseness across the shoulders of the horrible oatmeal cardigan he had on over his smart black cashmere polo top. Celebratedly youthful-looking all his life, it was a shock to catch myself thinking he was starting to look nearer ninety than seventy-one.

'Hello, dear child.' He kissed me and held out a trembling hand to

Jack, who quickly set down the bags in order to clasp it firmly in both his, as if he would iron out the hateful shaking if he could.

'Ralph, good to see you.'

'I'm so glad you're staying for a decent stretch,' Daddy went on brightly, slipping his hand into his cardigan pocket the moment Jack let go. 'I've asked Anya to put you in the blue room this time, because it's so much larger than Helena's, and has the biggest and best bathroom in the house, the one your mother used to complain we should have designed for our own quarters.'

'That's super,' I murmured, wondering how many times we had heard the bathroom thing and feeling sad about that too. 'And you look well, Father,' I said firmly, looping my arm through his and briefly dropping my head onto his shoulder as we progressed inside, feeling its boniness through my hair. 'I'd love some tea. Is there tea?'

'There's always tea, and one of Anya's cakes, carrot, I believe, her aim being to keep me healthy.'

'Ah, well that sounds heavenly and carrot's Jack's favourite, isn't it, Jack, so I'll have a happy husband on my hands, which is always nice.' I tried to catch Jack's eye, but we had arrived in the big square parquet-floored hall and he was busy setting down the cases in order to turn the beam of his charm on the housekeeper, approaching with her usual deference, drying her hands on her spotless apron, her plump, ageless face beaming. She loved Jack. Everybody did. It was one of the endlessly endearing and galling things about him.

'Dearest Anya, I hear you've been slaving in preparation for us,' he told her, having to bend almost in two to place kisses on both the housekeeper's ruddy cheeks. 'You are a wonder. And Ralph says we're on the top floor in the executive suite, so I'll take these straight up there now – on my *own*, thank you,' he added, scooping up the luggage before she could reach it.

'Come down for tea,' I called, sounding more commanding than I meant as he headed off up the staircase, which forged through the middle of the house like an artery, branching left and right to its furthest corners.

'Dad had a complete freeze,' Christabel whispered, when we were seated with tea things in the drawing room, snug between the bright furnace of a crackling open fire and the treble-glazed windows separating us from the lawn terraces and their dramatic backdrop of sea, that day a choppy grey stew which made the greenness of the garden and its dividing white pathways gleam in contrast. Father, full of his old charm and some animated discussion about the markets which he played, successfully, like a seasoned gambler, had left us for a visit to the bathroom. And he was walking well, I had decided with a burst of happiness, watching his retreating back, an impression which made this news of Christabel's all the harder to receive.

'Freeze?'

'It's why the meds got adjusted. I told you that, didn't I? We saw the doctor. I mean, Dad said he just suddenly couldn't move.' She threw an anxious glance in the direction of the door and leant closer, folding her arms across the baggy brown jumper of a dress she was wearing, a home-knit by the look of it, though I disliked it too much to ask. 'He was trying to do up a shoelace, apparently. I think he found it terrifying.'

'Oh God.'

'We did know it would come to this...'

'But not so soon.' I hated how accepting she sounded, like the battle was already lost.

'Apparently learning taekwondo can help. Or ballroom dancing,' Christabel rushed on brightly, undeterred by my withering looks. 'I heard a programme on the radio all about it. Something to do with learning to use new neural pathways. There's also this amazing research place in Bristol – I found it on the internet – where they want sufferers to volunteer to be monitored with all sorts of new-fangled equipment for measuring fluctuations in symptoms, the point being that they can then get a detailed picture of how the disease is progressing and develop tailor-made treatments.'

'He's got Parkinson's,' I said dully, finding that my sister's efforts at being hopeful were even harder to take than bad news. 'And you are right, we did know it would come to this. Just as we know it's going to get worse.' I turned my gaze back to the view. The light was failing now, the sea blacker, the grass grey, the shingle paths like dimming strip-lights.

Christabel was staring at the orange crumbs on her plate, gathering resolve to speak again. At forty-three, she was two years older than me and the same tall, slim build, but with a consistent lack of interest in advertising the fact that left me admiring and mystified in equal measure. Looking good was part of my secret armour against the world, integral to how I stayed strong; I couldn't imagine being parted from it.

'Of course, Daddy thought it was all nonsense too, just like you. But then, the pair of you were always the obstinate ones.' She picked at a loose stitch on her sleeve, smiling ruefully as the memory of our mother flickered between us, the two of them, with their softer natures, having been more aligned. 'He says he's got enough doctors and appointments in his life, thank you, and that he's managing fine and that I'm not to mention it again. He got pretty furious, actually. Oh lord, do you have to, Helly?' she moaned, seeing me reach into my bag for my cigarettes.

'He likes it,' I retorted, 'it makes him feel less alone with his pipes.' As there was still no sign of our father, however, and because it was a habit she detested, I dropped the packet back between the small, open jaws of my handbag, and settled deeper into my chair, folding my arms across my stomach and stretching my legs under the table. I was wearing my favourite knee-high black suede boots, as soft as slippers, and couldn't help thinking what a stark contrast they made to the thick old socks on my sister's feet, revealed when the wellies had been tugged off. 'But how horrible about the freeze, Christy. Terrifying.' I shuddered, wondering suddenly where Jack had got to and wishing he would come. 'I didn't mean to snap just now – about your ideas for things that might help. Ballroom dancing, skydiving – whatever works. I've always quite fancied taking it up myself actually, dancing that is.' I nudged one of the socks under the table, forcing her to look at me and grinning when she did. We had each carved out our roles over the decades, and one of mine was to make her laugh. 'Have you packed in your stints at the crystal shop yet, like you said you would?'

'Yes... well, no... that is, I still help Marilyn out from time to time.'

'And you are a marvel with Daddy,' I went on quickly, because she truly was, and because an urge to say something disparaging was in danger of overwhelming me – on the subject of crystals, and the prices the witchy Marilyn sold them for, on the back of laughable claims about powers of healing and energy emission. It was no time for my sharpness, I knew. Besides which, Christabel was always an unfair target anyway, tending – unlike Jack – to take everything lying down. I was also aware of being in something of a weird mood – because of Daddy no doubt, and the row with Jack. I could feel myself searching for something to lash out at. Something that didn't matter. And Marilyn did matter, I reminded myself, shooting my sister a smile, because she was Christabel's friend.

'I want to have a baby, Helly,' she blurted, 'before it's too late. I'm looking for a donor. Online.' She sat forwards, casting another look in the direction of the door. 'Please don't tell Daddy. Or Jack. Or anyone. It will probably come to nothing anyway.' Her expression was guarded, but her strong blue eyes blazed. 'And don't tell me I'm mad even though that's what you think.'

'It is not remotely what I think,' I countered hastily, attempting, through my astonishment, to imagine Christabel, barely in charge of her own life, coping with a child. A string of flaky relationships had got her nowhere near the temptation of marriage or motherhood that I knew of, and – apart from one brief flurry of panic in her mid-thirties – she had never seemed that bothered.

'I was also a bit worried that...' She paused. '...That you might mind. Or something.'

'Really? Well, I can assure you, I totally don't. Jack and I have never wanted kids, as you know. Having him to look after is quite enough, thank you,' I added, in a bid to be light-hearted that didn't quite come off.

'Yes, Helena, I know that's what you have always said. But that's not what I was referring to.'

I didn't speak, because I knew only too well what she was referring to, and it had been agreed that we would never refer to it.

She dropped her gaze to her hands, now twisting in her lap. 'I know what we always said, but we were so young and a part of me just wondered...'

'Well, you can stop your wondering right there, because I wouldn't change a single thing. Not one, Christabel, okay?' I stared her into submission, my eyes wide with castigation and warning. 'To go down the donor road is brave,' I went on, injecting a calmness into my voice that gave no indication of the churning in my belly, 'but I'm sure you don't need telling that.' The churning, I was certain, wasn't so much about the subject Christabel had raised, as from being caught unawares, on a day when I was feeling off-key generally. 'And, actually, if you were to go ahead with it, I think Daddy might be rather thrilled. Do you remember all the heavy hints he used to drop to Jack and me, until he finally got the message?' I rolled my eyes, even though the memory of my father's barely concealed disappointment was now churning along with everything else.

My sister seemed to be watching me more than she was listening. 'So, you are okay about it?'

'My god, Christy, yes. I think it's wild and amazing – like you. And please tell me as soon as you go ahead, so I know whether to keep my fingers crossed.' I reached across the tea table and squeezed her hand. 'Remember though, hon, babies, like puppies, are not just for Christmas – they're a lifelong ball and chain.' I pulled one of my old goofy faces and she laughed.

* * *

'It's okay being here, isn't it?' I flung an arm across the icy wasteland of sheet, finding Jack's hand, but he tugged it away.

'Yep. Let's get some sleep.'

'Although it's clearly not completely okay, is it? Why, otherwise, would you be behaving as if the person with whom you are sharing this sizeable piece of furniture has contracted the plague?'

'I am tired, Helena.' He sounded tired, but in a with-life kind of way, instead of with-sleepiness.

'The way you treated me at dinner – I might as well not have been there,' I continued.

'I was talking to your father, and to your sister, as you might recall. Being a good son-in-law and brother-in-law, as you like to encourage. And I treated you perfectly. I always do. But it is never enough with you. Nothing. Is. Ever. Enough. You dig. And dig. And dig. Now, please let me sleep.'

I hesitated, filing through my options of what to say next, how to get him to relent, play ball. He was still cross about the mess I had made with the red pen, I knew that much, but I had said sorry several times, both over the weekend and again in the car, and there was just so much humble pie one woman could eat. He was indeed great with all my relatives, perhaps because of not really having any of his own. An only child, he had lost his mother at nine and been ostracised by the woman who replaced her. A Canadian, she had packed him off to boarding school and whisked his father to Ottawa, where they proceeded to start a new family in which Jack had never felt welcome. It was a story that had evoked my pity when I first heard it, prompting all sorts of ingenious schemes for retribution and revenge – if only because of the money side of things, since the half-siblings were spoilt rotten and Jack never got a look-in – but Jack had always backed down or laughed them off; and now years had gone by without anyone being in touch with anyone.

Jack was such an ostrich, I fumed now, so bloody passive and bottled up, it was little wonder it drove me mad, even on a good day. Not even the revelation, bursting out of me as soon as we were upstairs, about poor Daddy's episode of paralysis had succeeded in breaking through this new iron wall. 'Oh dear,' he had murmured, looking vaguely dismayed, as if we were talking about some dim acquaintance, instead of *my father*, Ralph De Vere, once the fittest, brightest, most accomplished, cultured man either of us knew, now locked in battle with a body hurtling towards the prospect of becoming its own coffin.

I scrutinised Jack's outline, hunched away from me. A couple more inches and he'd topple onto the floor, I decided gleefully. But then he didn't budge and the room began to seem very quiet, which was more than a little unsettling, given how the elements were raging outside its hermetically sealed walls. Venturing into the garden after dinner, half hoping Jack, with his recent passion for fresh air, would follow, I had been almost blown off my feet, and received an unpleasant drenching too, from all the salty moisture in the lashing. I had felt quite sorry for myself, but stayed out long enough for it to appear as if I might have been enjoying the experience, hopping up and down to keep my feet warm and trying not to be seen as I stole peeps at Jack through the window, on the sofa in the glow of the fire, laughing and talking with Ralph and Christabel, as if I was the last thing on his mind, when I knew bloody well I was the first.

I found his calf with my foot. 'Guess what. Christabel wants a baby. She's trawling the net for a donor.'

'Good for Christabel.'

'Aren't you surprised?' I traced the curve of his muscle with my toes, thinking what great legs men so often had, keeping their shape and firmness even without proper sport and no matter how much the rest of their bodies went to pot. Not that Jack's body was doing any such thing. I loved Jack's body. I wanted him to wrap it round mine. Like he used to. More than I could cope with sometimes. It occurred to me suddenly that the last time we had, with any full, technical success, made love, had been under this very roof, downstairs in my smaller bedroom, well over six months before. It hadn't been great. We had both drunk a lot. But Jack had managed. Afterwards, I had used that very word, 'managed', in a bid to make a joke of it that had fallen flat. Nothing had been quite the same since, which was possibly significant, but also made me feel pretty helpless. 'Jack?' I snuggled closer, trying to tuck my knees into the backs of his, even though I could tell he didn't really want them there.

'Nothing about your sister surprises me.'

'And you don't have any regrets of your own on the subject, have you?' I asked softly. The conversation with Christabel was echoing back at me. It had been thoughtful of her to ask, I decided – very sweet and sisterly.

'What subject?'

'You know bloody well what. Offspring.' He had straightened his legs so my knees had nothing to tuck into.

'Not for a moment.'

'Good.' This was what I had hoped – expected – to hear. Jack had been totally happy about me explaining, very early on, that, despite my uncooperative reproductive system, I had no interest in having children anyway. More time for each other, we used to say. And yet there was something in this response of his now that felt like rejection. 'I can't imagine it though,' I pushed on, 'Christabel with a baby...' All I wanted – yearned for – was one of our chats, about my kind and hopeless sister. Instead, the weight of the silence grew, leaving me to ponder the power of all that filled it, the choices of what to grab at and what to leave alone. 'I would hate to turn out like Daphne though,' I tried finally, 'alone apart from her hats.' My voice had shrunk to something small and full of need, but Jack appeared to have fallen asleep.

I let outrage fill me instead, rolling away from him and onto my back. To be ignored. As if I didn't exist. When I was trying so hard. How dare he. How fucking dare he. And who was Jack Aspen, anyway, I told myself, other than a mildly talented semi-orphan of a painter with a decent body and ridiculously penetrating blue eyes who had chatted me up in a gallery fourteen years ago.

I wanted to stay angry, but now all the early memories were nudging their way in. Jack had seemed to let life wash over him, that was one of the things I had first noticed, adoring him for it, little knowing it would prove to be one of the biggest aggravations. While he, in turn, had liked how I did the opposite – calling out everything as

I saw it, attacking without fear, loyal as a rottweiler, even with a lost cause. I couldn't do eggshells or pussyfooting, and with his upbringing of exactly such horrors – stiff, false affections from a stepmother who wanted only to eject him from the nest and a father too weak to resist – it was precisely this forthrightness of mine that Jack had latched onto most keenly. He had seemed to like me for me, in other words, in stark contrast to all the other men always falling at my feet, not able to see past a head of long fair hair and a decent set of legs.

The art side of things had been key too; my contacts, my sense of taste, which Jack used to say could only be born with and never learnt. How I had loved it when he said that. And then there were his early canvases, some of which – even before the wedding gift – had stopped me in my tracks. At an early, tiny exhibition I had blagged into being – helped by a friend of my mother's – he had sold out. We had seemed like the perfect team. We were the perfect team.

Except my subsequent efforts had petered out because he was a touchy, lazy obstinate arse, I reminded myself, retreating even further to my side of the vast bed, making a commotion of it, punching the pillows and settling with noisy sighs. I already knew I wouldn't sleep, that I would need one of my knockout pills, and it was all Jack's fault.

I kicked my half of the duvet back and folded my arms across my chest, staring at the long cream curtains, ghostly in the dark. Jack and I were like two stone effigies on a tomb, I decided, dead and icy, lying side by side. Lord and Lady somebody in some forgotten dark corner of a chilly church. The heavy drapes seemed to stir and, before I knew it, the shivers of fragility that had been lurking all day were coalescing into something far worse; something that reminded me of the nameless anxiety that had intermittently dogged my teens and then briefly resurged in the aftermath of losing my mother. To be afraid when you couldn't see a reason. To be afraid of fear. It was the worst sort of invisible enemy and though Hugh had never been able to deal with it, Jack could. Jack had been steady, soothing, kind. '*I am here*,' he used to say. '*I'll always be here, Helena.*'

I was warm, but the shivering was getting worse and my throat felt curiously dry. Enervation was seeping through me, sucking me down. Even summoning the energy – the courage – to venture into the adjoining bathroom for a pill began to feel beyond my capabilities. I wanted the curtains to stir, but they were still as marble. At the window, a branch, bare and gnarled as a skeletal hand, waved in and out of view, tossed on the silent wind. I pulled the duvet back up over my sticky skin. I whispered Jack's name, but he still didn't reply.

CHAPTER 9

I

'So, Cornwall went well?' Hugh waved a menu at a waiter, indicating we were ready to order. We were in the most old-fashioned of his various clubs, an oak-panelled place with plush carpets and high ceilings, and a general atmosphere of such propriety that I always had to fight the urge to misbehave.

'If you call getting flu, and Jack being in the foulest mood, and Christabel drifting in and out with the ghastly Marilyn in tow, and Madeleine WhatsApping hourly with some new panic about the structural problems of her wretched gallery, and darling Daddy, of course,' I swallowed in time to catch the lump in my throat, 'deteriorating visibly by the bloody day, then, yes, thank you, Cornwall was a riot.'

'Poor Helly,' Hugh murmured, busy trying the wine with his usual seriousness, even though he had invited me to taste it for the waiter and the stuff was perfectly delicious, as evinced by my own glass already being in need of a top-up.

'Though Christabel was very sweet on her own...' I managed to stop short of mentioning the donor-baby plans. It most definitely wasn't a Hugh sort of subject, and I already felt a bit bad for having told Jack.

'Your sister was always sweet,' said Hugh mildly, taking a proper swig of his wine at last, 'though also always somewhat *in search* of herself, from what I recall—'

'Well, we're all on *that* goose chase,' I interjected, feeling I was defending my sister, who no one on earth was allowed to criticise but me. 'In fact, everywhere I go I keep an eye out... just in case I find myself lurking...' I made a jokey show of looking under the table, joining in with Hugh when he laughed. I could feel the alcohol lifting me up and carrying me towards the wonderful place where I needed to be, where the world could be looked at rather than lived in, a spectator sport.

We were well into April and it helped that Cornwall was starting to feel pleasingly remote, something to poke fun at rather than be depressed by. Whatever bug had laid me out, caught – everyone agreed – while I was so misguidedly braving the elements after supper on the first night, it had been fierce. By the middle of the following morning I had been vomiting, with fevers soaking the sheets and throat glands swollen to ping-pong balls. I promptly quarantined myself down in my old bedroom and forbade visitors, instructions that were nobly ignored by Christabel, Jack and Anya, who all took it in turns to check on me – gingerly, it has to be said – with offers of analgesics and mugs of soup, and then, on the fourth day, by a local GP, summoned at my sister's command, who checked me over properly before prescribing penicillin.

'So, you're better now? From the flu?' Hugh peered at me, an expression of such concern momentarily clouding his face that I wondered suddenly if all my efforts to look nice for the lunch had been in vain. Hair, feet, nails, eyebrows, teeth, facials – I had been doing the rounds since getting back from the West Country, feeling with each appointment that I was rebuilding and preparing my defences against something big, though quite what I couldn't have said.

'Oh, completely. It was a nasty bout, but I'm totally fine.' The waiter had delivered our starters with a flourish. I had ordered six snails, each curled in its slithery shell-nest of oil and garlic. At the sight of them, I was aware of a mild wave of revulsion rising and receding. I loved snails, I reminded myself. I was hungry, and one hundred per cent well. I started to eat, with determined relish, but could not quite shake the feeling of trying to swallow something other than food. The wine, thankfully, was a big help, and I drank it fast, making Hugh chuckle as he ordered a second bottle.

'I've got something for you,' he announced gaily, once it had been opened and our glasses refilled. 'That favour I mentioned?' He plucked a set of door keys out of his jacket pocket and laid them next to my side plate. 'For the flat. When you have the time. As you know, I'm off on one of my jaunts next week – New York, maybe Bermuda, definitely France—'

'Washing that girl right out of your hair,' I sang, picking up the keys, a yale and a Chubb on a heavy brass ring, and swinging them round my finger.

'Exactly. Paula Recovery Therapy. Actually, that's going well – the lawyers have everything in hand and there's no question of it reaching court, thank god.' He flashed one of his tight keep-off-the-subject smiles. 'As to the flat, it's just over Wandsworth Bridge, near Spencer Park, part of a new-build with underground parking, a gym and all that sort of thing, but I'll send you the details. It's easy to find and really rather nice, with a view of a bit of the river, if you look hard enough. Three bedrooms, two bathrooms, a big sitting room and a decent kitchen. All the basics and fittings are done. I just need furnishings – anything you like, within reason. I trust you implicitly, Helly, as you know. Email me the invoices and I'll settle as we go. By the end of the summer would be nice, but no rush. My accountant says I should hold back on renting till next year anyway, because of you-know-who, not to mention the taxman.'

'Permission to go wild then – a fun project. Exactly what I need.' I dropped the keys into my bag, on the floor by my chair and threw him a heartfelt smile of gratitude. Work always gave me a lift and I was good at it. 'Prepare for shades of purple and lime, in that case. Or scarlet and gold. Or Barbie pink.' I took another long swig of the glorious St Veran, still seeking something that it wasn't quite providing. The snail shells had been replaced by my mains, a rainbow trout nestling on a lush bed of samphire, all of it fringed with frills of radish and tomato. Like a still life, I kept thinking, too perfect to eat.

'And how's that husband of yours?' Hugh ventured, having, I sensed, bided his time to raise the subject.

I tore at the small, untouched brown roll on my side plate. I wanted to tell Hugh that – like my health – Jack was fine, but found that I couldn't. I lifted a piece of crust to my mouth and then put it down. If I couldn't be straight with my oldest friend, there was no point to anything. 'Actually, the Cornwall sulk I mentioned, it's still going on. I did something and he hasn't forgiven me.'

'Oh dear.' Hugh eyed me tenderly. 'And may I ask what it was that you did?'

I took a deep breath and launched into a description of the row that took place on the night of his visit and the act of graffiti with the red felt-pen that had followed. I made it sound as funny as I could – playing up the melodrama – but instead of laughing, Hugh looked aghast and said little wonder Jack was hacked off.

'But it was weeks and weeks ago, Hugh – two months in fact – and you know how drunk we all were. And it's not like I haven't apologised. I have. So many times. But he still won't be *normal* with me. He says normal things, but it's like he's keeping me at bay, like he's going through the motions. All he does is hunker down in his studio all day, or disappear off on *walks* – that's his new thing. He takes a sketchbook and is gone for hours, and even when he asks me if I want to come, I can tell he doesn't really mean it. It's like he's there, but not there. It's like I'm losing him, Hugh,' I ended miserably, framing this thought for the first time. I pushed my plate away, sickened suddenly by the trout's vacant, rheumy one-eyed gaze.

'Losing him to his work, right?'

'Yes...' This is what it should have felt like, I realised, but it didn't.

'But that's great, isn't it, Helena? It's what you've been wanting?'

'Yes, I suppose...' I was aware of how unreasonable I was sounding, after all the years of on-off complaining about Jack's cavalier attitude to his talent. 'But he's taken to locking his studio door,' I burst out, trying to explain to myself as much as to Hugh the acuteness of my feelings. 'I mean, Jack is literally *locking* the fucking door on me and hiding the fucking key.' I finished the last swallow of wine in my glass and refilled it. 'I keep asking him what's wrong, but he says nothing, and then I get angry and then...'

'Maybe let him be for a bit.' Hugh's hazel eyes were gentle, but his voice stern. 'Give the man some peace. You know how you can be, Helly, how you don't let things rest, even when you should. Now, do eat something, there's a good girl.' He pushed my plate back towards me. 'That's about ten quid a bite you're ignoring there.'

I pulled a face and picked up my knife and fork.

'Remember, Jack is Jack,' he said, all playful and sweet now.

'Yes, he is.'

'And you adore him.'

'Yes, I do.'

'And he adores you.'

'I think so, Hugh. I hope so. I mean, we are a good team, aren't we?'

'Yes, you are. A fantastic team. The best team I know.'

I began to eat, ravenous suddenly. It felt great to have confided in Hugh. He was right, I was letting things get to me – as I tended to – and needed to stop the rot. There were other matters weighing on my mind, that was the trouble, with Daddy being so sick and all Christabel's talk of babies. It would probably turn into another of her fads, but even so.

The trout was delicious, light and sweet, falling off its bones, and each bite of samphire like a snapshot of the sea, its saltiness working so well, so soothingly, against the cool buttery flavours in my wine glass, that it was all I could do not to groan out loud. I talked on between mouthfuls instead, expanding on my theory about Jack sometimes needing to get in a rage at me in order to galvanise himself, and seeing more and more the sense and comfort of it. 'Actually, Hugh, he's got some really interesting stuff on the go – tackling old half-finished projects and doing these new sketches of people on his walkabouts – he's going to work them up into a series of portraits, he says.'

Hugh laughed. 'I thought you said you'd been locked out?'

'Ah... yes.' I pretended to look guilty, though I didn't remotely feel it. 'He forgot the other day, didn't he, and being no fool...'

'You are many things, Helly, but never that.' Hugh shook his head fondly as I went on to confess that I had not only had a good rootle around Jack's studio, but found myself unable to resist the urge to take some pictures of what he was up to, out of sheer excitement. 'Go on then,' he laughed, 'let's see.'

I found the photos on my phone and handed it across the table. 'Thank you, darling, for this lovely lunch,' I said, my voice a little husky with emotion as I watched him scroll through the images, giving them his full concentration, as was his way. 'I am going to miss you madly while you are gone, you know that don't you, and I promise I shall try my hardest to give Jack a bit more... What?'

Hugh had stopped on one photo and was expanding and contracting it with his fingertips.

'Which one are you looking at?'

'The people picnicking by a lake – I like it a lot. Strong structure. Lovely colours. It could be Paris, early last century. Is it Paris?'

'I think it's Spain. It's from an old photo, one of the canvases he's been resurrecting. Lovely isn't it? I know I am only an interior designer with artistic pretentions, but Jack does water so well, doesn't he? And people, don't you think he's really good at people?'

Hugh chuckled as he handed the phone back. 'Yes, your artist-in-residence is good at people, and water, and a host of other things besides. And, if that particular one ever gets finished, I might be tempted to add it to my Aspen collection. Maybe find a space for it in the flat? For a proper price, naturally.'

'Oh, Hugh, that would be amazing. Wow. I'll keep you posted on its progress.' I picked up my glass to celebrate, but it was empty, and when I tried the bottle in the ice bucket, there was none left there either.

Hugh signalled for the bill and asked me what my plans were for the afternoon. There was a hint of solicitousness in his voice, which I wasn't sure I liked.

'Mayfair and Maddy. The bloody place flooded – did I tell you? – and that was after the boiler blew – it's like she's been cursed. All my hard work and we're nearly back to square one. None of it is the decorator's fault, I might add...'

Hugh settled up with the waiter as I chattered.

Reaching for my bag as we got up to go, I somehow managed to knock it over instead. I watched, faintly mesmerised, as several lipsticks, pens and a tampon holder, spun across the polished floor towards the legs of neighbouring tables and diners. It was Hugh who leapt up to retrieve them, apologising, cool and graceful, and snapping the bag shut before he handed it back to me.

'Are you taking a taxi?' he said once we were outside.

'What else?'

'Give me a hug then, and promise to take care.'

I pressed my face into his jacket, holding on a little too hard, a little too long as bleakness surged. A sharp breeze whipping down St James's was making my eyes stream.

'Perhaps go a little easier on the sauce, while I'm gone?'

I snorted, pulling free. 'Well, that is rich.'

'I know, which is why I can say it.'

'Fuck off.'

'Helena, I'm just saying take care of yourself.'

'Ditto.'

'Don't worry, I intend to,' Hugh quipped with his irksome calm, signalling for a taxi he had spotted on the opposite side of the street.

'Lots of pics and messages from your travels, please,' I trilled, as the cab embarked on a U-turn, dimly aware of a need to get our farewell back on track.

'Yes, and feel free to post some Befores and Afters of the flat on that website of yours, won't you. I took a peek yesterday and couldn't help noticing that it looked a little in need of some... refreshing? Another fun project, to keep you out of mischief?'

'Sure thing. Thanks.' I grinned, even though I knew I was still being chastised. Hugh was right. I had been letting things go and it had to stop. I had lost some perspective, but now I would get it back again.

I waved a little madly through the small back window of the cab, and then phoned Jack.

'Hello, darling, it's me.'

'All well?' He sounded a bit breathless.

'I've been having lunch with Hugh, remember?'

'Oh yes. And how was Hugh?'

'Fine. Heading off on his travels tomorrow.'

'Oh, right. When's he back?'

'I've no idea. You know what he's like. And now I've got Maddy.'

'Right. I hope that goes well.'

'Are you at home?'

'No, I'm... out and about.'

'On a *walk*?'

There was affront in his laughter. 'I'm working. As well as it being good for my step count.'

'Since when have you given a sod about your *step count*?'

'Since every health expert in the country started saying it mattered.'

'Right.' I had rung with such good intentions, but the conversation seemed already to be veering off track. 'I wanted to tell you some exciting news,' I blurted. 'Hugh is interested in one of your canvases – that beautiful one of the people by the lake – he said he would pay good money and it's been such ages, hasn't it, since he bought one?'

There was a silence before he spoke. 'That is good, of course... but how does Hugh even know what I am working on? How do you for that matter?'

'Because on Tuesday you forgot to lock your precious door and I had a sneak preview, okay?' I spoke in a rush, and more harshly than I meant, anger flaring at the fact these days of always finding myself on the back foot. 'Everything I saw was wonderful, darling,' I added hurriedly, 'and so I took a couple of pictures – please don't be angry.'

'I wish you hadn't done that.'

'Well, I wish you wouldn't lock me out. You've gone all secretive on me.' I knew I was snapping again. The warmth of the cab was fogging my head.

'I have not gone *secretive*. I have every right to some privacy with my work. *Every* right.' He sounded properly engaged now at least, like he was conversing with me instead of waiting for the conversation to find an end.

'I am glad you are working so hard, Jack, and I do care – I really do,' I whispered. 'Please don't shut me out.'

'You said it was the lake one that Hugh liked?' He was still gruff, but I could hear some hint of relenting.

'Yes, the people with sun-umbrellas and picnics. He thought it was Paris. I said it was Spain. Is it Paris?'

'No, you were right.' He was sounding properly mollified now. The old Jack. I closed my eyes. 'It's Madrid, from an old, very early photo – of a park in the middle of the city. The park is called Retiro.'

'Sorollo territory then.'

'Yes, exactly.'

'Your fave-rave.'

'That's it.'

'We were always going to go there, weren't we? Maybe we will one day. When you are ready for a break. A week in Madrid – it could be fun?'

'It could.' He paused. 'I'd better get on.'

'Don't go, Jack.'

'I'm not going anywhere, except home. I want to crack on while the light is still good.'

'Jack...'

'I'll see you later. Say hello to Madeleine for me.'

The traffic was clearing a little and the taxi moving faster. I leant forward and tapped on the driver's window, instructing him to go via

Selfridges and keep the meter running while I popped inside for a gift. Some champagne would cheer Maddy up, I reasoned, slumping back into my seat, quite apart from her weary interior designer.

I rubbed my temples with my fingertips where a headache was threatening, wondering if I could be less in the mood for the challenges of the afternoon.

II

'Are you okay?'

'Of course, I'm okay.'

'That's not what Jack said.'

'Well, Jack is far from being the fount of all wisdom and truth.' I propped my iPad on a pillow so as to bring Christabel's face more level with mine. 'I assume he asked you to call.'

'He told me about your fall, if that's what you mean. How could I have *not* called? I mean, six stitches—'

'Four. And it's mostly glue. I just slipped over, that's all.' My fingers fluttered to the light piece of gauze covering the shaved and very tender patch on my crown. Outside the bedroom door, I could hear the creak of Jack's step on the landing, and then the quiet weight of his footsteps proceeding upstairs to his studio. He had got up at the abominably early hour that was part of his new work routine, tiptoeing in when he thought I might have woken, to place a mug of freshly ground coffee on my bedside table and open the curtains to the grey daylight that seemed to have settled on May like a shroud. That morning, there had also been two pieces of toast and honey, which I had been touched and happy to see, but then found I couldn't finish because chewing anything remotely hard still hurt my head.

It was a month since my Hugh and Madeleine day. I had been doing my stoical best to follow Hugh's advice and give Jack the *space* he so clearly needed, focusing my attentions instead on sorting out Hugh's flat and not picking fights – not even when Jack, night after night and without apology, took himself off to bed barely moments after we had finished supper. Once, the pair of us had prided ourselves on being hopeless nightbirds, so it was hard not to feel abandoned. Impossible, in fact. Huddling alone on the sofa, with only Netflix and another glass or two for company, it sometimes felt like I didn't have a husband at all, like I was having to face the world – and everything in it – on my own. The only consolation, to which I clung whenever despair threatened, was that, as Hugh had pointed out, Jack was at least working, and that, given my husband's powers of self-containment were as unreliable as his bouts of industry, the phase would pass; and when it did, I would be let back in.

'Hey, and you better not have said anything to Daddy,' I warned my sister, picking up one of the crusts of Jack's toast and sucking the honey off. 'I don't want him worried.'

'Of course, I haven't. So, tell me anyway, what exactly happened?'

I dropped the crust onto the plate and carefully leant back among the wall of pillows designed to prevent bringing my patched wound into contact with the hard, mahogany bedstead. Christabel was wearing a bright lime-green T-shirt and looked lit up and lovely, despite being on-screen. In contrast, my face, with its spilling purple bruise round the left eye, resembled a police mugshot. 'It was embarrassingly stupid, Christy. One minute I'm finishing a quiet late-night ciggie on the patio, the next I've fallen flat on my face. I wasn't even in heels. It was just all the rain we've been having – the stones were slippery as hell. A fucking ice-rink.'

'Icy, you mean?' said Christabel in the dim way of which only she was capable.

'No, dummy, it's May.'

'But it's been so hot here. Baking.'

'Well, *here* we have had a couple of downpours *between* the hot days and it leaves a coating of slime on the patio, which is very *slippery*. I suppose we should get the stones jet-cleaned or something, but the garden is Jack's department and so, of course, nothing happens. I literally took a step, and wham. It could have happened to anyone.'

'Oh, but your poor face,' Christabel crooned, ignoring my cutting tone and craning to get a closer look, her expression fixed in exactly the sort of horrified sympathy I had been most keen to avoid. Instinctively, I leant further back from the screen, only to wince as the wound on my head touched the headboard. 'You really look like you've been in the wars,' she persisted, unwittingly drawing on an old favourite expression of our mother's, which somehow made it harder to hear; 'it must have been such a bang, Helly.'

'I managed to fall against the glass doors, that's all,' I countered briskly. 'At least I didn't break them – now that would have been a drama. Jack was a star, getting me to A & E, and there was a scary amount of blood, because that's head wounds for you – we made a turban out of a bath towel – in fact, I could start a new fashion...' I let the idea hang, unable suddenly to pull off the old trick of being amusing. 'Tell me, how things are with you, anyway? How is Dad and has Awful Alistair been pestering yet? Isn't it early summer when he tends to come out of the woodwork?' My head was throbbing suddenly, as if the glue might give way.

'Dad's actually not too bad, but Alistair Unwin? God no. Why would you ask about him? He hasn't been in touch for years. He left his wife and joined that dating site for lonely farmers, remember, and found true *lurve*.' Christabel laughed, throwing her head back, making her long unkempt hair bounce and displaying her mouth of perfect teeth and suddenly looking so beautifully familiar, so warm, that, for one stabbing moment, all I wanted was to dive through the bloody screen and grab hold of her. Or rather, have her grab hold of me. She would hug me in her enveloping way, pulling me too deeply into the lurid green top, and though I would feel suffocated, and squirm to escape, in that instant, there was nothing in the world I wanted more. 'Look, just take it easy,' she commanded gently, giving me one of her penetrating looks, as if she guessed the longing. 'I'm glad Jack's being nice. You said he's being nice, didn't you?'

'Yes, Jack's been wonderful. He even brought me toast, he...' I nodded, unable to continue because of the recognition that my little accident had indeed prompted loving care from Jack, the first in weeks, it felt like. Months. I managed a smile, while inside a new black seed of a thought gleamed.

'So, you're all right, Helly?'

'God, yes.' The black seed was embedding, spreading, growing – a possibility taking shape, making sense. The possibility of someone else. Another woman.

Behind Christabel, Marilyn's pallid elfin face came into view, with its alarming array of eyebrow studs and nose rings. Since Jack's and my March visit, her long spikey black hair had received a severe shaving, but only above the ears – two symmetrical squares that allowed a fuller appreciation of her elaborate, asymmetrically punctured earlobes. 'Hey there, Helena. Get better soon, won't ya.' She did a grin that showed off her wide, gappy front teeth and signed a heart shape over her chest with her fingers before ducking back out of sight.

'Are you in the shop?'

'No, I'm home, but listen to this.' Christabel was beaming suddenly. 'The donor thing, I'm going ahead. I've signed up with this clinic where everything gets properly screened. I've even told Daddy, and you were right, he is totally fine about it. Pleased, actually. He's said he'll help pay, which is so generous.'

'So generous,' I echoed. I was still half inside my head, picturing how she would look, this other person. Tall and blonde, probably, like me. Jack had a type. 'But my goodness, Christy, are you sure?' I exclaimed, as what she said began to hit home. A wave of sisterly concern was overcoming everything else, a welcome reminder that I was the realist, the one who always made a better fist of managing life's pitfalls. Christabel's chequered history was about throwing herself at hopeless ventures – like scented-candle shops and washed-up, lying, cheating, promising-the-earth men; and now this new business of ordering sperm on the internet. 'It is such a huge thing, darling,' I murmured.

'Isn't it,' she shrieked, dropping her face into her hands and shaking her head. 'I am actually *so* excited, now the decision is made... it's like, exactly what I needed, what I have been waiting to want, if you see what I mean...'

'And so, what, you just choose by ticking boxes?' It was impossible not to be intrigued. 'Like on a dating site? Hair, eyes, skin colour – that sort of thing?'

'Exactly. It's unreal. Though I'm trying not to get my hopes up, being an old lady, relatively speaking. I mean, I'm still regular and so on, but knowing my luck, it's bound not to work. And it's not like I've ever got close, is it? Unlike...'

I waited, faintly spellbound, for her to continue, marvelling at this second reference to the forbidden subject in as many months. But, instead, Marilyn said something off-camera and, the next thing I knew, Christabel was saying sorry but she had to go.

'Get better, okay? And we'll talk again soon.' The screen froze for a moment, the pixels half dissolving into a fuzzy mosaic, before the 'end call' sign came up and she was gone.

The house felt very quiet. Could Jack have gone out? To see her. Was there a her?

I reached for my phone, diverting myself by taking a few selfies, pulling mad, comical faces, to send to Hugh. An early flurry of one-liner updates and photos from glamorous-looking parties and balconies with glittering New York high-rise backdrops had rather petered out, and a few snaps of my current hideousness would certainly jolt a response. But then I realised the selfies were simply too hideous – too close to being tragic, as opposed to hilarious – so I forwarded some photos I had been saving of the flat instead. I knew I had done a good job – a cream and Wedgewood green colour scheme, offset with rainbow-coloured rugs and scatter cushions to give it all some zing – and was confident Hugh would be delighted. I posted the same set of pictures on my website and then got out of bed. I moved slowly, partly because I was aware of my injury, and partly because I was listening out for Jack, wondering about him, working out what to do. The suddenness with which the new suspicion had arrived, somehow made it all the more disconcerting. Never in fourteen years had Jack given me cause for worry on such a front, the tacit power-game between us being that I – more overtly and frequently admired – was the one more likely to run off. If he found a woman attractive, Jack's habit was to say so – putting his admiration in the spotlight and thus instantly diminishing its threat.

In the bathroom, I took some analgesics and showered briefly, keeping my head out of the line of fire. I then sat on the edge of the bath with a towel round my shoulders, watching the drips form into pools round my feet. Beside me, the lid of the laundry basket was open, revealing Jack's blood-spattered shirt sticking out from the pile of clothes. It needed salt, soaking – something. I fished it out and pressed an unstained patch against my mouth and nose, breathing in the scent of him.

The events of Sunday evening floated back across my mind: my irritated sense of self-sacrifice at feeling obliged to smoke outside, the wine bottle I had taken with me, not bothering with a glass; the weird slow-motion of tipping over, seeing the window coming for me, it felt like, and turning my head at the last moment to avoid its punch; and then, how long later we were unsure, Jack's face directly over mine, horrified, pouchy with sleep, coming in and out of focus, along with the bright wetness of my blood on his white shirt and the flecks of glass from the broken bottle glistening around us in the beam of the security lights. He had been so solicitous, so calm, so attentive. His old self again. I had tried to speak, wanting to tell him thank you and how I loved him, but the words came out all chewed up and wrong.

I picked the T-shirt up and ran the worst of it off under the cold tap, reducing the stains to brown fringes and then had a little scrub at them with some soap before dropping it back into the basket.

* * *

I knocked softly on the studio door. 'Jack?'

Arriving on the top landing, I had hesitated. All had been quiet, but then I thought I heard the murmuring of his voice inside the room.

'Yup?'

I was in, the moment he answered, the duvet I had slung round my nakedness, trailing behind me like a bridal train. 'How's it going?'

He was standing at the window, holding his phone and staring out at the grey morning, up to his knees in the new mayhem of his work. His usual apron was slung over the back of a stool, gleams of fresh paint layered over the old ones. There was a thin dusty streak of blue across his left cheekbone, and a few smudges on his hands.

'Were you talking to someone?' I asked.

'No. Why are you wearing that?' He slipped the phone into his back trouser pocket.

'I just felt like it. I had a shower, then went back to sleep. I'm feeling a bit better actually. Thanks for the toast. Christabel FaceTimed me – gawping like I was some freaky animal in a zoo – but it was nice of her. Mystic Marilyn was there, so, of course, she also had to have a peek. Apparently, Dad's not too bad this week. Oh, and she's going ahead with this baby malarkey, Christabel, that is, not Marilyn.'

I picked my way to the little yellow sofa as I talked, resisting the urge to peer too closely at his various projects, for fear of riling him, and keeping the folds of the duvet tightly round me so as not to knock anything over. Out of the corner of my eye, I noticed several new sketches pinned to his cork board, an old man with a fishing rod, a petite woman with sombre eyes and long hair whipping across her face, a child holding onto the handle of a stroller.

'How about a break from your labours?' I patted the sofa.

The reluctance radiated out of him, but he came towards me, stopping short of the sofa and folding his arms. 'So, you're feeling better, that's good.'

'Can't you sit with me?'

He took a step closer and I snatched the mobile out of his back pocket, tapping in his code.

'What are you doing that for?' He had gone very still.

'I want to see if you are lying to me. If you were talking to someone...but you've changed your code.' I kept jabbing at the number pad. My throat had constricted so much it was hard to speak. 'Why have you done that? Why have you changed your code, Jack?'

'It's been changed since I lost the last one, remember? Give it to me. You've no right.'

'So what is your fucking *new* code?' I was still wildly punching in numbers – his birthday, my birthday, our wedding anniversary.

'Fine. I'll check your phone, while I'm at it, shall I?'

'Feel free. It's in the bedroom.' A panic was gripping me, making it hard to breathe.

'Give that here, or it'll lock.' Jack snatched the mobile out of my hands, holding it out of reach while he fiddled for a few moments, before handing it back. I'm the one who shouldn't trust *you*,' he said bitterly, as I began scrolling through recent calls and messages in every quarter I could think of.

'Oh yes?' I kept my eyes on what I was doing, the panic ebbing slightly. There was no evidence of a recent conversation, though he could easily have deleted it during the course of supposedly putting in the code. The most recent calls were from me, his old friend Brian, and the specialist art place he used for most of his supplies. 'Like I said, you can check all *my* devices any time you want. And my code is the one it's always been, the first six digits of our first phone number at Beaufort Mews, back in the day when we wouldn't have dreamed of even having this conversation... because, unlike you, I have nothing to hide—'

'Except,' he cut in viciously, 'the fact that you drink too much. Every day now, Helena. Every day.'

He was stock-still, but a punch in the stomach could not have winded me more. I flung the phone at him – I was done with it anyway – and he caught it against his chest. 'How dare you?' My voice was throttled. 'That is *not* true and *not* fair...' The tears, held in for Christabel were starting to roll down my cheeks.

'Sunday happened because you were out of it,' he went on brutally. 'Because, to use the parlance, you have a *problem.*'

'My problem is you,' I sobbed. 'Absentee fucking husband. Never talking to me, never touching me, never *there.* No wonder I have a fucking extra glass now and then.' I had bunched myself up into a ball on the little sofa, hugging the duvet and rocking myself.

'But I am here,' said Jack stoutly.

'We never go anywhere, we never see anyone, we never do anything. The truth is, you don't love me like you used to...' I was wailing now, unravelling, and though humiliating, there was something brilliant in the fact, at last, of letting go. 'I think you've found someone else, Jack. I think you've got another woman.'

'Now that is just ridiculous.' He was beside me in an instant, pulling me close, which made me weep all the harder for how lovely it felt – to be touched with tenderness, to be able to believe that, behind the new wall of steely self-containment, the old feelings really were still there; that all my suspicions were groundless. 'You just never make anything easy, do you, Helly,' he said heavily, placing a careful kiss on top of my head, far from the piece of gauze.

'I look so gross,' I wailed. 'I'll have to wear a hat for weeks. I'm going to end up like bloody Daphne, a mad lonely old goat...'

'Nonsense.' He laughed, kissing the same spot again, more fondly. 'You could never end up like Daphne, even if you tried. If I wasn't around, you'd have suitors queuing along the street...'

'But I don't want suitors, I want you.' I burrowed closer.

'All you need is to take better care of yourself, Helly, not just with the booze, but everything. You've got so thin... I mean, look at you...' Most of the duvet had fallen off, and I saw that he had dropped his gaze and was indeed looking, at my small, pointy breasts, and my slim girlish stomach and long bendy legs, concertinaed in two from how I was curled up next to him. And, in the same instant, I sensed something in the looking, an intensity I had not detected in months and which made me – with some deep animal instinct – drop my knees open a little wider.

'I've missed you, darling', I whispered, dabbing the last traces of tears from my face with the duvet. 'I mean, really...' There was a tremble in my fingers as I traced the line of blue along his cheekbone. Here it was, my old power, just when I was about to give up on it. Jack wanted me. I could feel his entire body tensing with it. I shook off the duvet, which landed in a billowing heap on the floor, and swung myself onto his lap, facing him, my knees tight on either side of his thighs.

'Helena—'

'Be quiet.' I kissed the bridge of his nose, and then the tip.

'This is mad, Helly. You are not well enough. You are upset.'

'Don't tell me how I fucking am,' I scolded softly, tucking my hair behind my ears so he could see I was smiling. 'And don't tell me you are not in the mood because... I would say...' I edged deeper into his lap as I talked, tightening the grip of my legs, 'that there is some strong physical evidence to suggest otherwise. You don't need to do a thing,' I whispered, running my tongue along the seal of his mouth, 'just stay exactly as you are.'

He dropped his head back with the groan of one happy to acknowledge defeat.

'I'll even do a dry June,' I promised, quietly and solemnly, while inside, the blurry face of whoever she might – or might not be – shimmered. *If you exist*, I told her, *then I've totally got this. I've got this and I've got Jack and I'm never letting him go.*

Jack lifted his hips to help with sliding his clothes off, acquiescent now, his breathing fast.

'Sex for sobriety, husband,' I whispered, making my mouth brush his ear in the way I knew he liked, 'how about that for a fair deal?'

He made a low guttural sound as I lowered myself onto him, gripping my waist so that he could move me to the rhythm he wanted.

CHAPTER 10

I

The underground car park of the block containing Hugh's flat was an airless dungeon compared to the breezy June day outside. As usual, the vehicles were packed and stacked like Lego, requiring two circuits to find a slot and making me glad that this would be my final visit. I had been putting it off anyway, in no hurry to chase up Hugh's somewhat imperious mention of a faulty blind – fired off the previous week from the French poolside where he was now pulling the strings of his not-so-busy life. Somebody from his property management company had 'identified the problem' while doing an assessment of the flat, he wrote, and he would be most grateful if I could check it out 'forthwith'. I had intended to let him stew for a bit longer, but looping back down the M11 with Daphne having pulled the plug on our lunch, heading to South London to see off the irksome request had seemed a way of salvaging something from the day.

The parking slot was tight. Getting out of the car required some shimmying sideways, holding in my breath and my stomach. The lifts were quite a walk away and I set off at speed, the heels of my shoes – gorgeous new orange ones – echoing pleasingly on the concrete floor. I felt good, having dressed up a little for Daphne, in a comfortable ivory-coloured linen dress with a reddish trim that picked up on the vibrant colour of my footwear, and with my hair arranged in an artful loose topknot – designed to hide my not-quite recovered shaved patch where the stitches had been. Jack assured me it wasn't noticeable anyway, but since my fall and its aftermath, he had been trying harder to say nice things, so I wasn't sure I believed him. That my embarrassing accident had proved something of a turning point for us was the most unexpected of silver linings. There were no miracle cures; not drinking was extremely dull, we still argued – because we always did – and Jack remained feverishly preoccupied with his work; but the locked-door routine was done with and, from time to time, we were even managing some mutually satisfactory lovemaking.

The flat looked even better than I remembered it, classy as well as bold, and I couldn't help feeling proud and thinking how Hugh should have no trouble getting the high-end tenants he was after. The blind in question was in the furthest corner of the sitting room and took thirty seconds. Supposedly stuck in the down position, it merely needed a firm, but standard sideways tug – as they all did – to be released.

Blind fine.

I messaged Hugh at once, lingering by the window, with its view across rooftops to the nearby park.

Misunderstood as opposed to malfunctioning (comme moi!).
Hope France still fabulous. Hx.

I jabbed the send-arrow with a bit of a so-there flourish and then headed into the kitchen for some water, pooling it from the tap to my mouth in the palm of my hand because there wasn't a glass.

I was turning the tap off when I heard a thump, from somewhere in the flat, it sounded like, impossible though that was. I tightened the handle of the tap, listening intently, but not able to make out anything beyond the faint drone of a helicopter passing over the park. All I wanted was to go – to get home – but then I pictured how bad I would feel if it turned out a window had been flapping off its hook for months, allowing damage, and I hadn't even bothered to investigate. Other, more drastic possibilities made my heart pound as I progressed along the corridor, gingerly checking each room while inwardly rehearsing appropriate challenges if faced with a grizzled rough-sleeper or a pallid teenager huddling in a corner, or – hideous thought – a trapped bird or squirrel. I would run if that proved the case – slam the door and never look back. For me, flapping animals in confined spaces were as nightmarish as it got.

By the final door, with no further noises or trapped creatures of any species, I was relaxed. It was the smallest room – one peek would be enough. I swung the door open, already preparing to walk away, only to see Jack, sprawled asleep on the bed. I let out a cry of pure shock and he woke instantly, his eyes wild and blinking. 'Jack, what the fuck?'

'Darling, good god, what the hell are you doing here?' He scrambled into a sitting position, rubbing his face, looking so disoriented, so utterly lost, that I was aware of a terrible pity surging through my astonishment.

'I might ask the same of you.' He looked painfully dazed, and there was a faint sheen of sweat on his skin and forehead, as if he was going down with something. 'I mean, Jack, why on earth are you here?'

'Stupid, I know, but I wanted to see the Hugh picture in situ.' He talked very quickly, fumbling to rake some order into his hair with his fingers, too sheepish even to look at me properly. 'Then I'm afraid I couldn't resist a snooze. Slept like crap last night, didn't you? Those fucking foxes...'

I didn't care about the foxes. Something like anger was infusing my concern now. I glanced at the Madrid picture, hung at my instruction after Hugh had given the go-ahead, agreeing to a handsome price. 'You gave me such a fright, Jack. I thought there was a bloody squatter or lunatic or something.'

'I thought you were on a Daphne mission, anyway.' He was sitting up, arms round his shins, looking about as discombobulated as I had ever seen him.

'She cancelled, the silly, when I was halfway there. A text. Said she was ill, when she probably just didn't feel up to it. Extremely annoying – not that I could tell her that. So then I decided to come here instead, check on a window blind Hugh's been going on about... though it was fine...' I dried up, the weirdness of finding him here coming at me again.

'Maybe Daphne really is ill.'

'I bet she isn't... but, Jack...how did you get in, anyway? I mean, I've got the keys.'

'Hugh gave me a set too, just in case, remember?'

I nodded absently, because I didn't remember. But then May had been full of hazy patches – more than I liked to think about – and I had been doing my best to play them down to Jack. 'So, you came to look at your own picture?' I repeated carefully. 'My God, Jack, that's sort of tragic.

'Yup. That's me. Tragic.' He shook his head ruefully, holding out his arm by way of an indication for me to greet him properly.

'Well...' I clambered onto the bed, bemused. 'You could take me to lunch, I suppose, now that I am here.' I ruffled his hair with my fingers, and kissed the spots of grey at his temples. He tasted salty, but not unpleasantly so. 'Unless...' I stretched myself out. 'I mean, darling, we do also have other options, seeing as you've already messed the place up.' I laughed, sitting up and kissing him again, on the beard this time, just beside his mouth. 'Why not, my Jackadoodle? A bit of *spontaneity*? Like in the old days, when ...' I moved my lips over his, but could tell at once, even though he made a show of responding, that this was not what the extended arm had been hoping for.

'Sorry, but it doesn't feel right,' he protested after a few minutes, pulling away and absently wiping his mouth with the back of his hand, so absently indeed that something inside me bristled. It was impossible not to feel that it was the taste of me he was erasing. *Me*.

'Oh, and you coming here to ogle your own work is all right, is it?' I snapped. 'And having an afternoon nap while you're at it?'

'No. Actually, I couldn't be more mortified.' His expression was, it had to be said, the picture of mortification. 'I feel such an idiot. I just hit a bit of a wall this morning. I needed to see something that had... *worked*... get some faith back... in myself.'

'And have you?'

He was off the bed now, swiping the creases out of his trousers and patting again at the ruffles in his hair. 'I'm not sure... I think so. I guess we'll see, won't we.' He picked up his bag of drawing stuff that had been leaning against the wall behind the door. 'Shall we get going then?'

'Aye, aye, Captain.'

'Helena, I'm just...'

'I bet you're pissed off that I had it hung in here, aren't you? You had imagined it somewhere more central—'

'No, I hadn't. I really don't mind about that. Come on now.' He had the door open and was waving an arm to usher me through first.

I remained where I was, sitting on the bed, my arms crossed. 'So, you've been hitting a wall with the Rogues Gallery – you never said.' The term for his new project was one I had come up with, inspired by the sketches from his rambles now queuing for attention round his studio walls. 'I am interested in your work, remember?' Out of the corner of my eye, I was aware of the Madrid lake shining from its slot on the wall. It was a gem and did deserve more prominence, but I had felt the decision needed to come from Hugh. When he saw it for real, I was certain he would chastise me for allowing it to be so hidden away; indeed, I had high hopes of it being promoted to the Hampstead mansion.

'It's just this past week it's felt hard... and then a bad hiccough this morning...'

'Okay, so let's talk about it over some lunch.'

'No... I mean, that's a lovely idea of course, but I already grabbed a sandwich earlier and really ought to—'

'Well then, we could treat ourselves to the Goya or something.'

'I'm sorry, Helly, but I'd really rather not today...'

'Great. And what about what I want *today*?'

'Don't start...'

'Don't start? What the hell sort of way is that to talk to me? Like I am some sort of *annoyance*... when all I am doing is suggesting *nice* things. In fact, do you know what, Jack?' I swung myself off the bed and stepped towards him, putting my face right up against his. The being nice was always on his terms, I realised. It was never allowed to come from me. 'You and your hiccough can just fuck right off.' I pushed past him and headed off down the corridor, experiencing a stab of gratification to hear him hotfooting it to catch up, like he was running after me for once.

'Helly, please... Let's pick another day for doing something nice. We've got the theatre tonight anyway.'

'Maybe, maybe not. I think I'll tell Maddy and Spence I've changed my mind. You go, by all means, I'm sure the three of you will have a smashing time.'

'Please don't pull out tonight. And look, I'd have loved the Goya, but I've got Brian soon –he has a meeting which might run on, but is going to let me know.'

'To be turned down for the *possibility* of Brian,' I hissed, 'wow, you really know how to make a girl feel special.'

'Anyway, haven't you got your yoga to get back for? At quarter to four?'

'Ah, yes,' I sneered. 'How kind of you to remind me. How wonderful is your command of our respective diaries. Let us continue with our separate lives then, and maybe catch up with each other in a decade or two. Be sure to wear a rose in your lapel, just in case I don't recognise you.' We had reached the vestibule. Pleased with my tart remarks, and the look of helplessness they had induced in Jack's face, I continued my march, on out of the flat towards the lift shaft, not caring that this time he made no move to follow.

In the lift, I glared at my reflection in the mirrored wall, thinking how my anger was invariably laced with other things, like hurt and rejection and incomprehension. Such a swirl, it always made it hard to think straight. I thought too of Jack, curled up like a tramp in the flat's back bedroom, wondering for a moment whether it was his mental health I should be worrying about more than my own. Artists were a temperamental bunch, as I had learned only too well over the years; but the need to go and see his own painting – the first sale he had made in at least two years admittedly, and only thanks to me – marked quite a low.

My wheels squeaked on the polished concrete floor of the car park as I swung out of the space and up the winding narrow channel towards the exit. There I had to sit and wait, while the giant grid of double doors slid open at their agonisingly slow pace, revealing, like a stage set, the blinding light of the cloudless June afternoon. A part of me half hoped to see Jack standing on the pavement, penitent and sheepish, pretending to thumb a lift by way of an olive branch, or, maybe even hunched and sullen, still nursing his grievance as he liked to, feeding it, hanging on to it like a lifeline. Christ, I might be the famously stormy one, but at least I blew over.

It was ten minutes later, sitting at a set of temporary lights causing another gridlock in this most gridlocked of days, that something in me paused – to breathe, it felt like. A space. And into the space tiptoed something – someone – that made the hairs on my arms tighten. The possibility, again, of *her*. The other woman. She hadn't entered my head for weeks, kept at bay by Jack's and my new, successful efforts at equilibrium; but suddenly here she was, back with a force that felt like certainty, the seed that had quietly germinated all on its own, putting down its little roots while I was busy looking the other way.

I clung onto the steering wheel, letting the events of the last hour reconfigure: Jack with his strange mood and Hugh's keys, batting me away like a pest on the back of an afternoon of half-baked plans. It wasn't right. It was off.

Behind me, a raucous blast of car horns drew my attention to the lights having changed. I lurched forwards, turned down a side road and then doubled back the way I had come, sitting in the opposite queue for the same lights, still stunned.

Back in the underground car park, a new, comfortably wide space had become available, right by the lifts. I swerved into it, turned off the engine and took a deep breath. It was important to think straight, to be sensible, not to rush. I got out and opened the boot, sitting on its edge while I swapped my heels for the old converse sneakers that I kept in the car for Cornwall walks. I felt nimbler in them, more capable, as well as much, much quieter.

In the lift going up, I exchanged smiles with a young woman, shorter than me, but lithe and blonde with pretty green eyes. She had sunglasses perched in her straw hair and a wicker basket over her shoulder containing, by the look of it, a book and a mat from a trip to the park. Jack would like her. She was right up his street. I braced myself, trying to prepare for anything now, but she got out at the floor below. Unless she had recognised me and was escaping... would Jack show a lover pictures of his wife?

I knew at once that the flat was empty. So certainly, that I wondered I had not sensed Jack's occupancy earlier on. I checked all the rooms, needing to be doubly sure. They were exactly as they had been some forty minutes earlier, empty and immaculate, even the back room, where Jack had clearly straightened out the rumples in the bedspread before leaving. I propped the door open with my bag and stood there, sniffing the air like an animal, trying to feel beyond what my eyes were telling me. I slid open the wardrobe door and scoured the empty shelves and hanging space. Then I dropped onto my knees to look under the bed, expecting nothing, but needing to see the nothingness. I lay on the carpet staring, wondering. It was dark, but clean from being recently decorated. There were lots of carpet fluffs, like it had been scuffed up, but new carpets could be like that. A small doughty spider perched on the lip of the skirting board.

'Do you exist?' I whispered into the space. 'Do you exist and were you here?'

I returned to the sitting room and stood by the window with the view of the park before calling Jack.

'Sorry for getting stroppy.'

'No, I'm the sorry one, for not being any fun. I was pretty embarrassed too, Helly, to be honest. Not my finest hour by any stretch. Though, do you know, I really think it helped.'

'Seeing Hugh's picture?'

'Yup.'

'Are you still there?' I asked brightly, having no clear idea what I would do if I caught him out.

'At the flat? God, no. I left straight after you. I'm in Spencer Park. Sketchbook to hand. I've found a great spot.'

'And then you're seeing Brian?'

'Yes, that's right. Turns out the meeting isn't happening, so he's coming here.'

'To the park? In the middle of the afternoon?'

'He said it would be good to get out – enjoy the weather. Look, I was saving this, but he's apparently got some city contacts who might be keen on buying art for their offices. I'm pretty excited, actually.'

'Gosh, yes, that does sound promising.'

'Are you home?'

'Almost...'

'Okay, well, enjoy your yoga.'

'Will do. And I won't bail on the theatre.'

'Great. I'll see you there. When did you say it started?'

'Seven thirty. Maddy's got the tickets.'

'Oh god, the joy of Spence awaits us,' he joked, by way of reference to Madeleine's much older partner, a New Yorker with an unerring capacity to kill every conversation by stating the blindingly obvious.

Jack sounded so normal. Everything felt so normal. I stared at my flat shoes, waggling my toes and thinking how alive they felt and yet how one would barely know they were there, hidden under the canvas. 'See you at seven-ish then.'

'Yup. See you.'

I glanced down at the park. I would have to be careful, but it wasn't one of the big ones. It wouldn't take long. Then at least I would know.

* * *

It was almost four thirty by the time I got home. The drive gleamed like black treacle in the sunlight. The roses, heavy with their flowers, brushed my hair as I unlocked the door. I took an apple from the fruit bowl in the kitchen and ate it as I went upstairs, where I rummaged for my stretch capri pants and a T-shirt and dropped them both into the laundry basket. Then I ran a bath with my favourite oil, demolishing the apple, core and pips included, until the foam had bubbled into thick inviting drifts.

I peeled off my clothes and went downstairs, naked, to choose a bottle from the fridge, which I slid into one of the icy sheathes we kept in the freezer, before taking a wine glass from the cabinet and heading back up to the bathroom. I poured some wine, set the bottle down on the broad tiled ledge at the end of the bath, and then took the drink with me upstairs. There had been a few, moderate, lapses since my pledge, but none had felt more warranted.

I waited until I was in the studio before I took a sip, toasting the air first. The place was as messy and cramped as I had ever seen it, two paint tables and all three easels on the go, canvases in all states of semi-completion stacked around the open eaves' cupboard doors and piles of sketches everywhere, including more than I could count pinned to the big cork noticeboard that for years hadn't contained much beyond the odd postcard and a calendar. It felt pleasingly wicked to be picking my way around it all, naked, sipping my cold forbidden drink. Everything I saw I liked. Here was a man truly at work. Here was Jack. My Jack.

I went to sit on the little sofa, wanting to prolong the pleasure of the moment, and the wine, which was an Albarino, dry, with a hint of flowers. It had been easy to spot Jack in the park, seated in the corner of a bench with his pencil box open beside him and his pad on his knees. A group of teenagers were kicking a ball around a few yards away and he appeared to be drawing them. As innocent as the day he was born. Spying from my spot among some not-too-near bushes had felt good and then bad, as doubts had crept back in, along with the growing fear of being observed. He fiddled with his phone once or twice, but made no calls. And then suddenly Brian, of all people, appeared, sauntering along the path, eating an ice cream – vanilla in a cone, clearly bought from the van I had passed on my way in.

I had watched them for a further ten minutes or so and then crept away, taking the longest route back to the road to be safe. I felt let off the hook more than anything. The possibility of the other woman remained, a shadow hovering on the periphery of my vision. But a shadow could be ignored, or dismissed as a phantom. I needed to hold my nerve, to keep my wits about me, but for now I had a reprieve, permission to go on in the hope, still, of being wrong.

II

'But to *cook* on stage...' Madeleine rubbed absently at the pink cres-
cents her lips had been imprinting on the rim of her champagne glass.
'I simply do not know how the poor girl is managing without fluffing
her lines. Onions, too, for heaven's sake. My eyes would be streaming.
And browning the meat, not to mention the spaghetti. I kept
wondering if one of them was going to start doing that thing of flinging
bits at the ceiling to see if it stuck, except, of course, they don't have a
ceiling, do they, only that door, which they all keep slamming and
which I can't help worrying about because it looks so flimsy.'

'Great play though,' said Spence. 'The power of love, I guess, in all
its gory glory.'

'The power of the prenup more like,' quipped Madeleine, shooting
an impish look at her husband through the swinging frame of her
always lively and very glossy hair, cut with geometric precision round
her dainty face and with new gold highlights that were on fire under
the bright wall lamps of the theatre bar.

Spence chuckled, looking proud. That they were extravagantly and
equally wealthy was a matter of binding importance to them both, as
was the existence of their now eight-year-old son, Sebastian, who had
come by the gallery with his nanny sometimes during my visits earlier

in the year, offering opinions which Madeleine fondly encouraged while I privately fought down the urge to throw up.

Jack glanced at Spence, perhaps in acknowledgement that 'gory glory' really wasn't bad, but then quickly picked up on Maddy's comments instead, saying he, too, found the cooking distracting, but thought the girl was good, and hadn't she been on the TV in something recently. Our encounter in Hugh's flat felt a world away. Jack looked transformed – cool and unflummoxed, his heavy brown hair smooth and tidy, his big easy smile breaking through the beard that could seem so austere and fierce in his more sombre moods. He had got to the theatre well before seven apparently, as had Maddy and Spence. They were deep in conversation at the foyer bar when I arrived – eight minutes before curtain-up – the three of them having embarked on the bottle of champagne which had then been set aside for finishing in the interval. 'We've been hearing all about Jack's latest projects', Maddy had reported, handing me a programme as we joined the entry queue. 'Hugh's commission and the plans for the portrait series. It all sounds wonderful'. I had agreed it was tremendously exciting, noting the bashful pleasure on Jack's face and thinking what a needy baby he was and how I knew that really and should just get used to it instead of fighting it.

'And how was Brian?' I remembered to ask Jack now, taking an absent swig of my own interval tipple of ginger ale, which clashed unpleasantly with the peppermints I had been sucking, like the jolt of orange juice after toothpaste.

'Brian was in fine form.'

'Who's Brian?' enquired Maddy companionably, handing her phone to Spence so he could continue negotiations with Sebastian, who had rung for support in an argument with the nanny about his bedtime. The child's pixie face and blonde hair lit up the screen.

'An accountant friend of Jack's,' I explained to Madeleine, widening my eyes in only the mildest suggestion of my own reservations.

'Helena thinks he's a waste of space,' said Jack affably, 'but we were talking art today, as it happens. He has contacts in several investor banks and says there's a fresh swell of interest in buying work at the moment – not for private clients, but for the banks themselves, to decorate their offices. Oh, and he was on his usual soapbox about fishing, trying to persuade me to give it a go. I just might.'

'Fishing. Now there's a sport,' put in Spence, returning to our little huddle and handing the now blank phone back to Madeleine with a shrug and a rueful grin suggestive of parental climbdown.

'Ah, of course, you are *the* fly-fishing expert, aren't you?' said Jack, with an eagerness so devoid of irony that it felt like betrayal. 'So, tell me why, Spence. Make your pitch.'

'You've got... er... two minutes,' I chipped in jokily, genuinely fearful of the floodgates Jack had opened. 'Your time starts now.'

'Shall we powder our noses?' said Maddy smoothly, depositing her empty glass on a nearby table. 'Are you all right?' she asked as soon as we were in the queue. 'You seem a bit... quiet. And you came by taxi, so why aren't you drinking? Is there some *news* we should know? Liking what you've done here, by the way,' she added in her quick-fire way, artfully reducing the pressure on me to respond to either question and cupping my topknot bun, which appeared to be holding its own despite the rigours of the day, 'really cute.'

'There is absolutely nothing whatsoever to *know*,' I assured her hastily, as my sister's ongoing plans of motherhood bobbed unhelpfully at the back of my mind, 'and actually, I *am* drinking, but not much, and not so Jack sees – because I made a rash promise to do a dry month and am regretting it madly. Life gets a little dreary otherwise, don't you find? And it's not like I've ever poured whisky on my cornflakes, is it?' I pulled a face, aware that I was still a little drunk from the bottle which I had finished during the course of my bath – but enjoyably so, not yet past the point of everything seeming better instead of worse. 'Mind you, it did get a bit merry at my last Mayfair visit, didn't it?'

Maddy was already laughing, clearly entertained both by my gentle deceit and the memory of the afternoon of champagne and setting the world to rights that had followed my lunch with Hugh – an afternoon which, as she had said at the time, with all the gallery's various cata-strophes, was exactly what she needed. 'It sure did. But there's having fun and knowing when to stop and I'd say you're good at both.'

It was all I could do not to kiss the life out of her.

'So, Jack seems pretty fired up,' she went on, once we were out of the cubicles and touching up our faces in front of the mirrors. 'From what you were saying before, about him never getting down to anything these days, I was kind of surprised. I mean, pleasantly so. Is he really pulling it out of the bag?' She leant towards the mirror, talking through a fish-pout stretch as she applied fresh colour to her mouth – never in need of the cosmetic enhancement it now regularly received – deftly converting the pink back into a vibrant cherry-red.

Beside her, I felt a wreck suddenly. Despite the kind comment, my bun, trailing copious straggles, was starting to look forlorn rather than chic, making me kick myself for not having taken the time to attend to it properly before leaving the house. I would have had a stab at redoing it now, had I not feared Madeleine's beady eyes alighting on the lingering evidence of my small head wound. 'Well, as you know, I have never pretended to be an expert – and am probably too close to be impartial anyway – but, oh my goodness, Maddy, he is definitely in a new phase.' The exciting chaos of the studio flashed across my mind. 'I've never known him have so much on the go, such drive—'

'These portraits?'

'It's early stages, but yes, they are the main thing. To be honest, he's not that keen on me looking – it's taking all my feminine wiles to stay in the loop.'

'Fear of failure, probably,' Maddy remarked, pinching some colour into her small cheekbones, 'or judgment, or just tripping over his own feet. Artists are a funny bunch.'

'Tell me about it,' I murmured, but taking heart from the insight.

A strident bell sounded a two-minute warning for returning to seats.

'Look, use those wiles of yours and keep me posted, okay?' commanded Madeleine, pushing open the door out of the Ladies, the brusqueness of her tone doing nothing to stop me recognising the generosity of the suggestion. 'Now, tell me quickly about Hugh. He was on a trip, you said.'

'Hugh is fine... at least...' We were back in the theatre throng now and it was hard to stay abreast of Maddy as I talked. 'He's still away and gone a bit quiet on me. In fact, I'm starting to wonder if he hasn't met someone...' I was interrupted by another shrill bell.

Maddy accelerated, weaving her neat, petite body, impeccably clad, as ever, in a salmon pink trouser suit, through the hordes. We were swimming against the tide. Or at least I was. Maddy looked unperturbed by it. And I was getting left behind – a fact that neither she, nor anyone else, knew or cared about.

I stopped, my legs leaden, my heart racing, the old terror lapping at my ankles, sucking me down. I didn't know where I was trying to get to any more. What the goal was. What I could be sure of. Whether Jack had someone else, whether he loved me. Everyone I knew seemed to be racing on to new things, reinventing themselves, floating out of my reach. Maddy. Hugh. Daddy. Jack. Christabel...

'There you are.' Jack caught my arm. 'I thought we'd lost you.'

'Jack...'

'The last bell's gone. We've got to get a move on.'

Everyone, including Maddy and Spence, was already back in their seats. Our two empty spaces, plum in the middle of the third row, stuck out like missing teeth. Reaching them proved an obstacle course of knees, bags, elbows, all negotiated to the accompaniment of disapproving tuts and sighs. Jack smiled and apologised, unruffled, but I felt on the edge of one of my old explosions; close to gagging on the need to be polite; nursing the growing certainty that if I opened my mouth a scream might come out that would never end.

Seated at last, the auditorium lights dimmed, I groped for Jack's hand, pulling it onto my lap. He gave my fingers a cursory squeeze and then left it lying there between my palms, like something caught and held, something with no reciprocal desire to return the holding.

The play was a suffocating, self-analysing, snarled-up cat's cradle.

None of the right people loved each other. None of them were honest. None of them were worth caring about. The set was the same as in the first half, the pokey flat of the girl who cooked. It was cupcakes this time – butter, flour, eggs, sugar, the works – the actor delivering her lines between angry blasts of a Magimix. By the end, all the protagonists were seated round her tiny kitchen table, defeated by the mess of their inner lives, as well as the cake mix, which had got caught up in the fray, instead of finding its way into an oven.

'Well, that was cheery!' laughed Madeleine, once we were back in the street, surrounded by swarms of people ordering cabs or heading for the tube.

'Powerful,' said Spence.

'Gruesome.' The word flew out with an intensity that made them all look at me. My head was pounding, and the apple I had eaten was sitting, a pebble in my otherwise empty stomach.

'By which Helena means, thank you very much for the evening,' Jack said, playfully tugging my arm and pulling a face designed to express shock at the rudeness of his wife.

'Oh, I'd be far more worried if she'd pretended to like it,' said Maddy sportingly. 'In fact, gruesome is the perfect word.' She had looped elbows with Spence, now busy scanning the lines of cars for their private driver. 'We would suggest a meal, but...' She waggled her phone. 'Sebastian is still up, apparently, and *missing* us.' She pretended to grimace, but the delight beamed out of her.

'And there's a taxi,' cried Jack, making a death-defying dart across the road as a black cab, its yellow light ablaze, edged out of a side street.

'You take care,' Maddy instructed, giving me a stern look. 'And remember what I said.'

'And what did you say, honey?' Spence asked, not seeming fazed when all he got in response was a never-you-mind and a cheek-peck of such motherly condescension that I found myself looking away. At least Jack and I still clashed and struggled. At least we were still alive and kicking.

Jack was signalling impatiently from up the street. I took my time. For my own safety, I told myself, walking the few yards in the opposite direction to the traffic lights and waiting lawfully with the cluster of other pedestrians until the little green man popped into view. It felt good to make Jack wait. Like I was getting some ground back, some sanity, after the roller-coaster traumas of the day. I would prove a more-than-equal opposite force to him, I vowed, and to another woman, for that matter, should such a need arise. I would keep my antennae up. I would bide my time. I would never give up.

'Do you want to touch it?'

'Not really. Thanks all the same.'

Christabel shook her head, smiling to herself as she placed her palms on either side of the small hillock of her stomach. Five months in and she was already huge and waddling, like some fattened goose, but also happier than I had ever seen her, her skin radiant, her eyes like blue planets. The bigness was mostly water retention, she maintained, and only partly linked to the new daily craving for pasta, ideally dripping with oil and salt and garlic, or burnt mince – it had to be burnt, so that it crunched between her teeth, she had explained gleefully. 'The baby won't bite,' she murmured now, shooting me a look under the lids of her eyes.

'I thought pregnant women hated everybody grabbing their bump, anyway,' I retorted, getting up from my chair and going to study the posters on the opposite wall, despite knowing them all by heart.

'Not if it's sisters,' said Christabel dreamily, folding her arms across the hillock, as if it was some sort of shelf.

A part of me almost wished I could turn down some of my sibling's radiance, which felt somehow inappropriate – disrespectful even – given our reasons for being in the hospital. Old reasons now, admittedly, the new year somehow having found its way to March, two months on from Daddy's accident with a wheelchair that had been prescribed because of a sudden decline over Christmas.

'Sweet of Jack to want to go in on his own for a while, have some man-to-man time.'

'Yes. Jack's a bloody angel.'

'I think he might be,' said Christabel quietly.

I pretended to read the poster on hand hygiene, not wanting to be subjected to more of the flaky quasi-religious notions that my sister had been flinging out since the baby quest got underway – egged on, I had no doubt, by the loopy Marilyn – cherry-picking nonsense from whatever seemed to take her fancy, God one minute, shooting stars the next. The sperm donor, one Scott Cabot, an ophthalmologist from New Jersey, was a case in point, having been selected both for his impressive gene pool and some astrological nonsense that I hadn't been bothered even to try and comprehend. It was all 'meant to be' Christabel had informed me solemnly back in September, when the man had managed to combine visiting distant relatives with a face-to-face meeting to coincide with the delivery of his treasured product to the donor clinic, both sides having agreed that this personal element of their interaction was important.

'I mean, Jack really is very special, Helly.'

'Is he? Wow. Thanks for telling me.' I belted my arms across my chest, leaning back against the wall as a trolley was wheeled past, the orderly in charge giving us a cheery hello.

'Sometimes, I think you could be nicer to him, that's all.'

I locked eyes with my sister. Since getting pregnant, her face had grown fuller, rounder, younger. She was wearing a girlish blue corduroy pinafore dress that highlighted both her striking eyes and the new swell of her chest. I remembered in the same instant, the memory bursting into my head like a rogue firework, exactly how that breast swelling had felt, the weird tenderness of it, like pain was just a beat away. 'For your information, Jack is not always very nice to *me*.' As I spoke, she – the other woman – flared in my mind – a genie bursting from a lamp – as was her wont these days. An imaginary companion, it felt like sometimes, always with the features of the green-eyed girl I had seen in the lift at Hugh's place, despite months and months of vigilance having produced no further proof of infidelity with her or anyone else. 'In fact, the only time he seems to acknowledge my existence properly is when we're down here.'

'But that's because of all this amazing work he's doing, isn't it? The Rogues Gallery thing. The best stuff of his life, you said—'

I let my mind drift while my sister repeated things I had told her – true things, about Jack's continued year of extraordinary output – pondering the difficulty of confessing to unhappiness, even to someone whose love I had no cause to doubt. My life, it occurred to me, had in huge part been about proving to Christabel that she did not have to worry about me. The teenage secret trouble, which only she knew of and had helped me resolve, was partly to blame. But even before that, while being the little sister who blazed more of an obvious trail, it was Christabel who had my back. Until Jack took over the job, filling the space around me, the gaps inside.

Nothing had changed, I reminded myself desperately, as the genie danced. Except the gradual discovery that reprieve was close to limbo. I had done as I had vowed all those months ago. I had tracked, watched, waited. I had demanded and been shown Jack's phone at random moments on scores of random occasions. I had taken to scrutinising his expressions, trying to *see* the emotions he wasn't confessing to. Jack countered with an inscrutability that was as calm as it was impenetrable. Whenever my suspicions got the better of me and I exploded, he would shake his head like a rueful parent dealing with a tantrum, waiting for the noise to subside. Confrontations, dogged denials and reassurances would follow. The look of distance – of absence – would leave his expression and joyous certainty, about him, about us, would flow back in. Until the next wave of doubt, arriving so vividly at times that it felt like one thrust of my hand through an invisible wall and I could grab hold of my green-eyed rival – an arm, a hem of a skirt, a fistful of hair. But, mostly, it just felt as if I was losing my mind.

The start of the year had seen a creeping fatigue with it all. My antennae were beginning to droop. The portraits project was due for completion by the end of March, Jack promised, and I had been fixing my energies instead on the drip-drip worry of Daddy's slow recovery. I sought consolations as I went: the obvious, unedifying one, that Jack, thank god, had ceased to bully me about, and the more promising challenge of sneaking photos to Madeleine whenever I got the chance – not easy, since Jack had taken to wrapping and storing the canvases the moment they were done, for safety, he said, and readiness for all the city contacts that bigmouth Brian was still going on about.

Christabel had stopped talking and I found myself saying into the silence that I thought Jack might have found someone else. 'Another woman. Over this last year, I've kept wondering.'

'Oh, but he wouldn't, Helly, not Jack. How would he have the time? And where would he be without you, anyway?' She laughed, but very gently. 'You're just stressed because of Dad, sweetheart.' She cast a furtive look down the hospital corridor, as if there was a chance of Daddy and Jack overhearing us. 'And maybe because of this?' She tapped her stomach with her fingertips. 'A little?'

I raised my eyes skyward, marvelling as always at my sister's quiet, wily determination. 'Of course, I am demented with worry about Daddy, but I couldn't be happier about you and your American baby, okay? In fact, I have even considered whether you and Scott might end up making a go of it...' I went onto describe exactly such a love story that I had read of in the papers, but it was Christabel's turn to look exasperated.

'Scott and I met once,' she interjected quietly, 'and that was that.' She closed her eyes, and the subject, by the feel of it.

I studied her tranquil, milky face, wondering if she was going to fall asleep, as she had been doing several times a day, with enviable ease, dropping onto any piece of furniture that happened to be handy and nodding off in whatever position she landed. And suddenly the memory of that same drugged tiredness was rushing back at me – not the peace of sleeping, but the scary weight of it, the muffling fog in my brain. I slapped my palms together. 'God, Jack's been in there a while, hasn't he?'

Christabel's eyes flicked open. 'Maybe he's saying goodbye.' Her voice was small and tight.

'Yeah, right, which, given that Jack's catching a train back to London this afternoon, would make sense.'

'Helena, I didn't mean that—'

'Dad needs a better chair, that's what we've got to make sure of once he's discharged. More stable. Something that isn't going to tip over on a bumpy path in the wind, almost catapulting him off the cliff. Christ, who wouldn't have broken a fucking hip. And, of course, the break is taking a while to heal because of all the other delights his body's dealing with...'

'Helena—'

It suddenly seemed important to keep talking. 'The lower bone mineral density, the risk of pneumonia, the bladder infections, the bedsores...' The months of doctor briefings had made experts of us all.

'It's all right, Helly.'

I appeared to be crying. Christabel had left her chair and was holding me in her bear-hugging way, meaning the bump I had not wanted to touch was pressed right up against my ribcage, such a weird hard solid thing, yet with a tautness, tangible even through the corduroy dress, that suggested one puncture might deflate it to nothingness. Mine had never got that big, I remembered, not even a month on, because I had been so young, so lean and tight-skinned.

'I don't think Jack should go back to London today,' Christabel said firmly, pulling back to examine my face. 'He should stay and drive back with you on Friday. It's only one more day. I'm going to ask him.'

'Don't,' I snapped, pushing her away. 'You're right, Jack has been an angel about coming down here and never once left early. He needs to get back to get on with the finishing touches, he says, and frankly, I have no desire to stand in his way. I can't wait for him to finish, Christy, okay? And now – 'I gently pushed her away – 'I need to go and have a fucking pee.'

I was sitting on the loo, lid down, when I heard Christabel come in. I knew it was her from the rustle of her thighs in the thick maternity tights, with the extra-stretch paunch round the waistband which she had flashed at me that morning, praising their comfort, endearingly unbothered at displaying the emerging ungainliness of her figure. I held my breath now, waiting for her to enter the cubicle next door, there only being the two.

'I think this will be easier through the closed door,' she said, the rustling having stopped. 'So just listen. Just listen and do not speak one word.'

My charged-up brain was already slinging out possibilities; the worst being that my sibling's laser bloody eyes were boring through the lavatory door to the 'water bottle' that had already put the fire back in my belly and heat back in my heart. Jack might have learned to turn a blind eye, but Christabel would be far too stubborn and tactless to do any such thing. I had been more careful around her than anyone.

'I love Marilyn and she loves me.' My sister's voice on the other side of the toilet door was steady as a roll call. 'I have wanted to tell you for ages, Helly, but Marilyn kept saying you had probably worked it out or would soon guess. I am not currently planning to say anything to Daddy, because I think he might find it hard and I do not want to run the risk of making him more unhappy.'

I stayed where I was, numb with surprise and obediently silent as I gripped the small eco-friendly cannister which I had filled that morning with vodka and a dash of lime cordial. I heard the door to the Ladies swish back open and then Jack's voice in the corridor, greeting Christabel and asking if I was in there too. I returned the bottle to my handbag and I found a piece of the mint gum I had recently switched to from sweets – fewer calories and less stress on the teeth. I chewed it slowly, my thoughts flicking to Hugh's reviled, long-gone ex, Paula, fan of all things pink, including bubble gum. He had someone else now called Denise de Court, a model and musician with a villa near his. The place with the helipad, he had reported exuberantly in one of his increasingly rare communications. He had sent a photo with the message, of a red-maned beauty in her late twenties, at a guess, clad in a black thong bikini that marked out – with the efficacy of a highlighter pen – the areas of her nubile body most crying out for attention. She had been lying on a beach towel for the shot, propped up on her elbows, the hover of a smirk in her Hollywood smile suggesting she had the heart of the photographer squarely in her palm.

I flushed the toilet, though theoretically there was no need, and washed my hands at the basin outside, deploying the extreme thoroughness recommended in the corridor poster. Between my fingers, up my wrists, under my nails. When I had finished, I did it again, aware of Christabel's news growing ever more obvious as it settled. Marilyn was right, I should have guessed. I had been sleepwalking through so much, for longer than I cared to think, my focus leapfrogging, not getting to grips with anything. Not to have realised was actually embarrassing. I forced myself to picture Marilyn and my sister with no clothes on, their womanly bodies pressed close, making love. I half expected to be repelled. Instead, a tremble of tenderness passed through me, so visceral I had to hold the basin. Inside it, a worm in the bud, sat envy. My clumsy, hapless sister had found love – found herself. I was the one back out in the storm.

II

Coming down the stairs the following morning, I passed Anya, at one of the big landing cupboards, folding linen. She glanced up and smiled her new sad smile, the one that communicated so many obvious things that none of them needed remarking on. 'A beautiful day,' she said.

'Yes, I thought I'd begin it with a walk down on the beach.'

'Wrap up warm, there's such a wind. Jack got his train all right yesterday then?'

'Yes, thanks. There was a delay once he got to London, he said, on the Northern Line, but he got home safely.'

'And your father...' She clutched the big towel she was holding to her chest, like a comforter, a glint of pleading in her wide brown eyes. 'How was he?'

'Not too bad. They've tweaked the medication yet again, and the gentle physio seems to be progressing. The doctor was pretty upbeat, actually.'

The housekeeper crossed herself, throwing a supplicatory glance at the ceiling where her invisible Catholic god resided, before returning her attentions to the linen cupboard, which she was rearranging, I realised – towels to the bottom and sheets to the top. Whatever it took, I reflected grimly, heading on down to the coatroom, where I pulled on my old converses and Daddy's favourite dark green fleece, which was absurdly large, but beautifully warm and comfortingly scented with his aftershave and pipe.

Outside, the wind pummelled me as I picked my way along the lower garden path towards the steps that some helpful person had crafted into the cliffside decades ago. At the spot where Daddy had managed to fall, I paused, but only for a moment. He had wanted the blast of the salty sea air in his lungs. It was the same urge that I had woken to, as the sun pushed through the curtains that morning, my head thick and my throat dry thanks to the no-brakes of an evening alone. I had cleaned my teeth with extra vigour and swigged half a carton of tomato juice, standing at the fridge door, before going back upstairs to dress, taking a big bowl of bran flakes with me. The milk, the sugar, tasted fantastic. The very last thing I would want to add to such a treat was alcohol, I reflected cheerfully, as the exchange about whisky and breakfast with Maddy in the theatre toilets the previous summer floated across my mind. Knowing how to party and when to stop, yes, that was me, Helena Aspen. It was just this period of unforeseen stresses that had been requiring a little relaxing of the rules.

The cliffside descent was always steeper than I anticipated, and took concentration. For most of it, I faced inwards, using the big deep steps like a ladder, so that I didn't have the distraction of the drop.

Down on the beach, the tide was high, leaving only a corridor of sand for walking. The waves rushed in, deafening and relentless, crested with foam. I kept near enough to the waterline for the pleasure of skipping out of the way, not minding the gradual dampening of my socks through the thin canvas of my shoes. The sea itself looked serene and blue under the clear sky. Not unlike a great painting, I mused, pausing to stare properly, aware of a small bubble of hope popping inside, one of the ones that had been helping me cope. Jack had worked so hard and the results were undeniably stunning. He could do well now. It might be a whole new chapter, for both of us. Especially if someone like Maddy, with all her connections, got behind it.

The wind was whipping at my hair, and blasting some calm into my fizzing head. Near the shore, a few seagulls bobbed in a flotilla. Out to sea behind them, one lone tanker tracked across the skyline. I watched as it shrank to a dot, using my right hand as a visor against the sparkle of the horizon. The low moment in the hospital the day before felt a universe away. Daddy really did seem a little better. The consultant who had spoken to me and Jack – Christabel having shot off back to Marilyn – had been as positive as I had reported to Anya. It helped that he had been such a fit man for his age, the doctor explained, making me feel proud on Daddy's behalf, because that made all the difference in a patient's capacity to battle everything.

I had saved reporting Christabel's announcement until Jack and I were pulling out of the hospital car park, Jack at the wheel. He had burst into affectionate laughter, agreeing what a pair of dunces we were for not having put two and two together. And suddenly, with me laughing too, at this ridiculous, shared oversight, the moment had been transformed into something special, something so badly needed that I found myself wishing it would never end. I had watched Jack for every beat of it, his beautiful slender fingers gripping the steering wheel, the boom of his easy bass laugh, the smooth slope of his handsome nose and the full mouth that softened the masculinity of his thick, close-cut beard. So here it was, I had thought, relief sluicing through me, our old wavelength, not lost after all, just a little buried. And Jack had to have felt something similar, because a little later, with his bag loaded into his Truro taxi, he had surprised me with a proper kiss, instead of his usual peck, arms tight around my back, telling me to take care – almost like we were saying goodbye forever and he was truly reluctant to let go.

I had reached the jutting segment of cliff that formed the natural end to the bay, forging through the sand and out into the sea like a rampart. The tide was already pulling back, exposing more of the big rocks clustered at its feet and expanding the sandy crescent back the way I had come. Seeing a lace had come undone, I perched on a boulder to attend to it. My head was throbbing suddenly, worse than ever, and I wished I had thought to bring something to drink. Water. Nothing more. Not till the evening, anyway.

Absorbed by the fight with the lace, which was knotted and sodden, a real challenge for my cold fingers, barely poking out of the too-long sleeves of the fleece, I didn't notice Marilyn until she had stepped into my peripheral vision.

'Yoo-hoo,' she cooed, despite being only a few feet away, and performing a wave when I looked up. She was bouncing on her feet in turquoise trainers, and a little out of breath. On her stocky top-half she wore a cagoule that matched the colour of her shoes, with the hood tied so tightly over her head that her face looked as if it was stuck in a porthole. Her legs were encased in stretchy black leggings that showed off surprisingly neat shapely muscles. It was news to me that she even ran.

'Hello, Marilyn.' I quickly straightened, abandoning the lace. 'So, Christabel told me—'

'I know—'

We both spoke at once, falling, a little clumsily, into an embrace, my face briefly plunged into the thick rough curls of Marilyn's hair. It smelt fresh and sweet, like breathing in a meadow. For one mad, fleeting instant, I was tempted just to stay there, to be held by this woman who loved my sister, safe against the sea winds and life.

She grinned as she released me. 'I am so glad it's all in the open and sorted now.'

'Me too. And I am really happy for you both.' I was aware of sounding somewhat inadequate, despite my sincerity. The worm of envy had eased. I had Jack, after all, and Christabel, of all people, deserved to be happy. 'Jack too. We both feel such idiots for not having figured it out.'

'Oh, it's fine. And isn't this wonderful?' Marilyn threw an arm at the sea and the stretch of widening beach, where a couple of dog-walkers had come into view, their hounds hurdling after sticks through the chop of the breaking rollers. 'I want us to tell your dad too,' she went on, 'but Chris won't have it. Do you think she is right? I mean, we're hardly living in the Dark Ages, are we, and even if he *is* shocked, which I sort of doubt, it won't last. Like with Chris going down the donor road, he was, like, *overwhelmed* with joy. And so he can only be pleased, surely, that this grandchild is going to have *two* parents, because obviously we want to get married.'

'My goodness, well congrat—'

'And even if he finds that hard to swallow, he's hardly likely to cut her out of his will, or anything, is he? I mean, truth is all that matters between loved ones, isn't it?'

Marilyn had started doing stretches during the course of expressing these views, her netting of black hair flopping as she bent this way and that.

'I am not sure if I can speak for how Daddy would feel,' I ventured, aware of an inner guard slamming back into place at the casual mention of marriage and wills. It made me want to call Jack.

'Hey, your shoelace is undone.' Marilyn was on her knees in the sand before I could stop her, her small quick fingers picking out the knot and retying it in seconds. 'There we go. Laters.'

I watched her spring off, a nimble deer hopping through the scattered rocks along the compacted wettened sand.

III

By the time I reached North London, the sinking sun had converted the dispersing storm clouds into a spreading bruise of pink, purple, yellow and red. Blossom was bursting in every garden and on every street tree, glistening snowy clusters, gleaming in the dusky light. When the clocks went forwards at the weekend, the corner of the year really would have been turned. It was six hours since I had left Cornwall. I had stopped just once, for a toilet break and to buy a bar of chocolate and some water.

A dull ache sat deep in my eye sockets from the effort of focusing for so many miles through the fury of the windscreen wipers and the hazards of navigating the slosh and splash of the motorway. The notion of leaving a day early had blown into my mind as I picked my way back up the cliffside after meeting Marilyn. With Jack gone, and Daddy stable, it suddenly felt like waiting twenty-four more hours would just be marking time. My throbbing head also told me that I was in a mood penitent enough to justify having one of my sensible days, which suited the long drive, at the same time conjuring the appealing prospect of greeting Jack with whole-hearted abandon for once – conscience clear and smile easy, no lurking fear as to what messages might sit in the warm ripples of my breath.

After turning onto the drive, I switched the engine off and sat for a minute, savouring the quietness, the release from the need to concentrate. I loved our house, with its handsome stucco walls and sandy brick trim. Upstairs, a couple of lights were on and a cosy glow from the hall was showing in the glass panel over the top of the front door. Somewhere nearby, a bird sang a repeated note, perhaps celebrating the end of the storm. My body felt stiff, moulded into the shape of the seat, and my feet had grown chilly from being so long parted from the ankle boots I had tossed onto the passenger seat after my motorway stop. Twisting to get the boots back on, I experienced a wave of dizziness, the sense of being chiselled out inside. Apart from the chocolate, I hadn't eaten since the bran flakes and a home-made ginger muffin when I stopped off to say goodbye to Christabel.

'Oh Helly,' she had said, grabbing me in her mumsy way on the doorstep. 'Darling girl. Marilyn told me she bumped into you on the beach and the two of you had a lovely chat. She'll be down in a minute. She's upstairs showering.'

The cottage smelt of baking, laced with the smoke of a recently lit fire. I had let myself be pulled inside, arms limp as my sister tugged off my coat, scolding me for looking pale. I told her I had decided to head back a day early after all, but wanted to assure her how happy I was for her and Marilyn first. She was hugging me before I'd finished the sentence.

'I'd also like to give this a quick boost, if I can?' I waggled my phone once we were disentangled, a little sheepishly, since it was overindulgence that had made me forget the usual ritual of plugging it in overnight.

'But of course. There's a charger in the kitchen. I'll put the kettle on. Tea? Coffee?'

'No thanks – this is only a fly-past. I'm going to drop in on Daddy too.' I followed her into the cosy country kitchen, with its dark blue aga and spotty curtains and oak dresser. 'About you and Marilyn...' I glanced upwards where a faint creak of footsteps had started and stopped. There were heavy dark beams criss-crossing every ceiling in the cottage, but here they were studded with prancing porcelain animals – a fox, a rabbit, a duck – hand-painted and expensive, but with that hint of tweeness that was typically Christabel. 'Marilyn mentioned your future plans...' I paused, wary of the delicacy of the subject I wanted to address, not wanting to botch it, 'which I'd love to chat about properly, darling – on our own – in due course...'

'Oh, chat away,' said Christabel gaily, holding out a plate of gingery muffins, which were emitting faint whorls of steam from their recent spell in the oven.

It occurred to me that my sister's faintly blundering manner was never unintentional, that she deployed it deliberately, and effectively, like armour. 'It's just... well... like I said, Christy, I truly am so happy for you both, but I hope you won't let Marilyn...' I cast another glance upwards, '...rush you into anything...' The intense way Christabel was staring at me made it hard to go on. '...On any front.' I took a muffin just to be polite, nibbling its crusty edges, but then peeling off the paper case and eating properly because its warm moist texture, sweet with honey and the tang of ginger, was so delicious.

'You mean, about us getting married?' Christabel had demolished her own cake in three quick bites and was dusting the crumbs off her fingers. 'And here she is,' she cried, clapping her hands in royal welcome as Marilyn appeared in the doorway, barefoot in a long purple smock dress, her hair a glistening black mesh, her face shining.

'Hey, Helena, long time no see.' She fluttered her fingers at me.

I left soon afterwards, with little more said and the urge to talk to Jack swelling again. If anyone understood the potential threat of grasping outsiders to families, it was him.

The quick stop at the hospital only fuelled such concerns. Daddy was fast asleep, pink-faced, eye-lids translucent, his once thick, silvery hair sticking up in wisps; despite the doctor's reassuring words, he looked as vulnerable as a baby and should certainly not be harried with talk of unexpected weddings, I reflected fiercely, let alone the future implications of Christabel signing half her worldly goods over to a person we barely knew. It wasn't about meanness, it was sheer good sense.

Back in the hospital car park, I checked my phone, boosted into a little life thanks to its fifteen-minute charge at Christabel's. A message from Madeleine sat at the top of the emails. It was the one I had been waiting for. Hoping for. The thought of Jack's reaction to such momentous news made my heart skip. I would surprise him with it, I decided, along with my early return home.

Hope you are having a useful day

I texted him, because no morning communication would have been odd, then quickly switching the phone off, both to resist the temptation of spilling the beans and to save what was left of the battery.

* * *

'It's only me,' I called, hearing music upstairs. I dropped my bag in the hall and headed straight to our small downstairs lavatory, tucked under the staircase beside the door to the basement. Thanks to the bottle of water, I was in something of a hurry.

I fished my phone out of my jacket pocket while on the loo, going straight to emails because I wanted to see Madeleine's words again – check I hadn't read too much into them – before sharing the news with Jack. My eye was caught instead by an unread message further down the page, standing out from the others because it was in bold:

UrgentInformation134@mail.com

I hesitated, wary of scams and phishers. The low-battery warning was already on screen, so I opened the message anyway, resolving to ignore any attachments, no matter how enticing. There was nothing suspicious, however, and no name either. Just one line of typed capitals saying:

YOUR HUSBAND IS CHEATING ON YOU.

I carefully set the phone down on the edge of the basin. Around me, the white tiled walls shifted, floating, edging in.

The extractor fan, humming like a swarm of trapped bees, brought me round. I swayed at the basin as I washed my hands, scared to raise my face to the mirror in case it was her I saw, not me. Her. She. The Someone. Not imagined, but real. A person who breathed, whose skin had touched Jack's. All these months, the deflections, the lies, masked by the saintly camouflage of his beautiful canvases. I tried to picture her, but for once nothing would come, not even the woman in the lift. In becoming real, she was unimaginable.

It took courage to raise my gaze to the mirror, but there was still only me. The eyes the same dense blue as Christabel's, but smaller and feline; almonds instead of globes. Eyeliner, hastily applied after the beach walk, had held up well – a firm sweeping line along the upper lid, with a little dash of a tail into the creases at the outer corners. I opened them wider, trying to make the tiny lines disappear. Intervention would be required, but not yet, not yet. Madeleine was a wax doll these days and who would want that?

Nothing should be done until it absolutely had to, that was the point. Nothing. Not in any quarter. Like with the thing Christabel seemed hell-bent on raking up. An early life lesson. It went to the wire. It got messy. But, with her help, it had got sorted. Despite what got lost, the price paid.

I leaned closer still to the mirror, shovelling my hands up under the streaky blonde tumble of my hair, digging my nails into my scalp until it hurt, resisting the urge to go further, to draw blood. Hair was different to skin. Hair needed major intervention. Regularly. Not a penny wasted there. My tresses were indisputably tremendous. I pushed at them more wildly, admiring the artful, inexact parting, and the way the long front strands opened like sleek curtains over my clear high forehead before curving in their cute way over the broad frame of my cheekbones and down to my chin. An English Rose, people had called me, back in the day, when it meant nothing, when the fear of being alone was beyond imagining.

Christabel was right about my being pale, but it still suited me, enhancing the darkish red of my mouth and the natural thickness of the upper lip – a prize asset, I had come to realise, long before reaching an age where I understood quite why. I tried to blow a kiss at my own beautiful self, but my lips would only tremble and I could look no more.

I opened the toilet door briskly, mechanically. I knew I was in shock. I moved like an automaton. Inside, my heart punched, a fist in a cage. Upstairs, the music wailed. *I would do anything for love.* It was coming from the pod in our bathroom, I realised. Jack still didn't know I was home. I unzipped my boots, shaking them off my feet as I walked through the kitchen and into the sitting room, to the cabinet that housed the lead crystal glasses once used by the same grandmother who had owned the linen of which I was so fond; blinded by cataracts for the last twenty years of her life, widowed, housebound and miserable, she had reputedly made liberal and frequent use of them, for whisky mainly, by all accounts.

I picked one out, stout and heavy, and turned on my heel, looking straight in front of me as I headed back to the kitchen cupboard where we kept spirits. A glance right or left would have meant having to see the evidence – the detritus – of Jack's and my shared life – chairs, cushions, tables, books, papers, ornaments, the television, the pictures. Worst of all, it might involve a glimpse of the little girl tearing through the wheat field on the wall between our bookcases, her white dress and yellow hair flying under the sun.

The ice machine made a racket as the cubes clattered into the glass. At the touch of the gin, and then the Martini, the cubes cracked like flexing knuckle-joints. I wanted a slice of lime, but there was only a lemon in the fruit bowl, shrivelled like an old face. I carved out a slice from its middle, picking out the best and costliest of our various knives for the job, the one that had come from Japan along with the easy one-swipe sharpener to keep its long blade razor-keen. I gave the glass a shake, jangling the ice, and then drank, deeply, until the tumbler was empty and my lips numb.

Upstairs, the music cut out. I strained my ears, the fist of my heart punching more wildly as Jack's footsteps came into earshot, progressing down the stairs, then stopping abruptly. I remembered my baggy red leather holdall with its gold buckles, dumped carelessly in the middle of the hall.

'Helena?' I could hear the clang of incredulity in his tone.

'Hello, darling,' I cried, leaping into action like a jack-in-the-box and skipping along the hallway, weightless with adrenalin. 'Thought I'd surprise you.' I swung round the bannister post to greet him, as carefree as a dancer, flexing a smile intended to give no indication of the effort or hurt it required. The smile withered as it arrived, however, thanks not so much to the shock of confronting Jack himself, the words of the email blazing in my brain, but because he was carrying a huge suitcase and two bulging art-bags, one over each shoulder.

On seeing me, he froze halfway down the staircase, like a burglar caught mid-getaway. His appearance was another shock. This was not the grey-faced, windswept husband who had hugged me close in Daddy's drive twenty-four hours earlier. This was a sleek handsome man, his hair burnished from the shower, his beard freshly trimmed, highlighting its gingery glints and the strong curve of his jaw. He was dressed in a favourite shirt, a cobalt blue cotton-silk one and his newest tan chinos, the waistband loops threaded with a hand-stitched multi-coloured belt that I had given him for Christmas.

'A surprise indeed.' His voice was firm and bland. He balanced the suitcase on the edge of a step, rearranging his grip on the handle.

'Jack, what are you doing? Where the fuck are you going?'

'To Brian's.' A strange wild smile played over his face. The mask of inscrutability, perfected, I now realised, for months and months, seemed to have deserted him. He dropped his eyes to his feet as he began to move again, descending so slowly I knew it was because he was thinking what to say rather than because of the encumbrance of his luggage.

'Brian? With that lot? What on earth for?' I was reeling, flinging out anything, while in my head my new knowledge spun, waiting for the right moment to be released. I had power over that at least. But not over Jack, it would seem, because the other woman wasn't a phantom, but a real person. Because, as I knew now for certain, he had been *cheating*.

I took a step back as he arrived with his load on ground level, managing to stumble into my red bag. I kicked it viciously out of the way, causing a stabbing pain through the toes of my shoeless foot.

Jack still appeared to be moving in slow motion. He put all the cases down, carefully propping the art-bags against the walls and then dusted his palms, with a strange fastidiousness. 'Brian thinks he's now got some potential buyers lined up – a group called Freemans – city investors, remember? So, I'm taking over as much of everything as I can. In whatever I can.' He nodded at the bags and hefty suitcase. 'He and I are having dinner.' His hands, sliding together, made light slapping sounds. 'Obviously, I thought you were in Cornwall. Until tomorrow. I tried to phone you, but your phone's been off.' He almost looked at me, but then brushed at something invisible on his trousers.

'Dinner with Brian – taking your stuff – why didn't you mention it before?'

'Yes, dinner with Brian,' he echoed, ignoring the question. His smile when he looked up, properly this time, was ghastly, a man dying.

I had shifted backwards, nearer the front door. I folded my arms, standing sentinel, gripping my elbows to hide my shaking. To my left was a spindly Victorian hat and umbrella stand that Jack and I had picked out together on a balmy Sunday afternoon in a Sussex town famed for its antique shops. There had been a cream tea too, jokes about whether the cream or jam went on first, Jack's admission that he liked lashings of butter too. 'Bring on the heart attack,' he had cried, delivering a hearty thump to his chest as he wolfed an entire, laden scone in two mouthfuls, depositing flecks of cream on the tips of the moustache that had eventually evolved into the beard. We had fallen in love with the stand, with its scratched skinny legs, brass hooks and brown speckled mirror. We had loaded it with tremendous care into the back of the car, putting the seats down and tucking it up with blankets like some delicate child. No speeding, no bumps, no sharp turns, all the way back to north London.

'I can hardly cancel now,' Jack said, speaking with sudden energy and precision. 'I said I'd be there by seven. I was going to Uber...' His eyes darted to the hatstand, drawing my attention to a small array of items arranged along the little shelf under its mottled mirror: wallet, keys, phone. And something else too, parked under the phone, its rectangular edges peeping out; burgundy-coloured. His passport. Somewhere inside me, the incredible offer outlined in Madeleine's email, of not one but two summer exhibitions, swelled and shrank.

'Open it.' I gestured with my nose at the suitcase, squatting next to him like a large, obedient dog.

'I am taking artwork to Brian's,' he said obstinately, pathetically, not moving. He looked less fresh now, pasty-faced. Dark damp smudges were dotting the front of his smart blue shirt.

'Open the fucking suitcase. Let's see the *artwork*.'

'No.'

I could sense Jack bracing himself. My time was running out. One wrong move and he could get the better of me – and the door – and be gone. She existed and he was going to her. He was leaving me, and sticking to his stupid little story. 'I'll phone Brian, shall I?'

'Helena, that really wouldn't—'

'Open the case then. Let me see all the work that didn't fit into the art-bags. For Brian's city investors. Let me see it.'

'No.'

'You are such a liar, Jack Aspen.' I spoke in a whisper and, perhaps because of the unexpectedness of that, managed to trap his gaze properly in the crossfire of mine. For that instant, he was truly a creature cornered, blinking in the glare. Exposed. A cheater. And afraid. Jack was lying because he couldn't face what was real. Like always. Because I was the one who said the difficult things. Even in this, it was all up to me. It was almost funny. 'Who is she, Jack? Your woman? Tell me about her.'

'Helena, I am going to Brian's, I swear it...'

A scream spiralled out of me then, a noise and force from which I felt oddly separate; a sound years in the making, it felt like, powered by comprehension as much as torment, everything at last making sense because of how it was falling apart. I spun in the same moment, seizing his little travel pack of things from the hatstand shelf and ramming them into my jacket pockets, the keys last because I managed to jab and twist them in the front door first. I was so quick that Jack was still in motion as I threw myself back up against it, his handsome face ragged with horror as he dived like a lumbering rugby player for my pockets, yelling that I had no right.

'Tell me who she is.' Indignation made me strong. To be deceived, to be made an idiot of, through all the long, hurtful months of tiptoeing on eggshells. Or had it been years? Was there one woman or were there hundreds? Nothing was certain, least of all the past. War cries blew out of my throat, but there were no tears.

'There's no one—'

'*Liar*—'

We had become animals, wrestling, badly. He had my wrists and kept trying to clamp them in one hand so he could reach into my jacket pockets with the other. His grip was brutal, but I was the more agile, the more mobile, the more furious. We tumbled as we fought, a mini-scrum, collapsing and reforming, until, in one violent twisting effort to free myself, I fell heavily against the wall, catching my face on the corner of a heavy gold-framed print of a harbour – an old birthday gift to me from Daphne. The picture swung violently before slipping off its hook and crashing to the floor. Jack let go and I hurdled the wreckage and sprinted into the kitchen.

By the time he appeared in the doorway, I had the Japanese knife in my hand. In my haste, I knocked the wizened lemon with its missing segment off the counter. It bowled across the chessboard floor tiles towards Jack's feet like a cricket ball. 'Tell me who she is.' I was panting hard. My cheekbone throbbed like a pulse.

'Helena, calm down.' He edged towards me, one arm out, like a poacher about to throw a net. 'You've hurt yourself. Your face...'

'You've hurt me. *You've hurt me.*' I could feel a warm trickle from the cut running down my cheek. I stuck my tongue out, tasting blood. 'If you leave, that's what I shall say. That you hurt me. That you did this. I'll get you locked up.'

'Helena—'

'Tell me who she is.'

'Your face is a mess. You should put something on it. Here, for god's sake.' He tore a piece of kitchen paper off the roll beside the kettle and handed it to me. I snatched it and balled it in my palm before dropping it onto the floor. Of course, there was blood. This was war.

'You've assaulted me.'

'No, I haven't.'

'Who will they believe, Jack? I'll take pictures of my face. Evidence. I've got others I can use too. From before.' He had been coming closer, but I waggled the knife and he took a step back.

'Evidence? From before? What are you talking about?' For a moment he looked so baffled – the old Jack – and it gave me such a tug, because of loving him and because, even in this direness, my catapulting brain was somehow keeping me half a step ahead. The never-sent photos for Hugh after my patio fall had flown into my brain from nowhere, like inspiration. Another weapon. In war, one picked up whatever came to hand. It wasn't about wanting to. It was about fighting for what you could not afford to lose.

'Just tell me the truth, Jack. Tell me everything. Or I'll ruin you.' I could hear the new, desperate register in my voice, but Jack held my gaze boldly this time, his blue eyes glassy with stubbornness – being loyal, I realised miserably; protecting her, as he had been all along. Her, not me.

I sprang at him, swishing the blade and he side-stepped out of reach, panic scudding across his face, eradicating all the traces of defiance. The damp patches on the front of his shirt were starting to join up, creating one dark map from his armpits down.

'Helena, for god's sake, put that thing down so we can talk sensibly...'

'Her. Name.' I was holding the knife handle so hard the joints in my fingers had begun to ache. 'I have known she exists. I have *known*, Jack. And today someone kindly wrote to confirm it. A *kind* and *honest* someone.'

I saw his expression shift – traces of surprise and dismay, followed swiftly by the close-down. The resistance was in its own way, astonishing. It made me realise how long it was since he had shown any genuine openness or talked to me properly, about *anything*. He had been 'managing' me, keeping me at bay, doing the minimum. He was still doing it. Even now, with the precipice so close.

'Her name, Jack.' I tugged up the jacket sleeve of my left arm and pressed the pointy tip of the knife to the soft white underside of my wrist. I was aware of him going very still. The vein was so narrow and blue. A tempting thread, just a pinprick from the surface. I stared at it, breathing hard.

'No, Helena...' His voice was a growl. He started towards me, but I swerved away, holding the arm higher, pressing the knife a little more firmly, but still with the flat rather than the point of the blade.

A few tears were spilling down my face now, soundlessly. 'This woman. What is her name?' I had to keep blinking to see properly. I wondered, as if from a great distance, what tiny adjustment of the angle of the knife would see the layers of skin part, how quickly the blood would flow.

A sob came from Jack's throat before he answered. 'She... Her name is Fr... Freya.'

'Freya what... *Freya what*?'

But Jack had picked his moment and launched himself, and we were wrestling again, the knife somehow staying in my hand as it scythed the air. My arms and legs were starting to feel hopeless and heavy, all the Dutch courage sucked dry. On the island across the room, the bottles of gin and Martini came in and out of view. They made me want to surrender, to stop caring, stop trying. I managed one last wild kick and Jack released me with a breathy whimper, dropping to the floor and clutching his groin.

I hesitated. But he deserved it, I told myself, he deserved it, and there were things to do. Important things. Like hiding the contents of my pockets. So that Jack could not leave. Yes, that was it, Jack must not leave, because if he did, I would be alone. There was no one else left now. No one but Jack.

I dodged round him and darted out of the kitchen, but it was getting harder, to move, to think what to do. The knife had gone limp in my hand. I slammed the kitchen door behind me, partly to buy time, and partly to help me concentrate. To see Jack on the ground like that was awful. It made me want to curl up behind him, to spoon together for comfort.

But there was no comfort now, only betrayal and hurt and the desperate need to stop Jack fleeing. I could not be left. It wasn't a choice; it was a fact. At the basement door I paused, opening it and turning on the light, but then rushed on, silent in my socks, to the hall instead. Doubt was suddenly fogging my brain. Doubt that felt close to hope. There was the woman. *Freya*. But maybe Jack hadn't been lying about going to Brian's. Maybe the passport was a coincidence. Maybe...

The suitcase was lying on its side, a beached carcass. I slashed at it with the knife. One slicing motion and the material parted easily, exposing exactly the entrails I had most feared to see: layers of Jack's bright cotton shirts and trousers, his blue cashmere jumper, checked boxers, carefully folded, neatly balled-up socks, his loafers, his phone charger, his large tartan washbag...

Hearing the rattle of the kitchen door handle, I froze, crouched over the case, expecting to see Jack's face at any moment through the banister posts. Inside, a part of me had collapsed. My faceless rival shimmered in my mind's eye, ready with her own suitcase, no doubt; a whole new life zipped into a bag. *He's yours*, I thought. *I am lost. You have won.*

But then Jack didn't appear and I heard his voice instead, muffled and calling my name, as he thumped his way down the basement steps. I only had a moment, but that was all it took. I ran to the basement door, pulled it shut and turned the key.

* * *

'Brian? Hello there. Yes, it's Helena. How are you?'

I had been lying on the sofa with my phone charging next to me and Jack's on my lap, willing it to spring into life. I didn't want Brian, I wanted Her. Beside me, the gin and the Martini bottles had started doing their job, though I hadn't gone mad. I knew it was going to be a long night. I had even eaten something – a bag of salted cashews and some chilli-flavoured crisps – and was feeling weirdly, wildly alert.

Half an hour on and the shouting and door-banging was growing more sporadic, more despairing. On the table next to me sat Jack's old paint-spattered laptop, fished out of the suitcase and scoured for evidence that I hadn't been able to find. Not one full stop. Not one comma. That the password hadn't changed had prepared me for the likelihood of this, but it was still disappointing. His phone presented the bigger challenge because of not knowing the bloody code, so the call from Brian was quite a moment.

'Is Jack with you?' Brian sounded understandably confused at my voice. 'I mean, this is his mobile, right?'

'Yes... yes, it is, and I'm sorry he hasn't been able to ring. Because I know he was due at yours tonight, wasn't he...'? I left the sentence hanging. I was flying blind, I realised. I knew nothing.

'Yes, for a bite and staying over. I was expecting him half an hour ago. He said you've been in Cornwall... that your father—'

'Yes, indeed...' The verification of going to Brian's took a moment to process, as did the reference to staying the night. Jack had made no mention of that. In my red-alert state I knew this had to be just part of the story, that Jack, depressingly, and like the best liars, had learnt to camouflage his deceptions with truth. 'Actually, Brian, it's all been very difficult...and look, I'm sorry, but Jack's not going to be able to make it tonight after all.'

'God, I hope everything is okay?'

'Oh, it will be...'

'So is your trip off?'

'Our trip...'

'I could swing by, if that would help, pick up the paintings anyway,' he chattered on, no notion of how hard I was holding the phone, trying to compute every scrap of what I was hearing. 'I know Jack was worried about security, with you two being away so long, and of course that would mean I could still follow up with Freemans...'

'That's the bank interested in buying some works, right?' I fudged, while my mind whirred. Jack had told Brian that he and I were going away. Me instead of Her. He had taken the precaution of lying even to his oldest friend.

'It's a hedge fund, but yep, that's it...' Brian was sounding more cautious, like it had dawned we were playing a game he didn't understand. Which we were.

'That's so kind, Brian, but I think not. Everything is on hold. For the time being anyway. Jack will be in touch as soon as he can.' Another round of door-hammering started and I quickly ended the call.

I topped up my drink, swigging from it as I took Jack's phone into the kitchen, where, after carefully placing it in the middle of our largest chopping board, I swung at it with the hammer from the odd-job drawer. Smithereens skittered across the counter and onto the floor. Before finishing the job, I picked out the SIM card and put it in an egg cup which I stowed at the back of the top shelf of the crockery cupboard.

I tried the same with the laptop, for good measure, but it was harder to destroy. I switched my attention to his passport instead, using the kitchen scissors to cut every page into tiny asymmetrical strips, standing over the bin so that they scattered among the muck of wet coffee granules, eggshells and cheese rinds that constituted the evidence of Jack's twenty-four hours of fending for himself.

Afterwards, I took what was left of my drink and stood in front of the little girl with the daffodil hair in the picture between the bookcases. I told her I had her back now, and that everything was going to be all right and she wasn't to worry. I told her that marriage was for better, for worse and this was the 'worse' and that's why it was worth hanging on. I told her, too, about the bloodied mess in the Norfolk woodland left by Christabel helping me get rid of something I hadn't wanted – not with a single cell of my being – only to find that, once it was done with, the same treacherous cells had gone and started missing it, mourning it, aching for it, all the more as the years went by and it transpired that the bloodied mess had been my only chance.

This business with Jack made me feel the same, I explained, like I was about to lose something that I would regret, in ways unimaginable as well as obvious, for the rest of my life. 'The point being, that one has to hang on to what one has in this world,' I explained, 'because not having it is...' I stopped, needing to cry a little. 'I love Jack, you see. I bloody love him.'

'Helena.'

I didn't turn round. I hadn't heard him come in.

'I forced the door.'

I swirled the ice cubes in my glass. The tears had stopped as suddenly as they started. I cleared my throat. 'I'm not going to let you leave, Jack. I will never let you go.'

'I know,' he said dully.

Only then did I glance over my shoulder. He looked as if he too had been crying. 'Not to give up on you, that's something, isn't it?' He looked so forlorn, so broken – so exactly how I felt – that my shoulders started shaking, as if more tears might be on the way when they weren't. 'I know this has got to stop, by the way.' I held up the glass, giving the ice slithers another rattle, before placing it carefully on the floor against the skirting board. 'Properly, not like before. The AA and all that palaver.' I wiped my nose on my sleeve. 'I truly will. You know what I'm like when I set my mind to something.'

'Yes, I do.' His voice was hollow. His eyes had glued themselves to some distant spot on the carpet.

'And... she... the woman... Freya...' My throat burned from having to say her name.

'I will give her up, but I won't talk about her.' He interjected in a fierce rush, clasping and unclasping his fists, still not looking at me. 'I will never talk about her. I'm sorry, but that's how it has to be.'

I bit my cheeks. I had so much right to anger. But for now he had bust out of the basement not to leave, but to stay.

'You are fearless, Helena,' he said bleakly, like it was the worst thing anyone could be, 'the most fearless, bloody-minded—'

'Oh, but I'm not, Jack. I'm mostly terrified.'

He let out a scornful laugh, his eyes at last meeting mine. 'Of what?'

'Of losing my mind – going under, like I did before. Of losing you, like I nearly have. Of there being nothing of me that will every truly last or matter...' I folded myself down onto the carpet as I spoke, shuffling back to lean against the wall beside the glass, under the picture.

Jack slumped on the floor opposite, propping his back against the side of the armchair so that we were facing each other. The air vibrated. We had been at war, and there would be more, but this was a truce.

'Brian phoned. I said you weren't coming. I implied there were problems because of Daddy. I said you'd be in touch in due course.' I hesitated. 'He mentioned something about a trip, which I guessed was you and her. I said it was off. Where the hell were you going anyway?'

Jack just shook his head, a prisoner hanging onto his rights.

I reminded myself not to care, to let it pass, for these moments. He was staying. He was defeated. She was defeated. He was mine. 'I've destroyed your phone, by the way. With the hammer.'

'Yes, I saw.' His tone was deathly.

'And your passport. I cut it up.'

He moaned softly, swinging his head.

'I don't want you to contact her again, Jack. Ever. I want her gone.

Those are my terms. Cauterised. Like she never existed. I want you back, Jack. You and me. I want us back.'

'And what about what I want?' he whispered.

'You've got me.' My voice was small and full of longing, and I couldn't bear to look at him because I knew that his expression could not – and might never again – hold what I most needed to see...fondness, respect, if not actual love. 'And...' I paused. We couldn't be further from the context I had envisaged for playing my masterstroke, but it was all I had. 'Maddy has come through for you. I have been working on her for months, not telling you, for fear of getting your hopes up. You've got two summer exhibitions if you want them. Edinburgh and London. Top spaces. She let me know today – it's partly why I came back early, to tell you. She'll take a cut, but she'll get everyone. Everyone, Jack.'

'Thank you.' There was a faint trace of amazement in his voice. He bent his long legs up, hugging them and resting his forehead on his knees.

'Did you ever bring her here? To our home? To our *bed*?' It was a truce and he had said no questions, but, really, it was impossible. I wanted her eye colour now. Her chest size. I wanted to know the sounds she made when she came and what she ate for breakfast. I wanted to gorge myself on every last hideous detail.

'No, she did not come here.'

'And do you... did you love her?'

It was torture to watch how he struggled. 'I loved how she made me feel,' he said at length, spacing the words, as if the release of each one caused physical pain. 'She was kind. She was nice to me...' He hesitated. 'Forgiving.'

'Different from me, then,' I said in a brittle voice, so he would know all the anger and hurt was just a beat away, that I was holding it in.

'Yes,' he whispered, 'different.'

'When, Jack? When did it start? How?'

'I won't tell.' He glared over the tops of his knees. 'It's over...' His voice cracked. 'Isn't that enough?'

It wasn't enough and I couldn't imagine it ever being so. 'Do you even love me?' I hated not being able to hide my desperation.

'Yes, Helly, yes... I do... everything just got so... complicated.'

I let a few moments pass. 'For how long then? I have a right to know that, at the very least.'

'Seven... eight months.' He shrugged, as if he wasn't sure, and it made me not believe him. A year would make more sense, maybe more. All that time, I'd been living with a ghost, I realised bitterly, an echo of Jack, rather than Jack himself, and it made me wonder suddenly if it had been the same for her. How thinly Jack had spread himself between us. What had been left to spare after the priority of his work.

'I think you are the most selfish man I have ever known,' I said quietly.

We sat in silence for a few minutes.

'You said someone told you,' he asked suddenly. 'Who?'

I was half tempted to drag out my answer, make him suffer. But we were both pared back, beyond sparring. There would be torture. I would not spare him in the weeks and months ahead. But not tonight. 'I've no idea. It was just an email with a random address. It said you were *cheating* on me. Maybe it was someone who felt betrayed, like me. Did she – does she – have a husband? A partner?'

'Yes, she does.' Jack covered his face with his hands. 'Jesus...'

'Are you even *sorry*?' I cried, sickened again to see how he cared for her.

'Yes, yes...' He peeled his fingers from his face.

'Say it then, for Christ's sake.'

'Sorry,' he groaned. 'Sorry. Sorry.'

'You must never contact her, Jack,' I repeated. 'Never. Then she'll know there's no hope. It's the only way. She can sort her own fucking life out. Jack? No contact.'

He nodded, his eyes locking onto mine with a flicker of something that gave me hope.

'Maybe she's been your muse,' I conceded bitterly. 'This Freya. I wondered that, you know, sometimes. Which isn't to say—'

'It wasn't like that.'

'Oh really? What was it like then? Fucking someone other than your wife?' The cut on my cheekbone was pulsing again, but every part of me hurt.

'It felt...' he shuddered, squeezing his eyes shut. 'It *felt*, Helena, as if I was a total failure and it didn't matter what the hell I did.'

'You are not a failure,' I murmured. I was aware of the girl in the picture above my head. I would have to tell Jack what I had told her, I realised. He needed to know everything if we were to go on. Just as I would need to extract every last detail about the affair. He was making his stand, but I would prevail. The story of Freya. I would wear him down. I had the SIM. We had barely begun. It was going to be unspeakable.

When my phone buzzed from the table, we both jumped. I crawled to it, aware of Jack's heavy gaze, fearing more anonymous messages perhaps, or maybe even Freya herself, finding a way through. But it was a text from Christabel, which I read in silence and then held out for Jack to see, the tears already streaming down my face.

You have to come back. An infection has got Daddy. The doctors are saying it's near the end.

'You'll have to drive,' I sobbed, after Jack had hugged me and we were both on our feet.

PART THREE

FRAN, JUNE 2019

CHAPTER 12

I

The colours charge at me in a mountainous wall, towering red, orange, purple, green beasts, ready to gobble me up. I try to run, but cannot move. I try to shout, but no words will come.

I wake to a tangle of sweat-dampened sheets and a rapping on my door, but think I must still be half-dreaming because I've no clue where I am. On a small table beside me, a raggedy moth dances on the bulb of a light with a green lampshade. Around it are whitewashed walls, a wicker chair, a cream rug on a terracotta floor, and slatted pine window-shutters, peeking between long muslin curtains. My wrist-watch seems to think it's half past five in the morning.

'I come,' Catarina calls, already in the room, master key in hand, her black eyes bright with concern, her long jet hair streaming over the shoulders of a flapping blue silk dressing gown.

The jigsaw of the last twenty-four hours reassembles in the same instant: the dingy Edinburgh hotel room, Pete wiping his belt on his trousers; his and Harry's appalled and incredulous faces as I brief the entire plane on the state of my mythical heavy period; the air stewardess with the glint in her eye that tells me she'll fight my corner; the carousel of the airport concourse, the taste of fear still swirling through the relief, and then the word 'Madrid' surfacing through the mêlée like inspiration, a star to follow.

I am mortified more than anything. I've not seen the hotelier since she introduced herself some eight hours earlier, when her hair was a tidy black pincushion, and she pressed a glass of orange juice into my hand, ushering me into the guesthouse's cubbyhole of a reception for checking in. A mystifying quantity of personal contact information in the UK was required, for which I used Rob and Jo's details, to be safe, as well as the Santander card, which didn't work, and then did. Endless signing and paper-stamping followed, to the accompaniment, in my host's near incomprehensible, scatter-gun English, of a list of the guest-house's modest amenities and the fact that my very reasonable room rate included breakfast.

'I am so sorry...' I stammer. The poor woman is staring at me. My sweating, the rawness of my throat, tells me I have been shouting – I dread to think for how long or how loud. 'I had a bad dream, you know? *Un Cauchmar*?' It is the wrong language, of course, and does nothing to allay the hotelier's stormy expression or encourage her to withdraw. 'I am okay, really.'

'You not okay,' she corrects me.

She remains, arms akimbo, in the doorway, surveying the room. Her eyes widen at the sight of the blood-dotted pink T-shirt slung over the side of the chair and then the calamity of the sheets, which, as well as looking as though they have been minced in a washing machine, also sport the occasional faint smear of blood. Oh god, as does the top I have on, I realise, my only spare from Edinburgh, pulled over my head before I crawled into bed.

I recognise it is time to wrest control of the situation and struggle into a more upright position, trying not to wince. 'Yesterday I had a silly accident? Acc-i-dent.' I tug at the shirt I'm wearing, doing my best to indicate that I am referring to my ribs. 'But okay now.' I do a thumbs up sign. Even this small action hurts. Indeed, it's as if, given the chance to rest, my body has gone into some sort of lockdown. I think of my handbag supply of paracetamol, remembering it has run dry and deciding that the first task of the day must be to find a Spanish chemist.

The rolling walls of colour in my nightmare had been about pain, I realise – physical discomfort rather than terror. All traces of that had started sloughing off me, like some weighty old skin, as soon as the airplane begun nosing its way up through the Scottish clouds on the way to Spain. I read the in-flight magazine. I ate, I drank, I dozed. When the little dot of Madrid came into view on the overhead screen, I didn't think I had ever seen a place so exactly in the middle of its country, so perfectly surrounded, so safe.

Following the Exit signs after Passport Control, fatigue and the inconvenience of my body hurting had not stopped the little bubble of elation growing. Yes, the man at the Tourist Information desk told me, Casa Maria did happen to have one room available until Saturday, thanks to a late cancellation. If my ribcage had been up to it, I'd have done a little jig. 'You a lucky lady,' he remarked, reading the delight in my face, his moustache as big as his grin as he handed over the printed confirmation of the booking and a receipt-cum-ticket for the bus ride into town. And on the bus, with the lights of a new land blinking through the darkness beyond the motorway, it was the sense of being lucky that I savoured. I had made this leap, all on my own. And so far, I was still standing, figuratively anyway.

'You sick,' says Catarina, ignoring the shooing motions I have been making with my arms. Instead of leaving, she pushes the door shut behind her, and starts tugging the bottom sheet out of its tight hospital corners, jabbing a finger at the wicker chair by way of an instruction for me to move.

I see no other option, but I am embarrassed at my bare legs and their scattering of cloudy bruises, which I hadn't noticed before. I hug myself as I sit, scrunching the T-shirt out of sight between my knees.

Catarina mutters to herself as she continues to tackle the bed, profanities from the sound of it. I try out hand signals for regret whenever she looks my way, but she doesn't smile. Soon, she is coming and going from a linen cupboard in the corridor, her thunderous expression fixed. I shall probably be asked to leave, I reflect gloomily, unable to suppress the hope that it won't be until after my included breakfast. I had been too tired to forage for anything resembling supper, and the early-evening meal on the Edinburgh plane feels a hundred years ago.

Medico, she says when she is done, placing what looks like a clean nightshirt onto my lap, the bed having been transformed into the plump, pristine igloo that greeted my arrival. She is pointing down the corridor, as if ready to find me some analgesics there and then; and tempted though I am to nod, I say no thank you but thank you, shaking my head, between assurances – and considerable doubt as to whether they are understood – that I shall be getting my own just as soon as the day dawns.

The garment turns out to be a man's shirt, soft from laundering and frayed at the collar and cuffs. I brave a bit of body-washing, splashing myself at the basin in my small en suite before slipping it on, glad that the mirror allows not much more than a postcard view of my eyes and nose. They look pretty normal. And my torso, under the gentle touch of the worn cotton, actually feels not too bad. The inside of my head feels even better – full of air, but in a good way. I crawl into bed and fall asleep.

* * *

When I am woken again, by more knocking, three sharp raps this time, I know there is no question of my having shouted out. The room is still blissfully dark and cool. Tiny slits of light line the edges of the window shutters, forming gold rectangles on the tiled floor. I have been in the deepest, dreamless of sleeps, weightless and held, like swinging in a hammock. And time is playing tricks because, somehow, the hands of my watch have flown round to eleven o'clock. Which means this could well be the eviction order, I reflect ruefully, as I call out 'Coming' and ease myself out of bed, unfurling from what feels like the exact position I fell back into it five hours earlier. My stomach growls as I move, presenting the more immediate, distressing realisation that I have now, after all that, managed to miss the set breakfast.

There is a man in the corridor, who starts speaking at once, in careful, textbook learnt English. 'Please to forgive my disturbance. My name is Guillermo Noguero. I am doctor, and the brother of Catarina. She say you are very sick and she ask me to come.'

I only have the door open a few inches and the face I see is one of those swarthy ones already showing a faint shadow where the razor has done its early-morning duty. The eyes are a rich chocolate brown, hooded by dark eyebrows and hair as jet as his sister's, swept off his face and curling round the backs of his ears

'Thank you, I really am grateful... but I am not sick.'

'My sister has concern for you...'

'No need, really, I just... It was kind of her to ask you.' I am self-conscious in the borrowed shirt, as well as a little discombobulated from my drugged sleep. 'Honestly.' I offer up my best grin. 'I just need a few analgesics – some *medico* – and I'll be right as rain.'

He shakes his head, looking momentarily bemused. '*Medico* it mean doctor and that is me; but if you need medicine, maybe I can help also. Catarina will not speak to me again if you refuse, and my sister she make a terrible enemy.' There is a hint of a smile in the broad mouth that is the exact replica of his sibling's. She is clearly the older one, while he, at a guess, is in his late thirties. 'She will be here soon herself, so please, allow me, Senora Grove?' His dark eyes soften and it dawns on me that I am not to be kicked out – not that minute anyway – for lowering the tone and doubling the laundry bill, and that only a fool would deny such ready access to a medical opinion, given the pain I am in.

I nonetheless think of trust as I invite this stranger into my bedroom. He looks decent enough, smart in his dark suit, white shirt and light blue tie, one hand firmly gripping the handle of a square black leather doctor's case. He also nods respectfully, shaking my hand before crossing the threshold, and then tactfully busying himself with setting the case down on the winged wicker chair while I scamper back under the bedcovers.

After that, he asks if he might make use of the bathroom to wash his hands, emerging a couple of minutes later, shaking droplets off his fingers as he reaches for one of the fat clean towels that his sister has left hanging over the bed rail. I see in the same instant a flash of a wedding band, and have one blindsiding moment as echoes of old pain and unanswered questions surge. Jack had had just such a ring. We had decided upon this place together on a tide of hope, and yet now here I am, alone.

'May I?' The doctor is at the bedside now and picks up my wrist, pressing his fingers to the pulse while he examines his watch. 'Your heart rate a little fast,' he remarks quietly, laying my hand down, 'but maybe that is some stress?'

I have lurched from Jack to all that followed and what I have just escaped from, and yes, there is stress. I glance sideways, taking comfort from my phone, dead and unchargeable on the bedside table until I lay my hands on an adapter. I might not rush to do that. Because I have five days, I remind myself. Five days in the middle of the dot on the airplane map. I may be a little bruised, but I am safe. Mel and Rob know what has happened and where I am. I wrote them each an email before take-off, not yet able to face the one-to-one spotlight of their anxiety and interrogations, but telling them everything, saying I would be thinking through next steps, and would definitely be back in the UK on Saturday, spending the weekend with Rob and Jo, as my brother had requested.

By then, my phone had also been exploding with fresh vitriol from Pete, on the Gatwick Express with Harry and milking the role of the wronged husband. I had replied just once, saying that he and I were done and – summoning bravado – the next time he heard from me, it would be via a lawyer. Then I blocked his number. I had started on a very different message to Harry, when invective started pouring through that too, either at Pete's hand or by dictation, from the sound of it. Or maybe Harry was as angry as his father. So, with a heart like a boulder, I had simply written, Harry, whatever you feel, I love you, so please get in touch when you can.

'And how much is this going to cost anyway, Doctor...?' I have a stab at his name and make a hash of it. I am aware of sounding unfriendly. I have been distracted by the remembered fear of Harry not being able to call even if he wants to because of my phone being dead, and by the sight of the Spaniard feeding the ends of his stethoscope in his ears. Yesterday, I had morphed into someone brave and sharp, but now my arms suddenly seem to be pinning themselves to my sides at the prospect of the doctor having to set eyes on the damage under my borrowed nightshirt.

For the time being, however, he appears to have found my attempt to say his name amusing. Possibly – it occurs to me – because the reading of my heartbeat tells him I could do with a moment. He unhooks the stethoscope so that he can chortle freely. 'Please to call me William – that is Guillermo in Spanish, so more easy for you. And for my prices...' He releases a low whistle, raising his dark eyebrows, 'What can I say. My sister she already tell me she give you one of my own shirts to wear... so we are talking big bucks.' He starts to laugh again, but then stops quickly, because I am not joining in very well. 'I joke, Senora Grove...'

The bedroom door swings open in the same instant, steered by Catarina's elbow since she is carrying a large deep-sided tray, so laden that the muscles on her upper arms are standing out. The smells alone make me salivate: a plate of scrambled eggs, grilled tomatoes, fried potatoes, a hefty, dark sausage; a bowl of freshly cut strawberries; a glass of orange juice; a milk jug; a basket of croissant; butter pats, mini jam jars, a pot of coffee. My first thought is that she is en route to another guest.

When she exchanges grins with her brother, saying, 'English breakfast for English lady, but with morcilla sausage,' I burst into tears.

II

I have been geared up for a proper museum – ticket offices, roped-off areas, signposts to toilets – but Sorolla's elegant yellow-bricked town house, with its white balustrade and leafy green fountained court-yards, cooling just to look at in the Spanish June heat, makes me want to move into the place and never leave. Inside, the rooms are spacious but cosy, chock-a-block with the everyday things of life – chairs you want to sit in, cabinets full of trinkets and books, desks with paper and ink ready to go, all set among walls of lustrous colours and tapestried rugs that seem to float on the polished sea of soft brown wooden floors. In fact, I decide, it's as if the artist himself – and all the beautiful family members swirling through his dreamy paintings – has just popped out for a promenade, or a cup of tea, or a shot of absinthe, or whatever the hell people popped out for between 1863 and 1923 in Spain.

It's easy to see why Jack raved about the man. I even see how he tried to emulate him in his own work – and not quite succeeding, I decide, smiling to myself as I step out to enjoy a final stroll round the tiled pathways and statues in the back garden. There is an ornamental pond, and I sit on the edge of it, trailing my fingers in the water, letting thoughts of Jack arrive, not out of defeat, but because of being here, in our chosen bolthole, and able to feel so beautifully secure and separate.

I peer into the water, seeing the pale blur of my reflection but thinking suddenly of Helena. Whatever happened to prevent Jack keeping his word on that dire day three months ago, I have a stab of certainty – of common sense and instinct – that she will have been integral to it. A formidable adversary, Jack made sure I knew that much from the start, that glint of unmanly fear I so hated, burning in his eyes every time he mentioned her name. We had to stay on our guard and outwit her, he said after the close call in Hugh's flat, and many times afterwards. Yet, it seems increasingly probable to me that it was Helena who must have ultimately done the outwitting. And, as I contemplate this properly for the first time, amid the peace of the Spanish painter's garden, with only a couple of other tourists for company and the canopy of leaves rustling comfortingly overhead, I experience a shiver of admiration, followed – even more surprisingly – by a sensation akin to gratitude.

Looking back to March, all I can see is a scared woman fleeing with a broken suitcase, taking no stock of her real needs, prepared simply to hurl her wounded life – her fragile hopes of happiness – at the mercy of another man. My body, my life might be in a mess, but it is heartening to realise that I am no longer that woman; that in losing Jack I have edged towards a truer understanding of myself.

'Photo? Yes?' The man in the couple is holding out his phone.

They pose by a large potted shrub and I take a string of pictures, after which they offer to reciprocate in kind. I hand over my mobile, charged now thanks to an adapter provided by the redoubtable Catarina, and stand against the backdrop of the ornamental pond and yellow walls of the house, grinning at the strangers because I am happy.

I dawdle at the exit, buying a few postcards, using my Santander card as I have for everything, assuring myself, whenever panic about money hovers, that there should be no worthier cause than my own well-being, and that Mum would certainly approve. The searing sense of closeness to her that I experienced in the Edinburgh coffee house the previous weekend still lingers, but Dad keeps springing to mind too; almost as if shifting the dark cloud of Pete has given the pair of them the first chance of a decent look-in in years.

Out in the street, the heat of the day is blinding, with none of the Scottish freshness to take the edge off. Even attired in a recently purchased straw hat, sundress and flip-flops, I can feel myself wilting. I had planned to go to the Prado next, but after three days of rest, venturing only to the shops and tapas bars nearest the guesthouse, I realise quickly that it would be wise to keep this first day of sightseeing more low-key. I am on vacation, I remind myself, off the hook, with nothing to prove to anyone.

I find a shady patch of wall to perch on instead, popping two more of the Spanish doctor's wonderful painkillers, glad to realise that the gaps between needing them are growing longer. I then fish out the city map his sister had pressed into my hands that morning, having spotted me lingering with my breakfast coffee in the courtyard, enjoying its tranquillity and the rampant tumble of the purple bougainvillea.

The kindness of my sibling hosts feels central to my recovery. The dreaded examination of my bruised torso had taken place naturally and effortlessly in the end, with the rapid diagnosis of some soft tissue damage and two fractured ribs, accompanied by gentle questioning as to how I came by such injuries. I opened my mouth to lie and found the truth falling out instead. I had a husband who hurt me, I explained, a man whom I had now left. I was in Madrid for a holiday and would be going back to a new life, the details of which I was still figuring out. Just being able to package it all in brief, basic English for so calm and decent an audience was somehow a boost. Like many things, it really was all so very simple in the end.

'Ribs, they heal good,' Guillermo had said quickly afterwards, doing one of his whistles and retreating to his bag to dig out the tablets and some soothing pink cream for my bruises. 'Five or six weeks and then, poof!' He clicked his fingers. 'They are better! The human body is very clever how it heal itself.' His kind dark eyes danced and then darkened. 'But this is serious, Senora, what has happened to you – you know that, yes? The other wounds you have – on the inside,' he tapped his head, 'these will take longer to mend. I am thinking maybe you are needing help?'

'Oh, I have a lot of help, don't worry.'

Catarina, who had been doing her muttering and swiping at her eyes during the course of this conversation, her capacity to understand English clearly surpassing her ability to speak it, had rushed up to the bedside to squeeze my hand. Remembering the still untouched breakfast tray, she then bounded back across the room, miming her desire to reheat it. It took all my efforts, and her brother's assistance, to persuade her there was no need. Lukewarm or chilled, I already knew that few meals in my life would taste so good.

The street map shows there is a cable car ride to some famously picturesque parkland called the Casa de Campo, just a few blocks away. This sounds like the perfect easy option, but then, rather than moving, I decide to admire the nice snaps taken by the friendly couple in the Sorolla garden instead, and before I know it, I'm on Instagram, posting one of them. I stick on a headline saying:

Happy, but missing Harry

which gives me a tummy-tug of hope and longing, even though all my recent messages haven't prompted a single word in reply, good or bad. I know Pete is unlikely to bother with my feebly maintained Instagram account – of which I have never made any secret – but Harry just might.

Before logging off, I click on Mel's latest post, unsurprised to see a ridiculously classy shot of her in black swimsuit and high heels, still hanging on to her curves, thank goodness, and looking gorgeous. She is beaming and the picture has a caption that says:

BE HONEST WITH YOURSELF

and it makes me want to call her there and then, even though I know she has her hands full this week with work and her mum, and we've already agreed to have a proper talk when I am back at the weekend.

I give the picture a like and then find my eye caught by the most recent comment underneath it.

Edcaulder3 That's rich, Mel, coming from a liar.

I bring the phone closer to my face and click on the profile picture beside the message. A slim, shaven-headed man comes into view, tanned and smartly dressed in a light pink polo shirt and crisp white jeans. A pair of bug-eyed designer sunglasses perch in the middle of his bronzed dome scalp and, even though the picture is small, the light blue eyes staring at the camera are unmistakeable. Other images in his feed remove all doubt. I work my way through them, struggling still to merge each snap of a polished forty-something adult with my recollection of the slightly dumpy, dishevelled seventeen-year-old who had been expelled for trying to force himself on Mel when we were at school. There had been hair then, thick and blonde, and kept in a low one-sided sweep across his forehead, which I had thought looked stupid long before there were other reasons to dislike him. Ed had been dangerously out-of-place-posh, I remember too, but saved from mockery because of scraping the status that came with making it into the first football team.

I hesitate for a moment or two and then fire off a direct message, desperate to do something before Mel has the chance to spot the comment and get upset:

Hi Ed, I was at school with you and Mel Simmonds and, for the record, what you did nearly ruined her life. Please apologise and/or retract your comment.

My heart is racing. The wording sounds a bit schoolgirlish, I know, but shock and outrage on Mel's behalf are making it hard to think straight. I wait for a while – Ed's comment is only a few minutes old – but then force myself to drop my mobile back into my bag and shake out the map to study my route instead.

I have barely set off when there is the buzz of a new notification. I scrunch the map up against all its natural creases and sit back down on the wall.

No. She ruined MY life. Every word she said was a lie. After I got kicked out, life was shit. We had to move away. My freaking hair fell out. My parents divorced. It was a total fucking shitstorm. And all started by that bitch. I never laid a finger on her. Not. One. Finger.

I read it several times, before messaging back, my fingers moving a little more slowly now. I cannot believe this has landed in my lap, such an expected horribleness, just when I had dared to hope I was getting a grip on things.

Oh really, Ed? And why would Mel do that? I mean, I would be fascinated to hear your theory.

I am aware of the importance of not revealing any hint of losing my cool. Bullies and tyrants delude themselves – it is how they carry on doing what they do, as I know only too well. Self-justification is their main game, along with booby-traps of their own false logic.

The reply arrives quickly this time.

Fuck knows. The girl was a screw-up. Maybe something was off at home. She came on to everybody, especially us footie lot. Most of us quickly learnt to steer clear. Not all. Like Pete Grove, he got stuck in, for sure.

Time is a funny old thing. How it can slow and whizz of its own accord. Years seem to pass before I begin to type my reply.

And how would you know such a thing?

Each letter takes an age now.

Caught them at it, didn't I. And she didn't seem to mind, if you know what I mean. Then word got out about what she was like and Pete dropped her. She had it in for me after that. Everyone took her side. The school just wanted it done with. Look, the past is the past, right? Life's good for me now, but if I see bullshit, I call it out. So no, not going to delete or 'retract'. Btw does Fran_123 mean you are Frances Clark? Can't think of any others.

I ram the phone and the rumpled map into my bag and stand up. I am not remotely tempted to confirm who I am. Ed wasn't at the school long enough to know about me going out with Pete, I realise, let alone that we married and I traded the name of Clark for Grove. My sundress is sticking to the back of my legs and my ribs have started to throb despite my recent dose of medication. I have lost heart for the cable car. I head back towards the guesthouse, pulling the brim of my hat low over my face, my flip-flops smacking against my hot heels.

* * *

Stepping through the stone arch entrance of the guesthouse an hour later, I almost collide with a football, bouncing high on the stone floor and so directly at me that I catch it without thinking. Behind it, a reedy little child skids to a halt. He looks about eight or nine and is wearing a red and white striped football shirt that reaches almost to his shins. The shins themselves are stick-thin and smeared with dirt. He stares only at the ball in my hands, looking crestfallen until I hand it back, whereupon he charges off the way he has come, barrelling straight into Catarina.

'Es mi sobrino, Enrique,' she says patting the shining floppy black hair, and holding onto the child despite his plain desire for release. 'Please to come,' she says, gesturing for me to follow as she steers the little boy, still clutching his football, through the archway beside them into the inner courtyard. 'English tea!' she cries, with some triumph, indicating the bench where I had sat that morning. *'Ella llega,'* she calls to her brother, who is in a chair next to it, reading a newspaper. On the table in front of him are an array of tea things that include several fat slices of a dark cake spilling cream.

'Ah, Senora Grove,' he stands up, folding the newspaper away. 'I tell my sister I want to see how you are doing. Another consultation for big bucks – and tea.' He laughs, ruffling the sooty head of the boy, whom I realise, from the striking likeness of their long-lashed, dark oval eyes, has to be his son.

He pushes him off to play, shouting a warning a moment later when the ball gets kicked too near some guests enjoying refreshments at a table on the other side of the courtyard. They are an elderly American couple in matching towelling visors, whom I think I recognise from the artist's house.

'So, how are you, Senora Grove? Feeling better, I hope?' There is water on the tray and he hands me a glass, which I drink steadily until it is empty.

'Yes, thank you.' I speak automatically. There was wind in my sails, but now it has gone. I wipe my mouth on the back of my hand, return the glass to the table and sit down. The bench is in the shade and has a sloping back, which is very comfortable, despite my still tender midriff.

'You do sightseeing today?'

'Yes, Sorolla.'

'Ah, and that is very fine, I think?'

'Yes, very fine, thank you.'

He hands me a cup of tea and a plate with some cake, which I place on the arm of the bench. 'But you look a little tired. How is your pain? Are the tablets helping?'

'The tablets are fantastic, thank you.'

'And the lotion, it helps also?'

'Yes, the lotion is also fantastic. I am so much better. You – your sister – have been extremely kind. Please make sure all costs go on my bill. I shall be settling up tomorrow night as I leave early on Saturday.'

He flicks his hand, as if to wave the notion away, returning his attention to his slice of cake.

I let my back rest against the slope of the bench. I had wanted my oasis of peace to last until the end of the week, but here it is already, life – reality – pushing its way back in, from the most unexpected, the most unwelcome quarter, demanding an attention and energy I could not be less keen to give. I spent the long walk back to the guesthouse telling myself that all Ed's claims were nonsense – some grabbed, limp effort to change history and clear his name. But somehow the conviction won't stick. To have to raise the matter with Mel fills me with dread, at how horrible the conversation will be, where it all might lead. I had been so looking forward to talking to her, sharing all the recent hoops I've jumped through, all my new wild thoughts and hopes, even about Helena. I had also been intending to ask if I could stay at hers, certainly until the end of the summer term, but now that feels in jeopardy too.

'You are tired, I think, Senora Grove?' His voice, full of kindness, breaks through my thoughts. 'You have done maybe too much today?'

'Maybe. A little.'

'In London, you are a teacher of young children, Catarina says. That is a nice job. Hard work.' He turns his eyes, affectionately to his son, now doing football tricks for the Americans. 'You must, how do you say, *take it easy*.'

I nod absently. The little boy is doing kick-ups, tap-tap-tap-tap. He is masterful at it – better than Harry ever managed at a much greater age – resuming quickly after every miskick. Tap-tap-tap. The sound is strangely soothing. 'I keep trying to get a handle on life, make sense of it. And just when I think I have, it changes shape.' I am almost surprised the words come out. I don't care if the doctor hears or understands.

I am not even sure he has noticed, until he says, 'Yes, life must always change shape. Sometimes for good and sometimes for bad. And sometimes it takes time for us to know which one it is.'

I glance at him, grateful to see his focus still appears to be on the mesmerising skills of his son. It helps me to voice the next irrepressible realisation to flood my head. 'We can't completely trust anyone but ourselves. It's almost funny how long it has taken me to realise it. That, in the end, the only thing – person – I can be truly sure of, is me.'

'And this chocolate cake,' he says amiably, licking some blobs of cream off his fingers. 'That it tastes good, I am truly sure of that. You will be too maybe, when you try?'

He hands me a small fork off the tray and nods at my plate, still sitting untouched on the arm of the bench.

I pick it up and he settles back into his own chair, rustling his newspaper into submission. A beam of the late-afternoon sun has found its way through the rooftops onto the back of my head. The heat of it cradles me as I eat, bringing me fully into the peace of the moment and holding me there.

III

I put off Retiro Park until the last afternoon. The city's vast, elegantly gated central green space, boasting a crystal palace as well as the famous lake, is obviously worth a visit – Catarina has assured me so many times – but given my Jack-associations with the place, I have reservations. Inside, I am still reeling from the previous day's Instagram exchange, freshly aware, as the doctor advised, of the need to treat myself with care. By the time I got back to my room, the comment had disappeared. There has been no word from Mel since and, so far, I have resisted contacting her. I have no idea what she thinks or knows, but the silence feels heavy.

On the way out of the guesthouse, I put my head around the Reception door to request an early look at the tally of 'extras' I shall be faced with when I check out, but the office is empty. I shake the little cowbell on the desk and wait a while, looking at the now familiar array of faded postcards, and guest thank-you letters on the board behind the desk chair. Further along the wall there is a framed family photo, which I take the opportunity to scrutinise. It is of Enrique's christening, by the look of it, since a baby with the distinct look of the small footballer, scowling in a flowing lacy gown, is being held aloft between Guillermo and a tall, pretty, raven-haired woman in a red dress, whose similarity to the child is even more striking. The doctor looks virtually unchanged, but it is a much more youthful looking, rounder-faced Catarina who poses on one end of the front row, both arms round the waist of a skinny man in a white suit and grinning at the camera with an openness that I find hard to imagine her displaying now.

After a few minutes, I give up and set off for the park. The afternoon is the hottest so far, with the double whammy of the absorbed heat pulsing up from the ground to contend with, as well as the roasting sun overhead. I take it steadily, glad of the protection of my flimsy hat, stopping frequently to check my paper map for my bearings.

By the time I pass through the imperious wrought-iron gates of the nearest entrance, I have decided that the area is so vast and the afternoon so sweltering that I won't even bother going anywhere near Jack's lake – such a central landmark on the map, it should be easy to avoid. Instead, I head down the smaller, shadier perimeter paths, only to find that they meander heavily, taking my bearings with them. Some twenty minutes in, I round a bend and there it is, the lake that gleamed from the wall of Hugh's spare bedroom a year and a lifetime before, providing the wherewithal for Jack to lie to Helena, while I lay a few feet away, hidden and cowering. As in the painting, the water glitters, crystal under the clear bright sky.

Yet, it is nothing like Jack's painting. For a start, there are no picnickers, except on a couple of benches near me on the path. The water might glitter, but most of it is a frenzy of tourists – and many locals, by the look of things – doing laps in rowboats, making not entirely successful efforts to avoid each other and the various water-fowl gamely trying to find some peace. From the top of a tall plinth backed by an arch of stone colonnades, a kingly figure on horseback surveys it all, a master of the domain, who either never made it into the photo Jack used or which he chose to ignore for the purposes of his canvas.

I lean against the lake railings as people stream past, visitors to the city, as well as promenading locals, many of them holding hands. The

Spanish, as I have noticed everywhere, are fond of strolling, preferably keeping a hold of their loved ones as they go. It makes me see with fresh clarity how snatched Jack's and my moments of togetherness were, pretending to be a proper couple when we weren't. I am also struck, gazing at the sun-soaked water, alive with light and people, by the extent to which art is not – and can never be – reality; how it was the looking-at-life that Jack excelled at, rather than the living of it. He was a dreamer not a doer, who would never have made me happy. It makes me wonder whether he is now making Helena happy; whether there might even be a part of her that wishes she had let him go.

I stroll on, buying a bag of grapes and a bottle of water from a food cart before settling under a tree far away from the busy walkways. I open my phone with all the usual hope, but there is still no word from Harry. Or Mel. Pete has sent an email saying *fuck off* – which I delete – and from Rob there is a follow-up to an initial outburst of shock and concern, reiterating his horror at what I have been going through and begging me to call. I do a bit of admin first, checking my money levels, before firing off an instruction to Chalfonts to make all future salary payments to the Santander instead of the usual joint account.

It is impossible not to grin when my brother's familiar gingery freckled face pops up on screen, but Rob couldn't be further from grinning back. He flinches at the sight of me, as if in pain, and then erupts into a rant of rage at Pete, anxiety for me, as well as needless self-recriminations. He is also clearly in the midst of a hectic family moment, with a puce-cheeked Marcus on his lap, trying to grab the phone, and a background noise from the twins that sounds badly in need of policing. Poor Jo is not well, I remind myself, and Rob must be feeling the strain of running the whole show.

'Hey, Rob, how—'

'Christ, Frannie, why didn't you *say*...'

'Look, I am fine, honestly.'

'I can't think how... And in Madrid... why *Madrid*...?'

'Look, we can talk about everything on Saturday. If it's still okay to come—'

'Of course, it's still okay to come. Jesus, I wish you were here now. I wish we had known. I wish—'

'It's all right, Rob.' I pause as the baby swipes at the screen and Rob briefly bobs out of sight. 'My flight lands at midday, so I should be with you early afternoon. It's Gatwick, so the train is easy. Now, tell me how Jo's doing.'

'Great thanks, really great.' He widens his eyes, so I guess she is within earshot and possibly not doing very well at all.

'Please give her lots of love. And I can't wait to see you all... and, Rob, I feel terrible asking when you're already dealing with so much, but is there any chance I could stay on for a bit after the weekend and be a commuter for a while? Just until I've got myself a bit more sorted. I promise I will earn my keep...'

He is saying yes long before I get to the end of my pitch, clearly too kind – or perhaps too distracted – to question why I am not considering the more obvious option of parking myself with Mel, five or so miles from Chalfonts, instead of fifty. I'm not ready to go into the Mel business yet. Not until I've decided what to think myself.

After the call, I prop myself up against the tree and pick at the grapes, which are black and juicy with pips the size of gravel. My hair is heavy and hot and I wish I had something to tie it off my neck. I spit the pips into my hand and arrange them into a small pile beside me in the scrubby grass.

It takes effort to bring Mel properly into focus. A tendril of a hope remains that Ed's claims are lies; but there is the other thing I need to think about too. That she got with Pete. It was before he made his move on me, and now I wouldn't wish the man on anyone, but still. She should have told me. Shouldn't she? Ed said the past was the past, but that clearly wasn't entirely the case for him; and wanting something to be true is no recipe for making it so.

IV

'Your hair, it is cut. It suit you well.'

I murmur a thanks, absently fingering the new outline of my head, the result of a spontaneous walk-in to a half-empty salon after my sojourn in Retiro Park the previous day. I had watched in something of a trance as the young girl wielding the scissors lopped great sheaves off, before starting to shape a slightly impish gamine look out of what was left. I wasn't sure I liked it, beyond the fact of it being pleasingly different. And something Pete would hate, that was a pleasure too. Long hair had been one of his things.

I peek at myself now in the car's rear-view mirror, deciding that maybe the all-round shortness is better for my slim head and the way it gives more space for my eyes. 'I got it done yesterday, on a whim.'

'Forgive me, but... *on a whim?*'

'Oh, I see... well, a whim... is just something you feel like doing, on the spur of the moment, sort of thing – not something you have to do.'

'I see. Like me driving you to the airport?'

'A bit, yes.' I can't help laughing. It had been such a surprise, emerging from leaving my room key on Catarina's desk with the sun barely risen, to see the doctor standing, formal and sombre in his usual dark suit, by the guesthouse front door. To say farewell, I thought, until he held up his car key, announcing that he would be driving me to the airport. 'Catarina order,' he had added with mock gravity, pulling the old trick of claiming his sister was a harridan as opposed to a saint.

The pair's continuing kindness was dumbfounding, humbling. Settling up the previous evening, Catarina and I had played a bit of ping-pong with the printed-out bill because all it contained was the basic room-rate, without an extra in sight. When I continued to protest, she had grabbed my hands, kissed the knuckles and laughed, before flouncing out.

Guillermo's car, a dusty white Toyota, was parked across the road from the guesthouse entrance. To my surprise, little Enrique, in another, better fitting, white and blue football outfit and sleepily clutching a large soft gorilla toy, was curled up on the back seat. 'I drop him at his friend house and then he have football training after. It is perfect timing,' Guillermo had explained, taking my shoulder bag and hat and stowing them in the boot.

'But I am definitely paying you for this,' I say now, as we accelerate out of the last threads of the city and onto the motorway. The doctor's expression remains impassive. I have already lost an early skirmish about settling up for my medicines and his consultation fee. 'What do you think a taxi ride to the airport would cost?' I continue.

'I think you are an obstinate lady,' says Guillermo affably.

I seek refuge in the view. The way he handles the car, his arms relaxed, his gear changes deft and smooth between neat, businesslike checks of his mirrors, suggests competence as well as enjoyment, helping me not mind unduly about the speed at which the scenery is flying past the window. But then I have a thing about men and cars, I remind myself wryly, the young Pete flickering in my mind. I did love him, in as much as any eighteen-year old can know what loving means. Mel being more in the frame didn't change that. It was the having-and-holding I should have given up on, or at least Pete's version of it.

'And you go to London now?' my chauffeur continues.

'Yes, the school I work at is in South London, but I shall be living for a while with my brother in Kent.'

'Ah, brothers, they are good, no?' He winks and I laugh again.

'So, Enrique's mother, your wife, is she a doctor too?' I don't know if I imagine seeing his fingers tighten round the wheel. There is definitely a pause long enough to make me start to regret the question, which I have been burning to ask ever since seeing the woman in the red dress in the christening photograph.

'Ines.' Guillermo releases the name tenderly, like something that has been saved up. He throws a protective glance over his shoulder, where Enrique is sleeping like a puppy in the tangle of his seat belt and the rangy limbs of his soft toy. 'Yes, she doctor too. A wonderful doctor. A paediatric surgeon. Very skilled. More skilled than me, for sure. But...' He shoots me a sad smile. 'She pass away, it is ten months...' His command of the grammatical rules of the past tense seem to have deserted him. '*Cancer de pancreas.*' He says the disease in Spanish, and with a bitterness that sounds weary.

'Oh, I'm so sorry, Guillermo. So *very* sorry.' I feel cack-handed and thoughtless.

'Yes, it is the greatest tragedy of my life,' he says simply, 'and for Enrique also.'

It seems natural to stay silent after that. We are turning onto the airport concourse before he speaks again.

'One day I hope you will learn to trust once more, Senora Grove. I am thinking of what you say to me on Thursday with the cake, but...' He pauses. 'Not, please god, the man who hurt you.'

'Oh no, don't worry, my trusting days there are definitely done.' I manage a smile, touched that he should even care, while inside the question of Pete raises its ugly head. The degree to which I should cut my losses. The balance of my freedom versus letting him off the hook.

'Women forgive, you know,' the doctor goes on heavily. 'They are the softer sex, the peacemakers – it is a big problem.'

'What I told you then was in fact to do with a different situation... an old schoolfriend... my best friend. It turns out she may have been lying about something – something big – ever since I've known her. I only found out that afternoon, just before I saw you and... and, well, I am still trying to work out what to believe, what still matters. I mean, it was about something that happened such a long time ago, you see – literally twenty-five years.'

'Well...' He drums the steering wheel with his thumb, appearing, sweetly, to give the question deep thought. 'It seems to me, Senora Grove—'

'Fran, please.'

'It seems to me everyone deserves more than one chance in their life, Fran. But if your friend has told this one big lie, maybe she has told others also? That is your difficulty.'

'That is it exactly, thank you.' I cannot help marvelling at his capacity for straight talking and wonder whether it might possibly have something to do with the language barrier – the inability to express more convoluted notions and sentences even if he wanted to. 'Guillermo, can I just say—'

'William, please, no?'

'*Guillermo*,' I insist, happy to show off how I have so totally got the hang of pronouncing the Spanish name. 'You have helped me very much, you and Catarina—' I have a bit of a speech lined up, but he cuts across me, choosing the same moment to reverse deftly into a spot right outside Departures.

'Forgive me, Fran... but with this question you just ask, about the lie of the schoolfriend, it tells me you have... how you say... a lot on your plate?' The car parked in one swoop, he tugs up the brake and turns to look at me. 'Is that the correct phrase?'

'Yes, it certainly is.'

'A lot on your plate,' Guillermo continues, his fingers on the door handle, but not opening it yet, 'and so I think maybe this trust problem with your friend, it can wait a little. For now, it is only important to look after yourself.'

Behind us, Enrique stirs. '*Donde estamos, Papa?*'

'*Estamos en el aeropuerto, querido. Senora Grove regressa a Inglaterra.*'

'*Ciao, Senora Grove*.'

'Goodbye, Enrique.' I turn, but the child is already sinking back into sleep, and I am glad because I want to hug the hell out of his father when the moment comes and would hate the little lad to be alarmed.

Standing by the car a couple of minutes later, however, batting away the euro notes I have been trying to press upon him, it is a pointedly formal hand that Guillermo extends for our goodbyes. 'Your plate is full, Senora, but I think you are strong. *Que tenga un buen viaje, y mucha suerte.* That means travel well and good luck.'

I lose my courage for the hug – it would be terrible if he thought it inappropriate – and I realise my sore ribs are nowhere near up to it in any case; but our handshake feels strong and sincere.

By the time I glance back through the terminal's big revolving doors, the Toyota has gone. With the doctor's wise, simple counsel still fresh in my mind, I park my bag between my feet and tap out a message to bridge the silence between me and Mel. I keep it simple. I tell her I am doing fine, all things considered, and that, for the time being, I am going to be staying with Rob. I tell her about seeing Ed's comment and give her the bare bones of the extraordinary exchange that followed, explaining that, for all my wanting to believe her, something about what he claimed rang true. I say I now need to process my thoughts, as well as concentrate on the million and one things from the fallout with Pete, including – most important of all – making contact with Harry. I tell her I love her and that we will talk it all out, but can she give me a breathing space first.

When I look back up, the Toyota has returned and the boot is open. A moment later, Guillermo is being spun out of the revolving doors. 'You are here, thank goodness.' He looks more flustered than I have ever seen and is clutching my straw hat. 'You forget this. In the car,' he adds, before turning and running back the way he has come.

CHAPTER 13

I

Marcus's sturdy legs paddle the air as I try and slot them into the front of the shopping trolley. He is in a hand-me-down pair of voluminous pink elastic-waisted shorts that fit over his nappy, and a new white T-shirt – a recent gift from one of his churchy aunts – bearing the words, *I AM A LITTLE MIRACLE*. Jo had groaned as she pointed out the caption during the course of handing him over, but Rob, crouched doing up his trainers in preparation for a run, fending off the two overexcited dogs, had pointed out that creatures growing inside each other was pretty miraculous, whether you gave the word a religious tag or not.

I certainly do not need God or the slogan stretched tight over Marcus' little pot-belly, to know that my square-set, wriggly, resolutely cheerful – unofficial – godson is a marvel. He has just four teeth now, chipmunk-style, two up, two down, and a darkening tinge of auburn to his still downy head. He does his fair share of crying, but unlike my memories of Harry at a similar age – and for years afterwards, come to that – has always the clearest reasons for upset: hunger, thirst, sore gums, a dirty nappy, tiredness, the desire for company. A solution provided to whichever of these problems it is – no matter by whom –

and he settles at once, sometimes with a spark of what-took-you-so-long in his beady stare.

I see this spark now as I place a wedge of apple – brought specially for the purpose – into the clasp of both his dimpled hands, as soon as our negotiation of the trolley has been managed. It means I have about fifteen peaceful minutes, possibly twenty-five if a second wedge proves acceptable, Marcus's preferred approach to such treats being still to suck rather than chew. I set off at speed round the huge supermarket, one of Jo's too-long, but beautiful skirts, catching round my knees as I lob things off that week's list into the trolley. It is a list Rob is now in charge of and which is kept sellotaped to the lower half of the fridge so as to encourage all contributors; hence my challenge this Saturday morning to find, among other things, *the blue lollies,* a request in Tilda's tidy hand, and why I chuckle at a jumble of letters underneath, composed by her more mischievous and optimistic brother, which reads, *my OWN iPad pleeeese.*

In the clothes aisle, I can't resist a few budget garments for myself – a couple of tops, as well as a blue and white stripy dress and some cheap flats that look smart enough for work. The generous pile of offerings from Jo that greeted my arrival, including shoes only half a size too big, have kept me going beautifully – with the aid of belts and a little imagination – but it is a boost to at least start a fresh stock of things I can call my own.

Originally, I had hoped to make a lightning, lunch-hour raid to collect some belongings from the house, but it turned out Pete had changed the locks. The cabbie, whom I had splashed out on and asked to wait, shook his head in bemusement when I hurried back down the path saying I had changed my mind.

I find it soothing being in the supermarket, obeying the list, pulling faces at the baby. Three weeks in and it is a ritual that already feels integral to my new holding pattern of a life. Other systems have been developing too. Ways of being. On weekday mornings, Rob drops me at the station to catch the very early train necessary for my commute to

Chalfonts, before heading back to cover the school run with the twins and managing his own work day. Or, if he is tied up, I drive myself to the station using Jo's little run-around. Though an exhausting routine, just to be back in the rhythm of school feels like a luxury, together with the added thrill of the promotion to aim for. I made sure to report my altered circumstances to Camille on the very first morning back, receiving exactly the response I needed – sympathy without drama, followed by a quick shift of focus to the challenges of the second half of term.

On the home-front, Jo remains the priority. Rob is a marvel, but if we are both out all day, then a local girl called Jenny comes by for a few hours to help with the children. 'You poor darling, you are so welcome,' was her immediate greeting when Rob and I walked in the door from the airport, along with a brief, intense embrace that seemed to leave her drained. 'And lovely hair,' she had murmured, falling into a corner of the kitchen sofa. Later, she talked expansively about being so much better, thanks to the medicine and the counselling to which Rob takes her on a Friday morning.

No words, however, can mask the fact that my once inspiringly vibrant sister-in-law is still an echo of her former self: glassy-eyed, remote, sleepy, between bouts of determined cheeriness that are almost harder to bear for the glimpses they offer of what remains lost. It's as if she has been turned inside out; her inner fragility laid bare for everyone to see. I have to pinch myself that the arrival of the sweetest baby in the world and the *saving* of dear Tilly's life, on that surreal, sunny Easter Sunday, are what have caused this unravelling. The riverside picnic feels more and more like part of another world now, a naïve, distant idyll in which Jo was healthy and I was hanging onto belief in Jack; when Harry was back in my life, his old gauche, loving self; a time when even his father – thanks to his jaw-dropping heroics with Tilly – could still provoke a sliver of ancient faith in our marriage.

The only good thing about Jo's plight is that it keeps mine out of the spotlight, which is exactly where I want it. On my own bad days, when

Harry's unrelenting silence in particular threatens to get the better of me, it is also a poignant reminder that being derailed by life is not my own speciality; that being happy, getting things right, is a tricky business for everyone. Best of all, I relish the opportunity it presents to be a useful houseguest, to give something back, instead of being yet one more burden in the midst of all their recent difficulties.

'You are family,' Rob had said simply, after I had I scolded him for the surprise pick-up at the airport, my heart still bouncing from the shock of spotting the beacon of his messy red hair among the waiting crowds of taxi drivers holding signs and people jostling for first glimpses of loved ones. Looping arms for the walk back to the multistorey, doing my best to answer all his questions, never had I been more aware of my brother's physical solidity, a life raft in a storm.

During the drive to Kent, he even tried to take a little too much charge. He wanted Pete confronted and punished, he told me. The police needed to be involved, as well as lawyers. He wanted justice for his sister. And when I got to Mel, he was a little too quick to denounce her as having always been out for herself, not deserving of my precious energies.

I had stared straight ahead while he talked, faintly panic-stricken, thinking how much easier everything had seemed from the vantage point of Spain. Once he had run out of steam, I explained calmly and carefully, digging deep into my still settling courage, that launching straight into a pitch battle with Pete would stop the lovely sensation of being free of him; that I wasn't yet sure about taking any steps that might convert Harry into some sort of cannon fodder, destroying whatever shred of a chance remained of he and I reconciling; and that, above all, I needed time to regroup. It was a relief to feel Rob's hand reaching for mine across the gearstick.

'Okay, sis, I get it. But there's this great local lawyer called Diana Shears, who you should at least talk to. She helped a friend of Jo's with a car-crash of a divorce a few years ago. She's kind and clever and won't charge the earth – and I can pitch in with money anyway until you get everything sorted. Just *ask* okay, if you need me? Otherwise I'll do my best to keep my big brother nose out. Scout's honour.'

* * *

On the drive back from the supermarket, Marcus dozes, his head lolling like a drunk, his new T-shirt stained with apple-dribble. The motorway is clear and the fields gold under a clear indigo sky. I wind the driver's window down to get a blast of air onto my face, savouring the summer scent of freshly cut grass and the pleasure of a little time alone. I think of Harry, trying to keep the worry at bay, telling myself he will come round eventually and drawing comfort from the fact that Diana Shears, Rob and Jo's warm, wise lawyer friend, who is now representing me, thinks so too. We have met several times in her converted garage office for sessions that have felt more like normal conversations than the sort of intimidating meetings I had imagined. A woman in her early fifties with a firm but gentle manner, she has the knack of making everything seem not only less daunting but highly possible.

'What do you want, Frances?' she asked after our introductions. And when I replied, almost joking, that my sole desires were a speedy divorce, half the value of the house and the cat, she said, 'Well, in that case, that's what we'll get you,' as if we were picking out items from a catalogue. And when, later, I got on to the grimmer stuff with Pete, growing emotional, she placed a box of tissues in front of me, murmuring a Tolstoy quotation about unhappy families, before outlining a pulling-no-punches summary of my options, saying pressing charges wasn't for the faint-hearted, but she would back me whichever road I chose. 'You have already been so brave, Frances, never forget that,' she went on as the meeting drew to a close. 'I completely take my hat off to you.' I walked out of her garage on air, believing, as never before, in my own strength to see everything through.

The lawyer is still half on my mind as I enter the final labyrinth of country lanes round Rob and Jo's and have to slow almost to a halt for a woman in a peppermint T-shirt and jodhpurs, leading a huge chestnut horse by a rope halter. The animal is doing a prancing bouncy walk, the sunshine rippling across its polished back. The road is very narrow and, with a bend up ahead, there is no question of being able to over-take. It is only when the woman half-turns, pulling the horse onto the grass verge towards a gate into a field, that I realise it is Diana Shears herself.

The lawyer recognises me in the same instant and waves, looping the rope round a fence post before approaching my open window.

'Your phone's off,' she cries, bending down so our heads are level, 'I've been trying to call all morning with the good news that...' Spotting Marcus on the back seat, she clamps her hand over her mouth. The baby is puckering his lips, as if in anticipation of his next meal, but otherwise still fast asleep. 'Oh, my word, what heavenly cargo. He's grown so much.' She speaks very softly, gazing dreamily over my shoul-der. 'I wanted a few of those for myself, but life had other plans. As it does.' A beat passes before she picks up her original train of thought. 'Your phone – it just cuts out.'

I have already pulled my mobile out of my bag and seen that it has indeed gone into some sort of lockdown.

'An unpaid bill perhaps?' she suggests helpfully, peering through the window.

I shake my head, what must have happened already dawning. 'It's Pete. He was the contract holder. He will have cut me off.'

'Well, how very lucky to have bumped into you in that case.' She speaks briskly. 'Because the *good* news is that your soon-to-be-ex has at last appointed a lawyer of his own, so we are in business.' The horse is getting restless and, in the rear-view mirror, I see a Land Rover approaching.

'That's great, thanks Diana. I'll sort it out this week.' I keep my voice strong, but inside I am quailing. No working mobile means any message Harry might at last choose to send won't get through. And if I do end up with a new number, there'll be the worry of him just passing it on to his father – the chance for more invective until I block him. The prospect of the additional cost is frightening too. I have been desperate to get a laptop, but my finances are simply too tight. My brain is whirring. Pete can still yank my chain. I am so far from being free. And Harry...

'Frances? Listen, everything is going to be all right. It will take time, but we will get there.' Diana is putting her face almost through the open window, as if she senses I am close to coming adrift. She raises a hand at the driver of the car to indicate we are almost done. 'I'll email you with more details today. We'll talk on Monday evening anyway – I'll call on Rob and Jo's landline. We have totally got this, Frances, okay? For the duration, I am yours. In your corner. Any time of the day or night. Understood?'

I nod and she reaches into the car to pat my arm before striding back to her charge, muttering what sounds like 'contract holder' and shaking her head. I drive on with the caution of a learner, fighting back tears, and pulling over as soon as the road widens so the Land Rover can pass.

* * *

At the house, there is a note wedged under the door knocker in Rob's writing.

Gone to the llama farm! (Jo too – yay)
    Back soon. Jo says she has done fresh batch of milk for M – on top shelf of fridge.
    (We took sarnies so don't wait for ur lunch)

I fumble with the keys, managing to drop them into the tub of lavender that sits by the front door. Marcus is on my hip and whimpering now, rubbing his eyes with his chubby knuckles. I delve roughly into the bush, leaving a horrible hole in its cloud of dusty blue flowers. The phone thing has winded me. I should have seen it coming.

Keeping my number might be possible, but a new one will feel like a cleaner break from Pete. I try to recall the balance in my account, what sort of monthly contract cost I could afford. Rob and Jo have been generously and adamantly refusing rent, but it can't last and there will be Diana's bills to settle up too. I hug the baby, all the fear in full spate again.

But Marcus does not wish to be hugged. Nor does the eventual opening of the front door cheer him up. Three of his major causes for distress are in full sway – hunger, thirst, a sodden nappy: a perfect storm that ratchets the whimpering into full-on hysteria. There is no question of unloading the shopping.

Jigging him madly, I race around the kitchen, deploying my one free hand to locate Jo's little bottle of expressed milk, fill and boil the kettle, pour the water into a bowl, stand the bottle in the middle of it to warm and then rummage in the baby-change bag for a clean nappy.

The baby's upset makes me tense and clumsy-fingered. I lie him on the hall carpet to wrestle the pink shorts off. They are damp and Marcus kicks hard at my hands. His skin is red and needing nappy cream, but that will have to wait too.

When I am done, the new nappy looks like an inexpertly wrapped parcel. I scoop him up and run back into the kitchen, catching my foot on Billy's skateboard, left where he is not allowed to leave it, and for a couple of long seconds think I am going headlong. The memory of tripping over poor Suki reverberates at the back of my mind like a siren. On such pinhead moments do lives turn. When I end up falling lightly against the kitchen door jamb, Marcus unscathed and still yelling, it calms me down. I do not need to run any more. The time for running is over.

'It's okay, little man,' I whisper, stroking the baby's hot head and giving up on the jigging, which wasn't working anyway. I let him sob, as I shake the drops off the warmed bottle and settle us both on the kitchen sofa. At first, he is too furious to suck. He wants Jo's breast far more anyway. I have to stroke his cheek and do my tuneless version of singing to get him to latch on. Relief floods his pixie face. The blue eyes glaze. The silence is like heaven. Soon he is cupping the bottle with his hands.

Afterwards, the precaution of winding him done, I settle him on the floor with his favourite wooden truck, so I can deal with the shopping, warm now from its stay in the car. Marcus quickly abandons the truck in favour of my handbag, plucking things out like it's some sort of lucky dip. I keep an eye, not minding much. When he finds my London house-keys, now useless, and flings them across the floor, I give a whoop which makes him chortle. Next, he finds my change-purse, which he shakes gleefully to make it rattle, and then my comb, and then some old buried receipts from Spain, which alerts me to the need to provide a fresh diversion.

I peel a banana, breaking off a segment and taking a bite myself. By the time I crouch down to offer the baby his portion, he has something new in his fists, a crumpled piece of yellow paper. One of the fliers shoved at me in Edinburgh, I realise, a month into its residency in the gritty bottom of my bag and definitely not for chewing. The banana trade goes well and I take the slightly soggy crumpled page to the pedal bin. As I flick the lid of the bin up, however, a word on it catches my eye. *Aspen.*

Slowly I unfurl the creases.

Cornish Painters Series: **Jack Aspen** at Parkhill Square Rooms, Edinburgh EH1 1AD

　May 31 – June 5 Private View Tickets @ArtsTicketOffice.com

　And at The Grange Gallery, Marylebone, London NW1 4AQ

　July 30 – Aug 5 Private View Tickets @Madeleinefinearts.co.uk

Arranged around the exhibition dates are a mini gallery of portraits, too small to see clearly, all of lone figures in outdoor places, though the colours are rich and Jack-like. I realise at once it must be the Rogues Gallery; the sketches that became the paintings he wouldn't even take photos of to show me, for fear of jinxing. His old school-friend, the one Helena didn't like, was going to look after them for him,

I remember, and maybe find some buyers while we were in Spain. Brian. The name pops up easily, along with the now tired memory of the Gatwick rendezvous that never happened.

I stare again at the venues and dates, sensing Helena's fingers on the project, the keenness of her ambition, what I was up against, and Jack too. I screw the paper back into a ball and drop it into the open mouth of the bin.

II

I am woken the next morning by an explosion that turns out to be Tilly bursting through the door, still in her pyjamas and clutching the prized games iPad she shares with her brother. Sunday mornings are part of their weekly screen-time allowance, supposedly to give Rob and Jo the chance of a lie-in, although things rarely pan out that way, since Marcus usually has other plans and the twins' fights invariably require parental interventions.

'Daddy said to wake you.' She talks in breathy, self-important bursts, perching on the end of my bed. 'Because there is someone to see you.'

'Someone?' I struggle upright, fuggy with sleep which had been slow in coming, thanks to worries about Harry, and money, and the Edinburgh flier, which I had ended up picking back out of the bin and folding into an inner compartment of my handbag, just as voices outside signalled the return of the trip to the llamas.

'Yes, they are downstairs.' Tilly is concentrating on her screen, where brightly coloured blobs are rolling up and down stairways and along corridors. 'Daddy said to get you.'

'Okay, sweetheart, thank you. Tell Daddy I'll be right down.' She walks slowly out of the room, still playing the game, and I tug open the curtains. It is another cloudless June day, the very last of the month. I can make out a few early visitors dotting the green undulations of the pick-your-own strawberry fields beyond the river, and the water itself, silver slithers peeking through its tunnel of foliage.

I hurriedly scrub my teeth and splash water on my face at the bedroom's little corner basin and then pull on some clothes – Jo's skirt and one of the new supermarket tops – before hopping into my Madrid flip-flops and flying downstairs.

No one is in the kitchen and the front door is open. I race outside and only just manage to contain a cry of disappointment. For it is not Harry, as I had so impetuously hoped, having fired off an email from Rob's laptop to explain about the phone problem and begging him, as always, to write back. It is Mel. She is leaning against her dusty little blue Yaris, arms folded. At the sight of me, she straightens, gripping the straps of a small silver backpack as she begins to talk.

'Ghosting me now, is it? I mean, I know you've been through a hell of a lot, Fran, but still.'

'Mel...' The hostility in her voice is a shock.

'You didn't like it much, did you? With your precious Jack? And neither do I. I give you the space you ask for, and then it's weeks and I really badly want to see you, but when I try and call, it turns out you've gone and bloody blocked me—'

'I haven't... my phone's been cut off... Look, Mel...' I had envisaged many openings to our too-long deferred conversation, but never this. 'Look, come inside so we can—'

'I don't want to come inside thanks.'

She has her feet apart and her arms knitted tightly across her chest, like her entire body is saying, mess with me at your peril. She is in black jeggings and a tight sleeveless pink vest top emblazoned with a cartoon open mouth, the tongue sticking out. Her hair is plaited into bleached corn braids that hang like whips round her face. She makes me think of Lara Croft, and also of the girl who could – and did – get every boy in the sixth form, with their tongues hanging out, even if, like Pete, they hid the fact. After weeks of not seeing her, the completeness of this reverse transformation, in the flesh, is little short of astounding. It also instantly – and perhaps unfairly – reinforces my certainty that every word Ed Caulder wrote in his messages to me was true.

She doesn't move as I approach. She seems welded to her little motor. And since both she and the vehicle are fully in the path of the sun, it is only when I get close that I am able to discern that, for all the first impressions of regained athleticism and attitude, she is in fact in a terrible state. Her face, heavily made-up, resembles a picture that's been left out in the rain, her eye-lids kohl-smeared, her cheeks streaked through layers of foundation, the whites of her beautiful grey eyes bloodshot, her lips chewed and trembling. And, for an instant, the sight really does somersault me back, to when I stumbled upon her, crouched and weeping, behind the school bike stalls, all lovely and messed up, a cornered feral animal hissing at me to fuck off and leave her alone. Which I duly did, till we exchanged a couple of words the next day, and the day after that, and on it went.

Pity is already edging its way in. 'Mel, it's great you've come and I'm really sorry I've not been in touch, but I've had my hands pretty full... Look, why don't we have a cup of tea or something?'

She shakes her head vehemently, making the braids fly out.

'A walk then?' I cast a doubtful glance at her open-toed, high-plat-formed shoes. Even crossing the loose gravelled drive to the front door might present a challenge, but Mel nods at once, launching off down the lane which runs past the house towards the fruit farm. I see no choice but to pull the front door closed and scamper after her, gripping my flip-flops with the pads of my toes to stop them flying off.

Despite her footwear, she covers the ground fast, lifting and clomping her feet in a way that makes me think of someone labouring through deep snow. She flings sentences over her shoulder as she goes, giving no time for answers. 'Why would I want to go inside? Your brother thinks I'm trash. Like everyone. And where's this famous river anyway, the one where Pete did his big number with the kid. Maybe I could throw myself in, save everyone else the bother. He stepped up that day, didn't he, and perhaps there's a lesson there even for you,

Fran, because not everyone is totally bloody perfect, like you want them to be. People make mistakes, Fran. Except for you, of course, because you are always the *victim,* the one to whom everyone else does wrong, meaning you always get a total land-grab on every inch of the fucking moral high-ground, leaving the rest of us without a look-in...'

'Mel. Stop.' I have to bellow both words

A couple of wood pigeons flutter out of a tree in alarm.

When she turns, it is me who has her arms folded, standing my ground in the bumpy lane. 'I refuse to be the one on trial here. It's not fair, and I don't have the strength or the heart for it – there's just too much else... on my plate...' Guillermo's phrase floats in from the wings, coming to my rescue. 'Jesus, Mel. Is what Ed said true? Was it all just one big fat lie?'

'It was not.' She wags her finger, like she is the accuser. 'I... allowed everyone to believe something. That's different.'

I let out a small shriek. 'It is not different, Mel. It is lying. And it wrecked Ed's life. They had to move, he said. All his hair fell out from stress... Mel?'

She has shifted her gaze to somewhere over my right shoulder. The silver bag glistens on her back like a weird snail-shell, heightening the unnerving sensation of not knowing her, of maybe never really having known her.

'And what about you and Pete? Where does that fit into your *truth*? Not that I give a monkeys now, but...' I stop because Mel is plunging down a path into the undergrowth. Brambles spring closed over her retreating back, and all I can think is how badly I do not want to follow her. How all I wanted was for the person in the drive to be Harry.

I find her sitting on the bank where a few cows had watched the dramas with Tilly, batting lazily at the flies with their tails, like viewers of a dull sitcom. Mel is on the highest part of the river edge, her legs dangling over the dancing eddies of the current. There are no cows today. Jo and Rob's house is just visible – the gable above my top-floor room poking through the treetops.

'I can't swim,' Mel says.

'Well, you might recall that I am rubbish at it too.'

'Good,' she sneers, sounding now – as well as looking – like the teenager whom I first befriended.

'So, don't go getting any stupid ideas, is what I mean.'

'I know exactly what you mean, and so the idea wouldn't be stupid, would it?' She peers at the water. 'Presumably I'd sink anyway, given these.' She waggles her heavy-bottomed shoes.

'Mel, then I swear I'm off.'

'Great. Go away.'

Exasperation is mingling with my anger, softening it into a real desire to understand. 'Just talk to me, Mel. Tell me your side. Presumably that's why you drove all the way from London.'

'I'll jump, God help me. I will.' She's scrambled to her feet and barely seems to be holding her balance just being upright. The edge of the bank is a few inches from her high shoes, a crumbly messy sculpture of dips and lumps created by the hooves of repeatedly visiting cattle. If Mel could see – as I do suddenly – as vivid as the day it happened, two strong men fighting to carry a lifeless child across the current, she would not be playing games. Or maybe they are not games. Either way, I realise resignedly, I cannot take the chance.

Though much slighter, and wary of my recently mended ribs, I make a little darting charge and we both fall sideways into the hillocks of dried mud and garlic skirting the border with the field. She then rolls onto her back and stays there, blinking up at the trees. After a moment or two, I stretch out next to her. Through the branches of the small oak above us, the sky is a broken blue jigsaw.

'I might start sneezing soon. I get hay fever now.' Her tone is mild and conversational, back to the Mel I know.

'Sneeze away.'

'Forty-two years and suddenly I get hay fever. What's that all about. I like your hair, by the way. I wouldn't have thought short would suit you, but it does.' Somewhere, a cricket clicks. 'I'm sorry for what I said about the victim thing. It was crappy and not true. I'm so glad you've finally left him,' she says with sudden urgency, 'and not being able to take Harry... that must have been really hard. You're amazing, Fran, and always have been.'

I don't answer because this concern for my welfare has taken a while to arrive, and because I am not up to even beginning an attempt to describe my feelings about Harry, the growing, desolate terror of maybe having lost him for good.

'I used to like Pete,' she continues quietly. 'Out of all of them, I liked him. We got with each other a few times and then he dropped me – said he didn't want to hang out with the class shag. And I knew that it was Ed's doing, stirring things in that footie clique of theirs. The idiot never let me alone either. He was a pest. So, I decided to get him back... Honestly, I only meant to land him in a bit of trouble, but it all kicked off. His parents spoke to mine and, next thing I know, Dad's going ape and the Head is involved... it was like a runaway train. I just couldn't stop it. At least, not without Dad killing me. I don't know if you remember Dad.' She clears her throat. 'Anyway, so I stuck to my story and Ed got kicked out.'

A haze of midges has filled the space on the bank where she did her wobbling act, a cloud of brown humming. 'Why did you never say?' I sit up to ask the question, needing to gauge her expression as she answers. Mel does the same, using her palms to wipe roughly at the smudges of make-up under her eyes as she meets my gaze.

'It just seemed more and more pointless to even mention it.' She scowls, squinting down at the streaks of colour now rubbed onto her hands. 'And... embarrassing?'

'I guess I can see that.'

'I love you, Fran,' she mutters, adding vehemently, 'When you and Jack happened, I couldn't have been happier, remember? God's truth, my only fear was of maybe losing you... to him?' She reaches into the grass to pick a buttercup and holds it under my chin. 'You love butter, did you know that? And by the way, it looks like I've met someone now,' she blurts, 'I've been dying to tell you, Fran. He's called Jason and he's a bodybuilder, but only as a hobby. In real life, he's a shipbroker, whatever the hell that is—'

'Mel, I think you should apologise to Ed. I don't know how, but I think you should.'

'Oh, I did that already,' she murmurs, the ebullience vanishing as quickly as it had appeared. 'After taking down that lovely comment of his I messaged him, trying to explain it all. He didn't reply, but...' She shrugs. 'Who knows, maybe he will.' She shuffles a little closer. 'And, Fran, I want to say sorry to you too. For not being straight – for everything. Hey, why don't you come back to London and live with me?' she cries, all jolly again, and leaping to her feet as if we might set off there and then. 'It's crazy being buried in the sticks down here. We could have so much fun.'

'That's sweet, Mel, but being with Rob and Jo is working well for me...'

We are interrupted by a yodelling from across the water. My brother is on the opposite bank, doing semaphore with his arms. 'Eggs and bacon...' He cups his hands round his mouth as he shouts. 'Loads for all. Ready now.'

I get to my feet, yelling back thanks and that we're on our way. When we reach the drive, Mel tries to chicken out, mumbling about Sunday traffic and needing to hit the road. But I tell her, with a candour that feels new and which I am determined never to let go of, that if she doesn't at least have a stab at winning over my brother and his beautiful family, us being proper friends again isn't going to stand a chance.

CHAPTER 14

I

'Go on, Fran. Everyone's on your side. No one will judge. I mean I'm back here in one piece, aren't I?' Aditi, sitting next to me after a turn at the mike, uses the latest bottle of Prosecco to top up the glasses round the table, spilling drops here and there because, like the rest of us, the end-of-term party has seen a lot of letting go. 'Would you say I am in one piece, Mr Goddard?'

The Chalfonts music teacher, to whom she addresses the question, and with whom she has recently been spotted – by me and Beatrice anyway – holding hands, laughs and says, very much so, last time he looked.

'So, what about it, Fran?' Aditi presses, her black eyes shining in the way that they do when you're falling in love – or think you are – which amounts to the same thing, I realise, because loving someone, in the end, is an act of faith, without rules or a crystal ball.

'Yeah, go on Fran,' urges Beatrice a little tipsily, from my other side.

I laugh at them both, shaking my head and saying it's time I was off anyway. Short of returning to life with Pete, it would be hard to think of anything I want to do less than have a stab at karaoke – even among a group of colleagues who, thanks to many other enjoyable social get-togethers, I can now count as real friends.

As I say my farewells, I catch Camille watching me from a huddle at the bar that includes Erik, lounging on a stool in his film star way, and give her a smile and a wave. She looks equally glamorous, in a long loose white dress that manages, beautifully, to suggest the new curves of her five-month pregnancy while not quite defining them. We had managed a quick talk early on, with me trying to express gratitude for the faith and encouragement that has now seen my name on the deputy head shortlist, and Camille brushing it aside with affectionate commands to enjoy my summer break.

Out in the rain-splashed car park, the night air is cool and lovely. I am staying at Mel's, and warned her not to wait up. There have been a couple of other occasions – a parents' evening and a book club night – when using her spare room has made things a lot easier; and though we've both still got our kid gloves half on, it's been fine. Sometimes, it's almost like we're new friends, still getting to know and trust each other, which is about right.

The plastic bag I tied over the seat of my bike has kept off the worst of the rain. I use a couple of tissues to wipe away the rest and then snap my helmet on, a black one with yellow fluorescent dots, which Tilly has christened my 'ladybird hat'. I pedal gingerly out of the car park, mindful both of my own slightly slower reflexes and the flapping panels of the skirt under my cagoule. The bike, a bright red little fold-up, is a recent budget eBay purchase that has been revolutionising my non-existent fitness levels and saving me the cost and discomfort of the London underground. Rob still insists on our car shuttle systems for the twenty-minute drive to and from Gillingham station, but it is good to know I have my new portable transport as back-up there too – another thread of precious independence in a life that is still far too much about leaning on others.

At the main road, I turn right, instead of left towards Mel's. Diana has warned me to stay away, especially now Pete has put the house on the market and the move north is imminent. She likes to say we are playing a game of chess, with her one step ahead on all the moves, still maintaining that Harry will come round just as soon as everything gets sorted. But she doesn't have kids and I've always hated chess and I want to see the 'For Sale' sign for myself, and maybe – if luck is on my side – catch a shadowy glimpse of my boy at the kitchen window. I have managed it once already, after the parents' evening the previous week, telling no one and being rewarded by a clear view of Harry pulling the blinds down – a good three seconds. It was all I could do to not run up to the house and beat my fists against the windowpane. I can hardly believe it is six weeks since the ordeal that drove me to leave him on the airplane with his father. Forty-two days, with nothing but my messages and no response, not even after I got a new contract sorted and sent him the new number. My bruises are long gone and my ribs now good as new; but the wound of no-Harry is growing close to unbearable. Every day, I read more weight into his silence, more resistance.

The bike wheels make a shushing sound on the wet tarmac. Turning into our street, my fat front-light beam catches a fox in its glare, its laser eyes checking me out. I am instantly transported to the night after dinner at Erik and Camille's, and I realise that this is another small reason why I am drawn back – to remember and be glad that what was once the present has become the past, not gone, but further away.

The 'For Sale' sign, pinned to our rickety front gatepost, shimmers in the soft glow of the nearby street lamp like a white flag of surrender. I slow my pedalling, keeping to the opposite side of the road, and then pull up and get off, positioning myself between two parked cars. Behind the sign, the house itself is dark. Empty, by the look of it. Like Jack's house that time. The memory rises and I flick it away easily. I am beholden to no man now, other than my son.

When the upstairs landing light blazes into life, and not Harry's but Pete's round pallid face presses itself against the window, I hop back into my little space, my heart galloping. It isn't just a passing peek either; Pete is really looking, scanning the street, like an animal who has picked up a scent. I am glad to have the bike to hang on to. My fingers tighten round its solid rubber handlebars. I am camouflaged in a spotty helmet, I remind myself, and a dark cagoule of the sort owned by millions the world over.

I force myself to keep looking at the house, and for a split second our eyes seem to lock. I consider throwing myself onto the bike and pedalling away, but then Pete's face leaves the frame of the window and the curtain is being pulled across it, one of my tatty efforts that never ran smoothly along the tracks.

I am trembling a little. Harry's bedroom window remains dark and I blow a kiss at it, hoping he is tucked up asleep. Not yet up to cycling, I wheel the bike along the pavement. As I draw parallel with Annie's Smiths, a streak of black fur bolts across my path and into the front garden. It looks like Suki. I peer over the low wall, not trusting my eyes or my senses. I am coming down from the alcohol, I realise, and probably shouldn't be in charge of a bicycle, let alone thinking of riding one along the South Circular.

I am almost at the end of the street when a couple in dark clothes round the corner. It takes me another couple of seconds to recognise Harry, partly because in the dim light he could be any young man in a hoody, and partly because he is holding hands with someone who looks very like Mrs Dawkins' son, Len, the city trader. As I am preparing to speak, lost to the rush of sheer joy, Len lets go of Harry's hand and crosses the road with a small shrug of farewell. Harry yanks the wings of his hood more firmly over his cheekbones and lowers his gaze to the pavement as he continues towards me – a fair-weather lady cyclist with a spindly red bike and a silly helmet, the long hem of her skirt looking daft below her waterproof.

'Harry?' It is almost comical how he stops – like a cartoon animal braking at an unexpected obstacle – arms up, head thrown back, legs bracing. 'It's me. Mum.' His first, heart-breaking response is an anxious glance over my shoulder towards the house. Then he peers under the lee of my eye-catching headgear, his eyes like saucers.

'Have you been visiting Dad?' I am glad he sounds incredulous.

'No. I wouldn't... I mean... I just came... a quick look at the house... and that was Len, wasn't it and... Oh, darling, I can't tell you how happy

I am to see you.' My voice is as tender as my first hello before he even had a name, and, in truth, it feels almost as if I am meeting him again for the first time – Harry, not as a connection to me, but as a person in his own right, to be wooed and won over. A part of me would like to try and explain this, but such momentous things are not easily expressed and he's already bouncing on the balls of his feet like a sprinter at a start line. I try a half-hug, one arm having to keep the bike upright, but he shakes me off.

'Mum, I've got to get back. Dad will be wondering.'

'Can I say... you and Len... I'm glad...' There is so much I want to add – about always having liked Len and being happy Harry has someone, especially with me not around; how fear of his father's reaction is completely understandable, but that as his mother all I care about is him finding a person who will look out for him and be kind. It is no moment for long declamations however, and as I falter Harry, perhaps detecting this very possibility, hastily jumps into the gap.

'Alfie died, and they were pretty cut up,' he declares, as if this explains everything, chewing his lower lip and avoiding my eyes.

'Are you okay, darling? That's all that matters. I have been so worried, ever since Edinburgh...'

He grimaces at the word, glancing again towards the house – towards his father – reminding me that I am the cheating wife – the cheating mum – who got found out. The worthless parent. The breaker of sacred vows. Pete will not have held back from any chance of embellishment.

'Harry... all my messages... all I want is to see you properly – the chance to talk. Please, darling, can we do that at least? Soon? I sent you the number of my new phone, do you still have it? I'm afraid I never gave it to Dad because...'

He nods, and I don't know if that means he still has the number or that he understands about my reluctance to enable Pete to make direct contact.

'So, shall I give it to you again? I mean, you won't just pass it on to Dad—'

'Of course, I won't *pass it on*. I would never.' He snarls the words, pulling his head deeper inside his hood and peering out, so much more like a scared little turtle than a lanky twenty-year-old, that the ache to hold him swells like pain.

'Because Harry, darling, I know how Dad can make you feel, like you *have* to do what he wants—'

'For Christ's sake, Mum, I know what he is like. I *know*.' He scrapes at the pavement with the toe of his shoe. 'And I've still got the new number, okay?' He pauses. 'So, have you left Uncle Rob's or what?' He looks at me properly at last, for an instant sounding almost normal.

'No, but tonight there was an end-of-term school thing, so I'm at Mel's...' He's fidgeting again, preparing to go. 'Look, Harry, call me any time, okay? Day. Night. It doesn't matter...' I have hoped for some sort of goodbye hug, but he's already hurrying off, shoulders hunched, head down, hands rammed into his hoody pockets.

* * *

All is quiet when I tiptoe into the flat carrying my folded bike. I remove my shoes as I prepare for bed, even resisting the urge to make myself a tea for fear of the noisy boiling of the kettle. I feel floaty and hyper-calm. I have seen Harry. He has my number. I know about Len. The house really is on the market. I will be able to buy a flat with the proceeds. It will be pocket-sized, but it will be mine. The room spins as I settle in bed, and it isn't from the after-effects of the school party.

No sooner have I turned the light off than the front door thuds shut. Muffled hilarity and scuffling follow, suggestive, I decide, of Jason trying – and only half succeeding – in carrying Mel through to the bedroom. From what I have been able to see, they are clearly good together, like a pair of exuberant teenagers a lot of the time, but also seriously supportive and planning for the longer term. Mel has even introduced him to her mother – a 'major risk' as she put it – which passed off well, and there is now talk of her meeting Jason's seven-year-old daughter, Aisha, whom he apparently took weeks to confess to.

When my phone rings, I am in a thin sleep, one of Mel's rubbery spare-bed pillows over my head by way of a filter for the sounds that have been coming through the wall. I think it is their third round of lovemaking, but I have been doing my best not to listen or keep count. As I take the call, I see that it is three fifteen in the morning. The number on my screen says it is Harry, but I am prepared for anything – it would be typical of Pete to lay a trap. I say hello and then hold my breath because of the silence that follows.

'Mum.' His voice is barely audible. 'Dad made me swear never to talk to you. He thinks I'm doing the move with him, but there's no way. I've got another plan. Len's going to help. And Mrs D...' His voice is both breathy and staccato, like he is having trouble breathing. It sounds like he might be under his duvet. 'I wanted to get everything sorted before telling you. Dad mustn't guess anything. I thought about trying to come by the school a couple of times, but...'

'It's okay, darling.' I slide under my own bedding, pressing my phone to my ear, feeling as if it is Harry I am holding close. 'Nothing matters except that you are all right. You do whatever you have to. And, sweetheart, please understand that if you do want to be with Dad, then of course—'

'I do not want to be with Dad.' The breathiness goes and I hear his voice break. 'Mum, at the hotel... I stayed outside the door. I listened, Mum. I heard. Then I walked away.'

'Harry, stop it.' He is crying now, and my overwhelming worry is that his father might hear. With me gone, it is only common sense that Harry will be receiving the brunt of Pete's hypervigilance, at the very least.

'I can't believe I did nothing.' His voice is thick.

'It was Dad's and my problem, not yours... unless... has he ever...?'

'No... I'm fine, Mum.' It sounds like the tears have stopped.

'Are you sure he's never hurt you, Harry?' It is a relief to spell out the most haunting of my recent fears, that Harry would have been made to pay the price for my own bid for freedom.

'No, he's never done anything...and Mum, I don't blame you for leaving,' he declares fiercely, the loudness of his voice making me afraid again. 'Also, before that, what happened... all the stuff with you and that other man... I don't care.'

It is no moment for explaining about Jack. More critically, I want Harry to get off the phone. I tell him so, issuing a strict instruction for him not to make any sort of contact again until it is safe. I also, with a wry flicker of a recollection at the precautions I once knew so well, tell him to delete evidence of the call. I then add, because I cannot resist it, that if he has found love with Len then I could not be more pleased.

'Oh, it's nothing like that.' He actually laughs. 'We just get along. Night, Mum. Good to talk.'

'So good. Goodnight, sweetheart.

I crawl out from under the tent of my duvet. I lie on my back, my head on top of the rubbery pillow, my hands resting on my stomach. I breathe deeply and slowly. The bedroom air is deliciously fresh after the heat of being under the covers. I seriously wonder if I have known happiness until this moment.

II

The chicness of Marylebone is a shock, though I should have guessed it. Jack and Helena would never go for anything except a fancy gallery in a fancy part of town. I am holding my own though, in a new pair of powder-blue linen trousers and a simple sleeveless cream top with a scalloped hem, both snapped up in a summer sale. My hair has grown out a little and now tucks neatly behind my ears, showing off simple pearl studs that had once belonged to my mother. On my feet are good-as-new cream shoes of Jo's with a little heel and fitting me perfectly because, as she explained, helping me prepare the outfit over the week-end, they always hurt like hell on her. She gave me a handbag too, one of those really small ones on a long thin strap, to be worn slung across the chest, announcing with the sigh of one proud at her handiwork that I looked a million dollars. Which was very far from the truth, but another wonderful indicator of my sister-in-law's increasing prepared-ness to engage with me and the world in general, so I had hugged her hard and said I could never thank her enough, which was absolutely true.

Harry lopes along beside me in his old black jeans and a grey T-shirt, his cheap green spectacle-sunglasses tight against his eyes. He too has had a haircut. Or rather, a head-shave, carried out by Len, with electric clippers, in the back garden of Mrs D's, while her new pug puppy apparently played havoc with the cuttings, running them round the flower beds and in and out of the house. Mrs D has been expressing strong interest in the animal-care business idea – offering the garage which backs onto her garden as possible premises for the venture and saying she'd like to invest. The prospect sounds like the surest recipe for catastrophe I've ever heard, giving me the jitters from remembering Pete's doomed schemes. But Harry isn't Pete, and for now it's all just castles in the air, thanks to a new junior management job at a gym that he seems to be enjoying. So I have maintained as enthusiastic a stance as I can, issuing only the mildest reminder about the hazards of mixing business and friends.

'If you don't reach for your dreams, no one else is going to do it for you,' Harry had shot back, parroting sentiments I had spouted at him during the nervy run-up to my interview for the deputy headship a couple of days earlier. In the event, the interview had hardly seemed dramatic enough to warrant such big-talk; not a car-crash, but not especially good either. Now I can hardly even remember what I had said during the course of it, beyond being aware that it was neither original nor visionary.

'Do you know what, Mum, I think I'm going to let you go it alone in this gallery.' Harry has stopped outside a bookshop window displaying pyramids of bestsellers.

'Oh no you don't.'

'Please, Mum.' Both words are pure groan. I realise that we are opposite the road we have been heading for, a cobbled mews strung with trendy shop signs and flowering plants in large tubs. Harry's late pull-out means he knows it too. His face twists with pleading. 'Come on, Mum...'

I am holding both the tickets, yellow like the original flier, in my hand. 'I just wanted some moral support.'

'Oh god.' He rakes his fingers over his face and scalp. 'But it's not really anything to do with me, is it? It's something you said you need to do for yourself. Lay to rest the last ghost of what happened with this man... and blah.' His expression has settled into a look of agony and he has shoved his flailing hands under his armpits to keep them still. 'A quick walkabout, you said. In and out. You could easily do that and I'll be waiting right outside... right here, anyway.' He points at the pavement. 'Then we can go and eat... unless you are literally saying I have to come in to earn my promised pizza.' He is being funny, but he isn't smiling.

Pizza was part of the deal. Pete is on a stint in Scotland, a fortunate aspect of the date I had picked, when the reckless decision to dig out the flier from my handbag overcame me, very late one night after having poured the whole sorry story of the affair out to Rob and Jo. A couple of bottles of wine had rather helped the process, along with a reception from my brother and his wife of non-judgemental sympathy. Buying two rather than just one ticket to look at Jack's paintings had made the act feel less reckless, despite having no idea whom I would ask to accompany me. The option to just throw both tickets away had helped as well; although, as early August approached, taking such a way out had felt, oddly, both more appealing and less acceptable.

'I checked that skank flat out with you, didn't I?' Harry counters, by way of a reminder of how we have spent the last hour. The flat in question, two bedrooms and a garden in Kennington, had sounded too good to be true and proved so – the dank windowless rooms and broken square of outdoor concrete bearing little resemblance to the enticing descriptions in the spec. Hunting for London accommodation is a new duty, triggered by a serious offer on the house, from a divorcee with cash, no chain and two kids at local schools. I have yet to meet the woman, one Katy Phillips, but find myself imagining her sometimes, sliding into the spaces that witnessed Pete's and my failures, making her own go of it with her little ones, her own fresh hopes. The image gives me the disconcerting notion of all human lives being nothing more than a constantly reshuffling pack of cards, the non-stop turnover of good luck and bad. 'I bunked off work early and helped you agree the place was horrible, right?' Harry continues.

'Yes, you did.' I can't help smiling. I am relenting. The two of us have covered a lot of ground since the first, furtive proper conversation from under our respective bedding four weeks before. With Pete's increasing visits up north and Harry's recent bold stand about the gym job – he'll soon pack it in and come crawling, had apparently been his father's response – it has been relatively easy for the two of us to find opportunities to meet up and to talk in peace. Studying his grave, pained expression now, I am overcome by a wave of embarrassment at my own selfishness – expecting Harry to cope with attending Jack's art show on top of everything else. He has already taken on board so much, shown such nerve and maturity. 'You are right.' I beam at him. 'It was hateful of me to ask you along. Plain wrong. I'll go in alone and be out soon for our lovely meal. You stay right here.'

'Are you sure?' He looks relieved, but also anxious. 'Or I could go nearer the place. Be there if you need me, sort of thing.' He peers uncertainly at the entrance to the swanky alley.

'I'll be fine. Don't wander too far though. I'll message you when I'm coming out. One quick look and I'll be done.' I give him a wave and turn into the little street, walking with my head held high even when the cobbles start playing havoc with my not-so-sturdy heels.

* * *

The sign for the Grange Gallery is one of those miniature ones that tell you the owners consider themselves too special to have to shout out their existence. The door is fixed open and inside it is teeming with people. My ticket includes a glass of champagne, but when I stop at the drinks table, which is set right by the door, no one asks to see evidence of my right to be there. They are too busy talking to each other.

I reach through the throng of arms and take a glass, more so I don't look as out of place as I feel than because I really want a drink. I take a sip for the same reasons, trying to scan the room and its occupants without looking as if I am. The champagne is the real deal – dry and arctic, the bubbles explosive prickles at the back of my throat. Beyond the sea of revellers, I can make out an archway through to a second even larger room. The gallery walls are a light eggshell blue and covered, at tasteful distances, with framed paintings, lit by a network of angled ceiling lights. Jack's pictures.

I drift to the nearest wall, getting a jolt when I realise the sugar-pink flower clusters are the quince blossom he mentioned a couple of times, joking, in his self-deprecating way, that it was one of many early projects to force the realisation that he would never be a latter-day Monet. Even so, the entire wall is about these flowers, as buds, as blossoms, and then as dark stubs when the petals have fallen. There are a couple of still-life pictures of the fruit too, hung as a pair, each showing three quinces nestling like eggs in the cradle of a huge bronze bowl. In the first, the quinces are yellow as lemons, outshining the gleam of their handsome container; in the second, they are gnarled and knobbly, highlighting the sleek beauty of the metal that holds them. *Before & After,* says the little title-card on the wall.

'Well, he's not James Peale,' says a man next to me in a black fedora, addressing a woman on his other side as they both tilt their heads to peer at the quinces through matching half-moon spectacles.

'Of course, there's only so much one can do with acrylic,' replies the woman, who is tall and also flamboyantly dressed in a long floral green and purple jacket. 'Overpriced, too, but that's Madeleine for you. I see they've all been selling anyway, like the proverbial hot cakes. Shame she couldn't be here tonight. The son is sick, apparently, though, goodness, she fusses over him so.'

I wonder if the woman is a painter herself and look again at the wall of pictures in front of me, which I only know have been done with acrylic paint because Jack told me that was all he had used for years, apart from charcoal or a pencil. The little orange stickers on the corners of the frames means they have been sold, I realise, perhaps for thousands. I wonder if this means Jack is now getting what he used to talk of – recognition, decent money. I wonder too, whether these were the reasons why he never came to Gatwick airport. The oddness of being in the gallery is starting to creep over me, the thaw after the shock.

Bits of Jack are on the walls, and yet they tell me nothing. They are just flowers and fruit. They give no hint of Helena either, which, I realise with a start, was another motive for coming – to glean some further, deeper measure of *her*, the half-glimpsed creature whose decisions and personality have, for the last nineteen months, been shaping and shadowing my own. An invisible enemy, but also an ally of sorts, in the turbulence.

Blinking at the paintings, however, I feel only foolish. There are no easy answers here, or anywhere else. It was good – brave even – to come, but now it is time to go. I am reaching into my white pouch handbag for my phone, to text Harry, when a finger taps me on the shoulder.

'Well, blow me, if it isn't the cleaner who wasn't a cleaner but a teacher.'

Hugh. Oh god.

He shakes his head in bemusement, smiling at me but addressing himself to the girl on his arm – a catwalk model surely, several inches taller than him in spiky gold heels and a jade minidress, with alabaster skin and a waterfall of red hair which she has draped over one shoulder so that its wavy ends sit prettily on the bare upper curve of her breast. 'Denise darling, I bumped into this lovely creature when I was doing that spot of house-sitting for Helly and Jack, back in April, remember? The poor loves were in the thick of all that unseemly family squabbling after the death of Helena's father, and kept having to charge westwards to fire-fight. I am not sure we got as far as exchanging names, did we,' he says, addressing me again, 'but I'm Hugh and this is Denise.'

'Frances,' I say, as we all shake hands. 'And, actually, I was just—'

'You were unwell, that day. I hope you are better. You certainly look better.' He is really staring at me. 'And please, humour me, by explaining how you come to be here. I mean, first, I encounter you outside Jack and Helena's house, and now you pop up again at this exhibition of Jack's work. The very same Jack Aspen,' he says in a teasing voice, though his hazel eyes remain probing, 'we're all here for?'

'Really? That was Jack Aspen's house? But that's ridiculous.'

'Yes. It is.'

Hugh is eyeing me with something like disdain, as well as disbelief. And I don't blame him. My fibbing is pathetic, but it is all I can come up with. The idiocy, the courage, whatever it is that has brought me this far, is in danger of running out. 'What a coincidence. I mean... I'm only here because I thought it looked interesting and bought a ticket... back in June...'

'I don't really believe in coincidences,' Hugh says, cutting across me. 'You don't look like a stalker, but maybe you are one.'

'Hugh, stop it, you're being rude.' Denise delivers the castigation mildly, as if it's something to say more than anything. She has unwrapped her arm from his and is beginning to look around the room as if seeking better-quality entertainment. An outburst of clapping delivers it. 'They're here,' she cries, flashing a radiant smile at Hugh as they both sweep away, leaving me alone.

The hubbub by the door blocks any hopes of an easy escape. I hover on the outer edges, a dawning dread merging with dizzying curiosity at what I am about to see. I glimpse Helena at once and feel I have known her forever, unmistakeable, whip thin and elegant as a cat, in a clinging black strapless cocktail dress and black stilettoes. Long streaky blonde hair falls round her smooth tanned shoulders and face, out of which piercing deep-set blue eyes strobe the room like search lights. They pass over me and I do not blink. I am transfixed. She looks exactly as I knew she would, and yet, utterly different for being so vivid, so fluid in her movements, so real. At her shoulder, a much frumpier, scruffier woman cradles a baby in a sling and, for one mind-bending moment, I think this must be a nanny and that the child is Helena's. Helena's and Jack's. The logic of the scenario is still settling when it occurs to me that the frumpy woman, still in a maternity dress by the look of things and with strong echoes of Helena in her face, has to be the drifting elder sister whom Jack mentioned from time to time.

Christabel. The one who had shocked everyone by deciding to take the late plunge to have a donor child.

I see the top of Jack's head first and his rich brown hair. People are reaching for him, shaking his hand, trying to hug him. I catch slices of his face – the beard looks tidier, more closely cut, the eyes a little more pinched around the corners than I remembered, but perhaps because he is grinning so deeply. Prime among the onslaught of feelings is astonishment at this confirmation that he still exists, that, as Mel said from the beginning, it is only me he wiped from the slate of his life, that to the rest of the world he could not be more alive. There was no mugging, no death, no incarceration. He just decided, for whatever reasons, to stay with his wife. Helena.

I look at her again, now holding an orange juice taken from a proffered tray of drinks. Did she use her famous wits to keep him, I wonder, or did he fight to be allowed to stay? A hot bubble of old anger breaks at the back of my throat.

The overwhelming imperative is to leave, not because I am weak, but because I am strong. I do not want or need a 'showdown'. The thought of Jack's reaction to my being there, aghast and pitying, like he thinks I am a sad stalker, as Hugh said, is abhorrent.

The only immediate option for escape is the inner room. I hurry in that direction, past the few stragglers taking the opportunity to enjoy the exhibits without the crowd. It is a longer room, more of a gallery, and lining its walls are all the outdoor sketches that became portraits. Once I wheedled for reports on their progress, but I don't care about them now. I care only about avoiding being identified by Jack.

The swarm is moving, a buzzing thrum at my heels, heading in my direction to see the famous 'Rogues Gallery'. I stride to its furthest end, keeping my back to the room and peeking through a porthole window that affords a snapshot view of the street: some railings, a little light rain, a parked motorbike.

There is something about being stared at. Your animal hairs bristle. I think that's why I turn and there she is, Helena, her wild blue eyes on fire, her lean sculpted body as poised as a prima ballerina. 'Jack.' She summons him without turning her head and I feel the power of her. He steps to her side, eagerness-to-please in the bounce with which he abandons the little group where he had been holding court.

There are some moments in life, the ones you have dreaded and fought with every fibre of your being to avoid, which, when they arrive, have an inevitability that makes you relax. Acceptance. When Pete imploded, it was like that. And now I feel the same – overcome by an almost Zen-like state of, oh, here you are, well let's get on with it then.

Jack, to my satisfaction, looks nowhere near such a mindset. Jack is the opposite of zen. His expression is one of pure, unguarded terror. Indeed, it reminds me of how he looked as Helena's footsteps clipped down the corridor towards the bedroom door in Hugh's flat, the unseemly fear of the liar about to be caught with his pants down. Literally. I was prepared to brave it out, but not Jack. He made me hide, like some cheap crook, under the bed. I thought we were done with then, and now I wish we had been.

But I am prepared to brave it out now too. I have had a little more practice at standing my ground. And so, while Jack looks like a man slowly having the breath squeezed out of him, I say hello to Helena and offer my hand. She takes it, and we regard each other, allowing a moment in which it seems to me we are perfectly balanced in our fearlessness.

Keeping a loose hold of my fingers, she says to Jack, still without looking at him, 'It's her, the woman on the bench.' Only then does her gaze travel from my face to one of the portraits on the wall beside us. 'Her hair is shorter, but it's her.'

Following her sightline, I see the toddler first – my favourite of all the sketches Jack ever showed me, here transformed into a rich portrait – the baby-hair frizzy from sleep, one hand gripping the pushchair for support, the other flinging bread towards some ducks, who look startled more than hungry. The picture Helena is pointing to, of the woman on a bench, sits above it. The woman is small-boned, with long mousey hair and an earnest face, lit up by large light green eyes. She wears a thick cream jumper and jeans tucked into scuffed suede boots.

She looks alone and lost. She looks, beyond any shadow of a doubt, like me.

A little crowd is gathering now, gawping between me and the picture and murmuring. I am tempted just to leave. Jack, from his haggard look, clearly wants nothing else. And Helena, for all the cleverness of the observation she has made, the hint of triumph in her extraordinary eyes, is also exuding an anxiety now. She is a woman who likes to be in control, I gathered that much from the get-go, and is now wearing the expression of someone who thinks a bomb might be about to go off, but isn't quite sure from which direction.

My courage hardens. I am the bomb, to detonate how and when I choose. 'I'm Fran, by the way,' I say. 'Very nice to meet you all.' I give a wave to the crowd. 'Jack, aren't you going to say hello?'

'Yes, indeed... of course. I was just surprised. Your hair, it's so different... from in the park.' There is a hint of hope in his face now, like there might be a script we can follow, a route out of this maze. 'How nice to see you again, Fran. And yes, look at what our encounter produced!' There is desperation in the way he swings an arm in the direction of the painting.

I clear my throat. 'Well, yes, but it produced a few other things too, wouldn't you say?' There is menace in my voice and Helena hears it. Her reaction is to take a step towards Jack. She passes her half-empty flute of orange juice to someone in the crowd.

'Jack, who is this woman?'

'She's just someone—'

I find myself interrupting with an 'uh-uh' and a castigatory raising of one hand. My entire life has been about staying in the shadows. But not now. A crowd has really gathered. At the back of it, I spot Harry hovering with understandable uncertainty near Hugh and Denise, who are both looking enthralled. 'I am not "just someone". I won't accept that.' I speak curtly and very clearly. 'My name is Frances Grove—'

There is the dawning of something in Helena's face as she cuts in, 'Oh god, is she after money – someone call security please.' She casts the words over her shoulder, but nobody moves. They can see I am in the portrait. It seals my right to be there, to be heard. And they are agog, as I would be in their shoes.

'I don't want money. I just want to say that Jack and I had an affair.' I deploy my teacher's voice, like I am explaining something the whole class must pay attention to. 'We used to meet at a friend's flat – I'm staying there tonight actually, Jack – I'm sure Mel would want me to say a hi from her.' I throw him a grin, but he is staring at the floor. 'Well, more than an affair, actually. We fell in love. I mean...' A sharp laugh of wonderment escapes me. '...We *really* fell in love. At least, I did. I suppose you can't speak for someone else though, can you, not with that sort of thing. Who knows what Jack really felt? Or, indeed, what goes on inside anyone else's heart. It's a bloody mystery!'

There are titters. They are spellbound, including Helena. Maybe some think it is a publicity stunt. A few are taking pictures with their phones.

Helena mutters, 'Jack, *do* something.'

Jack moves towards me, murmuring, 'Please...' He seems about to say my name, but stops short. I see the deepest, faintest flutter of something behind the fear in his eyes; maybe regret, maybe, possibly, a trace of old love, but nothing is going to stop me now.

'He had me convinced anyway,' I forge on. 'We made a plan to run away together – I left my husband – but Jack never showed at the rendezvous, and yes, I know, it's the sort of run-of-the-mill thing that happens all the time, another silly love-story gone-wrong – but this wasn't just a story, it was my story, my *life*...' I hesitate, because there is a sudden, inconvenient catch in my throat which needs swallowing away, 'and it was like falling down a hole and I got a beating from my husband on the back of it, because he is that sort of man. Which you knew, Jack, didn't you?'

I throw the question at Jack, but still in a voice that carries, 'So I guess it was a risk you were prepared to take. Don't worry though.' I grin at him, at the whole room. 'I've not morphed into a bunny boiler. I am truly fine now. Better than fine. And I'm about done here. Except to say...' I flash Jack another beaming smile and he's gawping back at me now, his features crumpled into what looks like a combination of revulsion and sheepishness, 'that if the same thing happens with another lover, give her a bell, yes? Tell her the show is off. Just so she knows? I mean, it's common courtesy, isn't it? The painting – all your paintings – are lovely, by the way, and do please feel free to make use of anything I've said for the one of me, like in those little summaries for catalogues and whatnot. People love a good backstory, don't they? It might even help sales.'

'Leave, now.' It is Helena who speaks, with a dignity that a part of me has to acknowledge as impressive. Jack looks small beside her, despite his height, and also utterly stupefied, which isn't far off looking stupid, I decide, as I wave at Harry to indicate I'll be right with him. The crowd are beginning to disperse, in the deferential way of those trying not to ogle the scene of an accident. Only Helena is coming properly to life. 'But the woman – you – are Freya,' she accuses, 'not Frances.'

'Really?' I pretend to think hard, surprised at the suggestion of an attempt at misdirection by Jack, to protect himself no doubt, rather than me. 'Nope. I'm pretty certain of my own name. Or maybe Freya was another lover? Only Jack can say. Jack?' He shakes his head, still beyond words and I give Helena a what-can-you-do shrug, finding myself adding, 'He doesn't speak much, does he? I used to find that sometimes even when we were together. I think maybe he's better at his art than his life? Just a thought.'

I stride off, about as pleased with this as any comment I've ever made, for the simple reason of it being managed under pressure and pinning a truth, which, instinct tells me, Helena knows too. This has been between us, I realise. Her and me. All along, I have been her other woman, and she mine.

The crowd parts, creating a path that I follow, while, inside, I can feel the collapse coming, as it must when you've been punching way out of your comfort zone and need to bawl your eyes out to recover. I am aware of Jack trying to come after me and Helena holding him back, and then Hugh saying, 'Let her go,' as if I'm dangerous.

Harry keeps several yards ahead, walking with his eyes on the floor, understandably close to crawling on all fours with embarrassment at having me for a mother. I am at the reception table by the door when the rat-tat-tat of trotting stilettos tells me Helena is not yet quite ready to heed her friends' advice.

'There are no others,' she hisses. 'I got muddled, calling you Freya because it sounds like Fran. And he says you were the biggest mistake of his life. And I was on to you two anyway. I *allowed* it to happen.'

I keep walking, smiling, as if she has said something about the weather.

'And someone else knew about the pair of you too,' she adds, raising her voice because I am half out of the door. 'They were kind enough to write and tell me so. An email. Just so you know.'

It should be no surprise that Helena would want the last word, she is that sort; but even so, as a parting shot this is pretty powerful.

III

I sleep so late the following morning that Mel, never a fan of the gallery visit, knocks on the door to check I'm all right. She is resplendent in turquoise dungarees and pink trainers and holding a mug of tea.

'Glad you went?'

'Very.'

'Phew.' She puts the mug down beside the bed. 'Can I hear about it later? I've got Mum now, but Jason's around for a bit.' She blows me a kiss before closing the door.

I enjoy the tea in bed, sending a message to Harry to apologise again for the evening's unplanned ordeal and joking that I hoped our pizza afterwards made it worthwhile. The luxury of several hours to myself stretches ahead. I have another couple of flats to see in the afternoon and then a train ride back to Kent.

I am only just out of the shower when the door buzzer sounds. I assume it's a delivery of some kind and am glad Jason is on hand to deal with it. I step into one of my Madrid sundresses, the smartest, of pea green cotton, and a pair of sandals. I am running a comb through my wet hair when there's a sharp rap on the bedroom door.

'Someone to see you,' Jason shouts, before his footsteps retreat along the corridor.

'I'll keep this brief.' Helena begins talking long before I reach the doorstep, adjusting the large tortoiseshell sunglasses that are keeping her heavy blonde hair off her face. If the evening ran on, there is no indication of it in her clear blue eyes or the freshness of her outfit – a lilac-coloured lacy top and white three-quarter-length trousers, tailored to accentuate her long legs. On her feet elaborately latticed gold leather sandals display long slim toes trimmed with dark blue nail varnish.

'How on earth did you...?' I make sure I have the door handle in my grasp.

'In your showstopper, you mentioned where you were staying – the *love nest* – so I asked Jack for the address.' She takes a step back, shooting a disparaging look at the pebbledash walls of Mel's block of flats. 'Jack told me everything long ago, by the way, and I mean *everything,* Frances-not-Freya.'

I start to close the door. Caught off-guard, my bravery is a little harder to muster, but mostly I have no desire to give Helena the satisfaction of further engagement. She quickly puts out an arm.

'Don't go, please. I have something for you.'

'Whatever it is, I do not want it.'

'Oh, I think you might. It's a letter from Jack, you see.' She reaches into the large gold-buckled white leather bag looped over her shoulder and pulls out an envelope. 'There are things he wanted to say, and I agreed he could.'

'Well, how mighty generous of you.' I make another attempt to pull the door closed – not with all my strength, it has to be said, since curiosity is burning again, along with recognition of the sheer nous of the woman, bringing her hurt pride and bottled rage to my front step. The very same nous – I cannot help remembering – that proved such an unlikely and vital source of inspiration during my final, crucial battles to escape Pete. Awareness of Helena – of her shameless, fighting spirit – was always hovering, helping me to dig deeper into my own reserves of courage; all of which is so strange, so upside down, that given different circumstances, a different universe, I would be tempted to talk to her about it.

'Frances, please.' Her voice is different all of a sudden, soft and exhausted. 'I am not good at this. I mean, this is hard... I... have... hated you so very much.'

'And me you,' I can't resist muttering, but adding hastily, 'once upon a time,' having no desire to evoke any misplaced triumphalism or – worse still – pity.

'He was never going to leave.' She tosses her mane of hair, the defensive stridency back in place. 'You know that, don't you? All he did was *use* you.'

'I see.' Her words do not even sting. She is in the ring, gloves on, doing and saying what she must. 'And is that what this supposed letter says?'

She shrugs, holding out the envelope. 'I've no idea what it says. I'm just the postwoman.'

I cannot contain a scornful laugh. There may be things to admire in the woman, but I am not going to pander to her. 'Look, Helena, I don't know what sort of sick game you and Jack are trying to play – but it's not going to work. You can both keep your stupid letter. I'm not sorry for what I did and said last night. In fact, the only thing I regret is that it might make it look as if I still care, when I really don't. I mean *really*. Please do pass that on to Jack for me, won't you.' I make a third, decisive attempt to tug the door shut and this time she lunges forward and grabs the outer handle. For a few seconds, we push and pull.

'He wanted to write to you,' Helena says, as we tussle. 'I promise I've no idea what he has said. All I asked was that I be the one to deliver it.'

'Right. Like you haven't read it – steamed it open – altered the wording probably – or maybe even dictated it, knowing you.' I expect an angry riposte, but she just freezes, as do I. Her face is so close to mine, the skin glowing and the beauty undeniable, but also chiselled and harsh, like something forged rather than born with.

Instead of speaking, she thrusts the envelope at me, managing to lodge it under my arm, before taking a step back and staring me up and down. There may be the game of keeping Jack on a tight rein, but she, too, had wanted a closer look, I realise, just like me.

'Take the bloody thing and burn it for all I care,' she says archly. 'I haven't read a word. I promised Jack and we're both keeping our promises these days. No thanks to you.' She is preparing to go, buttoning up the big gold buckle on her bag. 'I suppose to ask for an apology would be expecting too much?'

'Yes, it would.' I clasp my hands behind my back, gripping the envelope, my expression deadpan. From inside the flat, Jason calls out is everything all right and I shout back a yes. 'Jack promised me everything, Helena,' I tell her steadily, 'including himself, and then he vanished. I was in an abusive relationship, to which I had to return.' She flinches, tightening her beautiful mouth, but remaining silent. 'Thank you though...' I falter, wary suddenly of falling into the trap of over-protesting – suggesting a vulnerability that no longer exists – but also assailed, more vividly than ever, by the peculiar thrum of allegiance between us. Helena is clutching her big bag, still looking pleasingly disconcerted. 'Because I am in this great place now,' I explain quickly, 'and everything that happened – and didn't happen – with Jack, has helped me reach it. I'm glad he stayed with you. I don't say that to be hurtful, Helena, but because it is the plain truth. I've got a bit of a thing about truth these days. I'm doing my best to hang onto it.'

'Me too,' she says tartly, 'and actually, you helped Jack.' She pulls the sunglasses out of the tumble of her hair and rams them over her eyes, for protection it looks like, since the sun is nowhere to be seen. 'You were his *muse*, and I can't unwish that.'

'Muse? Really?' I almost laugh because this is so not what Jack's and my love for each other felt like, but I sense the comment has cost her dearly. She is back on the pavement and beginning to move away, her back rigid, her nose in the air. 'Can I ask who wrote to you,' I call, seizing this last chance for an answer to the only thing still bothering me, 'about Jack and me?'

She stops and turns, waiting for a woman with a buggy to walk past. 'I have no idea, honestly. And it made no difference. I was onto the pair of you, for months. Biding my time. I knew Jack would never leave me,' she says again, like the phrase has become a mantra.

'Okay. Oh, and please don't come back, Helena. Ever.'

'Same to you, Frances.' She shakes her head as she walks on, as if amused, her real expression safe behind the big sunglasses.

'Blimey,' says Jason, 'that sounded heavy.' He has arrived next to me with his sports bag, clearly on the way out.

'It was fine. My ex-lover's wife. As you do.'

'Fuck me. You would have hollered any time you needed help, right? Mel will kill me otherwise.'

'I didn't need help, Jason, but thank you, I really appreciated the offer.'

* * *

I prop Jack's letter against the toaster, keeping an eye on it while I put the kettle on. The same kettle that had boiled water for Jack's and my cups of tea, and for speedy cooking of pasta, and vegetables – all the grabbed eating between the grabbed lovemaking. The memories are so beautifully powerless now, buried strata of fading colour.

I take my coffee and the envelope and go to sit on the sofa. On the 'v' of the flap, there is a small unbroken circle of red sealing wax, suggesting Helena's claims about ignorance of the contents are to be believed. Or at least that's what they want me to think. They are a team again, I remind myself. A married couple. They always were.

Even so, I take a big breath before breaking the seal. No mended heart is entirely impervious to pain.

Dearest Fran,

Thank you for accepting and reading this letter.

I know words cannot begin to make a difference. Actions make the difference – we talked about that once and it has haunted me. I promised to be with you and I walked away. I will spare you the details, but please understand that circumstances unfolded in a manner that gave me no choice. I promised Helena I would never contact you again, and that is a promise I have kept and why this letter needed her blessing.

I am so sorry, Fran. You placed your faith in me and I let you down. Hollow though it may sound, I have been racked with anxiety about that, and about you, willing you to be okay, especially with regard to Pete. Last night was a tremendous shock, but my goodness, it was a relief to see you looking so beautiful and strong. You were amazing actually – amazing and terrible! Helena was as flabbergasted as I have ever seen her, which I know will matter little to you, but which is saying something. As was I. Every word you uttered was fair and cut deep. I treated you appallingly, despite loving you, and can only beg your forgiveness.

Oh, Fran, if Helena wasn't pacing up and down outside, I would be crossing out and rewriting, because there are many more things I would like to say and because none of this is coming out quite as I intended. You should know that she and I are working, slowly, to rebuild our marriage, but it is a long road.

Three things then:

Please accept my sincerest apologies, even if forgiveness remains impossible, which would be understandable.

I hope you are as well as you seemed.

I pray, with every ounce of my being, that you find the happiness you so richly deserve.

Sorry, a fourth:

Helena has decided you were a 'muse'. I think it helps her makes sense of everything. My recent work is certainly being well-received, including the portrait of you, of which I am especially proud. But please know that to me, what we had was, and always will be, so much more.

With love,

Jack.

CHAPTER 15

I have been for one of my Sunday-morning coffees with Diana, going by bike because it is only a twenty-minute ride. The late August weather is glorious, each day seeming to vie with its predecessor to offer the surest peak of ripened summer colours before the hints of autumnal decay set in. Today must win. Never has the sky been wider, bluer; nor the sun brighter, nor the hedges greener. For weeks, we have been eating Rob and Jo's home-grown raspberries – in our cereal, as snacks, as pudding – but the blackberries are starting to make their bid, I notice wistfully as I fly past the hedgerows, which means autumn is nearly here. On another day, I would have stopped to sample a few, but I am already likely to be late for the lunch summons – an unusually strict one from Jo, who, getting ever closer to her former confident and happy self, has recently reclaimed charge of the kitchen. I am also still a bit full from the hefty wedge of Victoria sponge that Diana served with the coffee. To my confusion and pleasure, there had been a candle in it too, up to its hilt in the icing sugar, along with a parcel, which turned out to be a copy of *Anna Karenina*.

'Because birthdays matter,' Diana insisted through my protestations and thanks, 'and because we have come such a very long way.'

All I need is for the house sale to go through. And it looks as if it really might, since the divorcee, Katy Philips, has now asked for a date when she might pop in to measure up for curtains. Which had made me laugh, since no one would want my curtains, not even me.

I have gradually been moving out my stuff, keeping bits, but storing most of it at Mel's in preparation for finding my own place; and Pete has now accepted the fifty-fifty deal, which he apparently dismissed out of hand when it was first suggested. The only remaining hurdle is his typical, needling insistence, that I pay the mortgage contributions which stopped when I rechannelled my salary to Santander. Diana wants me to refuse – she thinks I am settling for far too little as it is, Pete's salary being so much bigger and him having put me through so much – but I have asked her not to. With the process going relatively smoothly, I am like a distance runner with her sights on the finishing line. I just want to get there, to cross the line, and leave Pete behind.

We have even met each other once now, in the offices of his London lawyer, Pete with his brief and me with Diana, the four of us sitting across a mahogany conference-room table like characters in TV drama. Adding to the surrealness was finding Pete in full smarm-charm mode; Mr Affability, asking me how I am and saying how sorry he was that 'it had come to this' and yes, he would sign up to the archaic 'unreasonable behaviour' admission required from one of us – someone had to, and he didn't mind. The new stand-up-for-herself Fran had wanted to shout in his face, call out his fakery, but again, the finishing line had shimmered. Harry's guess is that he has found a woman in Edinburgh, and after this encounter, I am sure he is right, my thoughts flying, for some reason, to the girl who had shown us round the site in the half-built shopping mall, just a couple of hours before he had slid the belt out from its toggles to vent an anger that had been building for fifteen years.

In the company of our lawyers, Pete certainly oozed the self-contentment of one having his appetites met, enough oozing to slip on the stuff and fall flat on his face, I had decided, watching him as the meeting progressed and marvelling at how the conversation flowed. Yes, he was happy with all the small print, happy for me to be transferred my portion the moment the money from the buyer came through, happy at Harry's new job, the lad was a grown-up these days, after all, ha ha; happy indeed, about anything and everything in the whole wide world.

That this is because Pete is afraid only dawned on me afterwards. He will guess I have said some things about his treatment of me, but does not know how much or to whom. He will be wary of what might transpire and will not feel safe, not even with his new love; and he is right not to. Just as soon as things are settled, I am going to write to the new girlfriend, whoever she turns out to be, and warn her, woman to woman, of exactly what she is taking on.

In the meantime, the pros and cons of pressing charges myself remain very much alive in my conversations with Diana. The reasons not to – leaving the past behind, the potential trauma for me, not to mention Harry, coupled with the low likelihood of a conviction, given the passage of time and paucity of evidence – have not changed. I may take action, I may not; and it is precisely that doubt, I hope, that is keeping Pete on his toes. Will she strike back, or won't she? There is some poetic justice in being able to relish, a little, the new power of that; a power worthy of Helena, I catch myself thinking sometimes, marvelling how embedded the woman is in me, how impossible to dislodge.

* * *

At Rob and Jo's all is quiet, apart from two bumble bees hovering over the dusty blue dome of lavender by the front door. A heaviness to the silence makes me try the handle gingerly, half expecting it to be locked. Inside, the house, too, is silent. No babbling from Marcus, no shrieks from the twins, no thump of dog tails or the scrape of paws skidding along the hard wood floors for a hello.

I peer into the kitchen. Everything looks more or less as it was when I left, the scattering of glitter on the table from the twins' extravagantly decorated home-made birthday cards, the wrapping paper from

Rob and Jo's gift – a pair of pink and grey brush cotton pyjamas. There had been some travel company vouchers too, in the envelope with my card – because I have earned a proper holiday, they said, laughing and pleased with themselves when I gasped at the sum.

A dim sense of upset is edging in. It is my birthday after all and if they have gone out it will be hard not to feel a little abandoned. And for Jo to be so insistent about getting back for lunch rankles too.

I drift into the sitting room, supposedly – and rarely managing to be – an animal- and child-free zone, observing that, on this August Bank Holiday Sunday morning anyway, it is looking irreproachably spruce and tidy. Jo must have cleaned it instead of cooking lunch. Even the windows are sparkling. I wander to the French doors that overlook the back garden. The small patio bridges the gap to a wide lawn that rolls all the way down to the woodland fringing the river. I am thinking about a book, a deckchair and a sandwich as I peer through the glass.

Except the garden is full of people. Or, rather, there is a concentrated mass of people standing in the middle of the lawn, completely silent, facing me. They are all holding glasses in their hands and nudging each other like an expectant audience. Rob has the dogs on their leads, but they are slumped at his feet like bored children. Someone, who looks like Mel, is holding Marcus in her arms, and standing next to someone who looks like Jason, who has a little girl clasped to his back, who might or might not be Aisha, the eight-year-old daughter from a previous relationship whom Mel now adores and I have yet to meet. Jo and Rob are in the middle of the front row, like the parents of a massive family taking a photo call. Rob is holding a bottle of champagne as well as the dog leads. They are all facing me but haven't quite seen me, and I let a beat or two go by, savouring the anticipation – laced with a little trepidation – before opening the door.

The throng erupts with shrieks of 'Surprise!' The twins are first out of the pack, racing towards me, the dogs, leads trailing, bounding and bonkers at their heels. 'We *spied* on you,' they cry, shrieking over each other, as the animals bounce and wrestle, 'we saw you on your bike – we had to tell everyone you were here – we had to not make a sound...'

It is my first surprise party, and as I walk towards the group, breaking now in dribs and drabs to come and greet me, I am glad of Tilly's hand in mine. There are familiar faces everywhere, calling out, waving, making it hard to know where to look. Behind them, set in the lee of the woodland edge, is a makeshift awning, its poles garlanded with fresh flowers, and what looks like several big old bed sheets stitched together by way of a roof. Laid out underneath is a refectory-style table, cobbled together with an assortment of smaller tables, to judge from the tangle of legs showing below the tablecloth, and decked with chairs of all shapes and sizes, clearly gathered from every corner of the house. On the table itself, between fountains of fresh blue and white flowers bursting out of tall thin vases, is a central line of dishes spilling with food.

'But everybody is here... how on earth have you managed...' I mutter at Jo, who reaches me as Tilly skips off.

'Happy Birthday, Fran.' Her lightly freckled face is lit up with delight at my amazement. 'It's been lovely to do – exactly what I needed.'

Rob breezes past from the other side, depositing a kiss on my head, en route to filling glasses. 'Happy Birthday, sis – not a day over thirty, and you need a glass.'

'Being a bank holiday helped, so thanks for that,' says Jo. 'And everybody brought something food-wise.' She puts an arm across my back, giving my shoulders a squeeze. 'All I really had to do was the odd bit here and there, and the flowers, which are hardly a big deal.' I know she is not telling the truth. She will, despite her still very recent fragility, have been secretly baking all week. And the flowers are everywhere, not just snaking all over the awning, but hanging off the garden fence like bunting, and parked in elegant ceramic urns round both the dining table and another separate one serving as a bar. 'And your brother has been in Boy Scout heaven building a barbecue down there.' She indicates a large metal rack balanced across two makeshift, but sturdy walls of old bricks, positioned several yards away from the dining area. Rob is already marching towards it holding a platter piled high with sausages and steak. 'So much more fun than using the gas-fired plug-in on the patio. We thought it would be nice to eat down there, and easier to keep as a surprise.'

'Happy birthday, Mother,' says Harry with the irony that he injects into all displays of affection, as he arrives at my side. 'I don't mind if you don't like my baking – I went for vegan brownies and they taste a bit weird. Healthy though, right?' He grins, letting me kiss his cheek, but still holding back a bit, as is his way.

'They'll be lovely.' I beam at him, proud and thrilled to have him there, easier in his own skin now than I could ever have dreamed. 'Is Len here?'

'Yeah, somewhere. He drove. And, Mum, we popped in on Suki before we left – she's so happy at Annie Smith's, it's a total joke. I mean, like, she could hardly be bothered to say hi.'

'Good, that's nice.' The gradual kidnapping of our pet by our elderly neighbour has, we've both reluctantly now agreed, been a blessing in disguise, even though Harry thinks Suki only went along with it because of missing me. But Suki's idea of bliss is a warm lap and having a full tummy and it is hard to think of one more worthy of the privilege of providing these luxuries than Annie.

I am moving in a bit of a trance. People are still waving, waiting their turn to approach. Aditi isn't there, but I spot Beatrice, with her husband Sham, and Camille and Erik and their entire brood, sprawling on the grass, in close conversation with Diana, who presumably had to slip in after giving me time to get back from her place first. Everyone knows the truth about Pete now and this in itself is such a comfort, like having a huge invisible safety net as I move on to embrace whatever lies ahead.

'It is not even a big birthday,' I murmur to Jo. 'Forty-three – it's nothing.'

'Oh, but it *is* big,' she retorts, checking on the proximity of Harry, I am guessing, before adding quietly, 'you have been through a bloody nightmare, Fran, and now it is over. This is the beginning of the rest of your life, girl.' She gives me a solemn glare. 'Which, Rob and I agree, by the way, is going to have to be right here, in Kent, because we're all going to miss you too much ever to let you go...' I am distracted enough for it to take a moment to realise she is joking. 'In fact, I've phoned that agency with the flat you like and told them the deal's off...' She is still grinning as she hurries away to relieve Mel of Marcus, the baby having started the squirming act that means he needs a nap.

'Many happy Returns and you haven't even got a drink yet,' Mel cries, skipping over to me in her new energised way, despite the brick-thick white soles elevating her silver trainers. Shoes are a new obsession, thanks to a deal with a small online company now paying her to wear their styles for her pictures. 'Here, swig mine, and Jason will get you a fresh one.' She signals the command to Jason, who does a thumbs up, hoicking Aisha higher onto his back, making the little girl giggle and her long black pigtail flap as they gallop off towards the encampment further down the garden. Mel pulls an apologetic face. 'Sundays are his dad day, so I hope you don't mind. Jo and Rob were cool about it.'

'Mind? It's lovely. And having you... him, Aisha, everyone... here. I'm a bit lost for words, to be honest.' I raise the glass at her and take a sip. In truth, there is still the new trace of awkwardness between us. She knows it and I know it, but we have both been just letting it sit there, hoping it might fade with time. It is because of the question I dared to ask her after Helena's visit, about the anonymous emailer. I had to ask it, in a bid to lay the matter to rest, while also being aware that it could just have been a wind-up – a last try from Helena to get one over on me.

Of course, she hadn't written anything to anybody about me and Jack, Mel had retorted, let alone to the bloody wife, whose email she didn't know anyway. And when I reminded her of what she had said – the cause of my suspicion – about being afraid of losing me to Jack – she had got even crosser, saying that was something she had told me out of love and not as a weapon to be swung at her whenever I fancied it. I had apologised and backed right down, biting my tongue about the trust issues she had brought upon herself. True or not, it was no longer of any consequence, I assured her. And it wasn't.

'Happy birthday,' announces Jason, arriving back with my drink, 'and congrats on the new job... it's okay to mention that, right?' He looks urgently at Mel, making me suspect the poor man has been grilled with a checklist of Subjects to Avoid on the journey down.

'Thank you, Jason,' I offer him a reassuring smile. 'Though it's not exactly a new job, just an additional post, which I am going to be sharing with a colleague—'

'Which makes it no less fantastic and, excuse me for butting in, but I work with Fran at Chalfonts and want to say a big well done,' interjects Camille in her smooth domineering way, sidestepping up to my shoulder, 'as well as good wishes to the birthday girl.' She kisses my cheek and, behind the loop of her big hooped earring, I notice Erik marshalling all the children into a game of French cricket with a ball and a tennis racket. I observe some traces of tiredness in her today, a slight heaviness round the jaw and faint shadows under her big eyes, but her overall look is as vibrant as ever, her expanding girth still elegantly camouflaged by a floaty gold dress, matched with a thick gold headband set deep into her lush black hair. 'The governors came up with the idea and...' She starts to expand on the happy decision to offer the post to both me and Beatrice, while I take a quiet breath, still not quite able to believe the effort that has gone into the day.

A few minutes later, a blood-curdling clanking stops everyone mid-sentence; a sound produced with visible glee by the twins, banging wooden spoons against saucepan lids, clearly at the behest of their mother, who stands between them with her fingers in her ears, laughing.

'Luncheon is served!' Jo declares, once they have been persuaded to stop. She turns to lead the way down the lawn to the meal. She keeps one arm firmly round each child as she walks, her long mint green skirt blowing gracefully round her legs.

Everyone obediently starts to move. I hold back a little, wanting to take it all in, this unimaginably happy forty third birthday; glorious proof, as Diana had pointed out that morning, of the progress made, the vast distance covered.

* * *

Getting ready for bed many hours later, the party is still inside me, all the lovely things that got said, the generous gifts, the laughter, the bright summer colours, the music that Rob started up out of his laptop to try and get some dancing going, but which never really took off. The heat hung on into the evening. The dogs, played out with extra attention and games, never got walked. The children, including Marcus, were yawning even before they were carted off for their baths and then barely awake for the herding round of goodbyes and goodnight kisses that followed, their soft toys tucked under their chins, their pale eyelids droopy with sleep.

'Bless,' said Mel, as Rob led them off, looking pretty sleepy herself, hanging on Jason's arm for their own farewells. They came in his car and he had just got back from tucking Aisha into some portable bedding on the back seat. 'It almost makes me want one. Almost.' She pulled an unreadable face at Jason and then we hugged hard, neither knowing nor caring any longer quite who was forgiving whom for what. I stood in the drive to wave them off, the last of the London guests, apart from Harry, who had said Len was happy to go back alone and could he stay through to the end of the bank holiday weekend. It was the perfect news to end the day and I had told him so, my heart twisting at how much he must be longing for the sale to go through and his father's move done with. The plan then is for him to move in with Len, as friends, Pete thinks. How long his father is allowed to live under that illusion is another matter and one I know I must leave with Harry.

Deciding now that a herbal tea might help me settle, I pad along the landing in my new birthday pyjamas, past Jo's study where Harry is, and then Jo and Rob's closed bedroom door, behind which I can hear my brother's faint rumbly snores. The doors to the children's two rooms are open, their night lights glow-worms in the dark.

At the bottom of the stairs, I step over the dogs, who like to sleep as close to the forbidden upper floors as possible, lying back to back like mismatched Siamese twins. In the kitchen, the humming of the fridge in the stillness is soothing, as is the running of the tap, the filling of the kettle, the reaching for the tea bag. The Japanese are onto something with their ceremonies, I muse, flopping onto the sofa, remembering the yellow flier and thinking how distant it, Jack, and the sad woman who fell in love with him, now feel, almost like things that happened to someone else.

'Mum.'

'Hello, darling.' Harry is in his boxers and a T-shirt. 'Do you want a tea too?'

'No... yes... but I'll do it.' I watch and think about love, and how it changes shape but never leaves, not if it is real. Even what I felt for Jack sits deep inside now, somewhere quiet and safe, helped by the letter, which rang true, whether Helena had born witness to it or not. Us – it – happened, for him too. As things turned out it was just a stepping stone – the route to where I am now – and I wouldn't go back or resuscitate it for the world; but neither is it lost. Nothing, ever, is lost, good or bad.

Harry brings his mug to the kitchen sofa, but sits in the furthest corner. He drank a lot during the party, to the extent at one point of joining in with his uncle's efforts at galvanising some dancing – an act so un-Harry-like that I guessed it had to have something to do with letting rip after Len had gone. I had been bowled over by the courage of Len even being there, though, to judge from their body language, Harry had been keeping him at arm's length and Len hadn't liked it much.

The body language in the corner of the sofa is telling me something now too. Harry, despite outward appearances, is not in the opposite corner for a cosy chat. Cosy chats are not his style. So, I am waiting, breath bated, taking quiet sips of my tea, glancing round the room rather than at my son. On the wall beside me is the landline, slotted into a holder that looks as archaic these days as the message pad pinned next to it. I see now that it has a phone message on it, a message for me, by the look of things, since the writing, in adult hand but using a thick orange felt-tip that must belong to the children, reads:

FRAN. GIJERMO CALLED. HAP BIRTH. PLS CALL BACK.

A phone number follows, international by the look of it.

I let my gaze drop to my tea. I suspect the message has been sitting there since my outing to Diana's this morning, forgotten about in the shenanigans of the day. I am aware of a warmth in my stomach that may not be entirely connected to my hot drink.

'Mum, what that woman said. As we left the gallery. The wife?'

Oh my, so we are back there. I feel another rush of guilt. All my careful efforts to protect Harry from gritty details about me and Jack couldn't have been more spectacularly blown to smithereens by what I allowed to happen that evening. I am surprised though, having said sorry for it many times now.

'It was me, Mum.' His eyes are fixed on something in the bottom of his mug. 'I wasn't going to tell you. I didn't think I had to, but now I think I do. I wrote to the wife. Helena Aspen. I did it. Don't go mental on me, please.'

I balance my now empty mug on the broad arm of the sofa and swivel my head slowly. I seriously wonder if I have heard correctly, whether, somehow, I have been mashing Harry's words in my head. We are both very tired after all, many glasses have been drunk by me as well as him.

'That time he came to the house,' Harry says, doggedly. 'I was there. I saw you. I heard you. I hid upstairs.'

'But that was...' I am seeing Jack's one visit to the house, early on, awkward and awful. We had begun in the kitchen, moved to the sitting room, trying to lose ourselves in embraces that had felt stilted, against the fridge, in the passageway, then on the sofa. I even remember a noise upstairs just as we had decided Jack should leave, and the explanation provided by Suki, trotting down from the landing.

'I knew about you and him, Mum. All along.' Harry's hollow eyes are on mine now, dark with pleading and also a hint of accusation that makes me think, pennies clunking through the labyrinth of my head, of the sourness towards me that started so suddenly, the months and months of it, stopping only after the hellish scramble home from Gatwick airport. 'I kept track. Not of everything, but enough to get the gist.'

I gasp out loud, incredulity still overriding the logic of what I am being told. 'But how?'

He flinches, chewing his fingers and looking at them hard. 'There are ways. Len's good with tech, even better than me... Look, Mum, I didn't want you to leave, okay?' he blurts. 'Dad's a dick, but I didn't want you to leave. It was better with you there. It was always better with you there.' Tears are starting to spill down his cheeks. 'And then what happened happened, in that hotel, and I felt like it was all my fault...'

He is unravelling now, shoulders shaking, sobbing, head down. The mother in me is desperate to reach for him, but I give it a moment or two. Very little – possibly nothing – is Harry's fault. But I need the time to absorb the shock. Albeit for heart-breaking reasons, I have been monitored – played even – by my own child.

'Dad is Dad and what happened in Edinburgh had nothing to do with you,' I say steadily, after a while. 'And Jack would never have left Helena for me anyway.' It feels good to say this out loud. 'She was the strong one. He didn't have the balls.'

Harry glances up at the final word, which I have fired out with a certain venom. 'So, it's okay?'

'It's okay. It's not ideal, but it's okay. You shouldn't have done what you did, but it's okay. Desperation can make us do desperate things. I know that well enough. It's all over though, right? I mean, you're not still...?' It's a necessary question.

'God no. I am so sorry, Mum. I know it was a shitty thing to do. All of it. So shitty.'

'It's all right, sweetheart, really. Me and Jack, it was a big deal for me – the real thing – but it wouldn't have worked out. We were too different. Frying pan into a fire.'

'I'm so glad I told you.'

'So am I. It was brave.' I let a few more seconds pass. 'I am guessing you aren't keen for Dad to find out about Len.'

'You could say that.'

'It's not for me to tell you how to play that, but maybe he will be cool about it. And by the way, I know you will still want to see him, after he has settled properly up north. Because, for all that has happened – and may yet happen' – I add this carefully, because Harry knows I haven't ruled out anything – 'he is still your father and, in his own way, he loves you.'

'Thanks, Mum.' Harry comes to me, sliding across the sofa and holding me as tight as he ever has in all his twenty years.

I stroke his bristly head, thinking of the tangles of different sorts of loving and what they make us do. Across the kitchen, the fridge hums. Overhead, the clock, makes its electronic tick. One of the dogs ambles in sleepily, takes a noisy drink from his water bowl, and ambles out again. In the corner of my eye, I am aware of the orange phone message lighting up the pad. I do not need to look at it yet. But it's nice to know it is there, part of a future that's finally mine for the shaping.

ACKNOWLEDGMENTS

With my gratitude to University College, Oxford, where the writing of this novel began, during my tenure as Visiting Fellow in the Creative Arts – the first to hold such a post in the college's 780-year history.

Huge thanks to my publishers, Boldwood Books, for their continued faith in me, and for the insight and encouragement of my wonderful editor, Sarah Ritherdon, whose ability to see to the beating heart of a story remains second to none.

This will forever be my 'Covid Novel', wrested into its final form during the spring lockdown of 2020. I am indebted to my housemates through that incarceration, Grace and Ali, not just for their joyful company, but also for their patience, stoical support and willingness to act as sounding boards whenever I emerged from my labours. They had nowhere to run!

My wonderful goldendoodle, Mabel, also deserves a word – there for me through the thick and the thin, as only a dog can be, reading my moods and never being altered by them.

BOOK CLUB QUESTIONS

- Why did Fran stay with Pete for so long?
- In what ways are Helena and Fran each other's 'other woman'?
- Do you think Helena is right to stay with Jack at the end?
- Was Jack ever going to leave Helena?
- Is Mel a friend or an enemy?
- Can the deceit of having an affair ever be justified?
- Was Fran wrong to try and put her happiness before Harry's?
- Which woman's story provoked the most sympathy in you?

MORE FROM AMANDA BROOKFIELD

We hope you enjoyed reading *The Other Woman*. If you did, please leave a review.

If you'd like to gift a copy, this book is also available as an ebook, digital audio download and audiobook CD.

Sign up to Amanda Brookfield's mailing list for news, competitions and updates on future books.

http://bit.ly/AmandaBrookfieldNewsletter

If you'd like to read more from Amanda Brookfield, *Good Girls* is available to buy now.

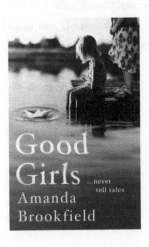

ABOUT THE AUTHOR

Amanda Brookfield is the bestselling author of 15 novels including *Good Girls* and *Before I Knew You*, and a memoir, *For the Love of a Dog* starring her Golden Doodle Mabel. She lives in London.

Visit Amanda's website: https://www.amandabrookfield.co.uk/

Follow Amanda on social media:

 facebook.com/amandabrookfield100

twitter.com/ABrookfield1

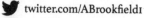 instagram.com/amanda_and_mabel_brookfield

bookbub.com/authors/amanda-brookfield

ABOUT BOLDWOOD BOOKS

Boldwood Books is a fiction publishing company seeking out the best stories from around the world.

Find out more at www.boldwoodbooks.com

Sign up to the Book and Tonic newsletter for news, offers and competitions from Boldwood Books!

http://www.bit.ly/bookandtonic

We'd love to hear from you, follow us on social media:

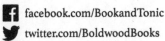

facebook.com/BookandTonic

twitter.com/BoldwoodBooks

instagram.com/BookandTonic